LORE & LUST
THE AWAKENING

Queer Vampire Romance Series Book Three

KARLA NIKOLE PUBLISHING

LORE & LUST
THE AWAKENING

KARLA.NIKOLE

KARLA NIKOLE PUBLISHING

First Karla Nikole Publishing Edition, October 2021

ISBN: 978-1-7355898-7-9 (paperback)

ISBN: 978-1-7355898-2-4 (ebook)

Library of Congress Control Number: 2021917001

Cover illustration by Thander Lin

Contact@LoreAndLust.com

www.LoreAndLust.com

Printed in the United States of America

10 9 8 7 6 5 4 3 2 1

To Monica, for sharpening my skills, and to Christa, who is always there and never too busy.

LATE SEPTEMBER

ONE

JAE

Humans can't be turned into vampires. People think it's possible because of questionable romance novels and TV shows with oversexed teens. But it's all rubbish.

"Can't you get me anything higher than this? You don't have any ranked vamps donating their blood? Third-gen, maybe?"

Wait, I'm sorry—am I some kind of back-alley drug dealer? This is a *hospital*. Smiling, I use polite Japanese. "Most of our donors are human or of lower-level blood. From a medical standpoint, either will provide the proper nourishment for your unique nature."

My patient huffs dramatically as she sits back hard against the chair. Teenagers. I really don't have time for this today. "Yukiko?"

She whips her head back toward me, her gaze serious. "I don't want to be 'low level,' Doctor Davies. I want *more*. How can I raise my rank? How can I be one of them instead of being on the outside like this? Ugh. I *hate* it."

Short answer? She can't. There's no shifting up ranks with

vampire blood. You are what you are when you're born. At least half of my job is explaining this. Part doctor, part counselor—stating the obvious one patient at a time.

In Japan, it's been more the latter. Almost every day I'm dealing with some lower-level vampire with Little Mermaid Syndrome. Groupies, to varying degrees. They ask me, "How can I be part of their world?" or "How can I become a full-fledged vampire?"

You can't. Get over it and carry on.

"Yukiko, you are a healthy young girl living in an age and culture where humans mixed with vampire blood can live comfortably. The stigma surrounding human-vampires has softened the past few decades. Instead of focusing on what you don't have, maybe you should focus on what's available to you? There's a particularly large community of human-vampire individuals here in Japan. Have you tried connecting with some of them?"

She scoffs. "Are you talking about *support* groups for loser low-levelers?"

I shake my head. "No." Although, that's exactly what I'm talking about. I spin it in my politically correct, Oxford PhD way. "I'm talking about like-minded communities. Groups of individuals with shared interests and circumstances. Do you have friends who are similar to you in nature?"

"Not really." She lowers her head, contemplating. Her long dark hair falls forward. "I still keep my nature a secret. Nobody at school knows. I'm only here because my parents caught me feeding from the dog. Again."

"Neither of your parents feed?"

"No." Yukiko sighs. She plays with the edge of her pleated skirt. It's way too short and she probably has the waist rolled over multiple times. I always wonder what came first—anime caricatures of high school girls or actual high school girls. Art imitating life and all that.

"My mother is fully human," she explains. "My father has the residual vampire genes, but he doesn't feed. He resists the urge since he's so far removed. I feel it, but I *don't want* to ignore it! I want to embrace it. I want to be like Hisaki-chan and Haru-sama. Beautiful and unearthly. Mysterious."

Thankfully, she's not looking at me, because I roll my eyes. I'm only vaguely familiar with "Hisaki-chan" because I've heard his name so many times from my teenaged patients' mouths. Apparently, he's some underground grunge–glam rock star. He's also a first-gen vampire, which automatically makes him posh and gorgeous. I haven't seen him, but I don't need to.

All ranked vampires are beautiful or rich. Usually both. They come in all shapes, colors and sizes, but those two factors remain consistent. It's not very easy to cross paths with a high-ranked vampire. The second- and third-gens skirt the edges of human society a little more, but first-gens and purebreds primarily stick to their own. I don't blame them, considering the fear, loathing and violence they faced when their existence was made known in the early 1800s.

Things are absolutely different now. But meeting a ranked vampire today is like crossing paths with a celebrity. People are giddy and re-tell the story to anyone who will listen: "You won't believe it—I was standing in the queue at the supermarket and a second-gen was *right* behind me. Buying cabbage! Astonishing." You have a better chance of meeting one if you frequent a vampire-owned business. Those places are pretty sharp on picking out the groupies though, so access would be quickly (and rightfully) revoked.

Some countries and cities are more populated with ranked vampires than others—depending on whether or not purebreds live there. The whole of Italy is a hot spot, along with Paris, Rio de Janeiro, Los Angeles, Hong Kong, New York, Auckland and recently Western Japan.

My home, jolly old England, is a complete dead zone. It's one of the few countries that have no purebreds at all, and nobody knows why. It's an unsolved mystery in vampire culture. I studied vampire health and medicine in a place with hardly any vampires. My friend Cyrus said I was ridiculous— like a fireman living in a city of igloos.

Moving to Japan has been an entirely different story. Fucking *brilliant*. The only downside is the weird anxiety I've had since arriving. I don't understand why, but it grips me sometimes, especially if I'm around a high-leveler. Mentally and emotionally, I felt well prepared for this incredible opportunity. I've been wanting something like this since I was a teenager. But physically, I don't know. Seems like my body is still adjusting?

"I heard a rumor that Haru-sama and Nino-sama came to this hospital." Yukiko blinks, her eyes wide. "Is it true? Did they sit in *this chair*? Oooh my God—"

"We never disclose information about who visits or doesn't visit our hospital." She'd have kittens if she knew that yes, Haruka has sat in that exact seat, and also that he and his mate will be here again tomorrow. Those two...

There's a row of pamphlets for different resources on the windowsill behind my desk. I grab one, but before I hand it to her, I take a pen from my desk and mark a star. "Look up this website in particular. There are a lot of communities listed here so you can talk to more teens and young adults with your similar circumstance. When I see you next week for your scheduled feeding, I hope to hear that you've at least reached out to one?"

She takes the glossy pamphlet from my hand and stands, awkwardly tugging on her thick checked skirt. "Yeah... alright."

"And maybe take a break from social media and vampire fan sites?"

Yukiko lifts her chin. "They're not fan sites. Hisaki-chan and Harunino are *my people.*"

She's looking at me, so I can't roll my eyes. But they are not her people. I've never met Hisaki-chan, but Haruka and Nino are in an entirely different league—an entirely different plane of existence. All ranked vampires are. Like kings and queens living behind a thick glass wall, unfettered by things like poverty and disease, racism, homophobia and the general hideousness that the mixing of human genetics often produces. Meanwhile, all of us humans are just standing here with our ugly faces pressed against the glass, breath steaming up the surface as we stare, wishing we could cross to the other side.

It's not possible.

I stand up from my desk. "See you next week, Yukiko." She bows in that hasty, flippant teenager way that reads more "Fuck you" than "Thank you, honorable and wise doctor who provides blood for me that is not from a dog."

Just as she walks out the door, an alarm sounds, and I realize it's my mobile. "Shit..." I'm already running late. I wonder if he's actually expecting dinner from me? I am *not* cooking.

Recently, a first-gen vampire named Junichi has been skulking around my office and insisting that we have dinner together. I met him by chance at Haruka and Nino's estate when I did a house visit to check on Nino's progress and drop off some books that his mate asked for. Even then, Junichi was eying me and blatantly flirting. It totally caught me off guard.

I don't know what the hell he's playing at or what he wants —calling me "beautiful." That's a stretch. Only my mum has ever said that about me, and I'm pretty certain that she was losing her grip on reality at the time.

Typically I get "weird" or "cute." Sometimes, if I'm lucky, the backhanded double-word score: "weirdly cute." One of my classmates in the medical program at Oxford said I was hot. That was nice. My friend Cyrus called me handsome once when he was rat-arsed. He denied it the next day and told me I look like something from that silly American Broadway show *Cats*—that I didn't even need makeup and I could walk right onto the stage. Tosser.

A quick fuck at my place and then I'll send the first-gen on his way. Truthfully, this happens to me often. Vampires get curious about me, and I have no idea why. It's only ever been low-levelers, though. *Never* a ranked one like this. Not that I've come across many, until recently. Until Japan.

These high-bred vamps make my insides feel twisty and bizarre, as if my stomach is tying itself into knots. Especially this one I'm meeting tonight. He's fit, though—leggy with jet-black eyes and dark curly hair. His skin is lovely and brown and reminds me of peanut butter. He speaks Japanese fluently, but he must be part something else?

Cyrus is brown, too, but with red undertones (Junichi's undertones are more golden). Cy's family is originally from Delhi in India. He says pricks who don't like people with brown skin are just jealous deep down. He and I disagree about a lot of things, but on that point, we are perfectly aligned.

The routine goes like this: the lower vamps come around to sniff and poke at me. If I'm up for it, we have sex. Sometimes they bite me. Then they move on like I was a shiny red apple rotten on the inside, telling me I taste awful. I told myself I wouldn't do this anymore after moving to Japan—that I wouldn't let them bat me around like a ball of wool. But I always know what I'm getting myself into. And I do enjoy it sometimes.

After packing up my desk, pushing the chair in and grabbing my rucksack, I check my watch. 6:05 p.m. Maybe I'll pick something up from the grocer, then stop by the corner shop for lube and condoms as well. Vampires are fussy about condoms, but that's where I draw a hard line. *Your* body might regenerate, but mine doesn't.

TWO

JAE

It's 6:50 p.m. by the time I'm showered and hastily pulling ready-made meals from a grocery bag. I run my hand through my damp hair, the waves there slick and heavy. My hair looks better wet, I think. Calmer. If I don't keep it trimmed low, I look like a bloody lion.

Or a character from *Cats*, apparently.

My mobile buzzes against the counter. Walking over to it, I see *Cy* on the screen. Speak of the devil. I honestly cannot deal with him right now, so I let it ring through to voicemail.

I'm nervous. That feeling like heartburn is settled in the center of my chest and my hands are shaky. I know Junichi won't hurt me. Ranked vampires don't actually do that. People who think so are either ignorant or watch too many films.

The truth is, Yukiko is right. Ranked vamps *are* other-worldly. They're much more emotionally sophisticated, cultured and genetically evolved than humans. And their eyes are always bright and focused. But at the same time blank. Curious? When Nino and Haruka are sitting across from me, their eyes are like an owl's and they keep their heads perfectly still, barely even blinking. It's both eerie and mesmerizing.

Junichi has black eyes—like pools of inky liquid. He's unreadable until he smiles with his full lips, and then his irises are playful and expressive. All three of them make my stomach feel weird. Sora, too. She's my nurse assistant at the hospital—first-gen, like Junichi, which means she's one generation removed from purebred status but still part of the elite group.

The majority of my intimate experiences have been with lower-level vamps—vampires very far removed from their pure-bred lineage. So much so that they read more human than vampire. In England, they just gravitated toward me, I guess, like hipsters to a basement record shop or a pretentiously eclectic café. One of them *was* a proper hipster. Blonde dread-locks, ripped jeans and earplugs. She was decent at kissing, but my flat always smelled like weed after she left. The second time we slept together she bit me, said I tasted like turpentine and left. Never saw her again... which is fine, really.

The doorbell rings and I jump, startled. I take a deep breath —where the hell are my glasses? I find them on the counter near my phone and slide them on, then move toward the front door. Grabbing the handle, I pause and roll my shoulders. Why am I doing this? Knowing he can't possibly want anything tangible or real with me...

If I'm honest, maybe it's just nice to be with someone, sometimes? I do well on my own, and I know how to take care of myself. I have for a very long time now. Admitting that I get lonely at times sounds pathetic, right? Nobody wants to acknowledge that, but there it is.

I unlock and pull the door. It's sunset. The weather is still warm although it's late September. Junichi is standing there, all legs and backed by an orange-purple skyline. He grins, charming as ever. He's holding... a bouquet of flowers. Bird-of-paradise?

"Hello, Doctor Jae."

"*God.*"

"No. Junichi, remember?"

"Flowers?"

"As a thank you for having dinner with me." He blinks his onyx eyes. "I noticed the painting on the wall in your office. I thought you might like them?"

My eyes scan his body, and he's wearing a clean white summery shirt, but it's fashionable with short sleeves and no collar. His trousers are dark and tapered at his ankles—perfectly tailored to his long legs. Bright yellow trainers. His facial hair is neatly trimmed and short, and he's wearing an expensive-looking watch. Made of wood? Christ. Everything about him is luxurious but effortless. I don't understand why he's standing on my doorstep.

"Doctor Jae?"

I stand up straighter. Was my mouth hanging open? Stepping to the side, I hold the door. "You have consent to enter."

Junichi crosses through the doorframe. Or rather, he swaggers, holding the elegant bouquet at his side. "So formal," he remarks, taking in my flat. He's speaking English suddenly. "'Come in' is equally sufficient."

I hesitate, but then answer in English as well. I'm proud of my Japanese and I studied hard. First languages are always more comfortable though, aren't they? Plus, this is *my* house. "Right. Well... it's not like I do this every day." Not with high-levelers, anyway. I haven't let any vampires paw at me in the three and a half months I've been here. Cyrus would be proud.

Only ranked vampires—purebreds, first-, second- and third-gens—need permission to enter a private residence. It's ironic though, because most ranked vampires would *not* be bothered with entering a human's home.

After closing the door, I move past him and toward the kitchen. He smells nice, like there's a haze of something very good hovering around his body. Not cologne. Something lighter, cleaner and elemental from the earth. Cypress and spearmint. A hint of lavender?

"Beer? Wine?" I ask, pulling the door to the fridge open.

"Are you nervous? You seem tense."

"No," I lie, raking my hand through my hair. It's nearly dry. "Which do you prefer?"

He moves closer to stand in the kitchen, then leans against the counter with his hip, flowers still at his side. "What are *you* having?" he asks.

"Beer. Probably."

"Beer it is."

I grab two bottles from the fridge with one hand. When I lift my arm to hand him one, he raises the bouquet and smirks, like he wants us to trade. There's an awkward pause of silence before I groan and take it from him with my free hand. He takes the beer, grinning.

"Thanks," I say, placing the flowers on the counter. I walk over to the round table off to the side. My kitchen space is small, but cozy enough for me and one other person. As a whole, my flat is very plain: beige walls, basic necessities and functional furniture. A tea kettle on the hob, a kitchen table, a gray sofa in the sitting area and a tall maple bookshelf pressed against the wall stuffed with all of my medical journals and research books. I don't even have a television and I don't care about decorating.

At the kitchen table, I pull a chair out for myself. "I picked up some food from the shop... in case you *actually* wanted to eat."

Junichi walks forward to meet me. "My understanding is that we're having dinner. It's what I asked for last week when I returned your book."

I blow out a breath. "Right." Sitting, I tell myself not to be irritated that he's playing some kind of uppity vampire game with me—asking for dinner and bringing me expensive flowers. I don't know what he's doing, but I don't need all this if he's just going to shag me and leave.

He sits across from me as I pop the plastic tops off our dinners. The food still feels fairly warm. I love supermarkets in Japan. They're neat and clean, chock full of ready-made, delicious foods like breaded pork over rice, all manner of crispy croquettes, giant makizushi rolls and even okonomiyaki—not to mention a wide array of bentos with veg and grilled fish. It's like they have some wonderful grandma in the back room, cooking up delicacies all day every day.

That sounds terrible, actually. Elderly-slave labor. I sincerely hope that's not the case.

"You said your schedule is very busy at the hospital?" Junichi's voice is cool and low in the silence, and his black eyes are focused on me.

I avoid his gaze by shuffling things around on the table. "Yes. Things were slow the first month, but it's getting quite hectic."

"You've been here for three months, right?"

"Almost four." I clap my hands over the food in gratitude as per the local custom before picking up my chopsticks. "Itadakmasu."

Junichi mimics the phrase and gesture, then picks up his chopsticks. "How do you like living here?"

I shrug. "It's nice. Clean. People are friendly and there's loads of work."

"I'm assuming from your accent that you're from England?"

"Yes. Born in London—East End. But I moved with my family to the outskirts of Bristol when I was thirteen. More rural."

"Bristolian." Junichi smiles. "South-west England is nice. I've traveled to Bath for work." He maneuvers the chopsticks with his long fingers, grabbing a slice of salmon and bringing it to his mouth. I'm watching him and wondering what he does for work. He's so tall. He could be a fashion model. Easily.

I also want to ask him, "What are you?" Which is odd because I *hate* that question. I've been asked that question my entire life. It's always awkward. I wish people would just wait and put the clues together on their own instead of being so focused on racial identity (my current hypocrisy aside).

Literally, it's the first question I'm asked sometimes, and I have to explain that my mother was a blonde Englishwoman and my father is South Korean: like I'm a dog at the Westminster Kennel Club offering my papers. Anyone with any subtle intuition and understanding of the world at large would realize my first name is Korean and my last name is not. It's right there in the name. Half and half. Jae Davies.

But Junichi Takayama... that's all Japanese. Looking at him, though...

"Have you had the opportunity to see any famous sites or cities?" Junichi asks thoughtfully. "Himeji Castle is popular. Kokoen is particularly charming in the fall."

"No." Shaking my head, I stifle my curiosities. He's only here to sleep with me, bite me and leave. There's no need for this small talk.

"What about other cities? Kyoto? Osaka or Tokyo?"

"No." I scoop up a chunk of rice with my chopsticks. "I've been too busy."

"That's a shame. I know I'm biased, but there's a lot to see and do here. If ever you have time in your schedule, I'm an excellent tour guide."

Seriously? I take the last bite of salmon and stare at him. I eat quickly. It comes with being a doctor. I do everything fast—read, eat, walk, sleep. Everything in my life is truncated so that I'm as efficient as possible. I thank the stress and anxiety of medical school for that.

The wall clock reads seven thirty, so I should get to bed soon. I'll probably shower again after we're done so I won't have to do it in the morning. We need to get this show on the road.

He asks more questions while he eats, slowly. I sip my beer and answer him, waiting for him to take his last bite. When he finally does, I stand. His gaze follows me.

"I know ranked vampires don't carry STDs," I say, "but I prefer condoms with whatever we end up doing. I have some. Hopefully that's not a problem for you?"

Junichi blinks his dark irises and breathes a clipped laugh through his nose. He sits back and folds his arms. "Excuse me?"

I glance at the wall clock again. 7:52 p.m. "I have an early start tomorrow, so it'd be best if we did this now."

Junichi narrows his eyes, his arms still folded. "If we did *this*... as in?"

"Fuck. I don't mind if you bite me, but I've been told I don't taste very good. So there's that. Since you're a high-leveler, I'll probably taste even worse to you."

Lowering his head, Junichi frowns—silent and obviously thinking about something. I'm about to speak again, but he looks up and beats me to it. "Do you think I'm some kind of monster?"

I draw back, shocked. "What? N-*no*—"

"I've only asked you to have dinner with me so that I could get to know you—as people often do in new encounters. I didn't come here because I needed charity sex, or to force you into some rash circumstance. I came because I thought you were striking and intriguing."

He stands up, but something inside me is indignant as I take a step forward. "'Get to know me'? Right. What else could a ranked vampire possibly want with a human other than to play with me for a bit like a toy? There's no long term here. I'm doing you a fucking favor and cutting to the chase, *mate*. I don't need flowers and this other bullshit."

The volume of my voice is increasing. I don't mean to yell, but I'm irrationally caught up in the moment. He's standing there looking eloquent and calm, like he's completely innocent. Like sleeping together is the farthest thing from his mind, when I know it isn't.

Junichi steps into me. He's taller than me by at least six inches, so it's annoying when I have to lift my gaze to keep watching him. His clean, lavender-cypress scent is wafting around me. When he grips my chin with his fingertips, the weird knot in my stomach jolts and practically sets on fire, making my eyes wide.

I swallow hard because I've never felt anything like this before. The sensation is so warm—pulsing and rushing down to my groin. But I don't want to acknowledge it. I'm supposed to be indignant right now, not erratically turned on.

Junichi looks me in the face with his emotionless black eyes. It almost feels like he's about to kiss me. If I'm honest... Shit. I suddenly want him to, and I want to lick my lips first.

But I don't. And he doesn't kiss me. Instead, his mouth pulls into a cynical smirk. "I don't need *any* favors from you, Doctor Davies. Not a damn thing."

THREE
JAE

I overslept, so I'm running late to the hospital. Which I *never* do. I get that from my dad. Growing up, he was adamant about three things: being punctual, speaking Korean and teaching me to make his native food. Well, maybe he was a stickler about two things? Since the latter items are indisputably related.

My schedule today is really busy, which is excellent. What's not excellent is that after Junichi left last night, I couldn't sleep. My body felt overheated. I was achy all over and my prick was insanely stiff. I've never had a sleepless night like that. Not even with Cyrus, and I spent *years* pining after that idiot.

I tried having a wank, which definitely helped, but then I'd think about those onyx eyes, beautiful lips and long legs... A few minutes later and I'd be writhing around in bed again. Pathetic. I acted like I was doing Junichi a favor. Turns out, he might have done *me* one if I hadn't acted like a dickhead. What a mess. It's like when I'm sitting in a seat on the Tube and a crowd rushes in and I don't want anyone to sit next to me. But then when no one does, I'm offended that no one wants to sit next to me.

Doesn't matter, really. I probably won't ever see him again.

When I step off the lift, Sora is already at the nurses' desk and watching me move toward her. Her eyes are deep brown and appear slightly less owl-like because she wears these neat, red-rimmed glasses.

I step up to the counter, smiling sheepishly. "Good morning. I'm so sorry I'm late. I texted you?"

She folds her arms and leans against the counter. "I got your message. It's not like you to be late. Is everything okay?" There's concern in her voice, which is nice. Honestly, I don't have many people in my life who express concern for my well-being. I've been self-sufficient for a long time now. No choice, really.

Sora had me over for dinner a couple of weeks ago. The thought of vampire children was always a little horrifying in my mind, but her twins were actually pretty cute. Funny. Like normal kids except they drink blood. *Thank God* I didn't see them do it.

"I didn't sleep well," I admit. "Are they already here?"

"They are. I finished the blood draw and now they're sitting in your office. I've already sent the bags downstairs to be shipped to Italy tonight. Separately, my kids are asking when you're coming to dinner again. How about next weekend, Sunday night? Since tomorrow night is the hospital gala with the board of directors. Don't forget."

Nodding, I turn to walk down the hall toward my office. I shouldn't keep vampire royalty waiting. "I won't—I already had my suit cleaned. And next Sunday sounds perfect. Thanks, Sora." Being my only day off, I usually play shōgi at the local temple with the old men on Sunday afternoons. Dinner with Sora's family is a worthy concession.

"I expect pajeon," she calls out. "Since you bragged about your father's recipe."

"Right." I smile. I'll need to make a shopping list and remember that. I walk through the doorway to my office, and there they sit. Haruka Hirano and Nino Bianchi. Century-old purebred vampires just hanging out and waiting to see me. No big deal.

I bow politely at the waist. "Good morning. I apologize sincerely for the delay."

"We're not in a rush today, don't worry," Nino says, blinking his honey, owly eyes at me. His irises are so bright they practically glow. His mate's eyes are the same way, except the color is maroon—like a glass of Merlot held up to the sun.

"Sora says you're never late. Is everything alright?" Nino asks.

"Everything is fine, thank you." I quickly hang up my rucksack, grab my lab coat from the rack and put it on as I shuffle over to sit at my desk. "How was the blood draw?"

He's holding Haruka's hand, of course. He smiles, warm, golden and open. "Great. The doctor in Italy says my father is getting stronger every day. Between my brother's blood and mine, he thinks we can relax a little and start sending blood every other month."

"That is excellent news!"

"Yeah, we appreciate all your help."

"It's my pleasure." I bow again. It really is. Helping them with *anything* is incredible. Even having them sitting here—I'm probably one of very few doctors throughout history to have worked with purebred vampires. Doctors are just not something they typically need. Their bodies naturally regenerate and have self-corrective biological components. Even if Nino hadn't come to see me a few months back, it might have been a much harder road, but he would have been fine eventually.

"Haruka, are you well?" I ask because he's been totally silent, and he's not nearly as easy to read as his mate.

He smiles politely and nods. "I am. Thank you, Doctor."

If Nino is like a bouncy, excitable and friendly dog, Haruka is a slinky, reclusive black cat. I have no idea how these two ended up together, but their adoration for each other is palpable. When Nino had been in the hospital a few months ago, Haruka never left his side. I'd walk in and he'd be running his fingers through Nino's hair and holding his hand, or at the end of the bed massaging his feet and legs.

They're unashamed and open about their love, as if only the two of them reside in this world—in whatever world they're part of. In vampire culture, they don't have labels and strict parameters around romantic relationships and identity like we do as humans. Love literally is just love, and you are who you are.

These two are so deeply enamored with each other, sometimes I think I should look away to give them privacy. I can't even fathom having a bloke and being like that—perfectly comfortable and carefree. The world *I* live in doesn't allow me to.

"Sora said the two of you wanted to talk to me about something?"

Nino's eyes shift over to Haruka. He gives his mate's palm a little squeeze as their entwined hands rest in Haruka's lap. Haruka takes a breath. "We are interested in expanding our family in the future. As such, we were wondering if you knew anything about—"

"*Surrogates.*" I gasp, smiling. "How—Did someone tell you I want to do this? Wait, no... I haven't told anyone here."

They're both blinking at me like I'm insane. "Sorry. I... I've been thinking about this topic for a while. Considering the steady decline in the purebred vampire population."

Haruka nods. "Yes. It is a matter of concern within our culture. Although the recent discovery of the Socotra population has put the masses at ease, for now."

"Right," I confirm. News of the Socotra purebreds has been covered in all the major human media outlets lately. It's incredible to know that there are more purebreds in the world than we originally thought, but still. This discovery is a temporary fix for a bigger, deeper issue.

"I... I was thinking that if we had a reliable surrogate program in place—perhaps a database of willing donors and carriers? It would help with the population issue. It's extremely difficult and time-consuming for same-sex vampire couples to find appropriate matches on their own. If we had a database available, it would be much easier. We have these kinds of programs more and more in human culture. They're very successful."

"Is there currently such a program in place for vampires anywhere?" Haruka asks.

"No. Not that I know of. It's just my idea for now. I lack resources... contacts and funding. I've thought about putting a proposal together, but I haven't even been here six months." It's a lot to ask for—a new database for keeping detailed records of vampire biology. Ranked-vampire records. Which creates added layers of privacy and cultural implications. No ranked vampire would willingly hand over their biological information to some weird human doctor.

If it were a purebred running this kind of database, though? If it were Haruka and Nino? Absolutely they would. There'd be no question about a ranked vampire's willingness to participate.

"Maybe we could help?" Nino asks, then looks at his mate. "You've been in the house so much lately, Haru."

Nino said the latter part in English. This is another funny

thing. Whenever they speak directly to each other, they always use English. Otherwise, everything is Japanese. Do they think I can't speak English?

"My love, this program doesn't exist," Haruka reasons. "I cannot help with something that has not been established. There needs to be a written proposal submitted to the hospital board. That is the first step."

Nino turns to me again, switching back to Japanese. "If you write the proposal and get it approved, maybe we could help you? It would be hard for you to get other vampires to comply. They would do it for us, though."

I nod, excitement bubbling in my chest. I've been thinking about this for years. It would be brilliant, and I could learn more about vampire biology and become even better at my craft. How long would it take me to write this up? Where would I even start? Who would I present it to? The department head? Board members? CEO—

"Now that I am paying attention..." Haruka is speaking in English, his deep, velvety voice smooth and calm. "There is something unquestionably vampiric about his nature."

"I was thinking the same thing," Nino agrees. He narrows his eyes. "But why? You're human, right?"

They're both staring at me with their owly eyes. I'm staring back at them, utterly confused. Do they know I speak English or not? Am I supposed to respond? Of *course* I'm human.

There's a knock at the door. Sora pokes her head inside. "Your next appointment just arrived. She's in the waiting room."

"Yes, thanks, Sora." Dammit. I wish I could talk to them about this more and flesh out the details. "I'm going to start working on the proposal, but there will be some details that I... It won't be easy to organize and work out on my own. I'm not sure how long it will take me."

Nino smiles. "Haru can help." Haruka's shocked eyes widen and shift over toward his mate as he continues. "He's not busy these days, so it'll be a good project. I'll help too, where I can. But he's the Historian. Historians in our culture have tons of connections and information at their disposal."

I look at Haruka, feeling apprehensive about the mood I'm suddenly picking up on. "That would be great, but... is that okay with you, Haruka?"

He nods, his composure recovered. "It's perfectly fine. I am willing to help. If you have questions, make an appointment with Asao as you've done in the past." Nino lifts his and Haruka's clasped hands from his lap and closes his eyes. He presses his lips to the back of his mate's knuckles. The moment is so tender and sweet that I'm wondering if I should look away.

"Doctor Davies?" Nino says.

"Y-yes?"

Nino is talking to me, but he's staring at his mate. Haruka is looking off and away, as if he doesn't want to acknowledge whatever is about to happen. "I know you need to go, but... with the Socotra purebreds being discovered and The Great Vanishing solved, we've received a lot of attention lately. And... *we* have been very reluctant to leave the house for the past couple weeks. I was wondering if you had any recommendations? Ways to cope with this loss of privacy? What we're doing now, I don't think it's healthy for us."

I can't read Haruka's blank expression, but clearly this is about him. His and Nino's faces have been plastered everywhere the past couple weeks. I've even seen people wearing pop-art T-shirts with Haruka's face on them. Knowing Haruka the little bit that I do, I'm sure this situation is a nightmare for him.

"Hm... Try leaving the house for something you really like."

Nino nods. "Okay, for example...?"

"For example, if you really like playing tennis. At least leave the house once a week to do that. If there's an ice cream shop you love, go there a couple of times a month? Try to think of something you truly enjoy, so that the reward outweighs the risk. Plus, you have a direct objective to focus on. That could be a good starting point?"

Nino looks directly at his husband and speaks in English, his voice low. "I think that sounds good. Can we please try, tesoro? Mm?" He lifts his hand again, but this time he flips Haruka's palm up, sprinkling kisses on the inside.

I look away and take a deep breath because they're making my gut all shifty and weird again. I have an urge to clear my throat, but who am I to interrupt century-old bonded and internationally celebrated purebreds making out in my office?

Gay vampires. Bloody hell.

FOUR
JUNICHI

Dios mío, ahí viene la misma vaina. My mother always used to say that whenever she heard my father shouting through the halls of the house—arrogantly posturing his purebred aura, flaring it outward and generally being a dick. *Here we go with the same shit.*

It's exactly how I'm feeling right now.

"Haruka's hair is growing out again."

I briefly glance up from my sewing machine to look at the pompous little vampire sitting on my couch. He's perched there with his legs crossed. His long white-blonde ponytail is slicked back tightly against his head. He's holding a cup of hot tea. The way the steam swirls up from the surface only adds to the ridiculous drama of his overall demeanor.

Hisaki lifts his chin. "We had him over to the house for brunch last month. Mother was pestering him about rehabbing the Socotra vampires and what he thinks happened to the British purebreds. That's all everyone in the aristocracy talks about lately. Why does it matter what happened to them? They've been gone for decades. So *boring*."

He takes a breath and sips his tea before continuing. "Anyway, I do appreciate Haruka's shorter hairstyle, but I think I prefer his hair long. I loved the way it emphasized his refined, elegant features. It reminded me of a black, flowing river—quietly reflecting the stars as it streams through rocky passageways in the darkest of night... I should write that down."

I sit up straight and stare at him—this dramatic little twerp waxing poetic on my couch. He takes another sip of his tea.

"Haruka is *married*," I say. "Bonded. For life."

Hisaki shrugs, unbothered. He shifts his blue eyes toward me. Last week they were green. They're contacts. "Haven't you heard? Bonds can be broken."

"Delusional." I shake my head, bending to tinker with the damn tension disk on my sewing machine. It keeps sticking. "Get off my couch. Go home."

"Rude." Hisaki flips his head so that his ponytail whips like a show horse's. "Why do *you* get to freely visit Haruka's estate whenever you want? I always have to make a formal appointment with that old guard dog of a manservant, and if my request isn't deemed tangible, I'm denied. How do you achieve this? Tell me your secret."

I play with the dial, adjust the thread and sit up straight, then gently press the foot of the sewing machine. The material I'm hemming slowly passes under the needle. "Well, let's see. I respect his bond. I'm not trying to get in his fucking pants—"

"I am *not* interested in a sexual relationship with Haruka. My intentions toward him are altruistic. He is beautiful and glorious, and I only want what's best for his grace. He deserves someone who understands his magnificence—who can support him as the leader and king that he is. And that is me. *Not* the Italian—"

"Nino is half-Japanese."

"Whatever. Haruka hardly ever leaves his home lately to

attend aristocratic events. It deeply concerns me. I simply wish to be by his side."

I sewed these buttons on this shirt yesterday, but today I'm rethinking the choice. Maybe instead of black, brown would look more modern? Wooden toggles might be interesting—

"TAKAYAMA JUNICHI."

I jump and lift my foot from the pedal, moving my fingers just in time from being snagged by the needle. My patience is officially shot. "You little *asshole*—"

"Don't ignore me. I hate it when you do that—"

"Don't you *ever* yell at me like that." I point hard, staring. "Hisaki, I *do not* have time for your self-absorbed bullshit today. I need to finish this by five o'clock and I have a gala tonight. Leave. Now."

He tilts his head. "Really? What kind of gala? For the aristocracy? Why wasn't I invited—"

"Estoy cansada de decirte—"

"Fine, I'm leaving. I hate it when you speak Spanish. You know I don't understand what you're saying." He stands with his teacup and shuffles his pale, narrow ass toward the door.

He's a young vampire—only twenty-three years old. There are thousands of teenaged humans and vampires who adore this brat. His music hasn't hit it big on an international scale yet, but he's a star in his own right nationally. I listened to his album because he kept pestering me. It's not bad, but definitely not my thing.

As his elder, I should be nicer to him.

I cannot. He annoys the shit out of me. He's everything that's wrong with ranked vampires. Self-important, snooty and prejudiced. He's barely been alive two decades and already exudes the arrogance of a vampire five times his age.

I tap my foot on the sewing machine again. From the corner of my eye, I notice that Hisaki is still hovering in the doorway.

He lifts his chin and clears his throat. "When... when will the jacket I ordered be here?"

I sigh, focusing on the material underneath my hands. "Two weeks." I almost add, "Don't come back until then." But he wouldn't listen. He comes to my studio every week on Sunday, rain or shine, whether he's ordered something or not. I have no idea why. I'm just lucky, I guess.

"Alright," he says. "I'll see you next Sunday." He washes out the teacup in the small kitchen off the hallway, and soon the door to the main entrance chimes to let me know he's left.

I sigh, pressing my foot down and threading the material under the needle again. "Pretentious little twerp."

WITHOUT HISAKI there to distract and demand my attention, I finish my client's shirt early and he's able to pick it up sooner than scheduled. This is nice because now I have time to stop by the bar and sit with my favorite old vampire before going home and getting dressed for the hospital gala.

Asao is Haruka and Nino's manservant, but he's a third-gen vamp. It's unusual for a ranked vampire to be a servant, but that's what I love about their entire household. Everything about them is refreshingly unusual. Relaxed.

I lock up my shop and walk down the cobblestoned road of the historical quarter. It's a pretty, breezy afternoon and the willow trees are fluttering in the wind. I love this sleepy little town. I grew up in Hiroshima, but this place feels more like home to me.

It's only a five-minute walk before I'm stepping into the bar. It takes a moment for my eyes to adjust from the bright sunlight outside. I hear a chorus of greetings.

"Hey, Jun!"

"Welcome back, Junichi."

I lift my chin in acknowledgment and smile. The bar is vampire owned. Our aristocracy in Western Japan is pretty tightly knit—but growing. Our realm leaders have gained a lot of attention the past couple months, so now, every vampire and their mother wants to live here.

Asao is waving me down, and I'm surprised to see Nino sitting beside him. No Haruka. Figures. Getting him out of the house the past few weeks has been like trying to coax a cat out of a tree. Usually I can tempt him with a good restaurant recommendation, but lately even that's not working.

I weave my way through the bar—through the noise of happy chitchat and laughter, glasses and plates clinking, enka music playing low in the background. The air is warm with the scent of grilled veggies and meat, and it makes my mouth water.

"Hey, Jun." Nino smiles warmly as I sit beside him in the booth. Asao is across from us. "We're celebrating."

"What, pray tell?" I ask, grabbing the half-empty pitcher of beer and a glass.

Asao grins. He's more than a hundred years older than me, but he's still square and handsome with salt-and-pepper features. He's obviously had a good life. "Haruka went out today. On his own," he says, grabbing his beer.

"Really? How the hell did you manage that?"

"We had an appointment with Doctor Davies yesterday to talk about surrogacy options," Nino says. "While we were there, I asked him about things we could do to cope with all this new attention. He and I talked about it more last night, and he agreed to try. We found a fairly safe activity to get him started."

I lift my beer in a toast. "This is excellent news." They lift theirs as well, and we tap glasses. After Nino takes a sip, he sighs.

"I don't want people to think he's a snob, you know? If he

keeps hiding and ignoring everyone, the tide could turn. They pulled a new group of vampires out of Socotra. The detective is pressuring us to take on more refugees, and she keeps blabbing to the news about our involvement. Haruka hates all this attention."

Haruka could easily be a pompous jerk given his ancient family roots, looks and upper-crust breeding. I wouldn't even blame him if he were. It's almost expected. The quality of his nature makes him a beacon for other ranked vampires, and his bloodline is clean and very old, which means he probably tastes like heaven. I can't imagine what life was like for him being unbonded. He told me he hid himself in England for a decade, and I immediately understood why.

"Speaking of Doctor Davies..." Asao is smirking at me. I frown, rolling my eyes and pulling my beer to my lips because I know what's coming. "How was your date?" he asks.

I take a long sip before setting the glass back down on the table. "Shit."

"Really?" Nino raises his brows. "Why? Doctor Davies seems nice."

I nod, diplomatic. "Yes, the doctor is very nice to his patients, which is excellent for the hospital. I have no complaints."

Outside of the hospital, he's a prejudiced jackass. A beautiful jackass that smells delicious. Well, fuck him and his good smells. Since when is it a crime to have dinner with someone you find attractive? What's so terrible about wanting to eventually make love? Now I can't ever have sex with him, because if I do, I'll just prove him right.

"He definitely has something funny going on," Nino says. "Both Haru and I took inventory yesterday. He's human, but... I don't know."

Asao lifts his chin toward me. "You should bite him. See what he tastes like so we'll know for sure."

I roll my shoulders. "Nope. That's not happening." As a ranked vampire, feeding from humans isn't fun. They taste like dirt, and if you do it too much, it can permanently ruin your bloodline. A few years ago, in the throes of passion, I fed from one of my human lovers in Paris. An exquisite young opera singer whose family had originally immigrated to France from Kenya. Lisette Noelle Moreau. I couldn't go out into the sun at all afterward because my skin burned. I had to cancel *two days'* worth of appointments and sit around her loft like a fucking squatter. Not worth it.

"Haru says it feels like there's a wall inside Doctor Jae," Nino says. "Like something is blocked. But he doesn't register as a low-level vamp either. It's confusing."

"Well, he'll need to find someone else to deal with his blockage." I raise my eyebrow and lean forward to drive the point home. "Because it ain't me."

Asao sits back and folds his arms. He's examining me in that paternal way that makes me uncharacteristically self-conscious. "The doctor didn't fall at Casanova's feet, so you're upset?"

"*No*," I say, then realize it makes me sound like I'm pouting. "It just wasn't a good match."

"Why?" Asao pushes. "You chased him for three weeks. What happened?"

"Technically, *two* weeks, since he said yes on the third week. And I didn't 'chase' him. I was returning his books... slowly."

Nino snorts at this, which doesn't help my case. I ignore him. "Anyway, he made it perfectly clear that he's not interested in me or what I have to offer." I open my palms in a curt gesture, like I'm a prosecutor and I've laid out all the obvious evidence. Or like I'm a magician. Voilà.

Asao laughs and shakes his head. "Casanova is a control freak. If someone isn't following the perfect little script he's laid out for them, he cancels the entire production."

"Wow." Nino blinks, lifting his beer to his mouth. I shake my head, dismissive.

"That's not true."

"It *is*, Jun." Asao grins. "You dumped a new client last week because he was getting too rigid in his custom order. You do it all the time! You're just lucky that you're wealthy and good-looking enough to get away with it. And that's really why you don't ever want to bond—because you can't control that kind of situation. Because you can't *trust* and be vulnerable with anyone."

"Shit! *Relax*, old man." I hold my palms up against the full-frontal assault. "I came here for a damn beer—not to be psycho-analyzed. God." I roll my shoulders again. Nino is laughing.

Asao smirks. "I just call it like I see it."

"Keep 'it' to yourself."

"You don't want to bond? I didn't know that," Nino says. His innocent amber eyes are blinking at me like he couldn't possibly understand. Of course he can't. He's mated with the love of his life, and their bond triggered on the first try. That shit is unheard of—like playing golf for the first time and getting a hole in one on the first swing. The stars practically aligned for them. But they're the exception, not the norm.

"I don't want to bond, but I'm not opposed to a healthy long-term relationship. I've had quite a few with some lovely humans over the years... Dammit." I pick up my glass and tip my head back to finish the golden liquid.

Asao's face is smug. "That's why he only has relationships with humans, Nino. Can't bond with humans. And being a ranked vamp, you always have the upper hand, too. You're always the one in control."

I grimace. "You're really on one today."

He wiggles his eyebrows at me.

Asao is wrong. It isn't about me controlling people. *I* just don't want to be controlled and forever beholden to anyone.

This is my worst nightmare: I'll look up and be in a situation with someone who outranks me. Who is controlling and manipulating every aspect of my life. That I'll be miserable and stuck like that until one of us dies—which is exactly what happened to my mother.

FIVE

JAE

Why does holding a person's hand feel more intimate than sex? What does that say about us as complex, physiological beings? I've had sex with quite a few people and vampires over the years, but I cannot remember the last time I held hands with someone (and what does that say about me?).

Right now, this is all I can think about as I walk into the flashy banquet hall. There are crystal chandeliers hanging from the ceiling and illuminated ice sculptures. Waiters with silver trays of champagne and hors d'oeuvres. It's impressive. Equally impressive is Lucy in her fitted black dress. She's standing at my side as my date for the gala tonight.

Lucy is a dietician and works a few floors down from me at the hospital. Human. Not vampiric at all. I was speaking to a lost hospital patient in Korean one day and she happened to be walking by. I had the language he needed but not the actual sense of knowledge to tell him where to go, so she stepped in. She grew up in America—Korean-American. We've been dating (mostly having sex?) off and on. Dating is hard for doctors. Sometimes it's easiest to get straight to the point.

We've been casually sleeping together, but it feels *very* weird to try and hold her hand. I won't, even though it's literally the dominant thought in my mind right now. Lucy often tells me that I'm, quote, "cute but kind of sexy." I don't quite understand how that works, but I like her so I'll take it.

"Hey." Lucy gently bumps my shoulder with her own. We're the same height tonight because she's wearing heels. "Your vampire friends are coming."

I look up, and Sora and Kosuke are walking toward me. They're dressed up and cleanly put together, like a couple in a model home advert. Sora's hair is down tonight, which is nice. Usually, she has it tied back or in a massive bun.

"Hi, Jae." Sora smiles. Kosuke, her mate, offers a friendly nod. "It's Lucy, right?" Sora asks.

"Yes... Tell me your name again? I'm so sorry." Lucy's smile is awkward. Privately, I know she has weird feelings about vampires. She doesn't understand how or why I work with them every day. She told me she'd be terrified that one would haul off and bite her. I told her they don't typically do stuff like that—that most ranked vamps probably think she'd taste disgusting. I also told her not to believe everything she sees on the Internet or in films.

We all engage in the typical banal small talk until an announcement is made. The formal presentation is about to begin. The lead CFO who helped this hospital reach its current success is retiring, and a new chap is being ushered in. Normally, I wouldn't care. I'm here on a grant and my position is only guaranteed for a year, depending on growth and need since this area has seen a major influx in vampires recently. I'm running a test program for the hospital to see if my services are valuable, which is why I'm apprehensive about pitching a major, potentially expensive long-term project.

I've been getting more and more patients though, and this

surrogate proposal could launch the hospital into an innovative space pertaining to vampires. Not many hospitals uniquely cater to vampires' needs (because their bodies are complex and self-sufficient), but we could become an authority on something very important and topical to an old, powerful race of creatures. So I'm paying attention tonight, wondering who I'll need to present my idea to once I have it fleshed out.

We all decide to sit at the same table. It's round with a thick white tablecloth and a full, Western-style dinner setting: porcelain plates and butter dishes, crystal glasses and cutlery all gleaming in the dim purplish lighting. The centerpieces are stunning white orchids. Lucy is sitting on my left and Sora on my right. The latter leans into me.

"I didn't know you were dating Lucy?"

I shrug. "It's fairly new." Are we dating? We picked up food from the corner shop once on our way back to my place from the hospital. Maybe *this* is our first proper date?

"Hm. I thought you might like Junichi. He certainly seemed interested in you."

My stomach clenches from the mere mention of his name. Christ. I scratch the back of my head because I'm not sure how to respond.

I consider myself bisexual. It took me a long time and lots of heartache to get to this place, but I know that label suits me. Being gay, queer or trans is not openly accepted or celebrated in mainstream Japanese culture. Sora is a vampire and doesn't care about all that... but still. I'm changing the subject.

"Who is this onstage now?" I whisper. A youngish bloke in a typical "salary man" black suit and tie is at the glass podium. He's giving a long-winded introduction for someone. The hospital's CEO? He didn't say a name.

"He's one of the board members," Sora says, adjusting her glasses and matching my whisper.

"If I wanted to write a proposal for a new hospital program, who would I need to present that to?"

Sora's brown eyes widen. "Are you thinking of doing something vampire related?"

"Yes. And maybe Haruka Hirano will help me? It's still in the early stages. He told me I need to get the proposal written and approved first."

"That's wonderful, Jae. Your best bet is to talk to Junichi."

My stomach clenches again and I frown. "Why would I do that?"

"Because he's Haruka's best friend, *and* he owns and personally finances our hospital."

"*What?*"

"Shh." Lucy turns and scolds me, but my head is spinning and I'm focused on Sora.

"He what?" I say more softly.

"He's the CEO, Jae. The 'Dean of the Hospital,' although he doesn't like being called by either title. You didn't know? He signs your paychecks."

"I don—I don't *get* paychecks. Everything is direct deposited."

"Your employment contract then?"

"Kawaguchi-san signed that!"

Sora shrugs. "Well, nonetheless. I thought you knew?"

"*No.*"

"*Shh!*"

Sora scrunches her face and leans past me. "Sorry, Lucy."

I shake my head, trying to rattle the information into place so I can process it. Junichi owns the hospital. He's the CEO... The owner of the hospital where I work asked me to have dinner with him for three weeks, came to my flat, brought me expensive flowers, and I told him I had condoms. I gave him a lukewarm, ready-made meal and said I was doing him a favor.

I press my fingers against my forehead and close my eyes from the massive headache forming there. "Bloody hell—"

"*Jae. Jebal, joyongheehae. Mooseun il itnee?*" Lucy is whisper-shouting at me in Korean when I just want to crawl underneath the table, curl into a ball and die.

"See?" Sora taps my shoulder as she whispers, "Look. He's there."

I don't want to look. Because if I look, then it must be true. Everyone is clapping politely as I lift my head.

He's there, bowing to the young salary-suit man and stepping up to the glass podium. He's smiling, his black eyes glistening, and his warm, peanut butter skin looks radiant underneath the spotlights. He's clean-shaven now and wearing a beautifully tailored plum-colored suit with a deep, rich and satiny tie. On anyone else, a suit that color might look ridiculous. On me, it totally would.

On Junichi Takayama, it looks like an absolute dream.

———

AN HOUR LATER, I still feel like I want to die. But now, maybe I'll throw up first. Clean myself out and do the mortician a favor. Junichi is walking around the room and greeting each table while dinner is being served. The closer he gets to my table, the more knotted and twisted my stomach is getting.

Sora and Lucy are politely chatting over me, both leaning forward. I'm leaning back and not touching my plate. I'm so embarrassed it's painful. Why do I care about my behavior now? When I thought he was just some arbitrary vampire, I wasn't quite as bothered. Now that I know he's my boss and the sole proprietor of a massive charitable institution, I'm gutted.

And I need to submit a proposal to him. I told Haruka and

Nino I would... I want to help them and other couples like them. But I've really screwed this up, haven't I?

Junichi is standing at the table next to ours, smiling and being charming. I can hear everyone swooning and laughing, praising him. I stand from my seat to excuse myself. I can't face him right now. Not here. Maybe later I'll send an email or something and apologize? Shit. That's cowardly. Am I apologizing because I'm genuinely sorry? Because he's my boss? Or because I need something from him?

D? All of the above?

A waiter directs me toward the bathroom and I'm grateful when no one else is inside. I tuck myself in a stall, lock the door and press my back into it. I close my eyes, just breathing and trying to get this shifty, knotty sensation in my body to subside. It's so uncomfortable.

It started when I first moved to Japan and began working with Sora. It was a low hum then, like background noise inside me.

Meeting Haruka and Nino made it worse. The hum shifted to a light pulsing, but I could still ignore it. Still manage it. With Junichi... It's the worst it's ever been. Like pounding and twisting at the base of my spine and in my stomach. Ever since the night he came to my place it's flared up at the mere mention of his name. I feel like a teenager with butterflies over a crush, except the butterflies are on fire and fighting each other. I even had a colleague give me a check-up to see if there was something medically wrong, but nothing out of the ordinary turned up.

I'm breathing now, but it isn't getting any better. In fact, it's getting worse—things have escalated and the fiery butterflies now have tiny knives. I hear the door to the men's room swing open as I shift my spine to the left against the stall door, needing some kind of relief. Footfalls echo against the marble, moving toward the center of the bathroom, but then stop. Shifting my spine to the right, I breathe in deep, and that's when I smell it. Cypress and lavender.

"Doctor Davies."

My eyes widen. My heart is beating out of control from the stress. I swallow, turn and unlock the stall door. Slowly, I open it and peer out. Junichi is standing with his arms folded, leaning against the counter. His black eyes are staring directly at me, but I can't read him at all.

SIX
JUNICHI

This is my mistake. When he hadn't agreed to have dinner with me after two weeks, I should have dropped it. I was adamant because he's perplexing and smells like something warm, sweet and straight out of an oven.

But damn all that. This ends now. I can't have the staff at Mom's hospital running from me and hiding in bathrooms—like I'm a literal monster.

He's looking at me as if he's scared of me, peeking his head around the stall door. Why is he so fucking tense all the time? I wait until he's out of the stall before I start. I'm glad no one else is in here. I speak in formal Japanese since I'm not feeling particularly playful and I want him to know that.

"First—forget about what happened on Friday. That was my error in judgment, so you don't need to run away from me or feel uncomfortable. I won't bother you anymore."

The doctor's shoulders drop, and he reaches up to scratch the back of his golden ombre hair. How the hell does he get it perfectly highlighted like that? His suit looks like it's his father's. It doesn't fit his square shoulders and lean frame as well as it should. He's almost swimming in it.

"Second. Sora just told me you might have an idea for a new program in your field of study. I'm not your boss and I don't oversee the day-to-day operations of the hospital. But all major financial endeavors need to be approved by me, since I'm funding them. When your proposal is ready, contact Risa Suzuki and set up an appointment. She manages my calendar for hospital meetings."

He's blinking at me from behind his glasses. After a few seconds, he bows in a quick, polite motion. He follows my lead and speaks in formal Japanese. "Yes. I understand. Thank you."

Good. I don't like drama. I get enough of it with my feeding source. Typically, I don't date while I'm in Japan. I conduct my romantic liaisons abroad and away from my home. Sleeping around within an aristocracy is frowned upon, and it can get serious fast since most ranked vampires want to bond. Humans and low-level vampires are just easier to be with—not nearly as fussy or demanding.

I turn away from him and wash my hands since I'm in here. He steps up beside me and washes his as well. When I put my hands under the dryer, it's loud, but the doctor turns his head toward me and says something. I pull my hands back, frowning. "What?"

"It's nice," he says. "The color. I like your suit."

He's speaking in English with that airy, subtle accent. Reluctantly, I follow his lead in my response as I quickly scan him. "Thanks... Your suit is ill fitted."

The doctor looks down at his plain gray suit, white dress shirt and hideous plaid tie. "Really? How so?"

"It's too big in the shoulders and cuffs. It looks like something your father owned in the nineties."

He laughs at this and runs his damp hands into his hair. "It *is*. I've had it since I was eighteen."

"How old are you now?"

"Thirty-two... thirty-three in March next year."

God. Tragic. He's smiling at me now with perfectly white, straight teeth. I think this is the first time he's been somewhat relaxed in my presence. I don't get it, and part of my brain is telling me to walk away now. But...

"Why did you act like that?" I ask. "When I came to your house. Did I offend you in some way?"

He shakes his head. "No... I—"

Someone walks into the bathroom. I recognize him, but I can't think of his name. He sees us standing there, bows politely and walks out. The doctor had turned to look at the new arrival, but he looks at me again. "Truthfully, every experience I've had with a vampire... They've been pretty direct with what they want. And I am genuinely busy with my schedule, so I just thought—you know..." He shrugs.

I frown. "Had a lot of experiences with vampires, have you?"

"Not *a lot*. Christ. Some. Never with ranked vampires, though."

I lean toward him, batting my eyes. "Well, I suppose we shouldn't walk around making sweeping generalizations about vampires, should we?"

He's looking at me, and I swear his gaze flickers down to my mouth for a split second. "Sorry about that," he says.

I stand straight, ignoring the quick flash of heat in my groin. "You're only sorry because you think I'm someone important now."

"No," he says sternly, frowning behind his black-framed glasses. "I felt like shit right after you left. But I didn't think I'd ever see you again."

"Well, if your proposal is flawless, you'll only need to see me one more time." I smile. I'm being an asshole, I know. Stepping around him, I walk toward the door. Halfway there, the doctor speaks out from behind me.

"So you *weren't* thinking about sleeping with me then? Not at all?"

The brashness of his question surprises me. When I turn to look at him, I don't show it. "Is sex all you think about, Doctor Davies? It's starting to seem like that's what *you* want from me, and you've just been projecting this entire time."

He pulls his glasses off and breathes a laugh, running his palm down his face. I wait, but he doesn't deny it.

Maybe Asao is partially right? The script is all fucked up now, so I don't want to deal with it. He's messy. "Whatever the case," I say, "it's never happening, so don't worry. I look forward to reading through your proposal, Doctor."

I nod politely, turn and leave the bathroom. Case closed. As I walk down the hallway, my phone buzzes inside my jacket pocket. I pull it out and look at the screen. Two additional messages quickly pop up. All from the harpy.

[We're scheduled to feed tomorrow Violet. You sexy moth-erfucker.]

[11:00 am DON'T BE LATE.]

[If you've fed from some low-leveler or human in the past week, don't even bother coming.]

Sliding my phone back into my pocket, I groan. I *should* feed from some low-level vamp or human tonight, just to spite him and call bullshit on his empty threats.

SEVEN
JAE

Recently, I realized that I rarely ever make the first move. I've *never* done so with another man. I can think of a few times when I've initiated physical intimacy with a woman. With men, they always make the first move on me. I don't know why.

Have I not liked anyone enough? Or did they just choose me and I went along with it? Do I unconsciously expect someone else to make the first move? This deserves deeper analysis at some point.

Currently, I'm holding my journal as I pace back and forth outside a meeting room at the hospital. Junichi is inside. I hear his voice, but I can't understand what he's saying. I also can't hear anyone else talking. I think he's on the phone?

"Tu no dejes que esa gente te hable así."

I have context clues now, though. He's definitely speaking Spanish. What dialect, I have no idea. Could be Mexican Spanish, Puerto Rican Spanish, Spain Spanish and on and on. While this doesn't necessarily mean that he's part Latinx, it at least tells me a little more about him. My mind has been in a wild state of tug-of-war all week—half worried about this proposal and half thinking about him. Particularly how stunning his golden-brown skin looked in that plum suit.

"Por qué diablos tu ordenaste una caja de fideos? Qué tu vas a hacer con toda una caja?"

I have five more patients to see today. One of which is new, and I'm always chuffed to meet new patients and understand their unique circumstance. Something in it is thrilling, like a fresh riddle to solve, and I genuinely love helping.

"Oh, guineos! Ah bueno... tá bien."

Risa told me Junichi doesn't have a formal office in the hospital, since he's hardly ever here. When he is, it's usually for meetings, so he camps out in a conference room until everything is done. It's been a week since I saw him at the gala. I'm nowhere near finished with the proposal, but I need some parameters. Guidance?

When I think I hear him say "adiós" a minute later, followed by a stretch of silence, I take a chance and knock on the door. He tells me to come in. This conference room is one of the nicer ones.

There are some meeting rooms in the hospital that feel like they're made for hostages, with no windows and only harsh fluorescent lighting. This particular room is filled with natural light. It's at the back of the building, so the windows are facing the thicket of trees behind the hospital. The afternoon light is yellow gold, and the leaves are still bright green as they flicker in the gentle breeze. A month from now, I'm hoping everything will be washed in red and orange.

Junichi is sitting at the table, in a chair off to the side, not at the head. He's alone like I thought—dressed surprisingly casually. He's wearing a gray cotton shirt, but it's layered underneath a blazer that looks like a creamy jumper, and it's patterned with thin black horizontal stripes. His jeans are deep blue and he has on expensive-looking trainers. Black leather and laces with stark white soles, like it's the first time he's ever worn them.

He looks fucking delicious, and the room is filled with his clean, woodsy-lavender scent. He's texting on his phone, but stops and flicks his black irises up at me under his dark lashes. "Hello, Doctor Davies."

English today. That's nice. He sounded angry when he spoke in Japanese before. "Hello..." The table is too wide to sit across from him, and sitting next to him seems awkward. I sit at the head of the table and face him.

"Risa said you wanted to ask me about the proposal?" He's texting again, but then stops and pointedly sets the phone on the table, face down, giving me his full attention.

I swallow, ignoring the stupid anxiety in my gut. "Yes. This is my first time writing a proposal for this establishment... and for you. While I'm obviously answering basic questions—who this proposal is for, what it aims to accomplish, why it is relevant and so on—I was hoping for more finite parameters. Perhaps a better idea of your expectations when reading a proposal?"

Before I go blindly careening off a cliff, I figure it's best to know what he's looking for. This way I don't waste his time or mine.

"Very smart. Your idea is to create a database of vampire surrogates for same-sex mated couples, correct?" Junichi asks.

I blink. "How did you know?"

"Haruka told me."

"Right..." I'm sitting here with the owner of an award-winning major metropolitan hospital whose best friend is like the purebred king of vampires in Western Japan. I'm suddenly having an out-of-body experience. I have no idea how I ended up here and vaguely associated with this elite circle of creatures.

"Haruka suggested I help you with fleshing out the proposal, since I know things about our culture that you're not privy to," Junichi says. "So it's good you came to me. He said he'll help you with the back-end research and establishing contacts wherever needed."

I nod. "Okay, brilliant." I lay my journal on the table, open it to a fresh page and grab the pen tucked inside. "Since you already know the basis of the proposal, can you tell me what initial concerns you have based on your cultural insight?"

Junichi folds his arms and adjusts so he's sitting back comfortably. He crosses his ankle over his knee. "Well, I'm not concerned about participation, or how much we'll need to pay the surrogates. If Haruka's and Nino's names are slapped on this, you'll have plenty of vamps willing to sign up for just about anything for little or no compensation."

"Right. I was thinking that might be the case."

"My biggest concern is communication and how the information will be organized once we receive it. I think we should do a small test market first. How are we presenting this to the vampire community? We need to be careful about the language we use, because ranked vamps can be very haughty and indignant about their blood. And what about unranked vampires? Inevitably, they'll learn that we're doing this. Are we not accepting their biology and telling them to go to human agencies? We can't discriminate. If we do this for purebreds and ranked vampires, we have to do this for same-sex low-level couples who want it too."

I nod again, writing at a furious pace. I hadn't thought of that. "I agree. I absolutely do not want to discriminate."

"There needs to be a clear understanding," Junichi explains. "Once we have things firmly established, I think hospitals in other regions should have their own processes apart from ours, but we're all communicating with each other and using the same database. Does that make sense?"

"It makes perfect sense. We would create the framework, then offer it to other hospitals to adopt and administer."

"Exactly. You should consider the workload you're taking on. This is a vast project, and there needs to be a hard line for where you turn over the reins. Hospital by hospital? City by city? Country by country? These are also things to think about."

I'm still writing and nodding, but he's absolutely right. I hadn't thought this far ahead. I want the database to be available internationally—meaning anyone can help any vampire couple anywhere. But would it be better if one major hospital handled this per city? So the information is being funneled cleanly instead of through multiple hospitals and channels? More hospitals (and smaller ones, at that) means more complications. More room for errors. Shit. I have a lot to think about.

"I'd like you to have those things figured out in your proposal." Junichi unfolds his arms and clasps his hands in the gap of his thighs. "A clear, streamlined path for how this will work—without anyone being offended or excluded."

I put my pen down and flex my fingers. "I'll think it through, absolutely. I don't have much experience with ranked vampires, but low-levelers can have *massive* egos. I definitely don't want to step on any toes there. Even calling them 'low-levelers' is slowly becoming politically incorrect. They prefer 'human-vampire' or 'of human-vampire descent.'"

"What made you decide to work with and study vampires?" Junichi is blinking at me, waiting. The answer is long and complicated, but... I shorten it.

"I've always been really interested in vampire biology and how your blood works differently than ours. It fascinates me."

"Like lab rats?"

"*No.* Not *at all.* I just..." There's a heavy, historical insinuation there that I don't appreciate. And the truth of how my interest in vampires started is weird to explain. I've only ever told Cy—which I immediately regretted.

"It's fine." Junichi pulls his perfect lips up into a half-smirk. "You have a fascination. Lots of experience."

I narrow my eyes. "The way you say it connotes fetish. It's *not* like that. And I'm never the one who initiates. The low-levelers are always the ones up for sex. I'm not talking about my patients either, to clarify."

Junichi shakes his head, still grinning and cool as ever. "Why does everything come back to sex with you? I didn't even say anything."

"You implied."

"Did not. How are things with the pretty human dietician you went to the gala with? Are you dating her? Not that it's any of my business. She's lovely."

At this, I smile. The fact that he noticed and is asking about it is fantastic. He seemed totally put off by me at the gala last week. All business. I don't blame him, and he basically said my suit was crap. "Not dating, exactly." I stifle my urge to grin.

"God." Junichi scoffs in a laugh, running his long fingers up into the soft curls atop his head. "Is there anyone you aren't just having sex with?"

"You?"

He pauses at that, and I'm suddenly feeling brazen. He's kind of my boss, but he's not my boss. He smells incredible and is so shrewd and suave. Ever since he held my damn chin in his fingertips and looked down at me with those black eyes, those beautiful full lips... I keep wondering what it would be like to kiss him.

My *chin.* That's what's set me off. Christ.

He leans in and against the table, resting his elbows there.

His irises are focused on me like rich, shiny marbles. "I didn't think you were interested."

"I never said that."

"You weren't very receptive to my advances, Jae. Like I was something to hurry up and get over with. You act as if you're afraid of me."

"I'm not, and I'm sorry... I explained that already." I take a breath. How many times do I need to apologize? This is the first time he's said my name without "Doctor" in front of it. I was "Doctor Davies" the night of the gala, which feels even more distant and like a hard boundary. He keeps staring at me. My heart is in my throat.

"I don't know what kind of experiences you've had," he says, "but I don't do things flippantly or thoughtlessly. I don't 'fuck' people. I take my time. If I'm interested in someone, I give them my undivided attention."

I inhale another breath because my stomach is twisting in crazy knots again. I'm sitting up straight, but the way he's leaning now, it would be easy for me to shift forward and catch his mouth. It's silent as I watch his lips. I pull my own bottom lip into my mouth to wet it with my tongue. I don't know what's come over me, but I *need* to kiss him.

EIGHT

JUNICHI

This human doctor is licking his lips and staring at my mouth like it's something he can eat. Something he wants to devour.

The way the sunset is reflecting off the window makes his chestnut-brown irises bright behind his glasses. His eyes are shaped like sideways raindrops under heavy, dusky and dark golden lashes. I'm tempted to pull his glasses from his face so I can get a better look at him before I take his mouth. His lips are already slightly parted for me, like an invitation.

There's a knock on the door, and I shift my eyes toward it and sit back comfortably. "Come in, Risa."

Jae drops his head and runs his fingers into his thick mane. He looks like he's in pain. I share his frustration, but I do a better job of hiding it. I look up and smile warmly at Risa as she walks in. "Yes?"

"Doctor Izumi wants to know if she can sneak in a few minutes before you leave? She's waiting for my callback."

"Of course." I flip my wrist up to check my watch, then look at Jae with his head still lowered in his hands. "We're finished here?"

He looks up at me from underneath those lashes, practically glaring. "Yes," he says, stiff but matching my polite Japanese, his face calm and professional. It's a façade, though. Doctor Davies is not pleased. He uses both palms to push himself up from the table, grabs his notebook and pen, then nods his head in a bow before he turns to leave.

It's for the best. I barely even know this male. For some reason, the tension between us is already running abnormally high. It's never this complicated with humans, which is why I like them.

I tried to take it slow and talk to him first—to understand his mind and experiences as the individual he is. What makes him tick? I *enjoy* that part because it makes me a better lover when I finally indulge. A lot of people go for cheap thrills and quick conquests. Not me. I've been alive for too long, and that shallow shit does nothing for me. Making love to and being in a relationship with someone is much more satisfying when I know them, and when they're fully unraveled, open and trusting of me. *That* is what gets me high.

But he wasn't interested. Told me it was bullshit.

He's attractive and obviously used to getting laid by lots of vampires and humans alike, and I'm not sure how I feel about that. That he quickly lumped me into the same category with every other "human-vampire" who's tried to bang him and bite him in the past.

I know I'm being a hypocrite, but I'm a first-gen vampire. I have a fucking ego.

———

THE NEXT DAY, I'm sitting in Haruka and Nino's kitchen, which is like a second home to me. We're having an early lunch since I'm leaving for Europe tonight for two weeks. I usually go abroad to see clients once a quarter, but last quarter was cut short because the lovebirds were having a crisis. I came back early for moral support.

Haruka walks into the kitchen, actually dressed. For the past few weeks he's only been wearing the casual robes I design for him. That's fine, but it's also a clear indicator that he's not leaving the house.

"Hello, Jun."

"Your grace." I smile. I don't need to call him that. Mostly it's to tease him. He takes it in stride. I jokingly called him "purebred prince" once, and he didn't like that at all.

When he sits down at the head of the table, his hair flops forward, grazing his temples and cheeks. He sighs as he rakes it all back with his fingers. When he brings his hands down again, it all rushes forward. I laugh. "Your barber won't cut your hair, will he? You waited too long, so he wants you to grow it out to donate it again."

He groans. "Correct. It has reached this awkward length where it is not long enough to properly pull back. However, if this is my biggest problem, I gladly accept it."

I smile at that. "Good perspective-taking." Haruka and Nino had a rough couple of months this spring. Awkward hair length is a welcome problem in comparison. "Nino?"

"Shower."

"Is he having lunch with us?" Nino doesn't have issues leaving the house. He manages aristocracy business affairs in both Kyoto and Osaka. It keeps him busy. He loves his work and is great at it. He turns struggling bars and restaurants around and makes them into success stories time after time.

Haruka yawns. "No. He has a meeting. Although we agreed that he should not work on Sundays. He assures me that this is the last one he'll schedule."

Sydney, their young purebred live-in, walks into the

kitchen with grocery bags. He offers a cheerful greeting before shuffling around to put things away. "Good morning, Junichi!"

"Hello, Syd. How was the market?"

He stops, blinking his sage-green eyes under the mop of his sandy-brown hair. "It was wonderful. Busy! There are pears now for autumn—and persimmons. Asao taught me..." He takes a deep breath and smiles bright. The look on his face, you'd think he just described the moon and stars in the sky.

Sydney is one of the rescued purebreds from Socotra—one of the first to be accepted into our realm. He came without a mate and was pretty scrawny and emotionally withdrawn at first. Nino and Haru tried putting him in an apartment and implementing their fixed program the way they do with other refugees, but it didn't go very well. They'd go check on him, and he'd be sitting in the dark in a corner and refusing to eat or feed.

Since they've transitioned him to living here at the estate and helping out, though, he's done a one-eighty. Plus, he loves cooking and is pretty damn good at it.

"How is Doctor Jae's proposal coming along?" Haruka asks.

"We talked about it yesterday. I think he's confident in figuring things out after our conversation. I'll let you know when I get the official report."

Haruka nods, then rakes his fingers through his hair again. "The doctor perplexes me. Why is he somewhat physically appealing to my nature? And you mentioned before that you could discern a scent from him. Not the typical unembellished human scent, correct?"

"Yeah," I say, leaning with my elbow on the table and cradling my face. It feels like Doctor Jae Davies is slowly occupying more and more of my world. "You don't smell any unique scent from him?"

"I do not. What does he smell like? May I ask?"

I frown. "Why does that matter?" Scents are a very subjective experience for ranked vampires. It is literally a case where one man's trash could be another man's treasure. My source smells like ham to me. Flat out. I like ham, but it's not very appealing to my nature and intrinsic thirst as a vampire—I don't necessarily want to fuck ham. If I told him that he would die.

I should tell him.

"Talking about scents is a little personal." I turn my nose up, brushing it off. But then I tilt my head in a pointed gaze. "What does *Nino* smell like to you?"

"Cinnamon. And oak. Sunlight."

I sit up straight, scratching my head. "Alright, apparently we're not embarrassed... How does sunlight *smell*, exactly?"

"It is difficult to describe. The sunlight aspect is more of a perceptual sensation."

"Got it."

"Hey, Jun." Nino walks into the kitchen, smiling. Handsome sunlight.

"Hey—what does Haruka smell like to you?" Double or nothing.

Nino pauses at the counter, folding his arms. "It's complicated. The simplest answer is roses. But when I feed from him, it's very visual—transcendent. As if I'm in a different place altogether... like the soul of him is a rain-soaked garden with lush greenery and roses in full bloom. Sweet and fresh. It's perfect."

Haruka is openly grinning now and staring at his mate. Nino walks over as if a silent beckoning has occurred. Haruka lifts his chin and Nino leans down, smoothly placing two firm kisses on his mouth. When he stands straight, he reaches into his back pocket. "Oh, here." He pulls out a thin black stretchy headband. Haruka scrunches his face as Nino quickly maneuvers it over his head, then works it back up to rest against his scalp. Haruka's overgrown hair is officially out of his face.

"Thank you, my love." Haruka sighs, then looks at me with his eyebrow lifted. "Your turn."

God. I have to confess after transcendent roses in a rainy garden? "Like something sweet... a baked dessert. With spiced peaches?"

"What's spiced peaches?" Nino asks. "Sounds delicious."

"How Doctor Jae smells to Jun." Haruka blinks his burgundy eyes at me. Examining me.

Nino laughs. "Aw, that's cute."

"Yeah, whatever." I frown. Fucking humiliating. Like I'm a kid with a fruit cup obsession.

"Do you all want coffee? I can make some before I start lunch." Sydney is already at the coffee pot, tinkering.

"Yes, please." Haruka smiles in his genial and sincere pure-bred prince way. "Thank you very much, Sydney."

The young vampire flips around smoothly, opening cabinets to get mugs. "It's my pleasure!"

Haruka told me candidly that it makes him uncomfortable —having this young, emotionally and physically traumatized purebred serving them like this. But Sydney genuinely enjoys himself, and in combination with his weekly therapy sessions, his progress is irrefutable.

When I took him out for his first beer, I asked him about it—if it would be better to have his own place and be more independent. He told me he likes Haruka and Nino's estate because he can keep busy, and it feels happier and safer than any place he's ever known. I couldn't argue with that.

"Typical humans *do not* register such distinct smells to our senses, Jun. Have you specifically asked Doctor Davies about his biology?"

I shrug. "No. He's human." But he's apparently been fucked and bitten by quite a few lower-level vampires, so maybe there's some kind of buildup? I keep that inelegant information to myself.

Haruka folds his arms. "There is more to him than meets the eye."

"Uh oh..." Nino says. "The vampire Historian is officially invested in this case."

Haruka shifts his gaze toward me, serious. "You should feed from him."

"No. A month ago you snapped at me for even joking about biting him."

"Feeding from humans long term and as a primary resource is detrimental to our biology and bloodlines. Doing so once or twice in a long while won't cause much damage."

"'Much damage.'" I scoff. "The last time I fed from a human, the sun literally burned my skin immediately after. I couldn't go outside for two full days. It was terrifying... My flesh looked like the paper burning off a cigarette."

Nino draws back, his teeth clenched. "Ew. *Jesus.*"

Sydney hands Nino a coffee cup, then walks around the counter to bless me and Haruka as well. After we thank him, he walks back to the inside of the counter and starts pulling pots and pans from the cabinets. He glides around the kitchen as if he's always been here. Effortless.

"I have never known you to properly pursue anyone within the aristocracy," Haruka says. "Aside from Ren—"

"I am *not* pursuing Ren."

"Of course." Haruka nods politely, graciously stepping over that particular conversational landmine. "I have always wondered, do you exclusively date humans? Are you opposed to your own kin?"

The question is loaded, and when I flick my eyes up, everyone is staring at me and frozen where they stand—Nino,

Sydney, and even Asao is suddenly here. He smirks when my gaze falls on him.

"When the hell did you get here?" I ask him.

He lifts his chin, haughty. "I *live* here. Or did you forget? Answer his question."

Sitting back, I take a breath. Asao already knows the answer to this question. We talk about it at length when we go drinking.

It's rare for the spotlight to be turned on me when I'm in this house. Usually I'm checking on *them*, making sure they're okay. Staying humble. I'm much older than both Haruka and Nino. Even though we don't operate by strict hierarchal standards (which is one reason why I like them), I'm not blind to the age gap. Instinctively, I feel big-brotherly toward them.

I fold my arms because this topic makes me defensive. My perspective is not the norm. "I don't like dating ranked vampires because they're arrogant and fussy."

"You're a ranked vampire, Jun," Nino says. Captain Obvious.

"*And* he's arrogant and fussy," Asao chimes in.

"Right." I nod firmly. "Why the hell would I want to be in a relationship with someone exactly like me?"

"Considering we cannot form bonds with humans," Haruka says, "you don't wish to mate?"

"Nope," I say simply.

"Why?" Haruka asks. "Before my first bond was broken, I was genuinely excited about mating. It was not until after I was betrayed that my stance drastically changed."

Haruka had been mated with a purebred female named Yuna when he was younger. He's never explained in great detail, but the gist is she did something intimate with another vampire, causing their bond to break. The event was unprecedented. We all thought bonds *never* broke.

"I grew up in a house with two vampires who forced their bond," I explain, taking a deep breath. "My father was a manipulative, demanding and strict bastard that used his purebred influence over my mother and all of us every chance he could. I never want to be in a situation like that again. I'll never bond with a ranked vampire—especially a purebred. No offense."

"Not all purebreds are strict and controlling," Haruka says thoughtfully, unoffended. "Do you think that Nino and I are that way?"

"Of course not. But you two are off the market, aren't you?"

Nino laughs and shakes his head. "I hate that I need to leave right now. I'll see you guys later." He drains his coffee, and we send him off warmly before I look at Haruka once more. "Can you truly sit there and tell me that most ranked vampires aren't arrogant assholes?"

Haruka shakes his head. "I cannot. However... if I was capable of meeting a vampire like Nino, perhaps there is hope for you as well? Your nature couldn't possibly be satisfied this way—having emotional intimacy with one source and apathetically feeding from another. You will be deeply gratified when the two are merged into one being. Feeding from the vampire you love... Junichi, there is no sensation more satisfying. Nothing."

I stretch my arms up and smile, mocking. "All fantasy. Whimsical dreams."

"It happened for me."

"Well, you're the purebred prince, aren't you?"

He frowns and rolls his eyes, distinctly looking away from me. It's Haruka's way of saying "fuck you." He would never say those words, though. I wish he would. Maybe I would pay to hear it. Either way, it works for me, because at least I've shut him up.

NINE
JAE

"*Oi*. You wanker. Why the *hell* haven't you been picking up your mobile?"

I rub my palm down my face as I hold the phone to my ear. "To avoid being shouted at?"

"Smartarse," Cyrus says. He's upset, but I can hear the laugh behind his voice. "You're in Japan for what, four months, and I'm to fuck off now, am I? Don't need old Cy anymore. To hell with him."

"Dramatic." I sigh. Have you ever had a close friend as a kid, and everything was pretty fine back then as far as adolescent relationships go, but then, as you grow up with that person and reach adulthood, you think, *If I met you now, with my fully matured brain, maybe I wouldn't fancy being your friend?*

That's me with Cy.

It's Tuesday night. I'm sitting in front of my laptop, trying to send an email about the proposal to Junichi. According to Risa, he's in Europe for the next two weeks. You'd think he would have mentioned that.

"I worry, alright?" Cyrus says. "You and your weird

vampire obsession. Japan is rife with them. I'm terrified you'll let one of them drain you and leave you in the gutter."

"I'm not obsessed. I'm not some fanboy—"

"Right. You're a professional fanboy. *Doctor* Fanboy."

"*Piss off*, Cy. Is this why you called me? To start an argument?" I hate it when he does this—picks at me about vampires, even though he knows why I am the way I am.

"No," he says, his voice finally softening. "I worry, alright? Pip does too. She just asked me when's the last time I spoke with you, and I couldn't remember. Don't let more than a week go by, Jae. Please?"

I'm massaging my forehead with my fingers. Why can't he just say that without all the other bullshit? "Fine. I'll do better." Cyrus and my dad are like the only family I have. Mum died when I was in secondary school. Dad stayed with me and saw me through my A-levels before he moved back to Korea. I went off to university in Oxford, and it didn't make sense for him to stay in a cottage in Bristol alone. We agreed.

His family is not very fond of me, although I've never met them. I suppose, technically, they're my family too. They hated my mum because Dad defied his mother when they got married and moved to England. Apparently, my grandmother was totally against all of it. Now that Mum is gone, the animosity from that situation has been transferred directly to me, it seems. I try not to think about it too much—that I have grandparents, an aunt and cousins I've never met. Maybe never will. Mum was raised in the foster system, so no reliable family history there.

We talk fairly often, me and Dad. He always wants to know how I'm feeling, like he's genuinely concerned for my health. I'm not welcome in his family's house. He apologizes to me for that. I haven't seen him in person since I was twenty-one. That was when I finished undergrad and he flew back to England for the ceremony. He also paid off the cottage in Bristol and signed it over to me so that I would always have a place to go. It's my home, but I have renters there now. It's a quaint, neat little house that my mum picked out before her health went completely downhill.

The cottage makes me a bit sad though, so I don't stay there.

"What are you doing?" Cyrus asks, finally calm.

"I'm working on a proposal, and I need to email the hospital director about something."

"A proposal for...? See, I don't even know what's happening in your life anymore."

I grin. "If you shut up, I'll tell you. It's a program to help same-sex vampire couples have kids."

"Sorry I asked."

"Tosser."

"Have you been dating?" Cyrus asks. "I mean normies. *Humans.* Don't tell me about your dodgy vampire banging."

"I hate you."

"You *love* me. Pip says hi."

"Hello, Pippa." I sigh. Pippa is Cyrus's very blonde, blue-eyed, pixie-like fiancée. Growing up, Cy and I spent so much time together that his little sister used to joke that we were gay. I didn't mind because... well, I was, wasn't I? Sort of. I hadn't quite figured myself out yet. But Cy *hated* it, and so did his parents. When Cy got engaged to Pippa before I left, his parents weren't thrilled over her blonde-hair, blue-eyed-ness, but I suspect they were grateful about her female-ness.

I once told Cy that the two of them sound like a children's book about a boy and his dog who solve mysteries. *Cyrus and Pip: Something's Fishy at the Beach* or *Cyrus and Pip at the Fair: Disappearing Clowns are no Joke.* He didn't think that was very funny.

"Can we catch up this weekend?" I ask. "I need to finish this email before I lose my train of thought."

"Promise?" Cyrus says.

"I promise. Cheers."

"Later."

I hang up and exhale a deep breath. Cyrus has been stressing me the hell out ever since I moved to Japan. We've been around each other almost constantly since we were tweens. It's like I'm trying to gently detach the umbilical cord and he is *not* having it. He was very against me moving here, saying I didn't know anyone and it was too far away. He's about to be married and start a new life. I honestly have no desire to be his and Pip's third wheel.

I read over the email in front of me one more time.

To: takayamajunichi@giannagraciamedical.org

Subject: Proposal Questions

Hello, Junichi,

I hope you're enjoying your trip. I have two more questions regarding the proposal details:

1. In addition to data on bloodlines and ranking, should we also collect biographical components? Such as interests and hobbies.

2. Can you give me a range as far as what it might cost to launch a new hospital program? How much have other programs cost in the past? I'd like to estimate a budget.

Cheers,
Jae Davies

Staring at my name, I wonder if I should put "M.D., PhD" behind it, or if I should sign it "Doctor Davies," since that's what he usually calls me.

I remove my last name and hit send. Sighing, I sit back. It's obscenely late and I should probably try to sleep, but my body has been wired lately. I'm about to stand when my email notification pings. I look at the screen, and Junichi has already emailed me back.

From: Takayama Junichi

Subject: Re: Proposal Questions

Hello, Doctor Davies,

1. That is an excellent idea. Please include biographical information in the data we collect with specific questions so I can review them.

2. Email Risa.

Thanks,
Junichi

I quickly type up my response.

Will do. Thanks!

When will you return from your trip?

Jae

Biting my lip, I hit send. He's online now, so... I figure I'll try. Maybe he's not interested anymore and I've blown it. Or, he might still want to get to know me? I remember his statement about taking his time and giving his full attention... Whenever it flashes in my head, a warm rush of blood races up my neck and heats up my entire face, and I start imagining what that might be like—having Junichi's full attention.

My email chimes and I sit up again.

October 10th. Why? Do you need something before then?

I don't, technically. But...

No, I'm fine. I was just curious. Are you on holiday?

About a minute later, his response pops up.

I'm working. Why are you up so late?

I consider for a minute. Truthfully, I can't sleep.

I'm working as well. Busy schedule tomorrow. Are you doing work for the hospital?

Now there's been silence on his end for about ten minutes, and I think I've lost him. It's a gaping, slightly anxious feeling... like I've asked one question too many and he might be annoyed.

After another ten minutes of mindlessly scanning the Internet (I tell myself I'm not waiting for him to respond—I *do* actually need to know "where Freddie Prinze Jr. is now"), I give up and stand to get myself a glass of water.

As I turn, my email chimes.

What's your phone number? Can I call you?

I'm chuffed. I type *Yes*, pound out my mobile number and hit send. My phone is on the end table near the sofa. I quickly grab some water, and by the time I'm sitting comfortably, my phone rings.

"Hello?"

TEN

JUNICHI

"Why are you interviewing me via email at three o'clock in the morning?" I ask. "Is this part of the proposal?"

"No..." the doctor says in his warm accent. When he speaks, it sounds like he's singing a song. Even in one syllable, I can hear the smile in his voice. "I was just interested."

I raise my eyebrow as I sit back in the plush armchair, making myself comfortable. "You're *interested* in me now?"

"I am. You had my number before..."

"That was before."

"You deleted it?"

"Why would I have kept it?" I ask.

He's silent, but after a pause, he asks, "Is this your personal mobile?"

"It is." I hear him fumble with the phone. Seems he's keeping my number.

"Where are you?" he says once he's done. "If you don't mind my asking."

"I'm in Paris. In a hotel room."

"Paris, wow... Why?"

"Because I have a couple clients in the city that I design for. In three days I'll go to Amsterdam for the same reason."

"What... do you design exactly?"

"Clothing," I say. This conversation is bizarre to me. Up until now Jae has not asked me a single question pertaining to myself. Not that everything needs to be about me, but I figured he genuinely didn't give a shit. Now, all he's doing is asking questions.

"Amazing—you design clothes and run a hospital?" he asks.

"I don't *run* the hospital. I just approve big decisions and review financial reports. Clothing is my passion."

"Ah, got it. That makes sense... You always look so perfectly put together. The plum suit. Did you design that for yourself?"

"I did. But I don't typically make things for myself. Just the odd piece here or there. I'd rather spend my time designing for others and making them look good."

"That's thoughtful."

"I'm a thoughtful vampire," I say. "Such a thing exists."

"A thoughtful vampire... Sounds like a melancholy romance novel in an airport gift shop."

I shift in my chair and cross my ankle over my knee. "Is that what you're into?"

"What? Airport gift shops? Romance novels?"

"Well, we know you're not into romance."

"That's not true," he says. "I'm just... not accustomed to it. Especially not with vampires... or with blokes."

I raise my eyebrow. "Looks like I'm a double negative. The chips were stacked against me all along."

There's a pause on the line. I'm about to ask him another question, just to keep the conversation going, but he beats me to the punch.

"Can we start over?"

I blink. The sincerity of the question catches me off guard. "From where?"

"From the beginning. From you asking me to dinner."

"So we're going to pretend that none of those other things happened?"

"No..." he stammers. "I don't mean forget. But... you said you wanted us to get to know each other—"

"I do. And I said you're beautiful, because you are." Hearing him take a breath, I quickly add, "But that doesn't mean that all I want is to sleep with you. Is that unfathomable?"

"Well, no," he says. "It's not..."

"Good." I smile. Finally, it feels like we're getting somewhere. Why was that so difficult? Remembering his reaction toward me that first night and the things he said... I still think he's messy. He's definitely got some stuff bubbling beneath the surface, but I like him like this—calm and with his guard down a little.

"I would like to get to know you, too," he says simply. Again, the naked confession catches me off guard. In my silence, he asks, "Will you have dinner with me? When you come back after your trip? A proper meal—out somewhere."

"Why, Jae?" I ask. "What's changed?"

He's silent for a moment, obviously thinking. Finally, he says, "Me. I'm seeing you... I'm looking at you now without all my ridiculous personal baggage in the way. Is that alright?"

I let that sink in for a moment. It's not sexy, but I like this answer—that he has the self-awareness to notice something like this and correct it is impressive. Most people look outwardly, blaming things on others. Zero accountability.

Actually... maybe, it's very sexy. "It's alright. I'll have dinner with you. I'm looking forward to it."

"Me too. In two weeks, then?"

Two weeks seems like a long time... "If we can make our schedules work, would you like to talk like this while I'm traveling?"

"Yes. I'd like that."

I smile. "Not at three o'clock in the morning though. I can't have the doctors at Mom's hospital functioning at half capacity. Why aren't you asleep?"

"Just restless. What do you mean by 'Mum's hospital'? Does she own it? Sora told me that you did."

I check my watch, and its 3:25 a.m. where he is. "When do you go into the hospital for your shift, Jae?"

"Six. I'm up now. Just tell me."

Laying my head back in the armchair, I close my eyes. "Yes, I own the hospital. When she was alive, my mother worked there as an RN."

"That's impressive. Not many vampires are comfortable working in hospitals—what with all the human blood smells and ailments attacking their senses... Like working in a warehouse filled with skip fires."

"What the hell is a 'skip' fire?"

"Er... maybe you'd say trash can? Garbage fires."

I laugh, shaking my head. "It's not quite that bad. But yes, it takes a strong mind and sense of willpower. That was definitely my mother. She loved helping people and working as a nurse. I always admired that in her, so when she died, I bought the hospital and renamed it in her memory."

"That's beautiful. Really. Such a lovely way to honor her. What about your dad?"

"My father has been dead for over fifty years. I don't miss him."

"Oh, well... alright then—"

"What about your parents?" I ask, realizing I need to

lighten the conversation. "Are they proud of their vampire-doctoring son?"

"Um, well actually my mum also passed away a long time ago. When I was still in secondary school. My dad is in South Korea with his family. He's fine with what I do. No strong opinions from him either way."

I pause, picking up on something odd. "I'm sorry about your mother. You said your father is with *his* family? Are they not your family, too?"

Jae takes a deep breath over the line. "Technically. By law and genetics? They don't recognize me as one of them. Messy business with my parents getting married without my grandmother's approval. But it's not a big deal. I talk to my dad pretty regularly. It's alright."

I can hear the shrug in his voice, but I'm sitting with my face scrunched up in disbelief. It definitely doesn't sound alright. "Understood. Is your mother's family more accepting of you?"

"Mum grew up in the foster system in London, so no relatives to speak of on her side. I've heard it said that relatives are a pain anyway, so I'm not torn up about it." It doesn't escape me that he's attempting to make light of the fact that he essentially has no familial ties. He's trying to sound breezy about it, but something in it makes my chest tight.

"Have you met people in moving to Japan?" I ask. Living in a new place can be lonely as hell all by itself, but not having family back home to reach out to either? Where is his tribe? His community? No man is a fucking island.

"Not really—but Sora had me over for dinner a couple of times. And I'm really rather busy with this new patient load and taking on the surrogate project. This is just how I operate best. I'm pretty well accustomed to handling things on my own

—have been for years now. It's really not as bad as it probably sounds. I'm not some loner... How did we get here? Christ."

"Maybe when I'm back, I can take you to Okutsukei Valley before dinner? It'll be beautiful by then with all the fall colors— since you said you haven't done any sightseeing. Or maybe Himeji Castle?"

I can almost hear the relief in his voice when he responds. "I'd like that a lot. It sounds fantastic. Sundays are my days off."

"What do you usually do on Sundays?" I ask.

"Hm, I mostly catch up on household chores. I also play shōgi at the local temple for fun."

I pause, my eyebrow raised. "You play Japanese chess with old men for fun on your only day off?"

He laughs. "Well, they're a kind lot. Very welcoming, and they like to bring me snacks and souvenirs any time they return after a holiday."

"Alright, well, if you've got your eye on any of them, tell me now and I won't intrude."

Jae snorts. "I don't!"

"If you're into older men, I'm probably twice the age of anyone in there. I'll bring you better snacks, too."

Jae keeps laughing, and it's a happy, open sound from his chest. It's nice. I can feel the walls coming down just a little bit more.

OCTOBER

ELEVEN

JAE

[I'm not walking. That's not what I do.]

I smile. I've been smiling so much this past week that my cheeks are numb. I can't remember the last time I felt this excited about something in my personal life. It's like there are stars floating around inside me. Wonder. A child on Christmas Eve.

My fingers move swiftly across the screen before I hit send.

[You could model. Of course they want you to walk. Legs for days.]

The bubbles immediately pop up in our chat, and Junichi's response soon follows.

[If you keep this up, I'll get the wrong idea about your intentions.]

I laugh, feeling wicked as I type.

[Please get the wrong idea. Terrible, very bad, no-good ideas.]

[You're a tease, Doctor Davies. Will you be shy when I get back home?]

[You'll just have to see, won't you? Good luck with your negotiation today.]

"Five minutes," the elderly man at the front of the room calls out. Before I put my phone away, it buzzes once more.

[Thank you. Shall we talk later tonight?]

[Yes, absolutely.]

[Perfect. Enjoy the old men... but not too much.]

I shake my head and tuck my phone underneath my folded legs against the tatami and sit up straight. *God.* I cannot wait until Junichi gets back.

We've talked and texted every day for the past week. I'm learning so much about him: how he really likes classic jazz and it's what he and Haruka instantly connected over. How he played kendo in high school and won a championship (at a prominent high school for vampires only, no less), and how he loves to travel but hates flying, because he says it's like being trapped inside a human-stuffed can for hours and he can smell *everything*, like, humans past and present... I know I'm human, but I wasn't even offended by that because it honestly sounds like a nightmare. Just thinking about that perpetual fart smell mixed with dead skin cells and stale armpits is enough to make me gag with my meager senses.

Fart smells aside, Jun's smooth, cool voice is becoming like an aphrodisiac. We talk late, and I'm such a slag because I keep wanting to say dirty things to him about my cock, or *his* cock and what I'd like to do with it.

If I go down that path, though, I'm not sure he'll follow me, so I keep it light and flirty and he doesn't dissuade me. When he comes back next weekend, it'll be all I can do to not wrap myself around him and lick him the moment I see him.

"Three minutes."

It's Sunday, and I'm at the local temple where I play shōgi with the old men. The temple is tucked in the back of a woodsy park here in Himeji, and the players are nice. Harmless. I haven't been in two Sundays because of the gala and then dinner at Sora's house.

Hiroyuki—he runs the matches—told me someone new is vying for the top spot. A young vampire has started coming each week, and he's already beaten the two best players beneath me. I have to play him today to potentially reclaim my spot. Just as I'm beginning to wonder where the hell he is, I realize someone is standing over me. I look up. My jaw drops.

"Haruka?"

He blinks his owly, burgundy eyes. I swear they're always glowing. "Hello, Doctor Davies. What a nice surprise."

"I didn't know you played shōgi?" He sits on the cushion across from me, with the shōgi board in between us.

"Of course, I have played privately, in the past," he says, neatly folding his long legs. "Never competitively, like this. I am here at your recommendation. Remember?"

I think back to our last conversation. It was only a few weeks ago, but it feels like forever. "Right. Getting out and doing something you enjoy..." I frown, because I'm an idiot and realize we're speaking English. I have never spoken to Haruka in English before this moment. "How did you know I spoke English?"

Haruka casually pushes the sleeves to his black jumper up his forearms, examining the board. "Your last name is Davies. And Sora told me that you transferred here from England. You always initiate conversation in Japanese. Is that your preferred language?"

"I—No. It's fine—"

"Ready—start!" Hiroyuki calls out. There's a hush of concentration over the room.

"Shall we begin?" Haruka smiles coolly. The confidence radiating from him is thick.

I nod. Confident myself. "Yes, let's."

I'M EXHAUSTED by the end of the tournament. I literally have a headache. But I ask Haruka if he's willing to have a cup of tea with me at a nearby café. It's built into the temple grounds, and a lot of the tourney players go there afterward. There's a garden, a bamboo grove and a lovely rock waterfall outside the open patio. It's a very peaceful, Zen atmosphere.

Once we're sitting and we both have our tea, I share the good news. "I plan to submit the proposal to Junichi this week. My goal is Wednesday. I still have a lot of finite details to work through, but if he approves, we could launch the test program as early as December."

He smiles, and it reaches his mesmerizing eyes. "That is wonderful news. You were able to complete the proposal in an impressive amount of time."

I shrug. I've been making the most of all these sleepless nights. "I know it's important to you and Nino, and I've been thinking about doing this for so long. Junichi helped me a lot, too."

"Junichi is an impressive vampire," Haruka says, bringing his teacup to his mouth. I nod. He really is. After our first phone conversation, I searched him on the Internet. I don't know why I hadn't thought to do that before. Junichi is a private designer with notable clients all across the world. There were pictures of him with politicians and celebrities I actually recognize—historical figures as well. He made an outfit for David Bowie, for God's sake.

He also owns and manages the hospital solely out of his own pocket. The hospital, Gianna Gracia Medical, is named after his mother, like he told me. But there's also a picture of her at the main entrance. I've been walking past it almost every day for the past four months without even knowing the connection.

It's a black-and-white portrait and she's magnificent in it— long dark curly hair falling over her shoulders, mocha skin and a bright, wide smile. Sora saw me staring up at the picture one morning and told me Gianna moved here from Santo Domingo to marry Junichi's purebred father in a political arrangement. His mother is Dominican. Mystery solved. It always is if you wait long enough.

"Doctor Davies?" Haruka asks.

"You can just call me Jae."

"Jae, what is your biological ancestry? Do you know your family history?"

I blink. That's a random question. "Well, are we talking racial ancestry?"

"Bloodlines, specifically."

"Human. My father is a South Korean, human. No vampiric ancestors as far as I know. My mother was orphaned. She... I don't know her biological ancestry." That's a can of worms that I would rather not get into. I like Haruka, but I'm not ready to drop my maniacal conspiracy theories on him.

"Your mother was orphaned..." Haruka considers, folding his arms. "Where is she now?"

"She passed away a really long time ago. She was sickly her whole life, but she managed. She got much worse when she got closer to forty."

"I am sorry for your loss."

"Thanks, Haruka."

"If you don't mind my asking, what was her ailment?"

Can of worms. I wonder why he's digging. Does this have to do with his and Nino's deciding I was vampiric in nature a few weeks ago? I am not.

"The doctors always said her body just couldn't absorb nutrients like it should. They tried supplements and a ridiculous number of treatments. There was nothing they could do. Eventually her heart failed."

He's nodding and obviously thinking about something. I decide to take advantage of his silence. "How... did you and Nino get together? How did you know he was right for you?"

The process of creating vampire bonds is explicitly concealed from human culture. It's incredible how they manage it, as there are literally no written documents or research on the topic. For all I know, Nino and two other vampires did a flamboyant mating dance in front of Haruka and he chose the one he liked the most.

Or vice versa, I suppose. I can't easily picture Haruka doing a mating dance. If he did, it'd be glorious—with silk and flowing robes... Actually, I think I would quite like to see that.

Jokes aside, everyone assumes sex or feeding is involved. You'd think someone would have officially spilled the beans somewhere along the way. Some aspects of vampire culture are very private like this. No stinky humans allowed.

"Everything between Nino and me felt natural when we met. We openly communicated with each other and submitted to our instincts. Neither of us fought the organic pull between us."

"That sounds nice." I smile. It truly does. "Is that how it is for most ranked vampires?"

"Unfortunately, no. Past experiences, assumptions and miscommunications often cloud a vampire's perspective, hindering them from seeing the truth as it stands in front of them. I imagine humans struggle with the same predicament?"

His eyebrow is raised over his rich iris, and I nod. "We do. Absolutely."

"Perhaps as a means of celebration for your proposal submission, you might be willing to have dinner with us next Sunday? Junichi will be there as well."

"Dinner? At—at your home?"

"Yes. If you do not find our natures offensive?"

"No, of course not." Their natures just make me anxious with my stomach in knots. That's all. "I would love to have dinner to celebrate. Wow..."

"Perfect." Haruka smiles. "You can join us following shōgi next week."

I narrow my eyes at him, feeling absurdly competitive. "Yeah... shōgi. Next week."

Haruka tilts his head back, laughing in a deep sound from his throat. I want to shove him like we're on a playground in primary school.

TWELVE
JUNICHI

[Hey. You ready?]

After I hit send, I fall back onto the bed in the hotel room and make myself comfortable. I'm exhausted and it's been a long day. A minute later, my phone dings.

[Yes.]

I'm tired. But I've genuinely enjoyed talking to the doctor for the past week. He's more relaxed and open now, and he has interesting yet grounded points of view. He questions things, which I suppose is a fundamental characteristic of being a doctor.

As I relax against the pillow, I call his number and bring the phone to my ear. After a couple rings, he answers.

"Hi—are you going to do the show?"

I sigh. "No. I told you I don't model."

"I looked up the designer online," he says. This is another funny thing. If I mention anything that Jae doesn't know, he researches it. Then he's practically an expert on it the next time we talk. "You match the designer's aesthetic perfectly. All his other models from his last catwalk show favor you."

"In what way?" I frown, curious.

"You know, very tall and... perfectly dapper with liquid swagger."

"Liquid swagger?"

"Oozing. *Dripping* with it."

I laugh and shake my head.

"Like treacle," he says. "Bourbon-flavored treacle—"

"Alright, Jae. Where do you come up with this stuff?"

"You inspire me. It's my image of you."

Despite myself, I smile. "I bet you say that to all the vampires."

"I don't. Never."

I'm tempted to ask him why he fools around with low-level vampires. If vampires are just his thing. I think it'll sour the mood, so I don't. Besides, everyone has a preference, whether they like to admit it or not. Clearly, I prefer humans. Does that mean *I* have a fetish? I don't think so. They're just easier to interact with. No rules and cultural hierarchy. No threat of being bound and chained to them forever.

"Did you call your friend over the weekend? Cyrus?" I ask. "So he won't yell at you."

"I did—the knobhead. I video-called him, but then he was like... busy and distracted the entire time. Obnoxious. He wouldn't sit still."

"Is he usually like that?"

"Hm, I don't know. Ever since I've moved to Japan, Cy is weird. He screams at me if I don't call, and then when I do call, he's awkward and barely paying me any attention."

"Maybe he misses you?" I reason. "Doesn't know how to say it?"

Jae blows out a breath that reads disbelieving. "Who knows."

"Maybe he likes you?" I offer. "Is he gay?"

"No no—absolutely not."

I raise my eyebrow at this. Some humans have weird convictions about being attracted to someone of the same sex. So much so that when they are, they often deny it, and it manifests in the strangest ways.

"Are you sure?" I ask.

"Positive," Jae says. "We've been best mates since we were little. And I've always been open with him about my sexuality. He would tell me."

I shrug, letting it go. Like I said, the strangest ways.

"Do you have a preference?" Jae asks. "Male or female? Other?"

"Not really," I say, lifting and bending my arm to cradle my head in my palm against the pillow. "I don't like drama, and all genders are capable of it. What about you? You're seeing Lucy the dietician."

"Not really *seeing*—"

"Just sleeping with, then?"

"Not recently... I—Well..."

"I'm not judging you, Jae. You're not on trial. You're allowed to sleep with whomever you please."

"Am I?"

The silence is weighted, and I smile. This doctor is something else. "Are you going to answer my question? What's your preference?"

"I guess I don't really have a preference... but are we talking sex?"

"*You're* always talking sex, so I'm assuming so."

He breathes a laugh. "Christ. Well, women are more... comfortable? To sleep with. Men are..."

"Not?" I offer.

"I don't dislike it. It's just... Obviously, there are loads of ways to have sex. But in my experience, men are always a little gruff and vulgar, like they have something to prove? Some men act like you're a keyhole to stick their cocks in, don't they? Like, 'Oh right, this will fit nicely in here, okay that was lovely, ta-ta and cheerio.' They walk away whistling and adjusting their monocle because they don't give an actual shit about the keyhole itself. Or the fact that a person is *not* a keyhole in the first place."

"And women don't treat you like you're a keyhole?"

Jae laughs. "No. They don't. And I don't treat them like one either."

"I'm sorry that's been your experience."

"That's life," he says. I don't like the apathy in his tone.

"Not always, Jae. Not every male is like that."

"Yeah?"

I smile again. This doctor makes me smile a lot. Something about him is very honest and... Cute? Like he's not hiding anything from me at all, and I want to wrap his feisty and perverted little personality up and squeeze it against my chest. "Yeah. Don't give up hope."

"I haven't," he says. "Lately, I'm thinking about a rather leggy gentleman with obsidian eyes that reminds me of bourbon treacle."

There it is again. I'm smiling.

"Do you have any siblings?" he asks.

"I have an older sister. She's living in Jamaica." My sister is interesting. As soon as our father died, she exiled herself from Japan and never came back. She doesn't even speak in Japanese to me even though we grew up speaking it in the house. Only Spanish or English. When I was a child, I stayed out of our father's way and did what I was told, primarily because I was afraid of him and didn't want to be beaten. But she *constantly* butted heads with him. Mom always said they were too much alike. My sister really hated it when she said that.

"Do you?" I ask.

"No, I don't. Always wished I did, though. Are you close to her? Your sister, I mean."

"We talk pretty regularly—at least once a month. And I like her mate. She's also first-gen."

"Oh wow, she's mated..."

"She is. They've been together for about twenty years."

"That's nice," Jae says, then pauses. Dead space is hanging between us on the line, as if he wants to say something.

"What is it?" I prompt.

"Do you ever date ranked vampires?"

"No," I admit. "Ranked vampires are glamorized in human culture, but the truth is they're rigid and difficult."

"Is this a warning?"

I laugh. "Maybe? That's been my experience. I think yours will be different." I don't think I'm rigid or difficult. In my mind, I'm much more relaxed and easier-going than your typical ranked vamp. My only point of contention is feeling subjugated.

Only a purebred can assert their rank over me since I'm a fairly old-blooded first-gen. I would *never* be with a purebred. My father was purebred with an exquisite bloodline, and he used that fact to boss us all around and run a painfully strict household.

When I was young, my mother loved dancing. Merengue, salsa, bachata. Father forbade her from dancing (and eventually from working as a nurse as well). It was "improper" and "unso-phisticated." The wild swaying of hips to lurid music.

When he was away on business, we danced—the hypnotic rhythms of the requinto, bongos and güira floated through the house, and Mom was full of life. Spinning me and laughing. I remember her hair bouncing as we moved and her beautiful smile. We'd cook together and she'd make dulce frío with fresh fruit on top. Sometimes brownies with chocolate chips (usually at my sister's insistence).

I loved it when my father was away. Those were the best times of my childhood.

"You're already different, Jun. Not like anyone I've ever met." Jae is so sincere when he says these things. His smooth, lighthearted accent is like sparkly sunlight reflecting on a glassy river.

I could tell him I feel the same. That even though things started out rough, he's the most intriguing and delightful creature I've interacted with in a very long time. That he surprises me over and over, which is not an easy feat.

But it's too early to show my hand. Instead, I say, "I'm assuming you mean this in a positive way?"

"Obviously," he says, breathing a laugh. "In the best possible way. I'm looking forward to you coming home..."

I smile, giving in a little. "I am, too. I want to see you, and I need to compile a list of all the places to show you. You've been here almost five months and you haven't seen anything."

"That's not true. I've seen the inside of the Lawson's around the corner from my flat a hundred times. I've also seen multiple train stops on the JR Kishin Line—"

"Ha-ha." I smirk. "Maybe we should start with Kobe. There's a beautiful little town called Kitano that I love—lots of history there—and it has one of my all-time favorite Thai restaurants. Do you like Thai?"

"Y-yes, absolutely."

"Thank God. I've met more than my share of picky eaters. Always humans."

"Vamps aren't fussed about brussels sprouts or broccoli?"

"No, we're not. We're picky drinkers, though."

"Ah yes, well, that figures. Do you feed from humans, Jun?"

"I don't, as a practice. But I have. It's not the best."

"Makes sense..." Jae takes a breath, and I can almost feel the wheels in his head turning through the phone, so I wait. "If... something so fundamental to you isn't satisfying with humans, why bother? What's the appeal?"

"Feeding is fundamental to my existence, but I'm not bound by it. It's not the sole motivation of my everyday life. It's just a thing that I have to do to survive."

"That's... unexpected. I always imagined feeding to be a *very* important and pleasurable thing for vampires. But you make it sound mundane—like breathing oxygen or drinking water."

The thing is, I've been feeding from the same creature since my skin developmentally hardened. Also, I kind of hate him. So, yeah, feeding isn't some magical experience for me. If anything, I dread it and wish I didn't need to do it. I'd be much better off.

"For most vamps, it is," I confirm. "But not for me. Instead of being driven by the way someone might taste, I'd much rather look at the whole picture. Their talents and character, the genuine kindness they exude in their sincere desire to help others, their bright smile or the way the sun catches the warm blonde highlights in their hair. For me, those things are a higher priority."

"I... Yeah. That does sound much nicer."

"You do realize I'm talking about you?"

Jae laughs. "Well, I was hoping, honestly, but I wasn't quite sure."

"Rest assured." I smile. "You have my full attention."

THIRTEEN
JAE

I'm now working on the budgeting part of the surrogate program proposal, which I had intentionally saved for last, because I had likened it to digging my eyes out of their sockets with a dull spoon.

Good news, though. It isn't like that at all. In fact, I have learned some very fascinating things: realm leaders collect taxes from their aristocracy members. I had no idea. It works differently from region to region and country to country, but in Western Japan, there is full transparency between the realm leaders and their aristocracy members—delivered electronically in quarterly reports by Haruka's manservant. The realm leaders pay a lump sum of taxes to human governments to avoid double charging, then they collect and use the members' monies to fund various society events. The refugee programs for the Socotra purebreds are being funded by this.

Also fascinating, when you have two bonded purebreds from differing countries (as with Haruka and Nino), the money and resources between the two aristocracies become fluid—like an infinity symbol stretching between Okayama and Milan. We can't pull everything we need from this singular resource, but Risa assures me that at least twenty-five percent of our funding will come from that. She also thinks Haruka and Nino will make a healthy donation to the program from their private funds.

It amazes me, the way these vampires support each other and make certain that their people want for nothing. Incredible.

I'm editing a chart filled with line items and their projected cost when my phone buzzes. I yawn, and it makes my eyes water as I look down at the screen.

[Why aren't you sleeping?]

Smirking, I grab my phone and type out a response.

[Maybe I was? Until someone texted me and woke me up?]

The response comes quick.

[Should I stop?]

Now I bite my bottom lip, frowning.

[No...]

My phone rings, but it's a video call and it's like my phone has suddenly turned into a live explosive, the way it's stressing me out. I pull my glasses off, rub my fingers against the inside corners of my eyes to make sure there isn't any weird goop there and quickly run a hand through my hair. Shit. I wish I had time to wet it a little.

"Hey," I answer. I look like I haven't slept in days, and the lighting is yellow and dull from the desk lamp in front of me, but everything else around me is drenched in shadows. Not exactly the makings of a sexy late-night call.

Of course, Jun looks flawless. He's outside on a balcony of some sort and the sky is bright blue and partly cloudy behind him. "You're sitting at your desk and fully dressed. Clearly, I didn't wake you?" He cocks one eyebrow up, and his black eyes are shining and playful.

"I said *maybe*. I thought you'd be at the airport by now?" He told me he was planning to fly back tomorrow. He's currently in Prague.

"I got a last-minute request," he says. "So I had to delay my flight a couple days. When's the last time you had a good night of sleep, Jae? You're up every night."

Rubbing my palms against my face, I inhale and exhale a breath. My gut has been on a rampage now for weeks, and I have no clue what to make of it. "I can't remember, but I sleep sometimes. I'm alright—don't worry."

"If you need help with the proposal, don't be afraid to ask for it. Are you worried about budget planning? Remember, you don't need to have everything perfectly figured out. Just esti-mates, and I can help with that as well."

"It's not that. I've got it, I promise." Dropping my hands, I look into the screen and smile. I know it's a weak attempt, but I give it my best effort. It's nice that he's concerned, but I'm really okay. I always manage.

There's a soft moment of silence where we're just looking at each other and he's not saying anything. His face is serious. "You don't have to do everything by yourself, Jae."

The words hang in the air between us, but the impact is like a punch to my gut. Which is the last thing my gut needs—further agitation. I take a breath and swallow, but it goes down like cotton is stuck in my throat. It's too much and I'm too tired. I shake my head. "I'm fine, Jun. But thanks."

He stands, moving the camera as he goes. "It's just a feeling I get from you—like you think you're an island. But I'm here if you need me."

"Okay..." Definitely not going there.

He fumbles with the camera as he moves. "Look at this." The screen flips to the other side, and now I'm looking at an aerial view of Prague. It's like something out of a Shakespearean play: rolling hills backed against a blue sky and white, fluffy clouds hanging listless over red-brown rooftops. There are towers with pointed corners, a wide, glassy river and a series of stone bridges as far as I can see. I've never been to Prague, but this scene is stunning and makes me wish I was there with him.

"Wow. It's beautiful!"

"*You're* beautiful," he says, flipping the camera back to his face and the sly grin on his lips. I rub my hand against my forehead. Every time he says this to me, it throws me. Like I was riding along okay on my bike, but then he sticks a metal bar in the spokes and I go flying over the handlebars. I never know how to respond, except to tell him he's insane. But that's obviously not very nice.

"You dislike it when I tell you this?" he asks.

"It's not that I dislike it... I—I'm just not accustomed to it. So it catches me off guard. Actually... my mother would say that to me a lot, right before she died. So I... I don't know." Add to this, a model-esque first-generation vampire is saying it to me. Should he have his eyes checked? I thought they had amazingly sharp vision.

"Your mother was right. I don't know much about her, but from that, I at least know she was a smart woman."

This makes me smile. "Thanks."

"I have a meeting soon, but I wanted to let you know my plans were delayed. Try to sleep?"

"I will. Good luck with your meeting." We end the video call, and I'm staring at the screen, my mind fuzzy, gut twisty, but my heart warm. I don't know exactly what I'm doing with this posh vampire, but... it's nice. However long I'm on this ride for, I'd like to enjoy it. I'm going to.

I should go to bed. I should try, and I told Jun I would. But I really want to finish this section of line-item estimates. I'm so close to completing the proposal. Once I get it submitted and approved, the real work begins, and I *want* that. If I have to lose a few nights of sleep to bring it along faster, so be it.

WHY DOES the time between a plane landing and a person escaping the airport and reentering society feel like a black hole? Or some sort of gap in the time-space continuum where you can't reach them and you have no clue what's happened to them.

Junichi's plane from Hong Kong (a connection from London via Prague) should have landed two hours ago. I'm sitting in my office and leaning back in my desk chair, staring at my mobile like I'm waiting for it to sprout tiny legs and tap dance across my desk to announce that Jun is back. We've been texting and talking every day for almost three weeks now.

It's 10:35 a.m. and my next appointment is at eleven. An older gentleman who's had mild health issues his entire life—fatigue and rapid weight loss from malnutrition—is visiting me for the first time. The GPs have never been able to pinpoint the problem. His wife has convinced him to come here to be tested and see whether he carries vampiric DNA. I'm excited about meeting him.

Can you imagine? Going your whole life feeling mildly shitty, thinking that's your "normal," only to find out you just needed a little vampire blood to set you straight. I hope I can help him.

I sigh and turn toward my computer. I'm about to respond to an email when there's a knock at the door. "Yes, come in," I say in polite Japanese. The door cracks open, and Junichi pokes his dark, curly head inside. I stand and suck in a breath, eyes wide. Not cool at all. I should probably act less excited, but I cannot.

He steps inside. Of *course* he looks delectable. His fitted trousers are moss green, and he's wearing a crisp white jumper with an autumny, deep goldenrod trench coat over the top and brown leather trainers. His beard is back as well, neatly trimmed and framing his beautiful lips.

"Hello, Doctor Davies. My phone died in Hong Kong. My apologies for the silence."

"Hi..." I don't know what's come over me, but I feel entranced by him as I step around my desk and walk forward. Drawn toward him, and he smells incredible... Why can I smell him from across the damn room? And who gets off a plane looking like this? Did he go home and shower first? It doesn't matter. Vampires. "S'alright... How was your flight?"

"Long." He's smiling and leaning with his back pressed against the closed door, his fingers wrapped around the handle. "Believe it or not, I have an emergency meeting in..." He flips his wrist up to shift his coat sleeve back, looking at his elegant watch. "Eight minutes. I wanted to stop in and let you know I'm back first. I also read through the proposal on the plane. It's excellent. Once the rest of my board approves, you'll be green lighted and fully funded."

"Fantastic." I smile. I'm standing about two feet in front of him now, staring at him like an idiot, so I say, "Are we still meeting up before having dinner at Haruka and Nino's house tomorrow to celebrate the submission?"

He grins, his onyx eyes shining. "Yes. It seems our first dinner date has been crashed."

I shake my head and take another step forward as I stare up at him. "No. This doesn't count."

"No?" He lowers his head slightly to look down into my face. "You're asking me to dinner *twice* now? You may want to wait until after the first. See if I put out."

"Two dinners... three, four." I step into him, and the first thing I do is slide my fingers against the bulge at his crotch. When I feel the full curve of him against my palm, I give him a nice squeeze. He breathes, and a deep but subtle groan registers from his throat. My face is lifted, inches from his mouth. His breath is warm and spearminty when it brushes my lips. "I want as many as I can get."

I raise my chin in a quick motion to press our mouths together, still gripping and caressing his cock with my fingertips. But I pull back to make sure he wants it too. He does, because he slides one hand through my hair and against the back of my head as he leans down. I lick and part my lips so that when he dips into me, his tongue instantly connects with mine. The sensation is magnificent.

His mouth is warm, wet and clean-tasting with a hint of lavender. I moan because it feels like we're fighting—but in the best possible way. He presses his tongue into mine and I push back, like he's challenging me and I meet him every time. Now both of his hands are in my hair, cradling my head and holding me captive.

My chest is so tight and my stomach and groin are burning. The fire actually feels as if it's going up my spine. I've *never* felt like this kissing anyone. I'm still gripping him with my fingers, but I want him naked. I really liked these clothes a few seconds ago, but now I find them wholly offensive. Discourteous.

He lifts up from my mouth, slow, and I suck in a breath from the loss of him and his warmth. I swallow hard. My entire body is trembling. He bends to brush our noses together. I close my eyes because it's the sweetest and sexiest thing anyone has ever done to me.

"The doctor isn't shy," he whispers. My eyes are still closed, but I can hear him smiling.

"I'm not," I say, my throat dry. I swallow again. He's massaging my scalp with his long fingers. His scent is so strong that it feels like it's all around me.

"I'll see you tomorrow afternoon?" he says. He softly brushes his lips against mine. "I don't know how long this meeting will take, and I need sleep."

"Tomorrow," I breathe. I open my eyes to see him staring down at me, smiling. He surprises me when he kisses me quickly on the mouth again, then pulls out of my grasp and cracks the door open. He slips through and is gone.

I'm standing here, shaking like a wet Chihuahua and wondering how the fuck I'm supposed to see patients and get through the rest of the day.

I AM NOT FASHIONABLE. Or trendy.

The world (perhaps mostly the demographic of young women ages sixteen to thirty) has recently become obsessed with Korean pop bands. Young men and women with asymmetrical haircuts, bright, iridescent clothes and pouty, angelic faces.

I look *nothing* like this, and the fact that I am half-Korean is not immediately apparent. I get "something." As in, "You look mixed with something." I don't look like a typical English bloke, but I don't look thoroughly Asian either. I think if my hair weren't this weird lion's mane color and properly black or dark brown, I would visually identify more as the latter. I don't dye it or do anything to it other than get it trimmed. It just grows this color—upstairs and down.

It's Sunday. This particular Sunday has already been much more productive than my usual day off, which consists of lying around my flat watching Netflix and eating crisps until it's time for shōgi. But today I skipped shōgi altogether (I texted Asao to let Haruka know). I've gotten my haircut and gone clothes shopping. I've also picked up a gift for dinner. A fancy variety set of organic green teas.

By four o'clock I'm stepping off the local train at Kurashiki Station. Jun wants to take me on a little momiji viewing tour around his city before we head to dinner at Haruka and Nino's house at seven. He says he knows a quiet spot where the autumn leaves are particularly lovely.

When I'm standing outside the station, I pull my phone out from my back pocket and type out a quick message.

[I'm out front. Are you here?]

The little gray bubbles immediately pop up.

[Three minutes.]

The sun is already low in the sky like a work of art—brush strokes in gradient hues of soft pink, orange and gold. The clouds are heavy, but scattered and shadowy. Today definitely feels like autumn. I can smell rice fields being burned and prepped for the next harvest season as it drifts through the air.

The breeze is cool against my face. I breathe in deep, pulling all of it into my lungs.

Reaching down, I adjust the hem of my jumper. In my effort to avoid being flashy, I think I've gone too far in the opposite direction. My trousers are navy blue and so is my jumper (which fits my shoulders properly, thank you). Underneath, my shirt is black, but there's an embossed, subtle pattern there. Essentially, a mannequin at the department store was wearing this same ensemble in the window, and I pointed to it and told the shop assistant, "This. In my size."

I've made a genuine effort to *not* wear something I've had for two decades. At this moment though, I'm not sure what's more embarrassing—Junichi noticing that I've made an effort or his not noticing.

He's a fashion designer. Of course he'll notice.

When a black taxi pulls up to the curb, I watch as Junichi gets out, thanks the driver and shuts the door. His jumper is beige but has this intricate pattern throughout. There are brown suede patches on his square shoulders and his dress shirt underneath is beige as well. Stunning. It's unfair, really.

He's smiling as he walks toward me. He smoothly steps into me and whispers, "Hello, Doctor." Instinctively, I lift my face since he's so bloody tall, but when he places a firm kiss on my mouth, my chest tightens because we're in *public*. There are lots of people bustling about, and Japan isn't exactly keen on public displays of affection—especially queer ones. So the fluttery feeling in my heart is suddenly in direct conflict with the astute awareness of social constructs in my mind.

As if he senses my anxiety, Jun frowns when he pulls up from the quick kiss. "Everything alright?"

I take a breath to calm my nerves. "Yes. Hello…"

"You look delicious," he says, stepping back and looking me up and down. "Who dressed you?"

A mannequin. The shop assistant? I bought the shoes it was wearing, too. "I dressed myself, you cheeky sod."

He breathes a laugh, smirking. "I don't understand your weird British lingo sometimes, but it's cute so don't stop doing it."

Again with this "cute" business... I'm alright with this, but if he calls me weird, I might be triggered.

"What's that?" he asks, looking down at the thick paper bag with handles that's hanging at my side.

"A thank you to the hosts for inviting me to dinner."

"How thoughtful."

I lift my chin, haughty. "I'm a thoughtful human."

"Hm... *A Thoughtful Human* isn't nearly as good a book title." He takes advantage of my gesture and sneaks in another soft, quick kiss. My heart skips. Christ. I don't know if I've ever felt this excited about someone. It's slightly terrifying.

But I'm grateful, because it seems that my effort yesterday to make the first move has paid off. We've been talking on the phone for three weeks, so I was worried that being together in person wouldn't translate—that we'd be awkward or uncomfortable. Doesn't seem to be an issue, though.

"Shall we? The temple is only a fifteen-minute walk from here." He steps forward and smoothly grabs my free hand, clasping my palm. He pulls me forward and my heart is in my throat: half from the sheer thrill of this little bloom of physical intimacy and half from being hyper aware that people are *actually* staring at us. I'm looking around, my eyes meeting all of theirs, when Jun suddenly stops.

He looks at me, then lifts his head to take in our surroundings and gives my palm a little squeeze. "You're uncomfortable with this?"

"Ah, well... not really, I—"

Gently, he drops my hand, sliding both of his into his

trouser pockets. He smiles. "Understood. Forgive me, Doctor. I'm very old and presumptuous at times. Follow me?" He walks on. I follow him feeling like... what? Shit? A coward? I'm on my first proper date since I can remember when, and with this leggy, statuesque creature. I'm not in the habit of being openly affectionate with another man in public, but... Why the hell should I feel shame or care what strangers think?

I take a few extra steps to meet his long stride. I hesitate, but reach out and wrap my fingers around his wrist. He slows, looking over at me as I urge his hand back out of his pocket. "Not uncomfortable, just... not accustomed." I smile. Having freed his hand, I slide my palm into his again and grip his fingers. He squeezes me in turn as we continue walking down the pavement.

He's looking forward, a smirk on his lips. "I was wondering, 'What happened to the bold man from yesterday?'"

"Well... he was behind a closed door."

"Then I suppose I'll look forward to being behind a closed door with you again."

FOURTEEN
JAE

"I think it's too soon for this question to even be on the table," Junichi says. "Culturally, we're *still* not over the disgusting war crimes committed in the 1940s. We're vampires. We remember shit for a very long time, Jae."

"I don't disagree with you—at all. No question there. It's been in the news a lot though, recently, with the rise of human ailments. Crazy."

Jun has guided me through the most charming little town lined with cobblestoned roads and weeping willows. It's lovely and the air feels particularly clean here. Now, we're navigating up a graveled lane with trees shrouding us on either side. It's secluded. Silent, aside from our feet crunching against the rocks and the occasional breeze rustling through the drying, brittle leaves. The setting sun looks like firelight glowing dimly all around us.

"Did your family participate in the wars at all?" I ask. "I know from researching that many vampire clans stayed completely clear of both World Wars. Went into hiding, even."

"We did. I told you before that my clan was based in

Hiroshima? We left the continent as soon as the humans declared war on America and traveled to Switzerland through my father's network. But my father stayed behind and was at our estate when they dropped the bomb on our city. He survived, but he wasn't ever quite right afterward. It just took a long time for the radiation to finally finish him off."

"Christ, Jun... that's awful."

"Nino's family was heavily involved in the first war," Junichi says. "That's how his mother died. Any vampire that got tangled up in that disaster either starved to death or was captured and experimented on. So for scientists to be bringing up the topic of using our blood for genetic research again... It's disgusting. The experiments done on us might seem like a long time ago for humans—for their lifespan. But not for us. Let's try being diplomatic about this topic again in a thousand years. Until then, fuck all the way off."

"Agreed. Absolutely. As someone with a curious mind, I do hope that one day there can be mutually beneficial, amicable collaboration between the vampire community and the human science community. For the benefit of both parties involved."

"I respect that. And being part of the younger generation, we have adapted and learned better than our ancestors to live in the present—to take life day by day in order to avoid the weight and burden of time. To avoid becoming embittered and out of sync with the fluidity and progression around us. Even still, *we remember*."

I don't even know how we got on this heavy topic. I think it's my fault for bringing up the news? We've been walking along, and now the path has opened up to an enclosed clearing. Before me stands a mossy, hidden-away temple on a low hill. The stone structure is small, but set against a curtain of trees shrouded in hues of red, orange and gold, the leaves flittering in the twilight. I spin slowly, taking in the entire scene. It's breathtaking. Peaceful.

"Do you know what I like about you?" Jun says, walking toward me and taking my hand again.

"What do you like about me?" I ask, grinning as he pulls me toward the narrow steps. I genuinely want to know.

"That you *help* the vampire community. You don't try to take anything from us or poke at us for your own personal benefit. When the board told me they wanted a doctor to launch this new program for lower vamps at the hospital, I was cynical. I told them, 'Good luck finding someone that isn't Dr. Jekyll and Mr. Hyde in disguise.' Experimenting on the marginalized group of us for their own personal benefit. But here you are, sincere and true. I guess anything is possible."

I'm still smiling like mad when we're at the top of the stairs. He lets go of my hand and I walk forward to explore. The area feels ancient, but not decrepit. As with everything else in this small town, it's well maintained and cleanly swept through. Even the fountain at the entrance is in working order—the basin for washing hands is filled with fresh water, and it's trickling smoothly from the mouths of two small stone dragons on either side.

I take a breath, registering the feathery warmth in my heart. I want to be fully present in this moment. Being in this magical folktale setting with this elegant and provocative vampire... Suddenly, it unquestionably feels like anything is possible.

Setting my gift bag for tonight's dinner hosts down on the stone, I reach for the fountain ladle to wash my hands. "Have you ever met a proper ranked-vampire doctor?" I ask.

Jun is across from me, mimicking my actions. "Not personally, but I know they exist. Just very rare. Nurses like my mother and Sora are a little more common."

"Well, vampire doctors aren't high in demand, are they?" I

shake my hands dry before picking up the bag. I walk a little further into the temple grounds, taking in the low, happy chirping of birds in the trees around us when another random thought pops into my head. I turn to look over at Jun. "Do you ever read human novels about vampires?"

"Absolutely not."

I laugh. I guess I wouldn't if I were him, either. "You typically date humans... I'm sure you've come across some odd ones."

"Mm. I'm much wiser about who I choose to spend my time with now, but when I was younger and at the outset of my newfound freedom from my father, I made a lot of poor decisions."

"Like?" I ask, wildly curious.

"Like one male who eventually tried to recruit me for some devil-worshiping cult in the 1970s. Or dating a female who was convinced I was a walking fountain of youth and kept asking if she could taste my blood—'just once.' She ended up trying to stab me..."

"Oh God..."

"Another female in the early eighties asked me to come to church with her. She kept staring at me the whole time and later said she was expecting me to burst into flames. She laughed like it was a joke. Ridiculous shit."

"Wow... Like, was she setting you up to burst into flames? Was she hoping you would?" How bizarre. It took a long time, but finally by the early 1900s, vampires were officially designated as a legitimate species legally recognized by humans across most countries—as opposed to a malformation or experiment gone wrong. A true race biologically and fundamentally different from humans (it's insane to me that this would even need to be "officially" stated). Despite the mandate, socially...

well. There's a very slow trickle down in attitudes and perspectives, isn't there?

"Who knows. By the time I hit a hundred, though, I learned how to pick them better." Junichi winks. "Been smooth sailing ever since."

Now I'm wondering how long he usually stays in relationships with the humans he dates. Until the spark wears out? Until they get old? But that feels pushy, like I'm digging and I want some framing on this—on what he and I are doing now. Talking for three weeks non-stop, wandering through autumnal landscapes on secluded temple grounds and having dinner with his friends. It feels like, well... I won't say it. I'll just enjoy it, for whatever it is.

———

WE EXPLORE the temple grounds a little more before he takes me on a short walking tour of the historical quarter. Afterward, we head over to Nino and Haruka's house for dinner, which is surprisingly only a short walk away.

Their house is gorgeous—traditional Japanese architecture but with sleek modern accents. We're having dinner outside, in the courtyard off the kitchen. There are massive cherry blossom trees here, but it's October, so obviously there are no flowers. The leaves are turning golden with red tips. The canopy reminds me of a fiery sunset, and there are tiny white lanterns strung along the bottom branches. There's a pit of actual fire burning brightly near the oak table we're seated at. It's all utterly gorgeous and posher than anything I'm used to.

Their chef—his name is Sydney, I'm told—is an attractive but wispy young male with very large green eyes. He's definitely ranked (I can tell from his owly eyes) but I have no clue how old he is. I say young because his demeanor is quite different from Haruka, Nino and Junichi's.

Older vampires feel settled, like they've seen some shitty things and are surprised by nothing. Younger vamps seem a little too happy, as if the longevity of life hasn't worn on them quite yet. Nino is the exception to this, because he feels like a little bit of both. I know from his medical records that he's slightly older than Haruka, which is surprising. Haruka feels older. I don't know how old Junichi is. I keep avoiding the question because I think it will freak me out. Like, brilliant—here's *one more* thing that makes me question why the hell you want me.

We have wine and a first course of buttery, light farfalle with spinach, mushrooms and pancetta. I feel like an ass for being surprised by this. For thinking we'd be eating fried pork cutlets or some kind of rice, fish and miso soup combination.

The conversation is surprisingly comfortable despite my general gut-and-spine-related anxiety. We've talked a little about the next steps for the proposal, and Haruka and Nino have asked me questions about my personal background and how I like living in Japan.

Everything has been fairly innocuous, so I'm a little surprised when Haruka blinks his burgundy eyes at me and pointedly asks, "Have you ever had your blood tested?"

"Um... for what?" I ask. Diabetes?

"To see whether you have any remnants of vampire genetics within your bloodline," he says simply, waiting.

This is a basic test anyone can take—particularly humans and low-levelers, since ranked vampires know they're vampires from the outset. It's almost a novelty thing, something you do when you're a teenager and have a laugh about with your mates. But we do use it medically, on occasion (I did yesterday, in fact, for the older gentlemen—who tested positive for vampiric blood). It only means that somewhere in history, *maybe* you had a vampire in your family.

It only gives a positive or negative result. No details. Scientifically, we don't have enough information yet on how vampiric DNA works to discern concrete information. There's no Ancestry or genealogy bank to figure out your vampiric bloodline, because again, proper vampires are born and taught about their heritage.

"I... I have," I admit, not wanting to lie.

"What was the result?" he asks, point blank. Now they're all staring at me with their glassy eyes, and for the first time, I feel grotesquely out of place.

How did I even get here? Sitting in Haruka Hirano and Nino Bianchi's home, having dinner with elusive high-bred vampires and casually spending the afternoon with one that's an internationally recognized designer—one that knew Jimi Hendrix! What the *actual* fuck?

Answering Haruka's question feels absurd. Like I'm sitting beside Mozart at a piano and saying, "Yeah, mate, I like to play 'Twinkle Twinkle Little Star.'" Of *course* I shouldn't be sitting here, because I'm not a vampire in any regard. The stress of it is suddenly winding me up, and my face is growing hot.

What the hell am I doing here?

FIFTEEN

JUNICHI

The Historian is digging for something. Haruka has been digging for a few weeks now because something about Jae is setting him off. I understand. I definitely think there's something funny about him too. But Jae is turning red and rubbing his palm against his face, distressed.

I reach over and gently take hold of his opposite wrist against his thigh. He jumps a little and looks up at me. "Are you alright?" I ask.

"It is not my intention to make you uncomfortable." Haruka gracefully picks up his wine glass. "I was simply curious. Particularly based on the information you shared with me about your mother. Please do not feel pressured to answer."

I slide my palm down, and Jae automatically opens his hand to me. I entwine our fingers together and smile. "No big deal. We're not bullies."

Jae takes a deep breath. "No—I don't think that. Sorry. Sometimes I get in my own head about things. Human failing."

"We all do that," Nino chimes in brightly. "When I first met Haru, I thought he was so mature. He felt wise and experienced, like he knew everything about the world and I didn't know shit... Actually, I *still* feel like that sometimes."

Haruka turns and looks at his mate beside him, concern in his eyes. "You know much more about popular culture than me."

"Is that a good thing?" Nino frowns, pouting. "Tesoro, I don't think that helps my case."

"Business too." Haruka is openly pleading now, leaning toward him. "And finances. *Cooking.*" Nino shakes his head and picks up his glass of wine.

Jae laughs at this, and I smile. Haruka and Nino have this effortless charm, like the love they have for each other unintentionally melts outward and touches anyone in close range of them. After a moment, Jae smiles timidly.

"I tested positive... for vampire genetics. But it doesn't mean anything. It's just a yes-no test."

"May I ask why you took the test?" Haruka asks. "What prompted you?"

"A lot of humans do it for fun, right?" I ask, not wanting him to feel pressured again. Jae runs his fingers into the back of his dark golden wavy hair and takes a deep breath.

"We do, but... the reason why I did it wasn't necessarily for laughs. But... you'll think I'm mad as a bag of ferrets if I tell you."

I frown, blinking. "What the hell does that mean?"

"Crazy," Haruka answers.

Nino draws back. "How do you know *that*, but I had to explain 'banging' as a euphemism to you the other day?"

Haruka shrugs. "I lived in England for several years, and my realm leader there possessed a very colorful vocabulary."

I flick my eyes over to Nino, smirking. "Why were you explaining 'banging' as a euphemism, Nino?"

"Don't worry about it, Junichi." He raises his coppery eyebrow and sits back in his chair, smug.

"Jae?" Haruka says, re-centering the conversation. "Rest assured, we will not think poorly of you. Please explain if you're comfortable."

"Well... alright, I..." Jae takes another deep breath. "Growing up, I thought... I thought my mum was a vampire—but she clearly wasn't, considering she's gone now. She died at forty. At first it was in that way where you're a daft kid, and you think there's a monster under your bed or that the old chap next door is a serial killer."

Haruka turns to Nino, blinking in confusion. "Is this a normal assumption in human culture?" Nino shrugs and takes another sip of his wine.

Jae laughs. "Probably not. But when I was thirteen or fourteen, I started researching vampires. I saw pictures of what they looked like when they were very ill—gray, skin drying out and emaciated. That's how my mum looked in the end. Like she'd just dried up. She was sickly off and on her whole life, but things got worse and worse as she grew older.

"After she died, I told my dad that I thought Mum was a vampire. I'll never forget his response. He said, 'Why do you think that?' Not, 'Shut it, you idiot,' or 'Are you stark raving mad?' His face was totally straight, and he wasn't shocked by my question at all. When I told him my rationale, he just nodded. He didn't say anything else, and we never talked about it again. I had the test done when I was sixteen."

I swallow hard. We're all completely silent, listening to him. I don't know how to take this information, but I definitely don't think he's crazy.

"Have you ever wanted blood?" Haruka asks, his gaze focused. "Or been hungry for something you couldn't discern?"

Jae draws back. "Me? *No.* Of course not. Never. I'm totally, absolutely human."

"How does being around us make you feel?" Haruka asks. He's going in hard now, and he's the only one talking. Nino and I are watching it all unfold.

"Well, if I'm honest... I'm alright." Jae shrugs. "But I'm definitely nervous. Like my insides feel all twisty and weird. Anxiety."

"Does that always happen when you're nervous? Or is this a recent development?"

"Ah... maybe recent? Since I moved to Japan it seems to have gotten worse. It's a new country and new environment for me. I'm still adjusting to everything."

Haruka nods. "Of course. Jae, have you ever been sick? Perhaps a cold or the flu?"

Jae laughs, and I'm relieved. Haruka's questioning feels intense, but I also see what he's driving at. "I don't think so," Jae answers. "Lucky, I guess? Haruka, I am *not* a vampire. I don't drink blood and I've never wanted to. I'm just... weird. And..."

"Yes?" Haruka encourages.

"I... I've had lower-level vamps bite me before. They say I'm pretty disgusting. Bluntly, actually. If I were a vampire, I'm certain that wouldn't be the case."

At this, Haruka sits back and picks up his wine glass, bringing it to his lips. This last bit of information... It says something. Significant. Haruka recognizes as much and has clearly come to a decision. He raises his eyebrow before he takes a long sip. "Not necessarily."

The rest of dinner is much less tense. Whatever Haruka was digging for, he's satisfied with the result. Afterward, when I'm standing outside the stone walls of the estate with Jae, I exhale a sigh.

"Well, my apologies for our host tonight. He's usually much

more laid-back than that. I didn't think we were walking into an interrogation."

Jae shakes his head, smiling. "No, no. It's okay. It was... interesting to talk about those things. I've had the thing with my mother bobbing around in my head for years, so it was nice to hash it out, actually." Jae runs his fingers through the back of his hair and laughs. "And Haruka is quite... compelling? It almost feels like I *have* to answer him. He's like vampire royalty."

I narrow my eyes at this. His word choice, coupled with the tense discussion of whether or not Jae could be a vampire, raises a flag in me. "Do you feel compelled to answer him? In some innate way?" I ask. Haruka is young, but his bloodline is very old, which deeply impacts all ranked vampires he encounters. Whether they want it or not. We're all very fortunate that he's more of a levelheaded introvert than a power-hungry egomaniac.

Jae frowns at me. "Christ, Jun—not you too? I'm *human*. Do you really think I'm standing here as a vampire and wouldn't know it?"

"Truthfully? I don't know, Jae. You smell good to me and register as attractive to my innate nature, which is unusual. But you don't feed—don't want to feed—and you're healthy. So maybe you're right? Or maybe you're a low-level vamp and you ignore your diluted bloodline?" Although low-level vamps never smell as good as he does...

Jae shrugs. "Maybe? Anyway, I know what I feel. I'm human... a human with a great deal of anxiety."

This doctor with his radiant skin, chestnut eyes and this neat little outfit that he clearly picked off a mannequin at an upscale department store. I don't usually have sex in my house, but I'm considering taking him home with me. That sounds strange, but because of my circumstance with my source, I always conduct my intimate affairs and relationships when I'm abroad and stay clear of the aristocracy—my home. In the rare times I've met someone in Japan, it's usually Tokyo or Sapporo, somewhere far off where no eyes are watching me.

In this current context, there's no way to say, "Should we get a hotel?" without sounding sleazy and arrogant. That's not how I do things.

Jae is standing beside me until he does a half-turn so that he's directly in front of me. Our bodies are almost touching, but he puts his hands behind his back and looks up at me from behind his black-framed glasses. "You're quiet?"

I'm remembering yesterday, when he shocked the hell out of me and slid his fingers against my cock and gripped me. I don't know what I was expecting when I walked into his office to say hello, but it was *not* that. That... was a glorious surprise. And kissing his sensual little mouth was even better.

For some reason, I expected him to be shy. He's not exactly short, but much shorter than me and with a lean frame. I assumed I'd have to make the first move. He constantly shifts between insecure (ashamed?) and brazen, but I love his feisty, bold spirit. I never know what I'm going to get, and it's enthralling. It's not easy to catch a one-hundred-and-thirty-year-old vampire off guard, but he succeeds over and over again.

I look down at him, but I don't kiss him. I could. He's right there. "I'm thinking."

"About?" He's staring up at me. It feels like he's goading me to take his mouth. Earlier at the train station, he went rigid when I kissed him out in the open, but we're the only ones on this street now...

I lean down and brush my nose into him. He closes his eyes and sighs, returning the gesture. He really likes this. "You," I say, "and me."

"Doing terrible, very bad no-good things?"

I laugh. "Is that what you want, Jae?"

"Yes," he breathes, still caressing his nose into me. He tilts his head and lifts his chin, placing a soft kiss on my lips. "Do you?" he whispers.

Caving, I wrap my arms around his waist and bring him into me. He puffs out a breath when he hits my chest and groin, then smiles. I kiss him again before I say, "I would rather do wonderful, beautiful, very *good* things to you, if that's okay? Will you come home with me?"

He lifts, wrapping his arms around my shoulders and pressing his body even tighter into me. I squeeze him because hc feels marvelous and warm. He whispers against my mouth, "Absolutely."

SIXTEEN

JAE

Junichi has a cat. She's black, with a black leather collar and golden eyes. At first, I was shocked by this. And she likes me. Junichi is shocked by *that*. The moment I kicked my shoes off and stepped onto the hardwood floor, she started slinking around my legs. When I petted her, she arched her back up into my palm. Her name is Lulú. He told me she usually scratches and hisses at anyone who comes in besides him, and he has to yell at her to go upstairs (apparently, she listens, which I find remarkable). Anyway, I consider this a good thing. Lulú is definitely in my corner.

Naturally, Junichi's house is exceptional. It's like a fashionable rainforest. The walls of the hall are creamy and warm with soft lighting, but his main living room is painted in a deep, deep green (like, navy green). There are loads of plants, interesting pictures framed in black and white, and his plush sofa is the color of sunflowers. The entire back wall of the house is glass, and I can see grass outside, a privacy wall of bamboo and a patio with comfy-looking furniture.

I'm only able to glance at these things, because Junichi holds my hand and pulls me through the open living room and kitchen area, then down a narrow hall. It's thrilling. I'm in Junichi's house and it's saturated with his scent: the epicenter. His hand is warm and firm, sending something like electric shocks up my arm. I can't catch my breath.

His bedroom is dark. The glass wall continues into this space, so the soft blueish haze of the moon is the only source of light. He's pulling me toward the bathroom and smiling. "Can we shower first?"

I nod. I showered before I left Himeji for dinner, but what the hell? We can damn well do anything he pleases.

WHAT'S mind-blowing to me is that there's more. If we didn't do anything else besides that shower, I would feel like the luckiest man in the world.

Junichi has an impressive shower, like a large stainless-steel box raining down water from the ceiling. It was perfectly warm and his large hands were all over me, and mine on him, as if we were cautiously trying to figure each other out. People-shaped Rubik's Cubes.

While he was kissing me and my mind was focused on his mouth and the slippery heat of him against me, his hands slid down to my arse. He stuck one of his long fingers inside me, and it was so gentle and slow that it took me a moment to register it.

When I did, though, it made me feel dizzy because of how *good* it felt. It didn't burn or feel awkward like it usually does when a guy does that to me. His mouth was hard on mine—his cock sliding against me and his free hand stroking my lower back and the hot water raining down... It's like there were too many sensations to manage, and all of them felt incredible.

I'm in his bed now, naked and on my back with a pillow tucked underneath my hips. That's new too. I'm elevated slightly. A sex ramp. He's got two slick fingers inside me and his head is slowly bobbing between my thighs. My cock is in his mouth, and I can feel his tongue licking and sliding against me as he twists his fingers inside me. He keeps pulsing them, so slowly, in and out. I groan, stretching my lower spine. *God* this feels so good. All of it—the cool, soft sheets against my back, his free hand caressing my hip, the clean, lavender smell of him as I inhale. The orgasm is bubbling low and hot in my groin, like he's slowly pulling it from me. Cultivating and releasing it for me.

"*Jun.*" I breathe his name just before it rushes from me and all through me, making me tremble and stiffen until it releases its hold on my body. I said his name to warn him that I was coming, but he kept his head there, steadily licking and tasting me. My chest is heaving when he pulls his head up. He licks my tip, and it is the sexiest shit I have ever seen—like he couldn't get enough of me and wants every drop.

He lifts. I suck in a breath when I feel him press a third lubed finger inside me. It's incredible. Already I feel the warmth of pleasure bubbling in my groin again.

When he's hovering over me, he rests down on one elbow because his other hand is still busy inside me. His long body is perfect—beautifully brown and smooth like peanut butter and with elegantly defined muscles. A smattering of silky dark hair on his chest. I spread my thighs wider, letting him stretch me to his heart's content.

"Are we okay, sunshine?" he whispers. The warmth of his breath grazes my skin. I lift my chin, parting my lips as I take his mouth. I've never felt this before, but I want to taste myself *on* him—mixed in with his perfect lavender and minty flavor. I didn't think I was into that, but I am. Quite suddenly.

He does something with his three fingers inside me that makes me grunt in pleasure against his mouth. He lifts and I inhale sharply. When I can gather myself, I say, "I'm ready. I want *you*."

Junichi smiles, warm and frisky, like I'm not just some human he's fucking. Like he really believes I'm this beautiful, inexplicable creature. He slowly removes his fingers from my body, hooks his hand behind my knee and gently slides me and the pillow down further on the bed. The move surprises me, and I laugh, breathy and happy. I'm utterly euphoric. I don't know if I have ever been this happy and carefree with anyone in the sack.

There's a condom beside Junichi, and he grabs and tears it open. I push myself up, grinning. "Let me?" He hands it to me like he's passing the butter dish at dinner, smirking. I pull it from the package, feeling the wetness in my fingertips. He kisses my forehead, then my nose and cheek as I reach down to grip him. He goes in to kiss the concave of my neck, but I hunch my shoulder, laughing. "Fuck, Jun, you're distracting me."

He laughs, but stops to let me concentrate. When I have the condom on his tip, I carefully unroll it. That's when he ducks down to take my mouth again. I roll it up his length until he's properly covered, indulging in the rhythm of his mouth on mine as I finish blindly. Just feeling and gripping him.

Junichi pulls up from the kiss and presses his fingertips into my chest, urging me back. I flop back down somewhat dramatically and exhale a sigh. I swear to God this is the longest plow I have ever had. We just keep *going*, and he hasn't even fucked me yet. It feels like it's been hours of bliss, and I've already come two times (I came in the shower, too, from a nice mix of tobacco sandalwood soap and frotting).

"I warned you that I like to take my time," Junichi says. I'm gaping my thighs wide for him again as he settles down between them, leaning over me. I can feel the tip of his shaft pressed to my opening.

I smile. "You did. I have no complaints." He slowly presses himself inside. I plant my feet and shift my hips up and into him, urging him deeper. But he rocks himself against my body, making me lift my feet and pull my knees back toward my chest. He's warm and thick inside me, but not all the way in quite yet.

He's smiling with his full lips and hovering over me when he says, "No help, please."

I relax into the new position, crossing my ankles behind his arse and resting my heels there. "The cheek." I smirk.

"I don't know what that means," he whispers as he kisses my mouth, but I'm laughing so we don't quite connect. My arms are wrapped around his shoulders. Now that he's fully inside me, he relaxes his weight down, then guides my arms up until they're stretched over my head. My elbows are bent slightly, but I feel elongated like this, somehow even more exposed. He slides his hands into my hands, and we entwine our fingers together. The minute I squeeze his palms, he pumps his body into me, one good, firm time.

I open my mouth to gasp and he leans down and licks into me. It's happening again—an abundance of sensations. He's kissing me, pulsing his cock into me and gripping my hands tightly all at once. It's overwhelming. It feels amazing, but something about this... What he's doing is making me crumble emotionally. My heart is too warm in my chest, and my stomach is swarming with butterflies.

He's rocking against me, slowly and over and over. He pulls up from my mouth. Now he's watching me with his onyx irises.

His nose is brushing against my face, but he's lazily catching my mouth too. Watching me. I can't breathe.

"Let go for me, sunshine. Don't fight it." He shifts his hips harder into me, and I make a whimpering sound that I have *never* made before. That I've never, ever heard myself make. It's like he's hit something so deep within me, and it triggers my entire body. I didn't think I needed to let anything go, but it suddenly feels as if I do. I groan as the heat races up my spine and to my brain, to my chest and out to my limbs.

Junichi's heavy body trembles on top of me, and he firmly shifts his hips into me one last time. His body stiffens, and he's leaning his forehead against me, breathing into me.

For some very odd reason, I really want him to bite me. Right now. I know what he is, and what he needs. I wish... It's like my body *wants* to give it to him. Somewhere inside me. I never feel this way when I sleep with low-levelers. They just bite me because that's what they do. I never really want it. But I *want* it with Junichi. I suddenly wish I could satisfy him innately—deep within his unique nature. That I could give him what he's just given me.

When he's come down from his climax, he's lazily smiling and kissing me upside my face, my cheek and temple. I realize that *this* is making love. The physical act of showing deep affection and desire for another person. Expressing your emotions and fondness through the gift of intense pleasure.

Junichi showed me that tonight. He gave that to me. He made love to every inch of me, and I'm terrified that I might be ruined now because of it.

SEVENTEEN

JUNICHI

I get up first the next morning and take a quick shower. When I come out, Jae is still asleep in my bed—perfectly cozy and lying on his side, like it's where he belongs. Like he sleeps here all the time.

It's 5:30 a.m. I don't know what time his shift starts at the hospital (I think he works fairly normal hours, since he's a specialist). But I imagine he'll want to go home and get dressed for work. The train to Himeji from my house is just under an hour.

I walk over to my bed, lean across so that my hands are braced on either side of his body, then bend and kiss him in the concave of his neck. I whisper, "Doctor Davies? You need to get up."

He stirs. When he first opens his warm brown eyes, it's a dreamy, satiated daze. The expression quickly shifts to confusion, then something like humiliation as his gaze flickers and lands on me. Damn. A lot just happened in those seven seconds. "Good morning."

He rubs one hand into his messy golden bedhead and

slowly sits up. His shoulders are hunched, voice scratchy. "Morning."

"What time is your shift today?"

"*Shit*—what time is it now?"

I flick my wrist up and check my watch. "Five thirty-five."

He sighs. "Oh... Um—eight."

"You have plenty of time. I don't cook, but do you want coffee? Tea?"

"Tea, please..."

"Earl gray or green? I only have the two."

"Earl gray, please?"

Nodding, I head toward the door. "You can take a shower here if you want. There's a towel on the bathroom counter for you. Your choice."

When I'm in the open space of my living room, I crack the sliding glass wall open. The morning air is crisp, hazy, and it looks like rain. Autumn. I grab my remote and click on my entertainment system, then quickly switch to the streaming music channel with classic jazz. Dave Brubeck's "Take 5" is playing. Perfect.

I head to the kitchen and start the tea for Jae. Coffee for myself. I pause when I hear the rain shower head in my bathroom running, which is interesting because I never hear it from an outside perspective.

Making love to Jae was truly divine. He's trusting, relaxed, playful and perfectly warm and delicious. He has a little brown mole to the right of his belly button, one just inside his left thigh and another on the concave of his neck. God... It's like they're targets that say, "Please bite here, here and here."

I wanted to bite him. *Badly.* Which shocked the hell out of me. He smells so good, and I can't understand why. I'm trying not to harp on it like Haruka is doing. If Jae says he's human, he's human. I like him, and things are going smoothly between us.

Plus, he doesn't drink blood. No feeding at all. Regardless of everything else, *that* is what fundamentally defines us. So if he's not doing that, he can't be one of us.

It's another fifteen minutes before Jae is peeking his damp head through the doorframe of the hallway. His golden hair looks especially dark since it's wet, and his glasses are back on his face. He'd ditched them last night before our very sensual shower.

"Hey, there's a mug and tea bag on the counter for you."

"Thanks." He moves slowly toward the counter, then sits himself atop a barstool. I grab the teapot, walk over and fill his mug with steaming water, careful not to spill on my countertop.

When I'm done, I flick my eyes up to him. "Is everything alright, Doctor?"

He tears the tea bag open and slowly dips it into the cup. He's staring down into it, his face unreadable. "My baggage is clouding my view again."

I breathe a laugh. Not because it's funny, but because it's forthright. "Can I help with this? I appreciate your honesty."

He looks up at me, his lovely eyes serious. "Are we done?"

"Do you *want* to be done?"

"Well... not really."

"Did you enjoy last night?"

"Yes. Did you?"

I smile. "Very much. I would like to do it again. Plus, you said you wanted *two* dinners."

"I said as many as I can get." He smiles for the first time. It's a weak, hesitant smile, but it's there.

"I remember." I lean on the counter with my elbows directly across from him. "Because of who I am, and who you are, we can't ever have anything very serious..."

The doctor nods. "I know."

"But as long as we're both enjoying, I think we should enjoy?"

"I would like that." Jae smiles a little brighter, and I swear his eyes look like there's light behind them. I shake my head.

"Alright," I say. "Let's seal the deal."

Now, Jae is sporting his normal sincere grin. His perfectly straight white teeth are shining. He lifts from the stool and leans forward, tilting his head slightly as he presses his lips to mine.

It's a sweet, slow kiss, and it feels like we already have our own rhythm. We're learning each other. His mouth tastes like peaches and cinnamon to me, even though I know he couldn't possibly have even brushed his teeth and humans typically have terrible morning breath.

LATER IN THE WEEK, Haruka sends me a text message asking me to come to the estate. This is weird.

Haruka never texts me. Or anyone. Nino says he only texts *him* back (sometimes) because he's spent over a year fussing at him about it. The purebred simply doesn't like smartphones. Something about the light of it bothers his eyes. It's not an official summons with his family's seal delivered and written in Asao's voice, but knowing Haruka, something is up.

It's Friday when I finally have time to stop by the estate. Being in Europe for two weeks is fantastic, but it creates a backlog of appointments and requests for me at home. I told Jae I would try to come to Himeji for dinner sometime during the week, but I haven't had time. Maybe I'll go tonight for a little while? Sundays are just better for both of us because he's off and usually I am too.

Today's visit to Haruka and Nino's home is absolutely different, because when I walk in, Asao tells me Haruka is in his office. "Where the hell is his office?" I ask. "We conduct all our business in the kitchen."

Asao laughs at this as he guides me down the hallway opposite the kitchen. "Your doctor boyfriend has created a spark of life in Haruka. He's going to Hong Kong next week."

I draw back, surprised. "Hong Kong? He's not my boyfriend." I'm a hundred and thirty years old and Jae is over thirty. Nobody in this situation is a fucking "boy."

Asao stops, raising his eyebrow. "Are you sleeping with anyone else right now?"

I lift my chin, indignant. "How do you know I'm sleeping with him?"

"You're sleeping with him. *At home.* That in and of itself is telling."

"Alright, old man. Keep walking."

Asao laughs and moves forward. I tell him too much. If I'm honest, Asao is a little like the father I never had. Well, the father I *wish* I had. He tells me what I need to hear, but he's kind. Thoughtful, in a gruff way. I asked Haruka how it felt being raised by Asao after his own father died. He said he greatly respects Asao and values the role he's played in his upbringing, but that no vampire could replace his biological father.

I've heard that Haruka's father, Hayato Hirano, was an incredible male—both publicly and privately. Very sharp and notoriously affectionate. Mischievous. Vampires in Okayama are hard-core loyalists to the Hirano Clan in part because of him.

Haruka once told me that when he was little, his father used to hide in the house. When Haruka went looking for him, he'd jump out from somewhere and sweep him up, hugging and kissing him. Haruka said it was both exciting and terrifying.

That story and the image of it stuck with me. I can't think of one time my father ever played with me like that—or in *any* way. Haruka's situation was the exception. Mine was more the norm. Old-school purebred fathers... They're not playful and affectionate. They don't typically do hide-and-seek.

Asao slides the door open for me and I walk inside. Haruka's office is his father's old office. It's traditional, with tatami floors, paper doors decorated with elegant sumi-e artwork and a wall of glass windows on the opposite side that show a view of the back garden and koi pond. There are also rows of book-shelves lining the back wall, and Haruka himself is sitting at a low table on a cushion. He's wearing a casual black robe that I designed for him.

Aside from his clothing, it all feels a little too formal, so when I'm standing in front of him, I lift my palms. "Um, what the hell?"

He's writing something. He briefly flicks his sangria-colored eyes up at me before looking back down at his journal. "Your lover is a vampire."

I sit down across from him, folding my legs against the tatami. I quickly decide I'm more comfortable with "lover" over "boyfriend." I don't argue it. "He doesn't feed, so how can he be a vampire?"

Haruka sighs and puts his pen down. He pulls his long fingers up to the center of his forehead and massages. "I'm still figuring that part out. However, he is indisputably vampiric in nature—and ranked. *Not* low level. It is likely that his mother was vampiric in nature as well, and because she denied her body the resources it needed, she perished."

Folding my arms, I let that sink in. "These are big assumptions to make. And I don't think they hold water, given the fact that Jae doesn't *feed*. Doesn't want to."

Haruka leans forward on his elbow, lifting his hand and holding up a single finger. "One, Jae registers as attractive to our natures. Two, he carries a unique scent. Three, he said lower-level vampires find him displeasing to taste. What he does not realize is that lower-level vampires find *all* ranked vampires displeasing to taste."

At this, I sigh. Jae had told me this before. When he reiterated it at dinner, I remember thinking it didn't help his case. Lower-level vampires find our blood to be too strong, too potent. Like having vodka straight. No ice, nothing. There's this misconception—more like a fantasy—among some younger low-level vampires that drinking ranked-vampire blood would be this euphoric and life-changing experience. They're wrong. They would gag.

Haruka has all four fingers up and only his thumb tucked into his palm. "Four, he has never been ill—which is extremely unusual for a human. Five, he said that his body has felt uncomfortable since he's moved to Japan. 'Twisty and weird' is exactly what happens with our natures when we are drawn toward other ranked vampires. Instinctively, he probably moved here because of the pull of his kin. Six—"

"*Alright*, Haruka, I hear you." When he pulls his other hand up to count, I'm over it. I get it. "You think Jae is a secret ranked vampire."

"My theory is that he is repressed." Haruka folds his arms, sitting up straight.

"You can only repress your nature as a low-leveler. Vampires whose bloodlines are so far removed that they are predominantly human, so they can ignore the remnants of their natures, right?"

"Yes, typically, but... what if a ranked vampire figured out how to suppress his or her bloodline?"

"Why the hell would they do that? We take pride in our natures."

"Correct. However…" Haruka takes a deep breath, his brow crinkled. "This is conjecture, but Jae is of English descent. We know that British vampires have a particularly violent and bloody past with the clan wars. What if… to escape the immediate threats, the vampires of the past decided to shut their bloodlines down? Turn in on themselves?"

This is a lot to take in, this wild theory. Haruka is more alive and excited than I've seen him in weeks. It's kind of nice. "Again, I hear you. But I don't see how any of this could be possible."

"No one thought breaking a bond was possible until it happened to me."

I nod. "True…"

"And I did not think bonding on the first try was possible until it happened to me. So I feel this circumstance is feasible. Perhaps the details of my theory are fallible. Nonetheless, Jae is a ranked vampire. If you feed from him, it will solidify my claim."

I rub my hand into the top of my head, fluffing out the tight curls there, and sigh. "I'm not feeding from him. I'm busy. I can't afford to be locked up in the house for multiple days if you're wrong."

He shakes his head. "I am not."

I roll my eyes.

"Junichi—the fact that he is even closely associated with us is telling. We do not casually consort with humans."

"I do," I admit, shrugging.

"This is *different*. Jae studies vampires, he works in a vampire-owned hospital and is now living in a heavily populated vampiric realm. He is dating an elite first-gen vampire and working with purebred vampires to launch a very cultur- ally significant program. The signs are everywhere."

"Maybe he's just a very lucky groupie?" I jest, but I do believe him now that he's pointed all this shit out to me. It makes me nervous, and I don't want to think about it right now. "What are you going to Hong Kong for?"

"There is a Historian there, a colleague whose library reaches back further than mine. I contacted her recently, and she has some ancient documents on vampiric suppression. I am going there to read her materials."

"Wow, you're really taking this seriously."

Haruka frowns like I'm being stupid. "Something very interesting and rare is happening within my realm. It is my responsibility to understand and potentially help Jae should the need arise."

I steel myself and ask the crucial question. "If you think Jae is a repressed ranked vampire, does that mean I shouldn't be sleeping with him? Am I in danger of accidentally bonding with him?"

Haruka's face is flat now, but it's still a look that says I'm being stupid. "Jun. It takes two-way feeding and sex to bond... and I suspect even more than that, now that Nino and I have thoroughly manipulated the *Lore and Lust* data and spoken to many Socotra purebreds. You refuse to feed from him, and he has no interest in feeding from you. So *no*. You won't bond."

He's right. That was a stupid question—like I'm a kid asking how babies are born. Except I'm old as hell and know better. I exhale in relief. Sleeping with Doctor Jae was a deli- cious and fulfilling experience, and I genuinely enjoy spending time with him. I'm looking forward to seeing him again.

I don't like fooling around with ranked vampires. The larger part of me hopes Haruka is wrong about all of this.

But something inside me knows he's probably right.

EIGHTEEN
JAE

I think it's selfish to hide things about yourself. Especially if you're in a relationship. Essentially, you're taking control and deciding that your desires and well-being supersede your partner's. Seems a bit unfair.

"So what will happen if I stop?" It's Saturday, and I'm having a consultation with the last patient on my schedule.

"Well..." I consider. "You'll experience a noticeable difference in your energy levels and senses. Your nature is primarily human, but on the higher end of the low-level vampire spectrum. To stop drinking blood altogether will be much like going through drug withdrawal. It is something that has enhanced your body and senses for years. Ten, right?"

My patient rubs his hands into his hair, utterly stressed. He hunches, placing his elbows against his thighs. "Yeah... I started when I was twenty-one. It helped me get through my doctorate. Now that I'm with Ami... *Shit.* I don't want her to know about this. I don't want to do this anymore."

Ami is my patient's fiancée. He intentionally hides his "other" nature from her. She's human and he thinks it will freak her out, so he wants to stop drinking blood altogether. But that'll be hard since he's been doing it for so long. As a low-leveler, once you submit to that part of your nature, it's quite difficult to turn off.

"Sometimes... I want to bite her when we're sleeping together. I told you my teeth can actually sharpen into little points?"

"Yes, you mentioned it before. But this is nothing to be alarmed about. It's fairly common among people in your similar circumstance." His incisors won't fully elongate like a ranked vampire's, because his biology doesn't require as much blood. My understanding is that the higher the physiological need for blood, the longer, sharper and more intense the fangs.

"Doctor Davies, I *can't*. I don't want to do that with her. She'll *freak* if she knows."

"It's distressing, I do understand. And it is a very serious choice you're making. You could at least *try* opening up to her about it? If you would like, you can even bring her to your next appointment, and the three of us can talk about it together so that I can explain your nature in detail?"

He whips his head up at me, his eyes hopeful. "Really? You would do that?"

"Of course. I'm here to support you. Having a medical professional explain that you're not a threat, nor would you ever hurt her because of your nature, could be helpful?" I also want to say that if she does "freak out" about his true nature, perhaps he's better off? Maybe he should find someone who truly accepts him for who and what he is?

But I don't say any of that. It's not my place.

"Okay..." he breathes. "Let me think about it. Thanks so much, Doctor Davies."

"My pleasure. So does this mean you don't want a bag this week?"

He's still now and blinking at me. I stifle the urge to laugh. He lifts one corner of his mouth in a grin. "Ah... no, I'll still take one. Might as well not suffer until I have to?"

"Right. Stop by Sora's desk on your way out. She'll schedule our next appointment and set you up with the appropriate bags."

"Thanks, Doctor."

When my patient is gone, I relax back in my chair and pull my mobile from my lab coat pocket. I type out a quick text and hit send.

[Shall I meet you at your shop? Or at the restaurant?]

Junichi told me that depending on how his day went, he might be running late. There's some fancy vampire wedding event this coming week, and he's had some last-minute alteration requests.

[Come to the shop please. I'll be ready by the time you're here. We can go together.]

I nod and type out my response.

[Okay. Leaving the hospital now. Going to stop home first. xx]

[Safe travels. xx]

My gut is all twisty just thinking about him. We intended to meet up for dinner through the week, but we were both too busy.

We. Like I'm in a proper relationship. I just want that to settle for a moment and swoon.

We were going to wait until today to meet. That is, until he surprised me on Friday night. He stopped by my flat on his way to some aristocracy event, brought me a new bouquet of bird-of-paradise, then kissed me until I couldn't breathe. When he left me standing in the foyer, I was insanely wound up.

Ironically, Lucy called me shortly after, asking if she could stay the night. My body *desperately* needed an outlet, but I told her I was busy to save myself from treating her like a keyhole.

I GO HOME and change clothes before hopping on a train to Kurashiki. I have my leather rucksack with my toothbrush and a change of clothes because I'm off tomorrow and I've been invited to stay the night. I'm wearing another mannequin ensemble I purchased, but basic. Just a smart gray jumper and new jeans. The trainers paired with the mannequin were somewhat flashy (bright red, canvas), so I went with the same pair but in white. The shop assistant said it looked good?

Junichi's shop is in the historical quarter of downtown Kurashiki. I love walking through this area. It's so quaint and picturesque. When I tug the door open, a delicate little wind chime rings out. The inside of his shop is modern and clean. The walls are a blueish gray with white furniture and a modern art–looking light fixture hanging from the ceiling. It looks like a bird's nest puffed out into a sphere.

"Jae?"

"Yep." I hear him call my name from somewhere in the back, so I walk forward and down a narrow hallway toward him. There are stylishly framed photos of him with famous people on the walls. Some I recognize, some I don't. There's a framed glossy magazine cover with him on it as well. Three covers... five.

"Hello, sunshine."

Jun is standing near a white table and organizing bits and bobs, smiling. His golden-brown skin is warm and radiant. "Hiya." He's less flashy today, in a simple forest-green jumper and light jeans that are all ripped up like an angry cat got at him. I guess this is fashionable? He's still sporting delicious facial hair.

I walk over to him, and he stops what he's doing and faces me. He grips my chin in his fingers, lifts my head and leans down into me. Reflexively, I open my mouth to him. It's ridiculous, but he tastes incredible every time. Something about him... It's deeply comforting to me. Familiar in a way that's illogical—like I *know* him, or some aspect of him, deeply. He sighs in the kiss, as if I taste just as good to him. I hope I do.

When he lifts up, he's still holding my chin and blinking down at me with his darker than black eyes. "Who dressed you?"

I snort in a laugh. "*Me.*"

"Your clothing has changed since the first few weeks we interacted. Are you making an effort for me?"

I pull my face from his grip. "Don't point it out. It's embarrassing." It really is. He grabs my wrist and drags me back into him. When I'm close again, he wraps his arms around my waist.

"I love it," he says. "It's adorable."

"I'm not a bloody bunny rabbit," I say, snaking my fingers underneath his jumper at his waist. He has this short, silky-curly hair around his tight belly button, and suddenly I'm very determined to caress my fingertips against it. I'm distracted from my task when he slides his hands down to my arse and grips me against him.

"Are you sure?" He breathes a laugh, leaning into my ear and kissing me there. *God...* I might be a rabbit, because I could fuck him where we stand. I could fuck him on every surface in this room if he let me. No dinner. Just sex all over his studio, please, ta.

He shifts his face into me and does that thing with our noses that I love. It's getting hot and heavy with his hands gripping and squeezing me against him, and he's about to kiss me again, but the little wind chime at the front door rings out. He freezes and stretches his neck up like a giraffe that senses danger. "Dammit," he breathes, then releases me and moves toward what looks like a very large walk-in wardrobe.

"What is it?" I ask.

"Takayama Junichi?"

A young person's voice calls out from the front. Very proper. When the owner of the voice walks through the doorframe, they're not quite what I was expecting. It's a vampire, and his hair (I *think* he's a "he"? They?) is like platinum, slicked back in a long thick ponytail. The vampire's pale face is narrow and sharp, like a caricature of a half-moon, and their clothes look expensive but gaudy. Too many patterns.

The young vampire stares at me with blood-red eyes. Without warning, the creature opens their mouth and hisses at me, crouching slightly at the knees and bringing their hands up like claws. I take a step back because it feels like they're about to morph into some sort of feline. I don't think vampires can do that, but there are many things in this world that I don't understand.

Junichi pokes his head out of the wardrobe, clearly angry. "D-did you just *hiss* at him? What the hell is wrong with you?"

"*What is this?*" the gaudy cat-vampire says, circling me. I'm genuinely getting freaked out, so I take another step back. "Is he a human or a vampire? I can't tell!"

Junichi hesitates for a moment, looking at me, and I catch his eye. It's as if he's considering the question, like he isn't quite sure himself. He shakes his head. "Hisaki, stand up straight and stop acting like an asshole. You're being fucking rude right now."

Ah. This is Hisaki... He does as commanded and stands up straight, but points at me like we're fighting while looking at Junichi. "Why does he *smell* like this? He reeks of ambiguity and confusion. I'm around humans all the time and they have a very distinct smell—but his smell is not quite human, not quite vampire either..."

Hisaki whips his head back, ponytail swinging and eyes narrowed on me. "It's as if there's a vampire hidden inside him... or he ate one."

My eyes are wide, terrified, as if he isn't talking about me. That sounds *horrific*. I swear I've never eaten a vampire. I've never even had venison or quail... not that those things are comparable.

Junichi swears again, ducking back into the wardrobe. When he comes out a few seconds later, he has one of those fancy garment bags in his hand. He thrusts it at Hisaki's chest, and his face is furious. "*Apologize* to him. Then take your fucking jacket and leave."

Hisaki looks over at me like I'm a pile of stinky rubbish. "Why would I apolo—"

"APOLOGIZE NOW."

Silence. The force and weight behind Junichi's voice shock me, and I'm blinking at him as he stares at the pale little vampire. The latter turns to me and gives a curt bow. "My apologies."

"Go home," Junichi says, stalking back toward the wardrobe. Hisaki grips the garment and slinks toward the door. At the frame, he stops, turns back toward us and tilts his head.

"What about alterations?"

"Mejor lárgate de aquí!"

"*Alright*, I'm going... but I'll be back next week." He flips his ponytail and glides out of the room. Junichi takes a deep breath and apologizes to me. I tell him it's not his fault, but he's riled up.

He's pretty miffed all the way through dinner and for the rest of the night, too. Complaining about ranked vampires and how utterly self-important and rude they can be. Hisaki-kun (*the* Hisaki-kun) is the worst example of this.

Junichi also has a source named Ren that sounds pretty contentious. He only goes to see Ren once every nine or ten days. He told me he *should* feed once a week to be in optimum health, but he can't stand to see him that often. As a doctor of vampire health and medicine, this deeply concerns me.

After I've taken a gloriously hot shower and prepped myself (Jun did not want to join me and do the honors, oddly), we're drinking beers on his lush, velvety sunflower sofa. I try to take his mind off what happened by sliding my fingers against his thigh to get things started, but he's sweet in telling me he's not in the mood. Apparently, Junichi doesn't like having sex as an outlet to his frustration or when he's angry. It's not his thing, which I totally respect.

Instead, we end up talking about classic jazz and whether or not *Kind of Blue* is indeed the greatest jazz album of all time (he says yes, I say no. I argued *Sunday at the Village Vanguard*, but then that generated a heated discussion about live albums versus studio-recorded ones).

Later he tells me about the merengue and bachata music he listened to growing up with his mother, as well as some of his favorite modern artists. I'm making a mental list to research these next time I'm on my phone. That is, until I fall asleep facing him as we lie on the sofa together.

NINETEEN
JAE

When I open my eyes on Sunday morning, the sun is bright yellow. It's streaming in gloriously through the back-glass wall of Junichi's house. Today we're supposed to go have nabeyaki udon for lunch, then see the autumn leaves near Okutsukei Valley. The weather already seems perfect for it.

I'm warm. At some point in the night, Junichi wrapped us up in a very soft, luxuriously furry blanket. It's black, like the seeds of the sunflower. It feels as if we're lying on a bear (and I mean that in the most humane way possible). Junichi is behind me, and my back is against his chest. I can feel him solid and breathing deeply, cypressy and perfect.

When did I become a "little spoon" kind of guy? I don't think I ever made this conscious choice, but I seem to end up in this position a lot when I'm intimate with men in particular. Who would I be the big spoon with? Is it a height thing? Bravado? Do I need someone shorter than me (I'm not even that short at five foot six inches), or would some shorter bloke with a Napoleon complex still have me as the little spoon?

This deserves deeper intellectual consideration later. For

now, I'd like to properly get stuffed by this big, delicious spoon behind me. I keep having flashbacks about our first time. A random memory will hit me when I'm innocently moving about, creating a flash of heat deep in my groin and spine. It's almost crippling and my face flushes.

I respect his aversion to angry sex. I'm not sure what mood he'll be in this morning, so I just shift closer into him for a snuggle. He groans and pushes against me, sliding his hand underneath my T-shirt and holding my naked belly. My heartrate kicks up, but I'm perfectly still now. If we're progressing, he needs to make the first move. He's so warm behind me, and he's not wearing a shirt (he had one on before I fell asleep, so he lost it sometime after). I'm perfectly nestled into him—back to chest, arse to groin, thighs to thighs. His face is in the top of my hair, and I can feel him breathing against my scalp.

He shifts again, this time gently grinding his cock against me, then clenching his fingers to tickle my stomach. A moment later, his long fingers move lower, sneaking underneath the elastic of my joggers. When he slides his hand inside and firmly grips me in his palm, I suck in a breath. "*Christ.*" I arch up and into him, and my lips are parted and dry. I lick them, but it feels like I'm being tortured now.

Jun moves his head down, nuzzling against my hair. His voice is groggy. "Good morning."

"Good morning," I say, but it comes out scratchy. My body is aching for him, as if my spine is on fire and the flames are spreading outward.

While he grips me, he's kissing the back of my neck. Soft, flirty kisses that lead into the curve of my shoulder. I arch into him again, feeling his hard cock and it makes me feel primal—like an animal. God. I want him inside me again right now.

We keep playing this game of gently grinding into each other. I turn my head because I'm greedy and I want his mouth, too. He lifts up onto his elbow, leans down and gives me what I want. Now we're slowly rocking and kissing, his tongue twisting against mine. I might come from this alone. Dry-humping. Like I'm a bloody teenager.

I pull away from the kiss because I'm close to losing my mind and I don't want to climax like this. "I want *all* of you," I tell him. He pulls his hand out of my trousers and leans down to kiss my neck. He shifts away from me like he's getting up, but I grab his wrist, panicked. "Where are you going?" This all feels too sexy and lazy and perfect for him to move. I don't want to lose this momentum.

He smiles. "To get lube and a condom."

There's a pointed moment of silence as I stare at him. "You... don't have to." And I mean it. Usually I'm very particular about condoms. Lube is also always necessary. *Loads* of it. Ranked vampires can't even catch or give illnesses or STDs. Since I'm human, though, I can still tear and get infected, so I'm adamant about it.

But I have properly lost my marbles because I just want him inside me right now. No delay in the action.

He leans down, still smiling as he places a quick kiss on my mouth. "Yes, I do." He drags his long body up and smoothly moves from the sofa and down the hall toward his bedroom. He disappears.

I flop down onto my stomach and suck in a deep breath. I *really* meant it. What the hell has gotten into me? Thank God one of us still has some self-control. I need to have a good long look at the man in the mirror when I'm back in my flat. "Now we're willing to let vampires bareback us, are we?" I'll ask him. "Where's your sense of self-preservation, you horny bastard?"

I'm still lying on my stomach and internally berating myself when Junichi reappears with the proper tools for comfortable lovemaking. He drops them into the bend of the sofa as he straddles my arse, resting one knee into the cushions and his other leg bent with his foot still on the floor. He lifts the bottom of my T-shirt and uses his thumbs to firmly massage my lower back. I close my eyes. It feels incredible.

"Are we not in the mood anymore?" he asks. I can hear the grin behind his voice. My response is muffled because my face is pressed halfway into the furry blanket.

"We are." He slides my shirt up higher, bending and kissing up the length of my naked spine. Inch by inch.

"I firmly believe," he says, working his way down, "that good things come to those who wait."

I smile. "Do those who wait come good?"

He chuckles. I love making him laugh. "Let's experiment," he says. "You can report your findings?" He grips the elastic waist of my joggers and slowly works them down. I lift my hips to make it easier for him, putting my arse in the air slightly as he kisses my lower back.

"Oh, the scientific method and sex—two of my favorite things neatly rolled into one. You charmer."

I'm done being flirty when he shifts to his knees so he can kiss and lick my cheeks. I'm writhing because I'm not sure if he's about to do what I think he might do, and I'm also not sure if I'm mentally and emotionally prepared for it.

When his nose presses between my cheeks and I feel his tongue flicker against my opening, I realize that I'm *not* prepared. At all. I gasp and make another unfamiliar sound. I shift away because this feels wild and wanton and I'm ashamed. I know about this, but no one has ever done it to *me*.

Junichi grips the front of my thighs and pulls me back into him after I've tried squirming away. He intentionally breathes warmly on me before lapping his tongue into my flesh again, and I whine in a way I *never* have. When he's got me in his hands and his tongue is softly dipping inside me, I give myself over to it and try to let go of the shame I feel. To let him do this thing to me that really feels quite incredible if I get out of my own head.

Slowly, I relax my lower half, clenching the plush blanket in my fists in exchange and opening myself to him. Letting him have me. And he does—moving down to lick other parts of me that have never seen the light of day. Gently sucking and teasing me with his mouth, playfully pulling at me with his teeth.

Jun does this for what feels like an eternity, urging my body toward a new and extraordinary threshold where I've forgotten how to breathe. When I finally feel his slick finger carefully pressing into me, I come. Just one finger and I'm spent. Moaning and cursing with my face buried into the soft blanket and my eyes watering. What he's just done to me... it's too much. My skin feels hot and prickly from the raw pleasure of it.

Eventually, he urges a second slick finger inside and guides me to relax down. I do. I would do whatever he wanted at this point. I feel him lean over me, and his low voice is soft. "What does the data suggest so far?"

I'm just breathing—incapable of saying something clever right now. Brain is barely functioning. Does not compute. He pulls his fingers from me, and I hear him opening the condom. I can't even offer to put it on for him. Lazy sod. Just lying here waiting to be fucked.

"Do you still want me?" he asks. I feel the smooth tip of his shaft against me. "May I have you?"

"*Yes*," I manage, my face still hot and my heart pounding. *May I have you.* Jun was polite like this the first time we made love, too. He made me feel as if I was some delectable dessert that he very sincerely wanted to have a go at. Like I'm a piece of cake.

I'm feeling languid from the orgasm, but as he presses his

tip in, I manage a bit more by slowly shifting my arse up and into him. He's teetered on his side, holding himself up, but now I'm lifting myself into him and doing the work. He likes this, because I hear him groan deeply from his throat—almost like a growl—which gives me a little more moxie.

He rests more of his weight on me so he can relax his hips, and I take it. Steadily pulsing up and into his cock inside me as he shifts his arm down. He lays his hand over mine, encouraging me to spread my fingers until he can entwine them. This hand-holding thing he does while he's making love puts me over the moon. My heart can't take it.

I shift up into him harder as he holds my hand, determined. I hear and feel him losing himself as he's telling me how good I feel. He doesn't know why I surprise him all the time or why I smell like this. I want to know what I smell like, but I also want him to come, so I'm not going to distract him with my typical doctory curiosities: "And how long have I been smelling like this? Have you noticed a change in your stool?"

Just when I'm trying to think of what else I can do to get him there, he leans into my neck and licks me. It's a hungry, long lap with his tongue just in the concave. When he speaks, the words are warm and breathy against my neck. Almost desperate. "Can I taste you? Please?"

I didn't think it was possible, but my heart accelerates even more in my chest. I swallow. "Yes." The low-levelers *never* ask me like this. They just do it without warning, like if I'm sleeping with them, what else should I expect? I'm a lowly human and my consent is unnecessary.

This vampire and the things he shows me—the way he treats me and the way he makes me feel.... It's like I'll never be the same. How can I ever accept anything less?

He bites down into the base of my neck. Even though he warned me, I still flinch from the shock of it. The pressure takes my breath away and I freeze, like time is standing still. I feel his thick incisors slide deeper into me, smoothly, but it doesn't hurt? When he sucks at my flesh, he comes. His body jerks and stiffens as he holds me tight around my waist with his free arm. He groans, completely satisfied as he heavily breathes out.

He climaxes but I don't, because there's something else going on inside of me and it's distracting the hell out of me. It feels like the knotty, twisty thing in my gut is unraveling, and it's the weirdest fucking sensation. I don't know what to make of it. Like a block of metal melting? Hot candle wax? I'm starting to worry that I've ruptured an organ or something, but the melty feeling is moving like electric spiders up my spine and to my head. It's all so bizarre. I'm frozen, distracted, when Jun pulls his mouth from my neck, licks me and quickly shifts himself from inside me.

My body is shaking, hard. Trembling from the inside out, and I have no idea why. This weird feeling. Jun gets up and is removing the condom, readjusting himself. Despite my wobbly state (am I having a seizure?), I sit up and watch him. He's got a very peculiar expression on his face. One I haven't seen before. He's staring forward and blinking with the used condom in his hand. Unreadable. Blank.

"Jun?" I prod. He turns his gaze to me and it's still vacant. But when it subtly shifts into something like accusation, I draw back slightly.

He stands up without preamble, goes to the kitchen to discard the condom and washes his hands. All in silence, with me just watching him dumbstruck from the sofa. He moves from the kitchen and toward me. I think he's coming to me, but he keeps going toward the glass walls.

"Jun, what is it?" I ask. I'm getting irritated now, and my heart is in my throat. What the hell?

He unlocks one of the walls and drags the massive glass to

the side. Slowly, he walks out into his yard. He's just standing there, barefoot, shirtless in his pajama bottoms and with his head lifted to the sky.

I stand, adjust my bottoms and cautiously walk toward the door. I can't imagine what's happened. I told him I tasted like shit, so he couldn't be upset about that. I warned him—*multiple* times.

When I get to the door, I move to step onto the pavement, but the ground is really cold against my bare foot. I stay inside on the hardwood and call out, "Junichi, *talk* to me. What the hell is wrong with you?"

There's a long moment of him frozen, perfectly still and just breathing like he's waiting for something. When he turns, the golden autumn sunlight washes over his sculpted body. He looks radiant standing there. Like Adonis.

But his face is hard. "You're a fucking vampire."

I *almost* say, "I know you are, but what am I?" like a twelve-year-old.

I don't say that, though, because he doesn't look amused at all. He looks like I've betrayed him in some fundamental way—like I've lied about who I am. We've joked about this previously, but in this moment... it feels very serious now.

I shake my head, unblinking. "I'm not."

TWENTY
JUNICHI

Jae is standing in the doorway, staring at me with his chestnut eyes. His golden hair is a fluffy mess, and he's got a little trail of blood going down his neck from where I fed. He's shaking his head, serious. "I am not, Jun. I'm *not*."

I don't want to scare him, so I take a deep breath to calm myself. When I do, I notice how good I feel standing in the warm sunlight. Not burning at all.

I'm due to visit Ren tomorrow for my feeding. Since I constantly push feeding from him back until the last minute, I'm always running on empty by the time I get there. My energy is lower, I'm more irritable and my skin tone isn't as rich as it should be. But I feel as if I've had an energy shot. Jae's blood tastes exactly how he smells to me—like some brown sugar and rum dessert that my mom might make. It's pulsing through me now and giving me life.

Just like a ranked vampire's blood would.

I move back toward the door and Jae steps aside, staring at me as I pass him. I go straight to the kitchen, pull a clean cloth out of the drawer and wet it at the sink. After I ring it out, I walk back toward him, grab his hand and urge him toward the couch. "Can we sit, please?"

He sits, never taking his eyes off me. I reach up and gently dab the cloth against his skin to clean it. They're not bleeding out anymore, but he still has small puncture marks from where I fed and there's light bruising. I shake my head. If he *is* a ranked vampire, this should have healed instantly. Also, his skin was soft to bite into, not hard. Biting into another vampire is like biting into an apple—perfectly satisfying, crisp and juicy. Biting into a human is like biting into a jelly-filled donut. Jae's flesh is all donut.

Nothing makes any fucking sense.

I wipe the blood from his collar bone. "Your blood is that of a ranked vampire. You had no idea?"

"What? *No*. That doesn't make any sense—I haven't lied to you about anything. I'm not trying to deceive you... How would *I* know what my blood tastes like?"

When he's clean, I drop my hands in my lap and look at him. "You've *never* drunk blood? Not once?"

"No."

"You've never had the urge to? Even a passing thought?"

"*No*."

Now we're staring at each other, his eyes resolute and mine disbelieving. I sit back and rub my palms against my face, sighing. "God, you make me so fucking *nervous*. I have no idea what's going on with you and you're not helping."

"What am I supposed to do?" Jae asks, throwing his hands up. "I've been *me* my entire life. I know who I am—and what I am. But suddenly you're telling me I'm something *completely* different and I have *no* evidence of it. I have *no* tangible reason to start behaving differently or think otherwise."

His warm eyes are usually playful and teasing. Relaxed.

Now they're stressed. I'm pushing him, I know. He's right, but I'm right, too. In my silence, he goes on, calmer this time.

"Even if what you say is true, what should I do, Jun? Do you want me to start feeding? Even though I don't have any desire to do so?"

"You don't have to do anything you don't want to do."

"Right. Okay. So?"

I sigh. "So you make me *very* nervous. You're an unknown and it makes me uncomfortable."

When I say this, he sits up. His expression drops—hardens in a way I'm unfamiliar with. "So you're done with me, then? We're finished?"

I blink. I don't like this expression on his face. "Why do you say that? That I'm 'done' with you—"

"Because that's what it is, isn't it? No use sugar-coating it. I'm a fucking weirdo that makes you uncomfortable, so we're done."

He moves to stand up from the couch, but I grab his waist and pull him back down in a soft tumble. While I hold him, I sit straighter and face him. "Please stop. We're just talking. Can we talk?" I lift my hand and run my fingers into the back of his messy waves. He shifts his gaze from me, but he doesn't pull away. "I didn't say *you* make me uncomfortable. You make me feel very comfortable, Jae. Too comfortable—and that's what makes me nervous. And 'unknown' does not mean 'weird.' Please don't twist my words."

I lean in slowly and brush my nose against his cheek. "Are you showing me your baggage right now?"

He puffs a laugh from his nose, but he doesn't smile. "Maybe. Absolutely."

"I like you," I finally admit aloud, then kiss his cheek. Even now he smells delicious to me. Intoxicating and sweet. I could bite him again—this human-vampire hybrid. "I would like to continue seeing you, if you still want to see me?"

He finally shifts his head to look directly at me, his expression softened. "Yeah, of course, just—*please* stop accusing me of misleading you. Because I'm not."

I lean in to kiss him and he automatically parts his lips. I love that. Like walking up a pathway to someone's house and they open the door before I'm even there. A warm welcome. I indulge in his spiced, peachy mouth for a moment before I pull away. "Haruka is in Hong Kong until Thursday. I want to talk to him about this—about you—since he tends to be all-knowing with these things. Is that alright with you? We'll make a plan to see each other next Saturday evening for another sleepover and I can report back to you?"

He nods. "Yeah, okay." He surprises me when he falls out of my grasp and back onto the couch. Just plops down and rubs his palms to his face. "*Christ.*"

I stand up and shift his legs onto the couch. When I sit, I make him straddle me with one leg straightened behind me and the other in my lap. I smile. "I didn't mean to cause you stress. I apologize."

"Bloody hell." He takes a breath, still rubbing his palms against his face.

"You must really like me?" I ask, grinning.

He lifts his head and looks up at me, frowning. "Are you taking the mick? Is this amusing to you?"

"No," I say, literally holding in laughter. "I find you captivating. *And* delicious. Whoever told you that you tasted bad was an idiot."

"Thanks..." He sighs and drops his head back, adjusting his spine as I lazily stroke his thigh in my lap. There's a moment of comfortable pause before he says, "So... am I to always be the bottom when we have sex? Can we talk about this?"

Now, I laugh. "You don't *always* have to do anything, Jae." There's an awkward pause before Jae lifts his head again.

"Tosser. That sounds like, 'You can go and sleep with someone else and be on top if you like.'"

We both laugh now. Confession: I've had sex in a vast multitude of ways and with many, many people, but I've never been the bottom when sleeping with a male. I didn't think I had a complex about it, but maybe I do. Asao would say it's because I have serious trust issues... He might be right.

I caress my hand higher up his thigh until I'm sliding my palm against his cock. He moans, breathy, and spreads his thighs a little wider. I love how comfortable he is right now— relaxed and speaking his mind. It's like all the walls are down and I'm finally getting to the core of him. "Do you think I'm treating you like a keyhole?"

"No. But it would be nice to use *my* key sometimes. Since I've got one."

I laugh again. This creature. "I'll think about it," I say, squeezing him.

Jae groans, but in a kind of chuckle. He's smiling and writhing underneath my palm. "He'll *think* about it. The function and use of my cock are up for deliberation. The jury is out."

I keep laughing, and all the tension from earlier has melted. I adjust my seating position to face him directly so that I can reach up with my free hand and caress my fingertips against his jawline. "Feisty, delicious man..."

He surprises me when he snaps his head to the side and catches my two fingers in his mouth. He scrunches his nose at me, defiant as he reaches up and holds my wrist so he can suck and lick my fingers.

God, he makes me nervous.

TWENTY-ONE
JUNICHI

Monday evening, I'm sitting in the formal tearoom of the Miyoshi Clan estate in Hiroshima. I'm on an elaborate cushion with my legs folded underneath me and I'm alone. I feel like a sacrificial offering. I check my watch. 7:15 p.m. He's made me wait fifteen minutes like this.

The harpy is challenging me. Daring me to leave.

I could. After feeding from Jae yesterday, I still feel energized and satiated. But I'm also nervous. He tastes like a ranked vampire but doesn't drink blood and swears he isn't one. I feel like a test subject for a new energy drink that seems fine at first, but three days later I might burst into flames. That's why I'm staying. To get some proven, surefire purebred blood in my godforsaken system in case Jae's blood has some unknown ill effects.

Ren Miyoshi as my source is my father's doing. Even after his death, my father is still ruining my life.

Ren is purebred. He's the unofficial realm leader of Hiroshima prefecture. Haruka is the official realm leader of all Chūgoku. But it's a huge region, *and* he has Kansai. Being how he is (unbothered, procrastinating and selectively lazy), he lets the Miyoshi Clan manage Hiroshima and Shimane prefectures, while Haruka primarily handles Okayama and Tottori.

My father formally offered me to Ren's family as his source when both he and I were still kids. Technically, as part of the arrangement, we should be bonded by now. When we turned twenty-one, we were supposed to seal the deal. We tried for years, but it didn't work. Probably because I genuinely dislike him.

I've been feeding from Ren off and on since we were both sixteen. When I first saw him, I thought he was gorgeous. His eyes are like butterscotch, which is rare for a vampire of Japanese descent, and he has these long dark eyelashes that practically sweep against his cheeks when he closes his eyes. He wears his jet-black hair down to his waist, like we're in the damn feudal era. He did when we were young, too. He's always had an affinity for flowing robes with elaborate patterns, and they suit him perfectly.

The first time I fed from him, my eyes burned like fire in my head from the taste of him. I thought he was delicious. When he pulled back and saw me though, he smacked the shit out of me and told me I was being "unchaste." Called me a heathen or some other old-fashioned term. Savage? I can't remember. My eyes haven't alighted since. They're broken.

I don't want to feed from him, but my body is conditioned to him. I can feed from another first-gen or maybe a second-gen, but it isn't the same. Not nearly as satisfying. That's Ren's power over me—that my first feeding source was purebred. For years and during the pivotal, developmental phase of my vampiric biology, I was conditioned to this rich, clean vampiric blood. It's what my body is accustomed to. Even when I desperately want to stay away from him—and believe me, I've tried— eventually I come back. I always will and he knows it.

Purebred vampires don't just easily offer up their blood. They might feed from others freely, but they rarely ever give of themselves, because they're considered the lifeblood of our race. A purebred vampire might offer themselves twice in their entire lifetime. Max. So it's not as if I can just find another purebred to feed from. If I do, it means there's an arrangement to bond with them. Which I don't want to do either.

So I'm stuck with the harpy.

"Hello, Violet."

I'm staring straight ahead. I can see him leaning on the doorframe from the corner of my eye, wearing some silken deep purple and flowy robe that's gaped open at his chest. He knows I don't like it when he calls me that. I ignore him because if you reward children with your attention, they'll keep repeating the undesired behavior.

He strides across the tatami until he's standing directly in front of me. Over me. Then he flops down onto his knees in front of me so I *have* to look at him. His hair is perfectly glossy, swept and flowing over his left shoulder. His vivid eyes are full of mischief. He smirks. "Sorry for making you wait."

I scoff. "You are not."

"I'm not." He smiles, sweet malice, lifting his eyebrow. "You make *me* wait, so why shouldn't I make you?"

He reaches up with his fingertips to touch my lips, but I draw my head back before he makes contact. I frown. "I'm not making you do anything. Can we please get this over with?"

He sighs, then dramatically falls over in front of me. He twists onto his back and his robe fans out. He's naked underneath, so now he's indecent as he stares up at me, his ridiculous hair splayed against the tatami. He looks like a half-naked cat wanting its belly rubbed... or some ukiyo-e, erotic shunga painting.

"You're so cold to me," he whines, staring up at me with

butterscotch eyes as he runs his hand across his flat belly and down toward his exposed groin, drawing one knee up. "We haven't tried in decades. Not since your mean old father died. Make love to me."

"Nope."

He sits up with lightning speed and grips my chin in his fingertips, hard. No more playing nice. He leans into me so that our faces are inches apart, and his eyes are cold despite their warm, pretty color. "I should cut you off. *Never* let you fucking feed from me again. Then what will you do?" He leans in and drags his tongue up the side of my face. I let him. This is what we do.

I'm silent, so when he's done, he stares at me again. "*Well?*"

"You always say this. You never do it." I almost wish he would. That he would stop waiting around for me, thinking that we're going to magically fall in love and be together. It's not happening. He *should* cut the cord, for both our sakes. Let go of whatever childhood fantasy he has of us in his mind and force me to suffer through the withdrawal.

His long fingers move down to the top buttons of my shirt. He's playing with them, but he doesn't try to unfasten them. He breathes a laugh, haughty. "I never will, will I? How could I cut off Junichi Takayama? Exquisite, internationally celebrated first-gen designer. I *feed* him. I'm his source and I keep him going—keep him designing and charming the world over. And he feeds me. Why would I *ever* let go of that distinction?"

"You're realm leader—"

"*Acting*," he says, turning his nose up. Ren has so many insecurities toward Haruka, it's painful. What's funny to me is that they could be related—if Haruka had an evil, ostentatious older brother. Ren is jealous of Haruka's status in the aristocracy (locally and internationally), his older bloodline, his gender-ambiguous appearance and the fact that Haruka is younger in age. His "luxury, foreign-imported mate" (direct quote).

He's even more triggered when Haruka grows his hair out. That's *his* thing, Ren will complain. Apparently, no other vampire can have long hair. He doesn't like that I spend more time with Haruka than him, either. I've learned to avoid bringing him up in Ren's presence altogether.

"Still," I say, "you could open yourself up? Bond with someone else—"

"There is no one else, Violet." He drags his nose along my jawline, leaning down into my neck. "Only you." He licks me, then bites down hard into my flesh. He feeds, and I clench my eyes shut from the onslaught of twisted, possessive love he feels for me. Pours it all into me as if it'll change the way I feel and make me want him too.

It's overwhelming, the way purebreds can do this. I hate it. But I've gotten good at shutting my mind to it. To him and this influ-ence—this pull and deeply rooted desire to make me his. It takes me almost twenty-four hours to shake off his emotional baggage. Once I do, I'm fully energized, sharp again, and I can avoid him for another eight or nine days. It's not a great system, but it's all I've got.

IT'S FRIDAY. The week has been painfully hectic with last-minute alterations and trying to fit everyone in. But the wedding ceremony has concluded without a hitch. The bride and groom looked stunning (I designed their traditional kimonos and did alterations for half the vampires in atten-dance), and now we're having drinks in a Zen garden washed in dusky light. There are large lanterns glowing softly and hung in the trees surrounding us. It's stunning. Whimsical.

"Why not invite Jae?" Nino asks, sipping his drink. He's incredibly handsome in a slim-fitted sage-colored suit I designed for him a few months earlier. Green looks great with his honeyed skin tone and amber eyes. Haruka, not as much, so his matching kimono is deep silver with hints of the same color. Nino had considered wearing a kimono for this event but chickened out. I would have designed it for him. He'd look glorious in anything.

"For one, he told me he has the flu. Two, why would I bring a human-vampire hybrid to an aristocracy event? He'd just steal the attention away from the bride and groom."

Nino shrugs. "That's fair. I like Doctor Jae. He's funny. He reminds me of myself before I was with Haruka—a little insecure."

My mind suddenly flashes back to the first time he kissed me and slid his fingers against my cock. "Not always," I mumble, then take a sip of my drink. Also, Jae is a damn good kisser. That's not a distinction I usually notice about a person, but his kissing is confident *and* intuitive. He's not just hungrily slopping into me like some humans have. He's passionate, but he pays attention to what he's doing—like he's kissing but also listening.

"Hello, gentlemen." Sora casually walks up beside us with a glass of white wine. Her dress is a deep midnight color and fitted to her slim curves. The red glasses she always wears pop nicely in contrast with the blue. "Drunk any good blood lately?"

Nino raises his eyebrow in a sly grin. "Well..."

"Alright, lover boy." I smile. "Nobody wants to hear you brag about drinking ancient purebred blood." Nino smirks and takes another pull from his glass. I turn to Sora. "Where's hubby?"

Sora waves her free hand toward a general area. Unaffected. "Over there."

"How are things at the hospital?" Nino asks.

"Busy—especially this week, with trying to reschedule appointments and make different arrangements for feedings. The lower ones *love* Doctor Jae. Is he alright? Have you heard from him?"

She's looking at me, her head tilted. This week has been insane, but now that I think about it... "Not since... Tuesday?" I say. "Why? Have you not heard from him?"

"No, not since Wednesday morning. He no-showed yesterday and today, which is not like him at all. I tried calling him and texting him all day yesterday, but he's not answering me. If you haven't heard from him either, should we check on him? I don't think he has any friends here..."

"We should check on him," Nino interjects, his brow furrowed. "Jae said he's never been sick before. Why is he sick now?"

I flick my wrist up and look at my watch. If I catch the next train, I can be there in forty-five minutes. Dammit. Why do I feel nervous about this?

"He came in Monday and looked exhausted and pale," Sora says. "Gray."

I sigh, setting my drink aside on a round high table. "I'll go now."

"I'll go with you," Nino volunteers. "Let me tell Haru real quick. He's been invested in the doctor lately, but he definitely can't leave right now. I can probably sneak away, though." Nino stalks off toward his mate, standing in a crowd of vampires including the bride and groom.

I exhale a heavy sigh and run my fingers against the top of my head. My throat is tight and my heart is racing. God, I hope he's just sleeping off some human illness. I haven't had the chance to talk to Haruka and tell him I've fed from Jae.

Sora turns to me, grinning. "Jae's demeanor is brighter the past few weeks. Cheerful and much more relaxed. I'm sure he'll be happy to have the hospital director personally checking on him..."

I frown. "Sora, what's your point?"

She shrugs. "It's just interesting. For years, vampires in our aristocracy have been trying to figure you out and why you're not bonded with Ren. I'm not one for gossip, but I feel like I've got the scoop. Does Ren know you prefer humans?"

I straighten my back and raise my eyebrow. "Ren lives in his own world and doesn't care much about what other vampires like or don't like."

Sora laughs, bringing her wine glass to her lips. "He's a real piece of work, that's for sure."

When Nino walks back through the crowd and toward us, he tells me he's ready and we depart.

By the time we get to Jae's apartment in Himeji, it's eight o'clock, and there are still fissures of deep orange sunlight set against the darkened horizon.

We knock, then wait. No answer.

And again.

Nothing.

Shit.

"*Shit.*" I run my fingers against my scalp as Nino knocks a third time. When we're met with the same hollow silence, he turns to me.

"I think I can unlock the door..." He focuses on the handle. "But I've never been given permission to enter his apartment. Have you?"

"Yeah," I breathe. "If you open it, I can go inside."

Nino steps forward and presses his fingertips against the

lock mechanism. He closes his eyes, and I can feel the hum of his zesty purebred energy slowly radiating from his body. It's warm, and feels almost... carbonated? Soothing, prickling bubbles against my skin. He opens his eyes, and they're glowing. The color is like apricots. I hear a loud snap. He twists the handle, pulls, and the door opens for him.

"Impressive." I smile, momentarily distracted by the focus and power he just exhibited.

He smirks in a laugh. "If you knew how many things I've destroyed in order to get to this point, you wouldn't be."

We both peek in, and the house is dark. A stench hits us both at the same time, because we both draw back from it. It smells stale and like something decaying. I shake my head, nearing full-blown panic. "*Fuuuck.*"

"Could he be dead?" Nino's eyes are wide, his voice higher than usual. "I hadn't even considered that."

I frown. "*Not* helping." The pair of us: two grown-ass vampires freaking out and being squeamish on a human's doorstep. What good are we? "*Shit.*" I step past the threshold and straight into the main room, where the kitchen space flows into the living room. Nothing. Except a vase of wilting bird-of-paradise and lots of empty water bottles. So many. On the table, fallen onto the floor, on the counter. Like the man was dying of thirst.

Nino is standing in the doorway behind me. "I'll open the windows from the outside? Air things out?"

"Thanks, Nino." I look over my shoulder, and his eyes are alighted again. He lifts his hand, flicks his fingers, and the lock on the window just off the main room snaps loudly before the glass slides open.

Instinctively, I wander down a narrow hallway. It's even darker here because there are no windows. I pass a door immediately to my right, peeking inside as I move. It's a makeshift office space and there's a floor table, cushion and papers spread out everywhere against the tatami. The room looks like a tornado hit it. No Jae.

There's a door at the end of the hallway on the left. My senses are telling me he's there. I reach the doorframe, and it's a plain bedroom. There are more water bottles on the floor here, like the aftermath of sloppy picnic-goers.

Jae's back is facing the door as he lies against the bed. He's not moving at all.

TWENTY-TWO
JUNICHI

"Jae?" I call out. Nothing. I quickly move toward the bed and sit along the edge. His skin is all gray and chapped, peeling. I lean down toward his face. After a still moment, I thank God he's breathing. It's shallow, but he's not dead. "*Shit.*" What the hell is happening to him?

"You find him?" Nino calls out from the front door. "Is he alive?"

"Yeah," I shout. "Hold on." Gently, I grab his shoulder and urge him onto his back. He rolls over, no resistance at all. He's not wearing his glasses and his eyes are closed, lips parted as a faint breath passes between them. "Jae. Can you hear me?"

Nothing. I place my palm against his ashen cheek and put more weight behind my voice. "*Jae*, open your eyes." It takes a few seconds, even though it feels like ten minutes. Slowly, his heavy lids open like slits. His usually warm chestnut eyes are white and milky, and he's not looking directly at me. His gaze is vacant, lifeless.

Still holding his face, I lean down into him so that our foreheads touch. "Three words, okay? 'Nino, come in.' Can you do that for me, please?"

He closes his eyes against the warmth of my face, and I think he's unconscious. I've lost him. But a long moment later, the words come out in a whisper, faint and dry.

"Nino... come in."

I sit up straight and take a deep breath, hearing Nino's footfalls bounding toward us. Soon, he's in the doorframe and hovering behind me. "Jesus. He... he looks like a dried-out vampire. Haru was right. *Look* at him."

I turn to Nino with my eyes wide, the panic settling in my chest. "What the fuck do we do?"

Nino shrugs. "Feed him?"

"Jae doesn't feed. He's *never* drunk blood. Never wanted to. Should we take him to the hospital?"

Nino shakes his head. "He *is* the doctor! And he looks like a starving vampire to me, Jun. My father looked like this shortly after my mother died, and Haru looked like this once when we first met. I'm not a professional, but I *know* this condition."

"We can't just give him ranked-vampire blood. What if I kill him? What if I fuck up his body forever?"

"Alright, hold on." Nino pulls his smartphone from the pocket of his suit pants. "I'm calling Haru."

"He won't pick up—he probably doesn't even have his fucking phone!"

Nino dials and brings the phone to his ear. "I'm calling Asao. He's with him... Hey, Asao? Can you grab Haru, please?" He walks into the hallway. I stare down at this decaying husk of the doctor, shaking my head.

"What the hell is happening to you?" And why now? Did I do this somehow? Did *he* do something to trigger this? He said he's been with vampires before—that's practically all he dated in England. Has this happened in the past and he just kept it from me? Does this happen once every six months, like he's a fucking part-time vampire. A million questions are running through my mind when Nino walks back in the room.

"Right. Okay, I love you." He exhales a deep breath when he pulls the phone from his ear. "Haru said feed him."

"*Fuck.*" I rub my palm down my face and take a deep breath. I can't *believe* this.

Nino watches me, his gaze soft and his voice calm. "I know... offering yourself on a whim like this isn't ideal. But you like Jae, right? You've been spending time with him and he's a good guy?"

With my eyes closed, I massage my forehead with my fingers, trying to process this situation while simultaneously wrestling with my ego. "I'll do it. Just give me a minute, please?"

Nino nods. "Sure. I'll go clean up the kitchen and give you some privacy. There's a market down the street. I'll grab him something to eat. He's lost a lot of weight."

"Thanks." Slow breaths, in and out.

"No problem. You're not alone in this, Jun. Whatever is happening to him, we'll help. He's our kin." Nino picks up the bottles on the floor in the bedroom before leaving, heading toward the kitchen.

He's our kin... He's not supposed to be our damn kin. He's supposed to be a *human.* Shaking my head, I bring my palm up to my mouth, but hesitate.

What if we bond?

If he is a vampire, we've slept together *and* I've fed from him... What if this is the final piece? The second he takes a sip of my blood, we're locked into each other for the rest of our lives? The only possible outlet would be a broken bond, which I understand to be a painful and horrific process (*if* you survive it). I've only known this male a month. I like him, but do I want to be tied to him forever?

I try to take another deep breath, but my chest is tight. I can't let him die here. Do I waste more time by telling Nino and Haruka that we need to find someone else—simultaneously putting Jae's life in jeopardy and looking like a fucking coward?

I will my incisors to elongate and bite down into my own flesh before twisting toward Jae again. I swallow hard, bringing my palm down to his parted lips. "Jae, you need to drink this." I wait, terrified. Not even knowing if he'll do it. If he even hears me.

Slowly, I feel the flicker of his tongue against my hand, his eyes still closed. A few seconds later, he lifts his chin into my palm, his tongue flattening against my flesh to take in more blood. I reach down with my free hand and wrap my fingers against the back of his hair, then gently lift his head upright from the pillow.

He's feeding. His Adam's apple is bobbing from swallowing and he's breathing a little deeper. I'm staring down at him, watching him. Nothing is happening and the room is silent.

My mind is wrestling. I'm thinking about how I like to keep my life simple—I design and make clothes, I fund Mom's hospital and I date humans to avoid ranked vampires and their aristocrat drama. That's me. It's been me for the past fifty-five years since my father died. It keeps me free, unburdened. I love it.

How I ended up sitting in a messy apartment and feeding a human–ranked-vampire hybrid is beyond me. I'm beside myself. I don't know if I should be upset at him for hiding this from me or with myself for chasing him to begin with.

IN THE HOUR it takes for Jae to rouse, I tell Nino that I fed from Jae about a week ago, and that he does indeed taste like a ranked vampire. It's my big revelation, but Nino isn't surprised. "Haru found out a lot of interesting stuff while he was in Hong Kong," he tells me. He's sitting on the floor across from me with his legs drawn up, knees bent and his back pressed against the wall. "He thinks Jae has always been a vampire, but he doesn't know it. I guess there are clans that did this in ancient days—repressed their bloodlines, like reluctant vampires."

I draw back. "He thinks Jae is from an ancient clan?"

Nino shakes his head. "Not necessarily. He thinks Jae is repressed more recently than that, since his mother was sick and he feels anxious around us. He can't say how many genera-tions, but maybe starting from the late 1800s? It's all conjecture."

"So why is this happening now? Have I done something to trigger him?"

"Don't know. Possibly. Haru said there was *some* info on the process of actual repression, but none on reawakening the bloodline."

"You think that's what's happening to him now? An awakening?"

"Don't you?" Nino breathes a laugh, incredulous. "Looks like it to me."

After that, I stare into space, wondering what the actual fuck I've gotten myself into. The only thing that snaps me out of it is Jae's shifting behind me on the bed. I'm sitting on the floor with my back against the bedframe. I turn my head, and Jae is haphazardly trying to push himself upright.

I shift myself up to sit on the bed, then grab his arms to help him. His skin is flaky and rough, and he's shaking. His weary eyes are less milky now—like milk with honey mixed in.

"Take it easy," I urge.

"Wh-what's wrong with me?" His voice comes out in a scratchy whisper. "Why—"

"You don't know?" I ask. Because somehow, I can't believe that he wouldn't know. That he would be totally blind to something innate like this about himself. That he would have no inkling of it in his conscious mind.

He's still shaking as I hold his arms, but he meets my gaze. "I—I thought... I had the flu. This is *not* the flu."

"You don't have the flu," Nino says from across the room. Jae whips his head to look at him, as if he hadn't known he was there.

He clenches his fists and lowers his head, shaking it. "What's *wrong* with me?" He's scared. Genuinely terrified as I gently hold his wrists in my hands. I can feel the fear and confusion rolling off him. My frustration is melting. He didn't lie to me. If he did, he's in the wrong profession and missed his chance at being an Oscar-winning actor.

I lean into him, pressing my forehead into his temple because when I do things like this, he always seems to calm down. "*Breathe*, Jae." He does. His shoulders rise and fall in a deep breath. He does this a few times, and the shaking lessens.

When I lift my head, his eyes are closed. "We'll tell you what we think is happening, but you need a bath—probably some food too. How do you feel?"

Jae opens his eyes. They're already a little browner. "Confused."

"Physically..." Nino smiles from across the room. "How's your body?"

Jae blinks over at him. "Confused."

Nino laughs. I shake my head.

"Alright." I stand up. "Bath first. Can you walk?"

Jae offers a shaky nod. Nino stands from the floor and

meets us at the bed. He helps me pull Jae up, and we both guide him toward the bathroom.

He wakes up a little more as I bathe and scrub him. His skin is peeling off and shedding like I'm going to clean and leave him raw—flaking off and disappearing down the drain. But when I'm done, he's fine. His skin is soft and supple, and his color is normal again, like nothing happened. Like I dreamt all of it.

He's livelier by the time we're done scrubbing, so I leave him to rinse and dry himself off. Nino is still wandering around and cleaning up (I'm realizing he must be a neat freak, because he's gone beyond the bedroom and is now tidying up Jae's makeshift office in a different room, which he definitely does not need to do), but I head to the main living room area near the kitchen and pull out my phone.

I'm losing my shit and I need a sanity check. I dial Asao since he's more reliable to answer, then ask to speak to Haruka. It only takes a second for his deep voice to register through the line.

"Hello, Jun. How is he?"

"He's getting dressed." I'm pacing the floor and rubbing the back of my neck. "He seems better after the bath and drinking my blood—*Shit*. There was so much dead skin, but he's fine now."

"His improving after your feeding him and the decaying flesh are the final proof," Haruka says. "He is one of us and he is changing."

This is fucking unbelievable. "So what do I do? And he's still not vampiric—not totally. He doesn't have fangs and he can't feed for himself. Should I keep feeding him? Or maybe we should find him a different source? What's best? And why is this happening now?" I'm not trying to pawn him off on someone else. I'm not. But I also have no clue what I'm getting myself into and it genuinely scares me.

"Which question would you like me to answer first?" Haruka asks.

"Why is this happening now?"

"I believe your natures are drawn to each other. It is why you were uniquely capable of discerning his scent and noticing him before Nino or I did. After you pointed it out, though, it was obvious."

I'm standing still, thinking. "I fed from him last week for the first time. He tasted amazing. Too good."

"Perhaps your feeding from him is what has triggered this? The unique intimacy of feeding in combination with your compatible natures."

"So it's my fault he's like this?"

"Not completely, but in a sense, yes. Junichi, you need to make a decision."

"About?"

"Will you see him through this? We do not know much about this circumstance, but what is true of all vampiric vitality is that consistency is key. His feeding source should be the same as he slowly awakens—and high quality since he is obviously ranked. His source should also make his transition as comfortable as possible, without stress, since we don't know what to expect. Should we attempt to find someone else? Or are you willing to commit to this process of his awakening?"

Hearing something, I turn to see Jae quietly stepping out of the hallway and into the kitchen. He's barefoot, and his already slender frame is now gaunt from weight loss. He's dressed in clean sweats and his golden hair is darker than normal because its wet. No glasses. We lock eyes in a cautious moment before he goes to sit in the kitchen.

I nod, pacing again. "I am. Of course."

"I think this is the best choice. I will come tomorrow to speak with Jae directly about his circumstance. It is my responsibility as his realm leader."

I shake my head. "You've been digging at this for weeks—inviting him to dinner at your house, flying to Hong Kong and studying in that old library. You're tickled pink right now, aren't you?"

There's a slight pause on the line before he answers me.

"A little."

TWENTY-THREE

JAE

I had thought... that when I eventually took a bath with Junichi, it'd be this very sexy, steamy affair. Like something out of a lush erotica novella. Teak wood and steam and slippery hands and panting. Slow thrusts and deep kisses.

Never once did I fantasize about him scrubbing dead skin off my withered body because I was too weak to do it myself. Nor did I imagine Nino occasionally popping in to make sure we're both alright.

Nope. Not how I pictured that at all.

I'm sitting at my kitchen table, mindlessly eating the miso soup and rice that Nino has kindly purchased for me. Whatever happened to me... Whatever is happening to me, it went from zero to sixty. On Monday I felt tired at work. As the day progressed, it was getting more and more difficult to pay attention to what my patients were saying to me.

On Tuesday morning, I woke up simultaneously exhausted and feeling like a dried-up sponge left on the side of a kitchen sink. I've never felt like that—like all the moisture inside me had been wrung out or siphoned somewhere, leaving me brittle. I likened it to dehydration, but no matter how much water I drank, I wasn't sated. All it did was cause me to run to the bathroom every twenty minutes... until I was crawling to the bathroom. Then I couldn't move or do anything, and *everything* ached like mad.

That feeling... it's still there. Almost threatening to overtake me again. Nino is busy cleaning my whole flat, I think (God bless him—utterly humiliating), and Junichi is pacing back and forth in my living room, talking to Haruka on his smartphone. I know it's Haruka because Junichi changes when he speaks to him. They're friends, but he's a little less haughty.

I'm staring at him, and I want him. I *always* want him, but it feels different somehow. Before I felt wildly satisfied with his mere closeness and conversation. A kiss? Wonderful. Sex? Brill. I still want those things, but something inside me wants even more than that now. As I sit here, I can't really understand what it is.

Junichi hangs up the phone and is walking toward me. He's been oddly quiet since giving me a bath. When he re-dressed, he ditched his suit jacket. Now he's wearing a crisp white shirt (sleeves rolled up to his elbows) and his trousers. The entire suit was black, but subtly patterned in a satiny off-black matte paisley design. Gorgeous. Yet another thing that would make me look like a clown but makes Junichi look like the most dapper creature in all Japan.

When he sits down, I can't help but stare at him. His irises seem almost muted in color, but still vividly expressive. Right now, there's kindness there. "How are you feeling?"

"I'm alright." My voice is finally back to normal. It was weird and scratchy when I first woke up. "Thank you... for doing all this. I'm very sorry to have interrupted your event. I appreciate the help."

"Why didn't you call me?" he asks.

"Everything went pear-shaped fairly quickly. I thought I was coming down with something and I'd be fine after a day or two. By the time I realized I was wrong, I literally couldn't move."

Junichi nods at this, folding his arms as he leans back. "Two things. One—the board approved your surrogate project. So when you're ready, you can start your first trial."

Despite feeling like shit warmed up, I'm genuinely elated to hear this. "*Excellent.* I'm looking forward to it. Have you told Haruka and Nino the good news?"

"That leads me to number two. Haruka is coming to talk to you tomorrow."

My jaw drops at this, eyes wide. "*What?* Haruka—here?" Christ. It's already humiliating enough having Nino here, but Haruka existing in my shabby flat, too? Why didn't I decorate? I've been here five months, for God's sake. Do I have any food in my fridge? Wine? Tea?

"Yes," Junichi says, interrupting my worries of being a bad host and decorator. "You can tell him personally tomorrow. He also needs to talk to you. Jae, do you truly have no idea what's happening to you?"

"What's happening to me?" Dread is bubbling up from my stomach. "Will you *please* tell me?" I don't want to admit it, but the way I looked—the gray, ashen state of my skin—it reminded me of how my mother looked just before she died.

Junichi takes a deep breath. "We think you're turning."

I blink and draw back. "Where?"

"Where?" Junichi frowns. "What does that mean?"

"What do *you* mean? Am I a car? Left or right?"

"Jae. *Turning into* a vampire. Well, technically you've always been one, apparently. So shifting? Awakening?"

I don't know what my face looks like, but I can't speak.

Can't move. His statement is so preposterous and goes against everything I have ever studied about vampires.

"Jae?" He leans in. I stand up.

"*Are you mad?*"

"What? No—"

"How—how many times do I need to tell you lot that I am *fucking human*. Turning a human into a vampire is not possible. It's not bloody possible—"

"Jae, please calm down."

I don't calm down. No one has ever calmed down from someone telling them to do so. If anything, it has the opposite effect. But I do stop talking. I'm standing here thinking he's bonkers. They all are. Something *is* wrong with me, but it isn't this. *This* is not possible.

"Do you remember what I did to make you feel better?"

"What you did?" I parrot.

"*Yes.*"

Shifting my gaze away, I try to think back to a little more than an hour ago. For starters, I was half dead, wasn't I? I remember hearing Junichi's voice. His smell. His flawless, marvelous scent. He spoke to me, telling me to do something. Then he gave me something... something wonderful that tasted just like he smells. Perfectly clean, cypress and minty. Junichi undiluted. Amplified.

I glance back over to him, nervous. "You gave me something. What did you give me?"

He stares at me for what feels like an eternity, as if he's trying to give me anxiety.

"My *blood*, Jae. You drank my blood and now you're better. Do you understand?"

Silence. I'm waiting for him to tell me he's kidding. Like he's having a laugh with me, but I don't think it's funny. He doesn't say anything. I'm starting to feel legless, so I drop back down into the chair. We're both quiet for a long moment. Eventually, I look at him, serious.

"It didn't taste like blood." That's all I've got. In my defense, your honor, it didn't *taste* like blood. I haven't had blood ever (not even my own—never been scratched or hurt), but I hear it tastes coppery and salty, like a penny. I licked a penny once because I was curious. I cleaned it first. Maybe I shouldn't have? Perhaps the filth is an essential part of the organic experience.

"What did it taste like?" Junichi asks.

"Like…" I've never said it aloud, so I consider. "Exactly like how you smell—a forest, but a little sweet. Clean."

Junichi smirks. "That's because you're a fucking vampire."

"How is that productive?"

"Thank you for the compliment. Ranked vampires have very intuitive senses, which include our ability to uniquely perceive and smell other vampires' blood. It's nice that I register as something pleasant to you."

I shake my head, disbelieving. I don't say it, but I've given his smell a lot of thought. Just before I turned thirteen, we relocated from London to a rural area near Bristol. It was magical compared to the grit and noise of the city, and the woods were my new playground season after season. The cottage where we lived is just off a clearing. The area is lush and serene, full of flowers, sunlight, trees and life in the springtime. In winter, it's perfectly crisp and fresh, like you can smell the glittery snow piles blanketing the landscape. Preserving them.

That is Junichi's scent—it reminds me of home. When home was cozy and secure. Before Mum died and it became empty and lonely.

"How about Nino and Haruka?" Junichi asks. "What do they smell like?"

I shrug. "Very nice. Not unpleasant at all."

"Nothing specific?"

"Not really."

"Sora?"

"Same."

"What about Hisaki?" he asks. "Someone ranked but unbonded."

I consider for a moment. "Like black licorice." I *really* dislike black licorice. Even the smell of it turns my stomach. I don't say any of that, though, because it feels quite rude.

Junichi offers another of his playful smirks. "You make me nervous, Jae."

"Oh, *you're* nervous?" I frown, annoyed. "I've been human my entire life and you're casually declaring I'm a vampire like dinner's ready. But *you're* nervous?"

"This isn't about me—"

"Right."

"I *know*. But I'm nervous about this timing, and about the two of us."

I sit back and scoff, because I honestly don't know what else to do, but I'm put off. The two of us, what? He makes this sound ominous, which is *not* helpful.

"Do you want to feed?"

I stare down at the table and into my empty soup bowl, frowning. "No."

"You need to. Your skin looked good in the bathroom, but now it's just a little off color again and your eyes aren't right. You should feed intentionally since you're awake."

"No thank you."

He laughs. "*God.* You still don't believe me. You're really sitting here with no desire to feed from me? There's nothing compelling you right now?"

I lift my head and meet his gaze. I always want him. Ever since the first night he came to my flat, and even though I was being an idiot, I wanted him. It's been almost a week since we last made love. Maybe I want his weight on top of me? Maybe I just need a good fuck, followed by a human doctor to examine me and tell me what's actually going on.

Or maybe... whatever happened to my mother is happening to me?

Nino reappears from the hallway. He looks marvelous in a kind of sage-green modern suit that perfectly complements his warm skin tone and personality. "I'm catching the train back home. We'll trade off and Haruka will be here tomorrow. Did he tell you?"

"He did," Junichi says, staring at me.

"Jun, are you staying?" Nino asks.

"Am I?" Junichi reiterates, his gaze like a laser beam on my face.

I'm not sure if he wants to or if I'm burdening him. This all feels tricky because I know very well how Jun feels about ranked vampires. He's told me about them, and even a little about Ren—his purebred source that he practically loathes. Now, he's saying *I'm* one. I don't believe it, but I imagine him running away from me, screaming with his arms flailing, the first chance he gets.

I'm not selfish. I know how to be alone and how to take care of myself, but... it's been a hard week and I'm not too keen on being left alone so soon. Not right now.

"Yes, please."

"Good." Junichi grins. "He still needs some convincing."

Nino smiles. "Sure he does. It's not like we just told him he's a quarter German. He's an entirely different *species*—like he was happily grazing around as a horse and now he's a lion and needs to eat meat. It's a big change."

"You hear that, Jae?" Junichi smiles. "You're a *lion* now. King of the jungle. Top of the food chain."

I roll my eyes. I don't feel very lion-like. I feel like an awkward human whose anxiety is being heightened by two vampires, and the fact that I've no-showed for work for several days... I feel like an unemployed doctor.

"Take care of yourself tonight, Jae," Nino says. "See you both later."

"Thank you, Nino," I reiterate. "For everything, really. And I'm so sorry."

"I'm your realm leader, and your friend. I'm happy to help you." He nods at Jun, who in turn waves, before walking through the front door and shutting it behind him.

My realm leader? How awkward. I lean with my elbows on the table, rubbing my palms against my face. God help me.

"Are you ready to feed again?"

"*No.* I'm not drinking your blood, Jun. No offense, alright? I'd like a second opinion."

"You already have."

"Have what?"

"Drunk my blood, Jae. You already did."

I drop my hands. "Well I'm not doing it again. Not until I see a *human* doctor." Getting up from the table, I move toward my sofa because I'm getting sick of him staring at me like the cat who got the cream. Like he's unequivocally right and *I'm* loony.

I plop down and continue rubbing my face. My hands and skin are still so damn chapped. Psoriasis? Shingles? I'm creeping closer to forty, and weird shit starts happening around now. Maybe tomorrow I'll want a lover half my age or a sports car I can't afford. Good God. I need to go to work tomorrow—my *patients.* What the hell has been happening with them? Can I work like this? I run my fingers up and through my hair, and it feels too long. I need a trim. Will I have time before my shift? Impossible. "*Bloody hell.*"

I collapse back into the sofa and take deep breaths. My world is literally falling apart, and I feel like complete shit. I lift my head and open my eyes because I can feel and smell Junichi directly in front of me, kneeling. I don't mean for it to, but my question comes out as a whine. "What *now?*"

He doesn't speak, but wraps his long fingers at the backs of my knees and pulls. The action makes me slide closer to him but further down into the bend of the sofa so that I'm slouching. I am *not* in the mood for this. He pulls my arms, urging me upright so that he's beneath me as he rests on his knees between my thighs. When I'm sitting straight, he holds my cheek with the palm of his large hand as he stares up and into my face.

"Kiss me?"

I should not be kissing right now. Or even thinking about kissing. But he's looking at me with his obsidian eyes and full lips. And I always want him, don't I? He pulls me down toward his mouth and I let him. The moment we connect, I exhale. I love his mouth—so warm, clean and talented. Slow and rhythmic, like he's dancing with it, leading me and pulling me into him. He licks deeper and I meet his effort, gently twisting our tongues together. Tasting each other.

He pulls away slightly, pressing his forehead into mine as he whispers, "Sunshine, you need to feed. You'll feel better."

"It sounds mental."

"It isn't." He lifts his head just a little and sucks his bottom lip into his mouth. I'm confused at first, but then I see that he's biting the inside of his lip and I draw back, gasping.

"Jun—"

"Will you try, please?" He's staring at me with his pitch-black eyes as he leans in, but he stops. Waiting for me to meet him. To comply. I can see the blood pooling just inside as he parts his lips.

My throat is tight and I don't know what the hell I'm doing, but I lean in—just a quick touch of my lips to his. I pull back, hesitating and feeling utterly insane. I didn't even taste anything. He cups my face between his hands and tilts his head, pressing our mouths together.

He urges me to part my lips, his tongue softly sliding into me as I open wider, and I taste him. His blood is just as it was before—fresh and woodsy. Inexplicable, like wintery forest air and lavender.

Instinctively, I close my eyes and give in to it, wanting more because it tastes so good. Not like blood at all. Not coppery or salty. It's delicious in the heat of our mouths and I start chasing after it. He pulls me again and I slide off the sofa to straddle his lap, wrapping my arms around his neck—frantically wanting both him and the taste of him because it soothes me.

He breaks the kiss and my breath catches. My heart is going wild and I want everything from him. Anything. Something. He brings his hand up to his mouth. I watch as his fangs slowly appear, elongate as if by magic into thick, sharp white points. They're honestly beautiful, and I'm mesmerized as he bites into the side of his palm. There are two pools of blood there when he's done, threatening to drip and run down his flesh. My eyes are flickering between his irises and his palm.

"You need more," he says, perfectly calm. The blood is running now because I've waited too long. Hesitating, I bring his hand to my mouth, all the while beside myself at what I'm actually about to do and how senseless it is. Psycho. Someone should lock me up and throw away the key immediately after.

I drag my tongue up the trail of liquid, cleaning until I reach the epicenter. The path tastes the same as the previous two times I've had him, so I wrap my lips around his bite marks. It's so fulfilling, like having a whole basket of chips to yourself after stealing only one or two from your friend's basket for the past ten minutes. I feel greedy and I have the nerve to suck, like

I actually know what I'm doing. When the flow stops, I pull my head up, indignant. The holes have closed and healed over. I blink up at him. "Wh-why?"

He laughs, even though, as far as I can tell, nothing is funny. "You want more now?"

"*No.*" I shake my head, rubbing my palm down my face. "I... Jun, this is too much—"

He bumps me up with his hips, bringing me even closer into his body. "You can have more, if you tell me you want it." He's kissing my jawline, then up to my ear and down my neck. His hands are wrapped around my arse, holding me into him. He feels solid and secure, like he's got me and I can trust him. Like... for once in a very long time, I'm not just on my own.

I inhale a deep breath, deciding to let myself lean on someone. To try, anyway. "I want it," I tell him. "I... I do."

TWENTY-FOUR

JAE

In my mind, Haruka is a bit like the Pope. Except much younger and Japanese... beautiful and queer with a gorgeous, sun-kissed husband. Alright then, maybe not like the Pope at all. He *is* regal. Patient and kind. Something radiates from him, quiet and elegant, that tells me he's on a different playing field. All ranked vampires have this, but Haruka with his burgundy eyes and cool demeanor makes me feel like I'm in the presence of a very old soul. A king. Someone totally unfit for my shabby flat. He's sitting with me at the kitchen table. Junichi occupies the third seat.

"You have been a vampire since the day you were born, Jae," Haruka explains, his mesmerizing eyes focused on me. "You were never truly human."

He pauses. I have no idea what to say to that. "Alright..."

"Can you accept this?" he asks.

"Well..." I sit up straighter, rolling my shoulders. "I've been happily sipping Junichi's blood for the past twenty-four hours, so I'm definitely not human like I thought. Humans don't generally do that... If they do, they're considered mental."

"Correct." Haruka nods. "Do you find yourself enjoying the experience?"

Junichi purses his lips, frowning. "I feel like that's a very personal question." Haruka rolls his eyes. I stifle the urge to chuckle.

"Yes," I say. "I do... Why is this happening to me? Why now?"

"I have already expressed this to Jun, because he has asked the same question," Haruka says. "Based on what I know of vampiric natures and forming romantic bonds, it is likely that your natures are highly compatible—which is why your scent registers so strongly to Junichi, and why this emergence is occurring within you now. It is as if something about Junichi is compelling your blood to awaken and flourish. Like magnets."

Forming romantic bonds... Shit. I nod, vaguely understanding what all that means. I don't know exactly how vampire bonds are formed, but I do know they're serious business. Not like a human marriage where you can just "grow apart" or cite "irreconcilable differences" in a swift divorce. You're supposed to be in a vampire bond for life. You link up your genetic code with this person who perfectly matches you, and you match them, so don't be an idiot and try to look elsewhere or you'll die.

Distracted, I look up at Junichi. "What do I smell like—"

"Not right now, please."

There's a moment of awkward silence before Haruka shakes his head at Junichi and continues. "I feel that while your interaction with Junichi has undoubtedly stirred your nature, your bloodline was already in a state of unrest. You mentioned feeling 'twisty and weird,' or 'anxious,' around us?"

"Yes. Since I moved to Japan, it's been worse than ever."

"Vampiric bloodlines, particularly those higher in nature, are innately drawn to each other. We are creatures who flourish in a community. As such, we naturally gravitate toward our own kind. Where there is a purebred, other ranked vampires eventually follow. Your living here as opposed to England—where there are no purebreds and few ranked vampires—has also likely roused your burgeoning nature."

I'm wondering about my life and this path I've taken of studying vampires, becoming a vampire doctor and moving here. Was it my choice? Or was it this "nature" thing inside me compelling me the entire time without my consciously knowing? And is that thing *me* as well? I talk as if it's something separate from me—some foreign, alien thing that's inhabiting my body. Something that's taken control of my fate and actions. But he's telling me it's always been there, silently occupying the driver's seat.

It's unsettling.

I shake my head. I'll tackle that later. "So... do you think my mum was a vampire as well? What happened to me this week... is that what happened to her?"

"I believe so," Haruka says. "Your mother was likely vampiric in nature but never properly fed. Whether or not she knew as much and refused, we can never be certain. But it is possible you would have befallen the same fate—either yesterday or sometime in the future."

All of this feels unreal. "I didn't know what was happening to me this week. I knew I needed *something*, that my body was lacking something vital. But I had no idea what that was. How was I supposed to know? How could Mum have known? If you've never been a proper vampire, how could you know you need blood?"

"Given your upbringing, you could not have known.

Thankfully, you are uniquely close to high-level vampires who do and are capable of supporting you."

"I'm... I'm very grateful," I say, offering a bow from my chair.

Haruka smiles gracefully. "We are your kin. It is our responsibility to see you through this transition."

I whip my head up, blinking. "So... I'm a vampire, but not quite? And you keep saying I'm ranked. What... what rank am I?" This is all so bizarre. I can't even believe I'm asking these questions.

"You're still in the oven, sunshine," Junichi says, leaning forward onto his elbows. "Not quite done."

"Which means..."

"Your nature will take some time to fully awaken," Haruka answers. "We're not sure of your rank yet, but Junichi feels you are likely first-generation based on the quality of your blood. However, time will tell. Your skin is also still too soft, and you do not have fangs to feed properly, correct?"

I shake my head. "I don't... not that I know of."

"The more you feed from your source over time, your true nature will reveal itself. I do not know how much time, but I imagine weeks or months. Possibly days. Not years, considering the rate of change you're already experiencing."

"Okay..." I breathe, blinking. "Okay... I'm turning into a vampire... That's fine... Brilliant."

Junichi speaks up again. "You're not exactly *turning*, Jae. You've always been one of us. Your perception just needs to adjust, along with your body and nature. You're emerging."

Right. Adjust my perception. Easy to say, much harder to do. Deep breathing. Don't freak out in front of the vampires. Christ. I'm a vampire too. Deep breathing.

"I'll see you through this process," Junichi says. I hadn't even realized my eyes were closed as I shift my gaze toward him. "I'll be your source the entire time. Haruka thinks we need to take this slow, so I'll be with you and make sure your nature remains stable."

"Since this is an unprecedented and delicate circumstance," Haruka says, "I feel it is best to keep the same source throughout the process. When you feel the desire to feed, you should express as much. Try not to feed from other sources for now."

I draw back. "I absolutely would not. I would be utterly *mad*." The mere thought of drinking some random vampire's blood makes me heave. I'm barely accustomed to the little Junichi has given me. It's still fucking weird, but simultaneously quite nice... like spinach in a fruit smoothie or pineapple on a pizza. Who figured *that* out?

Haruka stands from the table, and Junichi and I automatically follow his lead.

"I have many resource materials within my library at home. It would be beneficial for you to read through my books to learn more... restricted information about our culture. Your culture. I can also answer questions should they arise. Is this something you'd be interested in?"

Oh, *God* yes. "Yes, absolutely. I can also keep you updated with the surrogacy candidate process. Jun let me know I can officially begin contacting people and collecting information."

Haruka smiles sweetly. "That is wonderful news. Shall we begin next week, after shōgi?"

"Yes, that's perfect. Thank you, Haruka."

"It is my pleasure, and thank *you* for helping us grow our family."

After he leaves, I realize I feel better. For me, knowledge truly is power. At the very least, I have a stronger understanding of what the hell is going on. There are still so many unknowns, and calling myself a proper vampire feels bonkers, but the load feels a little lighter.

Once he's seen Haruka to the door and we're alone, Junichi tells me he wants to hash out a few more details. When we're sitting on my sofa with beers, he turns to me, point blank.

"I don't think we should have sex while we're doing this."

I blink. "Excuse me?" We didn't make love last night. He said I needed to rest and recover, which I agreed with. Plus, who wants to make love with someone whose skin feels like tree bark? Apparently, though, his reasoning stretched deeper.

"You're slowly awakening, Jae, and I'm feeding you—*nourishing* you through this. I'm not going to feed from you, but I've already bitten you once. Since there are so many unknowns... I would feel more comfortable if we kept things simple. You're definitely ranked. We don't know when you'll turn, and... I don't—I just don't want things to get complicated, or for us to fall into something we're unprepared for."

Translation: he doesn't want us to accidentally bond. I don't know what has to happen to form a vampiric bond, but if I'm honest, I feel a little gutted by this. If you'd asked me which I prefer, "Junichi as a masterful lover?" or "Junichi's blood?", I would have chosen the former, without question.

"Okay," I say, keeping my real feelings to myself. "I understand. I appreciate your doing this for me. Being my source. I obviously respect whatever terms you have." I look up at him, but then quickly look away and take a sip of my beer. His eyes are staring down at me, and those lips...

Can we not kiss? Cuddling is off the table too?

"Also," he begins, "you live almost an hour away from me. I know this is closer to the hospital for you, but how do you feel about living with me during this process?"

"Will I be able to work without issue? Is my position at the hospital in jeopardy? The surrogate program..."

"Your position is safe. As long as you feel up to it, please continue as normal. You'll just be living with me so it'll be more convenient to feed you."

I consider the circumstance: living with Jun, but not sleeping with him or kissing his soft, full lips. Not running my fingertips against his tight tummy or brushing my nose into him. Smelling him all the time. Seeing him every day.

It sounds like hell.

"If that works best for you," I say. Poker face on. I can keep it in my trousers. I can. "I should not expect you to travel an hour out of your way to do this for me. Of course I can."

"Alright. I appreciate it."

My heart is sinking, because this is starting to feel like an icy business contract. It isn't how we came together, is it? Why should we do this now? And Haruka said he thinks we're highly compatible—like magnets.

Jun doesn't like ranked vampires, but am I really one? Even if I am by classification, am I by character? That's what he takes issue with. Their toff manner and stiff way of thinking. But I'm not like that. Which is why he liked me to begin with.

Just as I'm telling myself to take deep breaths again, the doorbell rings. I'm not expecting anyone, and the only people I know have all been here in the past twenty-four hours (except for Sora, but she rang me this morning to check in—so kind). I stand, honestly happy to move away from the now forbidden object of my intense desire. When I open the door, I'm gobsmacked.

"You *wanker*. Why the *fuck* haven't you been answering your phone?" Cyrus is standing there with a rolling suitcase beside him. His round, doe-like brown eyes are hostile.

Someone rude and too loud for the present circumstance is at the front door. I crane my neck to lean over the back of the couch, looking toward the entry since it isn't very far. A human man is there. He bumps shoulders with Jae, hard, as he passes him to enter the apartment.

"Cy—what the hell—"

"I have been ringing you *every day* since last Saturday, and you never pick up! What am I to do, Jae? You haven't got any family except for your dad, and you're stubborn as *shit* about making friends and asking for help. So what?"

"Dramatic," Jae spits. "Christ—is Pippa here too?"

"No, she's not, you tosser. Why haven't you been answering my calls? I'm supposed to be your *best mate*."

Clearly, this is Cyrus. Jae's best friend and childhood crush. He told me all about him during one of our late-night phone calls while I was abroad—how confused he felt as a youth because of his feelings toward Cy.

Turns out he was a fucking vampire. We don't label our sexuality like humans do. We are who we are, we like whomever we like. How painful to grow up not knowing who and what you actually are and what's driving you—to be shamed, burdened and discouraged in exploring it. Humans really get it wrong.

When I stand and walk around the couch, Cyrus finally takes notice of me. He turns to face me, then draws back, his eyes wide. And wide eyes he has. They're chocolate brown and shaped like oversized almonds. His skin tone is the same nutty color. He has short, silky ink-black hair, a very straight nose and a healthy shadow of a beard framing his thin lips.

Jae definitely has a type. And a sub-type—one level deeper than vampires. I realize I check two boxes for what he clearly likes.

"Who the hell are *you?*" Cyrus asks, his thick eyebrow raised. He and Jae are standing in front of me. They're the exact same average-ish height, but one is warm vanilla while the other is caramel macchiato. Jae steps in between, exasperated.

"Cy, *please.* This is Junichi Takayama—Junichi, this is Cyrus Dayal."

I smile. "A pleasure to meet you. I've heard much about you."

Cyrus sneers. "I wish I could bloody well say the same. You're a vampire."

"Correct."

Cyrus shifts his gaze to Jae, focusing like a laser. "Christ, man—are you *sleeping* with him?"

"For God's sake, Cyrus, please stop it, alright? Just calm down. You're *killing* me here. Literally murdering me. Blood bath. All manner of forensic evidence."

Jae's typically airy English accent has suddenly become heavier, his words less rhotic and his vowels longer, with Cy's appearance—as if he's been curbing his speech pattern for us

American-dialect speakers. As if we wouldn't understand him in his natural state.

The loose cannon pauses, seemingly taking his friend into consideration for the first time since Jae opened the door. He inhales and exhales a deep breath before he reluctantly looks at me. "Sorry, mate."

I raise my eyebrow and move around the two of them and toward the door. "It seems you both need some time to catch up. I'm going to the café down the street. Would either of you like anything?"

"No, thank you." Jae sighs, rubbing the bridge of his nose and lifting his glasses.

Cyrus lifts his chin, snide. "I'm good. Cheers."

I nod politely before I make my exit. God. Cyrus is like a ball of fire and tension—essentially the last fucking thing we need right now. I'm already on edge about this entire ordeal, trying to be calm. To take ownership for the fire *I've* started.

What Haruka didn't tell Jae is that he thinks my biting him was the trigger. I told him Jae has been fed from by other vampires before, but my bloodline quality is what makes this time different. Things have been tense between us since the moment I saw him almost two months ago, and the pull has only grown stronger the closer we become.

It scares the hell out of me.

It was one thing when I thought he was a special snowflake of a human. Knowing he's like me—that he's vampiric in nature and therefore capable of forming a bond—now it feels like I'm playing with matches in dry, dry brush. My entire lifestyle, everything I've built for myself, is being threatened. One wrong move and all of it goes up in smoke. I'll be chained to him forever, without even knowing what kind of vampire he truly is.

Who will he become when his nature fully awakens? How much will he change? Is stiff, arrogant, ranked-vampire pride inherited within our blood, or is it learned? Nature or nurture? I can't possibly know right now.

I like Jae. A *lot*. He's hilarious and kind, intelligent, insightful and grounded... endearingly anxious, brazen and warm. Beautiful. If that wasn't enough, he tastes amazing. I *like* him. But I can't give up my freedom for him. Or anyone. Not forever.

"Tell me you're not shagging him then."

Cyrus is pacing back and forth in front of me. I'm sitting on my bed, my back pressed into the wall and my legs folded in a sort of Zen yoga position. It's not helping me feel relaxed.

"Well?" He pauses, staring at me. Technically, I'm not sleeping with Junichi anymore. He just told me we can't.

"I'm not," I say simply.

Cyrus draws back. "So you haven't? *Ever?*"

Well... that's a different question, isn't it? I dodge it.

"Will you please relax?" I ask. "Why have you come here to shout at me? Ever since I've moved here you've been *completely* unsupportive. Even before that, you make fun of my career and research, my sexuality—"

"I was just having a laugh with you about those things. Don't be sensitive—"

"But it's *not* funny, Cyrus."

I *hate* it when people say, "Don't be sensitive." Such a twat thing to say. To me it reads, "Oh, don't be an actual complex, living and breathing person with feelings, different experiences and perspectives than my own. Just accept that *I'm* an insensitive arsehole, will you?" People are horrid.

"That's what I'm telling you," I say. "You've been even more of a knobhead about me living here—but I *always* support you. In becoming a dentist, in getting engaged with Pippa... when you decided to do that fucking 'juice cleanse' for thirty days and you looked like a walking advert to help feed starving children."

Cyrus folds his arms, pouting. "Prat."

"Can you just be supportive of me—*for once*? Our lives... We're changing. You're getting married soon. I'm learning a lot about myself here, and it's good for me. Can you please respect that and not scream at me all the time?"

Exhaling a heavy breath, Cyrus stalks toward me and climbs onto the bed. He sits beside me, facing me. His expression is sincere and relaxed for the first time since he's stepped into my flat.

"I don't mean to shout at you. I just... I *miss* you. You weren't very busy back home, so I could *see* you or pop into your office anytime and bring you lunch—remember? The number twenty-six pad see ew with fried tofu and extra broccoli?"

I sigh. "I do miss that Thai restaurant."

"And I miss going to the pub together on Saturday nights. I miss playing footie with you in Port Meadow on Sundays. We talked all the time, Jae, but now you're here and you're *Doctor Busy*, and it's like I don't even exist to you anymore... I want you to come back home."

Cyrus is staring at me and being so sincere that it makes me slightly uncomfortable. Usually everything is rough and tumble with him—a smack on the shoulder or whack in the back of my head. Some snarky, rude comment that makes me want to punch him. I don't know if he realizes how close to my face he is. I want to lean back, but I don't want to trigger him into being a knob again, so I shift my gaze down from his face. "I can't come back home. I have a contract with the hospital, and... I *like* it here. I enjoy being busy, and I like my patients and the people I'm meeting. You and Pippa are starting a life together. You don't need me to be your third wheel—and I don't want to be."

I think I've made my point when a comfortable silence settles between us. That is, until Cyrus blinks his chocolate eyes at me. "You don't have to be."

I frown. "What does that mean?"

"It can just be me and you, if you want that?"

Now I'm blinking at him, utterly lost. I'm about to ask him what the hell he's talking about, but before I can, he leans in and kisses me. Straight on. Cyrus's mouth on mine. It's like I've received a jolt of electricity, because I jump back and away from him. He's still leaning toward me and my eyes are wild. "*What in God's name are you doing?*"

"What does it look like I'm doing?"

"*Why?*"

"Because... because I fancy you, Jae. I *like* you."

Now we're both staring at each other—Cyrus like he's just told me the sky is blue, and me like he's suddenly sprouted a second head.

"*What?*"

"Is this really so shocking for you?" Cy scowls. "Even my bloody little sister saw it when we were still lads. My father had a *vicious* talk with me about it when we were teenagers... and once you'd finally left for Japan, Pippa said, 'My biggest competition is gone.'"

I shake my head. "*No.* Cy, you are *not* gay."

"What if I am?"

"You're not."

"Maybe I am, Jae... I'm gay for you."

"Oh—oh Christ. *Oh no*—"

"What?" Cyrus says, his brows tight. "What's wrong with that?"

"It's *awful*."

"It's romantic."

I scoff, shaking my head in disbelief. "It is not."

Cyrus finally sits up straight, folding his arms. "Why? How the hell isn't it romantic?"

I pause, still awkwardly leaning away from him. "Because all the weight and responsibility of *your* sexuality is on me, isn't it? As soon as things go to shit, you're not 'gay for me' anymore —it'll be *my fault* you're gay. My fault that your life is ruined and your family quarrels with you. No thanks, mate."

"No! I wouldn't do that to you. It won't be like that—"

"And what about Pippa?" I ask, incredulous. "You're to *marry* her in three months—"

Cyrus grabs my arms and pulls me upright toward him. When I'm close, he uses one hand to thread his fingers against the back of my head while he holds my upper arm tight with the other.

"Will you just—*Shit*. Can you *calm down* for a minute? You have no idea how long I've been wanting to say these things to you—how long I've wanted to touch you, you... absurdly clever, perfectly quirky and delightful man." He leans in, but I lean back this time, still looking at him like he has two heads. I feel as if I've entered some upside-down parallel universe.

"Can we please just *try*?" Cy asks. No, he pleads. His fingers are rubbing against my scalp and his eyes are so soft. He's never looked at me like this—with such affection and longing. "Please?"

Something inside me wants to give him this. He's showing

vulnerability like I haven't ever seen from him. He's my friend —my best mate. I care about him and his feelings. And he was the first bloke *I* ever had feelings for. My first love, even. My teenaged years were spent either with Cyrus or thinking about Cyrus. Daydreaming about him.

He's here now, telling me he's felt the same all along. That he fancies me too and he wants us to try. For some, this is the fairy tale twist. The golden path to a tidy, happy ending.

Not for me.

He's still holding me when he tries to kiss me again, chasing me as I lean back even further out of his reach. I'm halfway to being flat on my back against the bed when I hear a soft knock against the doorframe. I whip my head to the side and Junichi is there. My heart sinks into my stomach.

"I'm heading home," he says smoothly, his face unreadable. "Nice meeting you, Cyrus. And Jae, I assume you'll call me should you need my assistance." He offers a polite nod, then disappears from the doorframe. Cyrus looks at me with his nose upturned.

"What the hell would you need his assistance for? Who *is* he to you?"

Panicked and without a word, I pull myself out of Cyrus's grasp, stand from the bed and yank the sliding door shut behind me as I leave the room and follow after Junichi. Christ my life. Utter shambles. A fiasco.

I come into the living room space just as Junichi is putting his dress shoes on to leave. I'm standing there, but he's ignoring me. I keep my voice low. "That wasn't what it looked like."

Junichi stands, staring at me with his black irises. He says nothing.

"There's nothing between us," I say. "I'm not confused about who I want, Jun."

"What about who you are? Are you still confused about that?"

I take the few steps forward to close the gap between us so that we're about two feet apart. "I'm... getting there. That will take more than a day, I think. Is that fair?"

"It is." He looks down at me. His dark irises are totally unreadable, so I tell him as much.

"I can't read you when you're looking at me like this."

He reaches out and takes hold of my hand. My heart warms when he brings it up to his mouth then places a soft kiss into my palm. "You don't need to explain your actions to me, Jae. You can sleep with whomever you please."

I raise my eyebrow, triggered. "*Can I?*"

He breathes a warm, amused laugh into my palm, then kisses it again. He doesn't answer me, so I go on. "We can't have sex... but can we still be close like this? Can we kiss?"

He's essentially making out with my palm now. It's sexy, but I would rather he did it with my face. He speaks in between kisses. "I never said we couldn't."

I scrunch my nose. "We can have a snuggle sometimes?"

He laughs. "Do vampires snuggle?"

"Mm, it's good. We do it well. Expert snugglers."

He lowers our hands between us and entwines our fingers. "When can you come to my place to stay?"

"I was thinking this week. But now it depends on how quickly I can send Cy back home. Can I ring you tomorrow for an update?"

He nods. "Don't let too much time pass or you'll end up like you were yesterday."

"Understood... Thanks, Jun."

I wish I could kiss him—just to confirm that there is no confusion about this situation. But he's so bloody tall. It always puts me at a slight disadvantage. The minute I reach up and into him, he could just straighten his giraffe-like body and I'm left looking like some git that's leaning face-first into an open window.

He shifts down and places a soft kiss on my cheek, then presses his forehead into my temple. He's warm and smells divine. His voice is low and I can feel his breath against my skin. "Good night, sunshine."

When he stands, he slowly pulls our hands apart. I sigh. That was actually much better than my potentially thwarted kiss. A moment later he's gone. Only the soothing scent of him remains. I feel like I'm floating as I walk down the hall toward my bedroom. But I'm grounded when I slide the door open and see Cy there, looking surly with his arms folded.

"You know, I read a novel with that title once—*I'm Gay for You*. It happens a lot in those romance books—which is how my dad found me out when I was sixteen, by the way. He uncovered my stash of erotica."

I'm standing in the doorway, watching him and scratching my head. I literally have no words. He goes on.

"I always imagined you'd be chuffed to hear me say that, and then we wouldn't be able to keep our hands off each other. We'd have awkward, bumbling but sincere sex since I've never done it properly with another man, then we'd fight my parents and the world at large. It was my dramatic opening line. It was supposed to change everything between us."

I exhale a breath, considering. "Honestly? Fuck that book—and your line." Fuck bumbling, awkward sex too. I'm getting too old for that shit, and Jun has essentially ruined me for it.

Cyrus scoffs. "Whatever. In those books, one bloke is always *very* rich and the other embarrassingly poor. I could never decide which one was me or you, since we both grew up properly middle-class. Neither of us is white, either. They're almost always white—"

"You don't see the issue in your basing our relationship off erotica novels with mainstream plot devices?" I ask, folding my arms. "Feeding me lines from them?"

Cyrus shrugs. "Seemed like a good idea at the time."

"Well... you should try it again—on a different man, I mean. Some guys will really be into that—"

"Shut up." Cyrus pouts. "It only works the *first* time, doesn't it? Have you slept with that leggy bloke? That fucking posh vampire. What rank is he? What's his ethnicity?"

So many awkward questions. I avoid the first one. "First-gen. Why does his ethnicity matter?"

"Because I want to know!" Cyrus sneers, bitter. "You've totally fucked him. Don't even bother answering, you twat."

TWENTY-SEVEN
JAE

In the end, Cyrus stayed for five days. Which, honestly, is four days longer than I'd hoped.

His confession started off lighthearted and fairly ridiculous —quoting lines at me from his secret stash of erotica novels. But as the days went on, he opened up more about it and his feelings ran shockingly deep.

It started when I told him I was sorry for ruining his "gay holiday." He didn't find that humorous. I guess I should have known better because that's one of the problems with us. Whenever *I* joke with *him*, it never lands. He always gets mad and starts fighting with me. Meanwhile, he says whatever the hell he wants to me, and I take it. Let it roll off my back time after time.

That was probably his fantasy—that I'd always be his little sidekick and take whatever trite crap he threw at me, smiling and happy because at least we were finally together. My best mate, a straight guy, has turned gay for me. He wants me and *only* me. Oh joy.

Piss off. I have enough baggage of my own that I'm already

working through. I'm not shouldering his, too.

I did apologize to him, though. Later, I realized I was insensitive during his very first time opening up about his sexuality. That, I definitely regret—my initial reaction was wrong. In the end, I told him there could never be anything romantic between us. I also said that if he truly feels he's queer, he should explore that and gain a better understanding of himself —that he shouldn't hold anyone else responsible for his feelings and choices. It's not fair to the person he's in a relationship with. I also told him to be honest with his family, when he's ready, and on his own terms.

He told me to stop treating him like one of my patients, but I hope he listens. I usually charge an obscene amount of money for that kind of advice, and he got it for free.

I promised to check in with him at least once a month. That's shit on my end, but I'm busy, aren't I? Shifting into a vampire. I didn't tell him anything about that because we had enough on our plates. I *did* tell him that I'm moving in and have been sleeping with Junichi. He kept pestering me on that topic, so I finally admitted as much.

He asked me a lot of questions about Jun—what he does, where he grew up, his family background. Honestly, I was surprised I could answer him. The way I talked, I sounded like a bloke with a proper boyfriend. Someone in a stable relationship. I don't feel that I am, but the template is there. The only question I couldn't answer was how old Junichi is.

In an oddly sincere moment, Cy also asked if Jun makes me happy. I wanted to tell him he makes me feel like I've sprouted wings so I can fly over the moon for him and bring back the stars. He makes me so happy and comfortable that I'm willing to lap up his fucking *blood* after he bites himself for me. What kind of psychotic level of affection is that?

I settled with a simple "Yes."

I'm walking up to Jun's house now with my rolling luggage, rucksack and a reusable shopping bag full of groceries. It's Friday, late afternoon—one full week since Junichi essentially brought me back to life from the near-dead. He's left a key underneath the front doormat for me. He's working late in his shop, so he told me to let myself in and make myself comfortable.

I do just that. He said I can take the room down an opposite hallway from his... Fantastic.

Sarcasm aside, it's a nice room. There are lovely green plants set in glass jars full of clean water hanging from the walls, a slim window with a view to the quiet street, and the mattress is covered in white, fluffy down bedding. This feels quite the step up from my shabby flat. Maybe I'm the poor bloke in the gay romances Cy was going on about, and now comes the part of the story where the rich benefactor has taken me in?

I'm not exactly poor though. I'm not rich, but I do have a little more than a hundred thousand pounds in my investment portfolio and about fifty thou in my savings, plus the paid-for house in Bristol. Not too shabby, but I should probably be much further along in my retirement savings.

After I've unpacked my things, I head to the kitchen to unload my shopping bag and start dinner. Lulú is following me, slinking about all the while. I occasionally reach down and pet her, letting her arch her smooth back into my palm as she purrs. What's incredible is every time I speak to her, she responds.

"Do you think Jun will be upset if I take over his kitchen for a bit?"

"*Meow.*"

"He doesn't seem to use it much, does he?"

"*Meoooow.*"

"I know, right? Bloody shame."

His kitchen is lovely. Sleek stainless-steel appliances, porcelain backsplash with a blue-and-white paisley pattern and dark granite countertops. I open the refrigerator, and there's literally nothing there but two bright green bunches of spring onions, a pack of beer and some bottled water. "What the *actual* fuck?" I grab a bunch of the onions and stand straight.

"*Meooow.*"

TWO HOURS LATER, it's seven thirty and I can tell Junichi is home because Lulú goes padding down the hardwood hall and toward the front door, meowing excitedly. She's kept me company this entire time, jamming out with me as I cook and we listen to an Aventura and Romeo Santos streaming station. I'm just finishing up as Junichi slowly walks around the corner.

I grin in his direction. "Hiya."

I am not, but he's looking at me like I'm wearing a clown costume and clowns make him very nervous. "What's... going on?" he asks.

"I made dinner." I lift the hot pot from the hob using both handles, gripping them with two dishcloths that I found. I walk over to the kitchen table, where I've already set up the other side dishes. I look over my shoulder at him. "Hope you don't mind."

"No... I don't." He's slowly walking forward, still confused. "You cook?"

"I do."

"And like bachata?"

"More and more," I say honestly. "After you told me about the music you listened to with your mum, I looked up the names you mentioned on YouTube. I'm kind of stuck with Aventura and slowly branching out—Romeo Santos, Toby

Love. I do like that younger bloke that's popular now... Shit, what's his name? Ah—Prince Royce? Anyway, I just turned the entertainment system on and you already had it on this channel. I don't know how to change your channels, so I left it."

He's still looking at me as if I'm in a clown costume but he's getting accustomed to me. I'm a friendly clown that won't hurt him. "What?" I ask. "Why are you looking at me like that?"

"Because you're unbelievable. Like a sponge."

"I'm a doctor. It's what I do. Apparently, though, I need to start saying that I'm a 'vampire doctor.' I have no clue what that means yet."

He walks toward the table and stands beside me, examining the spread. "This is incredible. You made it all from scratch?"

I nod. "It's not hard. I just need to be motivated. I didn't make the kimchi though. I bought that from the shop."

He blinks at me. "You can *make* your own kimchi?"

I shrug. "If I have the time and the resources, sure. We're having kongnamul muchim, sigeumchi namul...Wait. Do you speak Korean?"

He shakes his head, staring at me like he's mesmerized. "Nope."

I don't know why, but I'm surprised by this. I've heard that most ranked vampires speak multiple languages, and with Korea being so close to Japan... "What languages do you speak?"

"English, Japanese, Spanish and French," Junichi says. "I can understand Cantonese, but I still screw up the intonations when I try to speak it. Do you speak other languages besides English, Japanese and Korean?"

"Nope, that's all. I can bumble about in basic German. I took it in school."

"I think three is pretty damn impressive, considering you were raised as a human."

Raised human. So weird. I shrug. "Bilingual household. And Japanese was self-taught after getting my doctorate."

"What made you move here? Why Japan? Any major city in Italy would have been closer and has a booming vampire population as well. Los Angeles in America, too."

I sit down at the table and Junichi sits beside me. I point to the dishes as I explain. "This is seasoned spinach, beansprouts, stir-fried courgette, here's steamed rice, and the big pot is galbi-tang—beef short-rib soup. And I guess I've always liked Japanese culture, even though the history between Korea and Japan is shitty."

"The human history between Japan and just about *every* country in Asia is shit." Jun leans over and lifts the top to the pot of soup. "This smells amazing. Can we eat?"

"Yes. Everything is ready. If there's some left, it's perfect for some brekky the next morning. You could have some before you leave for the shop."

He pauses and looks at me. "What the hell is 'brekky'?"

I laugh. "Breakfast. The soup works as a breakfast meal as well. With rice. Very filling and comforting with this colder weather settling in."

We both take a moment to fill our respective bowls and small plates, and once we're comfortably digging in, Jun breaks the silence. "Your father taught you how to do this?"

"Yup."

"Does he know you're here? In Japan?"

"He does. I don't know if it's because I'm closer, but he's been calling me a little more lately. Like, once a week. Usually it's once a month. Always asking about my health."

"That's nice," Jun says, taking a spoonful of rice and dipping it into the galbitang broth. Perfectly done. "Maybe he'll want to see you?"

I sigh. "I don't know. He told me his mother is ill recently, and that he has to do a lot to help her. I don't think he'd have the time to meet up with me."

"Did you tell him you're a vampire?"

I scoff, shaking my head. "God no. He doesn't even know that I'm bisexual."

"You're not bisexual, Jae. You just love. We don't think of ourselves in those strict terms. Your sexuality exists on a broad spectrum that you're free to explore."

"*Tosh.* That works fine for you, but it took me my entire youth to accept that label. Don't try and take it away from me now. It's mine."

Junichi chuckles at this. "Have it your way."

"I will." I lift my chin, smirking.

If I truly had things my way, we'd make love tonight after we finished dinner. Since that can't happen (apparently), I have another idea. It isn't until we've talked more, finished dinner and cleaned up the kitchen that I express it.

The music has been playing low this entire time. Junichi is wiping up the counter when I'm standing in the open living room space. The moon is full tonight, so even though it's dark, the sky shines in a deep, warm blue, with moonlight spilling through the glass walls at the back of the house. I turn to look at him, smiling. "Dance with me?"

He freezes in his wiping motion and looks up at me. I'm a clown giving him anxiety again. "What?"

"You heard me. Show me how. I know the basic step because of YouTube."

He falls back into the counter and covers his face with his palm. "Dios mío..."

"I'm not awful, I swear." I grin, realizing I'm this pasty half-English bloke and how I must look to him right now. "I can move my hips fairly well."

Junichi lowers his hand from his face, his black eyes shining and one eyebrow raised. "Oh, I am *fully* aware of how well you move your hips."

"Cheeky sod..." I turn my nose up, smiling. "Alright then, come on. Chop chop."

When he actually stands straight and swaggers around the kitchen counter and toward me, my heart jumps up into my throat. I'm excited. I'm probably coming into this overconfidently, but I really think I can do it because of all the videos I watched. Just like when you sit on the sofa eating crisps, watching Olympian-level gymnasts miss their landing, and think, "*Jesus*, what've you been training for all these years? *I might as well get out there.*"

He's standing in front of me and lifts his left arm. Instinctively, I clasp his hand with my right as he places his right hand at my waist. I put my free hand on his shoulder, and I can't stop grinning. "See?"

"We haven't even started moving."

"I *got* this."

"What's the step, Jae?"

"Bachata? Side-together-side tap."

"That simple?"

"Yup." I nod. The song playing now is slower, as luck would have it. I set my shoulders back. "I'm ready."

"Let's just make sure you can stay on beat first. Don't worry about your hips, alright?"

"My hips have their own agenda, so I can't make any promises—my hips don't lie."

"Alright, Jae. God..." He laughs, leading me to step to my right with him. I match his movement, keeping up with the slow beat as he leads me to the left now.

I have rhythm. I'm no Fred Astaire, but I can keep up with a beat. I'm following him well—side-together-side tap to the right again, then the same steps to the left. He leads me back to the right now, but then lifts my arm to guide me into a turn as we shift back to the left. I wasn't expecting that, so my footing gets a little clumsy. The person on the sofa watching us on their TV could have done it better.

"You should have warned me!" I smile up at him when we're doing the basic step again.

"You were doing so well, I thought I'd challenge you."

When he does the move a second time, I'm expecting it, so I nail it. He grins, impressed.

"Very good. But you're stepping too high—almost on your toes. Ground yourself more into the floor with the balls of your feet. That's where your hip movement should stem from. The pressure of your feet on the ground—like this." He shifts his hands down so that his palms are resting on my hips. For a moment, I don't know what to do with my hands. I can't remember watching a video like this.

"Shoulders," he says simply. I lift my arms and relax my palms against his square shoulders. "Watch," he instructs. I look down at the languid, easy sway of his hips, how he alternates their movement based on the pressure he's applying to each foot. I watch a few rounds, and it looks like hip-hip-hip tap instead of side-together-side tap.

Soon, he's guiding my hips with his palms to do the same and I mimic him. I try to use the pressure from the balls of my feet like he's told me to. Thank God this is a slow song. This is more complicated than I thought.

When the melody fades, he brings me close by sliding his hands around to the small of my back. I slip my arms around his neck, and now our bodies are pressed together. He's still gently rocking his hips to the quiet rhythm. The warmth of him against me is setting off a fire in my belly and chest. It doesn't get any better when he moves one hand down to cup the center of my arse.

TWENTY-EIGHT
JAE

Junichi leans his face down and I lift my nose into him, nestling and breathing him in.

"You did much better than I thought," he says. Gosh. I want to do this again, but naked next time. Dancing bachata naked isn't considered sex, is it? How far can we go before it's sex? I need some firm guidelines.

"I *told* you," I whisper, brushing my lips against his. My mind is getting fuzzy and my body overheated. He kisses me, and I moan because he feels so good and solid. He always does.

Junichi pulls up from the feathery kiss, slowly lifts his palm to his mouth and bites himself. I smile, self-deprecating. "Am I looking peaked?" He's told me to ask him when I want to feed, but I haven't really gotten accustomed to voicing it. Also, I don't know when I need to. It's a different feeling from my typical human hunger.

To start, there's a dry tickle in the back of my throat, and it just gets worse and worse—which is why I mistook it for the flu. I can ignore it, but I don't know how long I should ignore it. How long is too long before I end up immobile, scabby and in the fetal position? I feel like I should test this out in a safe environment to understand my new limits.

He pulls his fanged mouth from his palm. "You're a little gray," he says, distracted. "You don't feel the urge to feed yet? Like you innately want something?"

I take hold of his palm and bring it closer to my mouth. Once the blood is available, I'm not so shy about lapping it up anymore. "Well, I always want *you*. Now just much more so."

After licking the pooled blood in his palm, I bring the edge of his hand to my mouth and suck. I close my eyes. He tastes wonderful and soothes the dry ache in my throat.

Doing this... It's starting to feel a little less mental and a little more wildly intimate. Forbidden. Like he's giving me this very private thing from his body that he wouldn't normally share.

Junichi sighs heavily over my head, the warmth of it gently fluttering my hair. "You're a brilliant doctor with sincere motive and ideas, you're funny as hell, gorgeous, you can cook your ass off and now you're dancing bachata with me... Where did you *come* from? What am I supposed to do with you?"

I can feel the holes closing up against his flesh. Sad. I give his skin a quick lick to make sure it's clean. I'm examining it when I say, "I can think of loads of things you can do with me, actually." When he lists it out like that, I sound quite impressive, don't I?

Playfully, I lift my gaze and blink, but his face is serious, so I frown. "What's wrong?"

"You make me nervous, Jae."

"*Why?* You keep saying that. What am I doing exactly—"

"You know I don't do this with ranked vampires. I've told you this."

He has. Multiple times, in very frustrated rants usually having to do with his purebred source—among others. "I'm not a proper vampire yet, Jun. See, no fangs." I awkwardly open my mouth to try and lighten the suddenly dour mood. It doesn't work.

"But you *will* be," he says. "Any day now. And I'm feeding you. I've already fed from you, and if we make love and you've turned, we could bond. Do you understand how serious this is?"

I shake my head. "Not exactly. Is that all it takes to bond? There's so much mystery surrounding vampire bonds. Humans don't know exactly what it requires."

He takes my hand and leads me over to his sunflower-colored sofa. We both sit down. "The short answer is yes," Junichi says. "Mutual feeding and sex are the basic components for creating a vampiric bond. But there are other, more complex factors that dictate how quickly it happens or the quality of the bond—how strong it will be."

"Such as?" I ask. "What are these factors?"

"The biggest thing we've recently learned is compatibility. Haruka's family has a research manual about vampiric bonds called *Lore and Lust*. It highlights all the factors associated with vampire intimacy and bonding."

Christ. An entire research journal on vampire bonds. I wonder if he'll let me read it when I start visiting him this coming Sunday...

"If a ranked vampire couple is highly compatible, they bond faster," Junichi continues. "Haruka says he's learned that the best-quality bonds form within one to three tries. But it's *rare*. It normally takes vampires somewhere between five and ten tries before a bond forms, and we now know that those bonds are weak. Forced. They're low-quality bonds."

I sit for a few moments in silence, letting the abundance of information knock around in my brain. "Alright... how does a couple know how compatible they are?"

Junichi exhales a heavy sigh and sits back against the couch. "Talk to Haruka about it when you visit him. He says it's something you feel—a certain pull. He thinks trust is a major factor."

I nod. I will definitely ask him, but now I want examples. "So, how long did it take Haruka and Nino to bond?"

"First try."

"And that's rare?"

"*Insanely.*"

"So in a sense, they're perfectly compatible?" I ask.

"Yes. 'Choosing a mate is not absolute.' That's what we've always said in our culture—that there is no singular vampire who is 'perfect' for you. But this new information tells us that there are vampires so well suited for your nature, and yours for theirs, that the bond instantly and easily clicks."

"First try..." I mumble, considering. I think about Haruka and Nino and how obviously balanced they are. How soft and considerate they are with each other. How the loving warmth between them feels like the glow of the sun. It touches me and makes me smile just being in their presence.

I think back to what Haruka told me the first time we had tea together. That everything between him and Nino felt natural. That they communicated and openly accepted the pull they felt in their instincts. The magnetism. I'm sure that's a huge part of it. They didn't fight it. They didn't let their baggage, hang-ups and assumptions get in the way. They fully trusted each other.

I look over at Jun, deciding to get back to the fundamentals. "What does it mean to bond, Jun?"

"It means you're beholden," he says. "You're chained to a singular vampire forever. Breaking the chain has dire conse-quences. You can only feed and have intimacy with that particular vampire for the rest of your life, and your bloodline is shared. Deeply entwined and dependent."

The fact that his definition is laced with pessimism isn't lost on me. It was not an unbiased explanation. I want to ask Haruka the same question on Sunday. Maybe Sora next time I'm at work, too. Just to get as many takes on it as possible before I develop my own perspective.

Already, though, if I take what he's said and remove the bias, it sounds quite nice. Feed from and make love to a person you're perfectly compatible with forever? Yes, please. Absolutely.

What I wouldn't give to have that. To never go on a first date again, or deal with the awkward learning curve of a new sex partner (only to reach the end of the curve and find that you aren't even compatible—the sex is just dreadful). To always have someone to share moments, laughs and experiences with. To never be discarded, or paranoid about being abandoned or alone again.

For me, it sounds brilliant. To Junichi, though, not so much.

"You make bonding sound like a kind of prison," I say.

"In the home I grew up in, it was. It took me seventy-five years to be free of it. And even now my biology is still impacted because of my father's choices—even though he's been dead for more than fifty years. I'm still chained in some ways."

I nod and do some quick maths. Junichi's age is between a hundred and twenty-five and a hundred and thirty. So difficult to fathom. This life span.

I don't say it aloud, but *this* is Junichi's baggage: his childhood. The environment he was brought up in was damaging to his views on relationships. I openly acknowledge my baggage. I have abandonment issues and a toxic best friend, and I try to do everything on my own. I know it well, and I try to be aware of it when it's fucking up my lenses. I'm not sure if Junichi knows his baggage, or if he's willing to take ownership of it.

I want to test the waters, so I give a slight poke. "Not *all* bonds are reflective of what you personally experienced growing up. Look at Nino and Haruka?"

Junichi scoffs. "They're the exception, remember? Not the rule."

I nod, keeping my mouth shut. Zero awareness of the baggage. My mind is spinning in a million different ways, so I jump slightly when he reaches over and clasps my hand.

"Did I scare you?" he asks.

"No. Sorry. Just thinking."

"I want to be honest with you. Bonding is not something I want to do, Jae. I don't usually put myself in this kind of situation. I never offer my blood like this, or even let anyone stay in my home. But I care about you... and I like you."

"I like you, too."

He nods, returning my smile. "So I want to support you through this. I'm going to—I'm happy to. But we need to be careful. All jokes aside, can you respect that?"

"I can." And I will. I'll stop it with the flirty comments and trying to goad him. If he's truly terrified that we might accidentally bond, I won't provoke him. Not even for a snuggle.

What he's doing for me is unbelievable. Letting me move into his home, invade his privacy and take his blood. Of course I'll respect his wishes. I can behave myself. He'll see.

LATE NOVEMBER

TWENTY-NINE

JUNICHI

[When do you think you'll be back home?]

I'm staring at Jae's message and considering my response.

[It'll be fairly late. Maybe close to midnight.]

[Okay. I was going to make soondubu jjigae tonight…
Breakfast instead?]

[Yes, please. I'll try not to wake you when I come
home. xx]

I set my phone down on the worktable and breathe a sigh. It's been about a month since Jae started "awakening," and not much has changed other than his sleep patterns. He said before he'd stay up all night sometimes. Restless and jittery. Since I've started feeding him, though, he sleeps well—deeply and comfortably. It's not very exciting but definitely a good thing. I'm glad.

"There are rumors circulating about you, Takayama Junichi."

It's Sunday afternoon and Hisaki is perched on my couch, dramatically flickering his horse tail and looking at me. I should get rid of that couch. Can't flounce around in here like a dumbass if there's nowhere to sit.

"I wonder if that confounding creature I met here last month is the one everyone is talking about? The one spending time with Haruka lately. This *doctor*. Miscreant. What gives *him* the right?" he says. I'm hand-stitching a design on the collar of an outer coat for a kimono. New Year's will be here before I know it, and I'm thinking of asking Jae to go to the local temple with me. I'm not religious, but I think the tradition is nice. My mother used to drag me and my sister because she liked to dabble in Japanese culture despite her rigid circumstance. I think she was always trying to make the best of things.

I'm making Jae a kimono and coat as a surprise. I'm starting with the coat because I don't know his exact measurements yet. I'm estimating the neck and shoulders, but I can make adjustments later.

"Are you ignoring me?" Hisaki asks.

"I'm trying to." I'm threading the whip stitch, which is lapis blue. The fabric I'm using is a deep steel gray. The kimono underneath will be dark blue. I think he'll look good in these colors, and it'll stop him from buying some pre-made kimono combination off of a mannequin at a department store.

"Are you living with him? Is he truly residing in your home?"

I shake my head, focusing. I don't need to answer this twerp's questions or explain myself to anyone. What's happening to Jae is his business. Not the aristocracy's. Not yet. If and when he awakens, then they can know.

Living together with Jae has been surprisingly comfortable.

Easy. He's pleasant and keeps busy. His room is always a mess of papers and research things, but he keeps my common areas and kitchen clean. I've never had a roommate before, so I don't have any points of comparison. But I imagine he's probably the best kind.

"You know, my bloodline is unique among vampires," Hisaki boasts. "We have a very keen sense of smell. It has been passed down to each successive first-born child for generations. So it was easy for me to tell that something was off about your... friend?"

I have not said more than three words in at least ten minutes. It's unbelievable how he sits here, perfectly satisfied with hearing himself talk.

"Junichi, you are wildly popular within our aristocracy. Your bloodline and breeding are exquisite—fit for any purebred to mate with. You should not be engaging with this strange creature in this way. I am not interested in physical intimacy—and our age gap is significant—but... even *I* would be a more socially appropriate choice as a mate for you."

I dry-heave and quickly take a breath. I rest the needle and fabric down onto the table and close my eyes. "Hisaki. What I do in my private life has nothing to do with you, or *anyone* in the aristocracy. Do you understand?"

He blinks his red eyes at me like a calf at a new gate. "No. I do not understand. Because we are a tightly knit community, and we want to know more about this creature you've suddenly latched yourself to. Does Ren know about this?"

My first instinct is to say, "Fuck Ren." But I can't say that. Not aloud. He's like my drug dealer—the one with the good stuff. I have to keep things as amicable between us as possible.

Or maybe I *should* say it and completely sever the ties between us? That's what should really happen. Except I'm weak. I've been drinking his blood since I was sixteen... fucking purebred blood. I'm going to see Ren today, which is why I can't have spicy tofu soup for dinner with the bright, sexy doctor living in my home. I have to go get my damn fix.

Jae has been hustling for the past month. He's been taking patients part-time at the hospital, setting up and interviewing candidates for the surrogacy program and visiting and researching with Haruka. He's over at his house now. He usually goes twice a week. When Jae comes back home, he's giddy. I'm sure Haruka loves it too—having another bookworm to nerd out with over vampire lore. Add to it, Jae is an excellent student. Even his bachata has gotten better.

At night, he's cooking and spending time with me. The irony is that he's doing exactly what I asked and taking my stance on us not having sex seriously. But *I'm* the one harassing him when we're in the house together.

He's got that sexy little mole in the concave of his neck, so if I'm walking past him in the kitchen, I'll lean down and kiss it. Unprompted. He laughs and shrugs his shoulder every time I do it. I love it. If we're sitting on the couch together, eventually I pull him into my embrace so he's sitting against me while we talk. Then I rub my face into his soft, golden hair and nibble at his ear. He smells so damn good and sweet—I want to bite him so bad it's painful. Sometimes my mouth waters from his nearness.

I don't bite him. I haven't since the first time. He still can't produce fangs at all, and he says he feels the same. Maybe I'm being overly precautious, but how can I know? This is uncharted territory.

"I *said*, does Ren know?" Hisaki repeats, frowning at me.

"Again—my business. Not yours. Go home. I need to leave." I stand and walk toward the closet to store my side project there. I work on Jae's kimono at the end of the day after all my clients have come and gone. The respectable ones, anyway.

"It doesn't make Ren look very good... you shacking up with this mysterious creature. It's disrespectful to your purebred source."

I poke my head out of the closet, my eyes sharp like daggers. "Are you *lecturing* me right now?"

"No." He promptly stands, clearly having read the danger in my face and tone. "I'm leaving. I'll see you next week."

"I would rather you didn't." I walk back into the closet to finish hanging the garment.

IT'S a two-hour trip one-way to see Ren in Hiroshima. That alone should be enough to convince me to stop this shit. When I slide the door open to the small tearoom within his estate where we always feed and meet, he's already there. I'm shocked. Usually he makes me wait fifteen to twenty minutes, and then I have to sit through a dramatic entrance.

He's sitting on the floor on a cushion, his legs tucked underneath him. He's wearing a black robe with an intricate geometric wave pattern in muted gold. His long dark hair is pulled up into a hasty, careless bun at the top of his head. His arms are folded.

I made this robe for him, actually. A very long time ago. He rarely wears what I make. He says my aesthetic isn't bold enough. Well, fuck him.

I slide the door closed and move toward the empty cushion directly in front of him. "This is a nice surprise," I say. Maybe I can get the hell out of here faster than usual? His butterscotch eyes shift up to watch, following me as I sit across from him and match his formal position.

I would say he looks annoyed, but... he almost always looks this way. Surly. Like he's swallowed something distasteful. Even when we were kids. It's too bad, because he's genuinely striking: his lean, straight features are like a work of art—ironic, because he's also a pretty skilled painter. He even painted a portrait of me, once. But his personality renders all of this as irrelevant.

"What's up your ass?" I ask, raising my eyebrow. There was a time when I was more formal toward Ren. More polite. Those days are long gone.

His vivid eyes are expressionless, but his gaze is penetrating. "Who is staying with you? In your home."

"A friend."

"Who?"

"That's my personal business, Ren. It doesn't have anything to do with you—"

He reaches up and grips the top of my head by my hair. Fuck me for not getting my hair cut recently and fuck him for being so damn fast. My hand is wrapped around his wrist, but when I move to pull it away, he grips me even tighter. "*Shit*—"

"Are you *fucking and feeding* from someone under my nose? In *our* aristocracy?"

I'm about to tell him to take his damn hands off of me, but his eyes alight and I suck in a breath. My body suddenly feels like I'm a thousand pounds—like I'm a person-sized boulder anchored to the floor. I can't move. He's staring at me with vivid golden light in his eyes, furious.

He's only done this to me one other time. After my father died and I sincerely tried to cut the ties between us. I told him I wasn't sleeping with him anymore, and that I was going to try weaning my system off of his blood. He freaked out, weighed me down and told me he needed me. That I couldn't leave him.

At the time, I hadn't even known he was capable of doing this. He'd been keeping it a secret.

Some purebreds have powers but most don't—usually because their ancestors haven't done a good job in keeping their bloodline clean through the centuries. Someone fucked it up by feeding from humans too much, and their blood takes a couple generations to recover—if it ever fully does.

Ren's bloodline is clean (which only enhances my addiction to it). When he overpowered me that first time, it scared the hell out of me. *He* cried afterward, telling me he was sorry— that he accepted my feelings about us not bonding—but asked if we could stay each other's sources. We'd been together since we were kids and I was all he'd ever known. He pleaded, telling me he'd never do that to me again.

Obviously, I trusted him. But it seems he lied.

"Tell me." He grips my curls even tighter in his fist and presses me down as he lifts to his knees, using my head as leverage. I don't say anything. He can manipulate my body, but he can't make me talk. I can't believe he's asserting his power and rank over me like this. Knowing how much I hate it. Knowing what my father was like and how I tip-toed around him every day of my youth to avoid this exact situation.

Ren lifts his hand from my head like it's suddenly caught fire. I'm trembling even though I still can't move of my own free will, awkwardly hunched in a bow in front of him. He takes a deep breath. "Violet, why do you make things so difficult? You and I should be bonded by now—we should have been mated years ago. We're not supposed to be like this!"

He places his hands on the sides of my face. I can't move on my own, but since he's in control, he urges me upward. He's looking into my eyes like he's searching for something. "Why won't your eyes alight for me anymore? They did once. It was exquisite... I'll never forget that color."

I close my eyes because he can't make me look at him either. He's delusional. He smacked me hard the first and only time my eyes alighted for him. The first and only time they alighted for anyone. But he's recounting it now like it was a sweet memory. Like it was a good moment between us when it was not.

Ren's voice is calm but firm. "You belong to me. *Everyone* knows this. Whatever the hell you think you're doing, stop. Your father was a strict, tyrannical asshole—I get it. We all knew that. So I've let you play and have your freedom... I've been good about letting you tramp across Europe year after year. Enough is enough. We need to establish our bond. I'm done with this childish game."

He bends down and licks my neck in a long, wet stroke before he bites down hard into my flesh. I clench my eyes shut even tighter, bracing myself for the flood of his possessive, frustrated feelings that register as love in his mind. It flows into me like black ink—like a dark stain on my entire nature, stifling me. Suffocating me. It's usually bad, but it's horrible today. Unbearable.

When he's done, he pulls up, licks me again, then kisses me hard on my cheek in a loud smacking sound. He smiles, dignified. "I don't think I'll let you feed from me today. Let's call this punishment for upsetting me. Letting some strange creature into your home... You've never once invited *me* into your home. It's hurtful, Violet. I'm sensitive."

The hold he has over my body releases, and I shove him, hard. He tumbles backward and onto his ass, laughing as I stand up. I want to hit him, but I can't. Even with what he's done to me, the fucking moral code that's been drilled into me since birth won't let me punch a purebred vampire. If *I* were a purebred vampire and could match his power and status—if we were equals? I would drain him dead.

My legs feel numb and I'm still shaking. My breath is short when I point down at him. "You will *never* fucking touch me again. We're done."

He sits up straight, grinning as he lifts his arms to lazily unravel his long hair from the bun atop his head. "Oh, don't be dramatic. You'll need to feed within a day at maximum, and then you'll be back. Let's consider tomorrow night a fresh start for us, yes? You can make love to me and feed from me like you used to. You'll enjoy it, I promise. I will make certain."

I shake my head, walking backward and away from the monster sitting on the floor. My head is swimming and I feel nauseous as I leave the room. When I'm outside the estate gates, I actually do vomit. I don't think I've ever done that. What a terrifying sensation. I've never felt this bad after Ren's feeding from me. The weight of his subjugation is gone, but it feels as if it's lingering within me. My body and mind are heavy, weak.

I just need to make it home and take a hot shower. When I'm in my safe space and clean from his fingerprints and saliva, it'll be better. It always is. I'll sleep, and in the morning I can have spicy tofu soup with Jae and figure out what the hell I'm going to do.

That's what gives me the strength to get through the two-hour train ride and make it all the way back home. The thought of tomorrow and breakfast with warm, sweet Jae in my home.

THIRTY

JAE

"Knock it off."

I groan and turn over to my opposite side in the soft bed. I've left the window cracked open a smidge and it's perfectly crisp in my room. I love that. Winter sleeping—when I'm cozy underneath the weight of the duvet without having to kick it off in the middle of the night because I've gotten too hot.

"Meoooow."

"*Lulú.*" I drag my body upright because this cat is giving me hell. Meowing and bumping her fuzzy little head into mine like she's itching for a fight. I usually leave my door cracked as well, because she likes to sleep at the end of my bed some nights. Like a puppy. When she's not there, I think she's in Jun's room. She's alternating between us like we're divorced parents. But we're alright, Jun and me. No problems there.

"Meeeow."

"*Shit*, cat. What is it?" I watch as she leaps from the bed, steadily meowing. She walks toward the door and slinks through. I think she's leaving, but then she pokes her head back inside, meowing more. Christ. Am I supposed to follow her?

When we were younger, Cyrus was obsessed with very old American TV shows. There was one he made me watch sometimes called *Lassie*. I'm reminded of that now, like, "What is it, girl? Has Junichi fallen in the well?"

I pull myself out of bed. I'm only wearing my sleep trousers (less probability for me to become overheated), so I grab my robe as I head out the door. Lulú is already ahead of me, down the hall and in the open living room, still whining. It's quite obvious now that she wants me to follow her. Weird.

Eventually she's meowing in front of Junichi's room. When I'm standing there with her, she lifts onto her haunches and presses her front paws into the closed door, looking up at me with her bright golden eyes. I sigh. "Lulú, your father does *not* want me bothering him." Do I need to explain to her that Junichi doesn't want me in his bed because he's afraid of bonding with me? Do I really need to tell this cat that information?

When I hesitate, Lulú comes back down on all fours, then swats at my feet. "*Hey.*" I step back and away from her paws. She goes to the door and stretches up against it once more, fussing.

"Alright, alright." Later, when Jun is annoyed about me sneaking into his room in the middle of the night, how convincing will it be to say, "The cat made me do it?" I imagine not very.

I press the door handle and peek inside. It's very dark tonight. Not much moonlight pouring in through the glass wall. Jun is a long lump on his bed, above the covers and lying on his side. I will admit... immediately, something feels off. I don't know why, but the atmosphere is wrong.

"Meeeow."

"Christ—*alright.*" I step inside and walk forward. I've left the door cracked in case Lulú is joining me. When I look back, though, she's sitting in the hall, watching me. She's quiet now and her tail is flopping around behind her.

Stepping up to the bed, I keep my voice soft so I don't startle him. "Jun?"

He doesn't rouse. He wasn't home when I arrived from Haruka and Nino's house. I get really sleepy lately (which is nice), so I went straight to bed after showering. Speaking of, Jun must have done as well, because he's only got a towel wrapped around his waist.

It's chilly in here. When I place my palm on his bicep, his skin is surprisingly cold. I put a little more weight behind my voice. "Jun—"

His eyes flash open and he jumps away from me, startling me as well. We blink at each other in the ambient darkness for a moment before I say, "Hey... you alright?"

He's trembling. I can see it as he runs his hand into his thick curls atop his head, and his eyes are bewildered in a way I've never seen. Usually, Jun's black irises are so cool and calm. Sometimes I can't tell what he's thinking because he's got such a swaggery poker face. His face is not like that right now. It's distressed.

Worried, I lean onto the bed with both palms flat, careful not to invade his space or startle him. "What's the matter?" He'd glanced off, but now he's looking at me again. His hand is still shaking when he reaches, wraps it around one of my wrists and gently urges me onto the bed.

Understanding, I climb on. He slowly pulls me down. As I adjust on my side, he snakes his arms around my waist, pulling me into him. Embracing me. He nestles his body into me so that his face is at the center of my collarbone and just underneath my chin. I can feel his breath there as he holds me tight, so I shift and cradle his head in my arms. My chin rests against the top of his soft head.

He's not saying anything, but after a minute, the shaking subsides. His breathing is slow and deep with his arms wrapped tightly around me. His skin is a bit cold at first, but after a moment, he warms up as he relaxes against me. Perfectly still. Soon, I feel myself drifting off to sleep as well.

This is even better than a heavy duvet. This is winter sleeping elevated.

MY FINGERTIPS ARE PRESSING and rubbing up against something firm and taut. There are silky hairs there. I smile because it's nice and I remember this texture. This sensation. When I remember why I like it and why it makes me smile, I open my eyes wide.

It's morning. I'm halfway atop Jun's body, leaning into him on my belly. He's on his back. I push myself up slightly. He's got his fingers in my hair, caressing my scalp as I look down at him, panicked. I'm even more anxious when I realize he's naked. Wonderfully, perfectly, but the towel is gone—unraveled somehow in the night.

"*Shit.* Sorry, Jun."

He's awake and lazily watching me, a gentle smile on his lovely lips. "Good morning, sunshine."

I rub my palm down my face. God, he's gorgeous. "Morning."

"What are you sorry for?"

I look down the length of his naked body again. Shit. Stop that. "I shouldn't be in here... but, are you alright? The cat made me come in here to check on you. I am *literally* what the cat dragged in."

Jun laughs, and the anxiety in my chest eases a little. I keep rubbing my fingers against his tight abdomen because, well, he doesn't seem to mind it and I've missed this. Very much.

"I'm pretty sure my mother did something to that cat," he says. "She liked science and had a curious mind."

I frown. "The cat or your mum?"

"My mother... clearly."

"Right. Why do you think?"

"Lulú was my mother's cat. She's been alive and perfectly healthy for... Maybe it'll be eighty-three years this year?"

"You have *got* to be shitting me."

Junichi shrugs against the bed. "Nope. My best guess is Mom injected her with her own blood, but I'll never know. I only say that because she weirdly reminds me of my mother sometimes."

"God..." I shake my head. "A vampire cat." I'm one part amazed, one part anxious and one part wondering if I need to show Lulú much more respect going forward.

"Not technically. She doesn't bite or feed—at least, I've never seen her do that."

"Maybe she needs to be awakened," I whisper, slightly horrified. "Like me..."

Junichi is laughing when he pulls me down toward his mouth. The ridiculous B-list horror movie tension I feel fades. Normally, I part my lips immediately, but I don't now because I'm not sure how far he wants this to go. Soon, he's urging me to part them, so I do. Meeting the warmth and wetness of his mouth, his tongue is divine. I've missed him. He's been kissing and nipping at me for the past month, playfully. Innocently.

It drives me mad. I feel like a hungry bear, and he keeps petting and teasing me, but I want to turn around and swallow him whole. Maybe I'll dry-hump him first.

Just as the kiss is getting good and my skin is getting hot, he breaks it, staring up at me with soft black eyes. I'm preparing myself for the worst when he whispers, "May I have you?"

I *almost* say, "But what if we bond?"

I'm not stupid though, so instead I say, "Yes."

He lifts his head to kiss me again. This time, I put my whole self in it, breathing into him and shamelessly tasting him. Reacquainting myself with the texture of his tongue and the rhythm of his mouth as it moves. While we kiss, I shift my robe off my shoulders with one hand. Jun senses I want to be naked and helps me, freeing me from the material.

When it's off, he rolls me onto my back and sits up. I hook my thumbs into my joggers to start working them down. He helps me again, grabbing them at my thighs and pulling them toward my feet. The other two times we made love, Jun was so slow in all his movements, like we had all day—forever, even.

Now there's a frenetic energy between us, like we both desperately need this. I'm naked when he climbs back up toward my face. He reaches between us to align his cock against mine before he rests his hips down. Everything below and around my navel feels like fire—amazing heat that makes me groan and writhe. When he presses our mouths together again, his movement is hungry, but soon, it's slowing back down to our usual pace.

We're kissing softer now, and I'm just enjoying the heaviness of him on top of me. The taste of his mouth. My thighs are gaped open, and I lazily pull one of my knees up and slide my ankle against the outside of his leg. We break the kiss, and he stares down at me as I run my hands up the center of his back. I suddenly feel like we're in the eye of a tornado, perfectly quiet and still.

"What?" I grin. I'm so happy like this. Just like this.

He answers by leaning down and rubbing his nose into me,

which gets me every fucking time. Like my heart might burst. I close my eyes and try not to let it overwhelm me.

After a few more soft, lovely kisses, he sits up and off me again, smiling. "One moment, please." He stands. I watch his long, wonderfully golden-brown and finely muscled body move toward the bathroom. I hear a cabinet or two open and close, then he's walking toward me again with his hands full.

I'm surprised when he sits against my side and pops the lube open. Once it's spread on his fingers, he lies down, making himself comfortable beside me and propping himself up with one elbow against the pillow. "Do you have a preference?" he asks.

"I like watching you. I like seeing what you do to me."

Jun reaches down and grips his fingers around my shaft first, making me suck in a breath. He's stroking and pulling me. I lift my hips up into his movement because it feels excellent. After a minute he moves his fingers down lower. "Can you take over?"

I reach down and grip my own shaft while Jun's fingertips massage and caress lower and lower until they're flirting with my opening. He's barely done anything and I honestly might go crazy. Everything in me is ecstatic and wild. My entire body is celebrating this.

He presses a finger into me. I breathe and relax with the intrusion. It's good, but I'm already imagining the fullness of him inside me. I'm mentally past this stretching business and I want all of him. I close my eyes, imagining it as I pull and grip myself. Jun is pressing his finger in and out of me in a slow, steady movement.

Gradually, he pushes deeper. When he hits just the right spot, the rush of warm pleasure springs up on me from nowhere, like liquid heat shooting up my spine. I arch my neck, groan and let it take me. Let it engulf me from head to toe.

Jun kisses me as I slowly come down—on my cheek, my temple and my ear. My breathing is heavy, chest rising and falling. He keeps kissing me and it's so loving. Attentive. Like my climaxing is the only thing he wanted and he's thrilled about it.

"*God,*" I breathe, just as he presses a second finger into me. I shift slightly toward him now, angling myself to give him better access to my body. I'm right underneath him as I look up and smile. "Hi."

He laughs. I love making him laugh. "You're beautiful when you come," he says.

I feel the warm flush of embarrassment color my face. "Not something I thought I'd hear today... or ever."

"You are." He leans down and kisses me again while gently stroking his fingers in and out, twisting and flexing. "You give yourself over to it," he says, breaking the kiss. "To me and what I'm giving you. It's alluring, watching you... so trusting."

"Because it's you. *You* make me feel this way."

There's an irony here. When I asked Haruka what it meant to bond a few weeks ago, his definition was much simpler and more objective than Jun's. Haruka said, "To be truly bonded with someone is to trust them completely. To openly give of yourself and your affection."

I like this explanation. It makes sense and I *feel* it with Jun. I trust him. He's turning me, or "awakening" me, for God's sake. I trust him to do this utterly insane thing to me. *For* me. And I... I would honestly give him anything if he wanted it. Everything.

He's got a third finger in me now. My groin is getting tight again, so I reach my fingers up to hold his chin. I don't want to climax like this a second time. "Inside me now, please."

THIRTY-ONE
JUNICHI

Jae is looking up at me from the pillow, his chestnut eyes lazy with sexual gratification. My sweet prince—warm creamy skin and dark golden, messy waves.

Now that I know for certain what he is, it's obvious. How the hell did I miss it or even question it? He's stunning. Perplexing. The pull I feel toward him is unquestionable, buzzing inside me like a low hum. It's always made me nervous, so I've tried to ignore it. I've pushed it away along with the words Haruka spoke—that Jae's awakening is in part because of me. Our compatibility is so strong that his nature intrinsically responds to me.

I remove my fingers from the warm cavern of his body and sit up straight. Grabbing his hand, I pull him upright and toward me. He's confused but smiling. He trusts me.

"What's all this?" he asks.

I sit up straight, folding my legs in the middle of the bed. His hand is still in mine, so I urge him toward me. "Come closer," I say, smiling up at him as he lifts to his knees. I bring his hand over my shoulder like we're dancing, urging him into my lap. He gets it now and climbs onto my folded legs. I hold his waist while he places his hands on my shoulders to steady himself.

Soon, he's facing me with his legs gaped open as he sits in the hollow of my lap. The condom is beside me, so I pick it up and hand it to him. While he opens it and slowly unrolls it onto me, I'm lazily tracing my fingertips outside his thighs, up his hips and waist, then around to the small of his back.

Could I do this with him forever? Have him in my house, being warm, witty and delightful? Running my shop by day, then coming home to him at night... pleasing him and laughing with him. Dancing and eating with him.

I've never had the desire to bond. Even when I was expected to do it with Ren, I didn't want it. Being bonded with my father slowly killed my mom's spirit. I hated watching it year after year, knowing I couldn't do anything about it other than promise myself to never be in a situation like hers—permanently beholden to someone cold who outranked me.

I *still* wouldn't say that I want to bond, but... when Jae fully awakens and he's a first-gen like me, maybe... maybe I can imagine it. We'll be equals then—well matched and innately drawn to each other. Even if he's second- or third-gen when he awakens, if my nature responds this strongly to him, I should accept it, shouldn't I? I'll be rid of Ren and his fucking purebred blood. It'll be hard, but... maybe I should trust in this?

Jae is making sexy little moaning noises as he slowly settles himself onto my cock. I don't force or manipulate him in any way. I just kiss him underneath and along his jawline as I caress his lower back with my fingertips, waiting until he's made himself comfortable. When he's all the way down, he wraps his legs around me, sighing and finding my mouth to kiss me back. He feels so tight and hot around my shaft—the weight of him is marvelous. Not too heavy, not too light. Perfect. He's relaxed and already gently rocking his hips into me as he kisses me. He's so fucking sexy and brazen. He does these things and chills go up my spine.

I slide my hands down to his hips, urging his movement against me now. We're still kissing, but it's getting wild with Jae's rocking. Messy. Jae breaks the kiss and inhales like he can't breathe, lifting his face toward the ceiling with his eyes clenched shut.

"*Christ*, Jun... you feel so good."

With his eyes still closed, he removes his hands from around my shoulders and leans back on his palms, using the bed as leverage to rock himself harder into me. He's swearing and out of breath, like he's desperately chasing the release he needs from me.

I'm mesmerized by him. The feel of his body wrapped around me, the delicious scent of him and his shameless desire. I take one hand from his hip and firmly wrap it around his shaft between us to help him in his pursuit. I grip him hard, pulling and tugging, and a moment later he cries out, spilling over for me. He arches his neck and back, stunning and angelic in the golden sunlight pouring in through the glass wall.

Without even thinking, I grab his torso and pull him toward me while his neck is exposed. I lift my chin so that I'm just above his collarbone and I bite down hard. I hear Jae gasp, then feel his hands at my shoulders, swiftly wrapping around to embrace me.

His blood is flowing into my mouth, divine as I pull and swallow. He tastes just like he smells—sweet, warm and *every-thing* good. Anything satisfying I've ever known. Something freshly baked or a rainy day indoors. A winter night by the fire. Everything cozy and wholesome feels like its concentrated in Jae's blood and I don't understand why. How is he so unbelievably satisfying to me when he hasn't even fully awakened yet?

The sublime pleasure of his blood and the heat of his tight body push me over the edge. I climax while I'm still feeding from him, like electricity is running up my spine and through me, straight to my brain. Jae has one hand clasped at the back of my neck, the other in my hair with his fingers gently massaging my scalp and his arms resting on my shoulders. He's encouraging what I'm doing. Willingly giving of himself.

When I pull up from his neck and lick him clean, I notice he's trembling. Worried, I look up to check his face. "Are you alright?" I ask.

He's calm as he smiles. "I'm perfect."

"Why are you shaking like this?" I look him over, caressing my hands up his spine to embrace him tight, wanting to ease his tremors.

He wraps his arms tighter around my shoulders. "I don't know... This happened the first time you fed from me too. I feel gooey and melty inside. It makes me shake, but it passes. I'm alright."

I blink, lifting my head from the warm hug to face him. "Why didn't you tell me that the first time?"

He leans into me, brushing his nose against mine with his eyes closed. "You were a bit miffed with me at the time, remember? Having thought I was lying to you about being a vampire."

I smile, meeting his affection. "You were."

He lifts his head from me, his face serious. "Was *not*. Jun—"

I kiss him and wrap my arms even tighter around his waist. When I sense the tension in him relax, I pull up. "I'm joking, Jae. If you feel something strange happening with your body, please tell me. I'm sorry I wasn't in the right state of mind that first time."

"Don't worry," he says, nuzzling his nose against me again. God, he really loves this. "Are we... bonded now?"

I laugh. "No. If we were, you would know. I hear it's an

unmistakable feeling—like an anchor being dropped in your gut and at the base of your spine."

"I sincerely doubt it's as painful and horrific as you describe."

I shrug. "It's just what I've heard—and sometimes there are flashes of light and color." I pinch his ass so he jumps slightly in surprise. "If you'll release me, maybe we can shower, have some spicy tofu soup and then make our way back here?"

Having fed from Jae is like a palate cleanser. The residual, emotional muck that Ren dumped into me is gone, but I still feel tired. I didn't have a lot of appointments today. The ones I had, I'll cancel. I know Jae usually researches and works on the surrogacy program in the mornings, but...

He grins, occasionally wincing as he slowly lifts himself from my shaft. "Lazing about all morning in bed? With you? Yes, please... So sex is back on the table for us?"

Distracted, I carefully take hold of the used condom. "Obviously." When I have it in my fingers, I scoot toward the end of the bed.

"No—I mean... This isn't a one-time thing? Like you just wanted a refresher course."

I'm standing to walk toward the bathroom, but pause and look at him. "I think... if you're open with me about how you're feeling, maybe we're okay? Since you're not fully awakened... we don't need to be so strict." And deep down—deep, deep down—I tell myself that if it happens... it happens.

Jae falls back, smiling as he stretches his arms up over his head and writhes against the comforter, happy and naked. "I promise to tell you everything—open communication. No secrets... Are you sleeping with anyone else? Currently?"

I'm in the bathroom, but I still hear him. "No." I poke my head through the frame. "Are you?"

Jae spins himself and flips so that he's lying on his stomach and facing me. His feet are in the air behind him and he's resting on his elbows. "Nope. I don't want to."

I smirk at his matter-of-fact response. He's watching me like he wants to say something else. When he doesn't, I ask, "Are you showering with me?" He nods and scoots to the edge of the bed. As he walks toward me, I'm already thinking about how I'm going to make him come a third time before we finish this shower situation.

I WOULD SAY that every time Jae cooks, it's like eating at a restaurant. But it's not. It's better. As if each dish is especially made with his unique style—flavorful, filling and light. He's not heavy-handed with seasonings, so it's always just right.

We're showered, well fed and in my bed again. Clothed this time—comfortable in sweats and long-sleeved shirts. I'm lying on my back against the pillows with my hands cradling my head. Jae is sitting upright beside me with his legs folded. Our only points of physical contact are his left thigh resting against mine and his left hand snaked underneath my shirt. He has his palm on my stomach, gently caressing his fingers against my flesh—in and around my belly button. He switches back and forth between playing my abdomen like a piano and rubbing me like I'm a very good boy.

"What happened to you?" he asks, his expression serious but sincere. "What was wrong last night?"

I suspect he's been wanting to ask this question since before we took a shower but kept hesitating. Jae is good about reading the room and finding the right moment to say something—our first dinner date excluded.

I inhale deep then blow it out. "Ren acted like a shithead yesterday when I went to feed from him."

"How so?"

"Well, let's see... He physically assaulted me and exerted his rank over me by suppressing me with his aura, dumped his twisted emotions into me when he fed then sent me on my way without letting *me* feed."

"Christ, Jun..."

I shrug. "He's usually a self-absorbed wretch of a creature, but yesterday was especially malicious."

"Why?"

I consider that for a moment, and everything Ren said to me. Bottom line? "He wants me but I don't want him. Technically, we should have bonded a long time ago."

Jae nods. "You told me that. I remember..."

"It'll *never* happen. I haven't even slept with him in decades. I thought he understood where I was coming from, but apparently he's just been 'letting me play' all this time—like I'm his fucking pet and he's always been the one in control. Now he's done with that, it seems. He's insane."

Jae's hand hasn't moved in a couple minutes—just resting flat against my stomach as he stares at me, worried. "When you say he 'suppressed' you, what do you mean?"

"Purebreds can radiate their vampiric energy outward. And if their blood is especially clean, they can manipulate it in such a way where it's like having unique powers. It's originated in their blood and emotions, and they can use it to compel or control their prey—to make some poor sap do what they wish by force. It feels like shit and it's painful."

"It sounds terrible."

"I hate it."

"So, what will you do?" Jae asks.

I shift my hands from behind my head, rubbing them down my face from stress. I had pushed the reality of it aside until now. "I need to quit him, obviously."

"Right. He's legitimately abusive, Jun. Physically and emotionally."

"I *know*. It's just... It's easier said than done. I won't go back. I *won't*. But... I don't know what that means. How my body will respond to that decision."

Finding another first-gen or lower-ranked vampire to feed from would be pretty easy. But how long before my body starts to act up? And can I successfully push through the withdrawal? How long will I have to suffer before I can function normally? Comfortably? I'm stressed just thinking about all this shit.

When I flick my eyes back up to Jae, he has that look again —like he wants to say something but he's hesitating. I reach my hand down and meet his underneath my shirt, wrapping my fingers around his. "What is it? Tell me what you're thinking."

THIRTY-TWO

JAE

I'm thinking two things. One—I never want Jun to go see Ren again. Ever. I know there's a hierarchy within vampire culture, but it's difficult for me to imagine anyone subjugating Jun. He's confident and independent. Debonair. He's such a mentally strong person that anyone getting the better of him—no, *abusing* him—is beyond me. I can't fathom it.

Two, I clench Jun's hand a little tighter at his stomach. "I know I'm not quite out of the oven yet, but... when you feed from me, is it satisfying? Are you fulfilled in your nature?"

"Mm." He nods against the pillow, watching me. "Strangely."

"Right, well, why not feed from me then? Don't go back to Ren. Just have me as your source?"

On record, this is not a snap decision. Every time he's gone to Ren in the past month of us living together, I've thought this. I don't know Ren, but I don't like him. Junichi is never pleased to go to him, so I'm displeased right along with him. Junichi always has a contented air about him—until the day comes when he needs to see Ren. His entire demeanor shifts on those days, and I really hate it.

Jun is watching me carefully with his black irises. I can't read him. "You're offering yourself to me?" he says.

I blink, sensing some formal nuance I don't understand hidden within the words. "Well... yes. Is this particularly special in vampire culture?"

"It is." Junichi cracks a smile. "It's kind of a big deal, Jae."

"Should—should I get on one knee or something?"

Junichi laughs. "*No.* You're thinking of marrying me now?"

"I—" I swallow hard because my heart has leapt up into my throat. Shit. I... What?

"As ranked vampires," Junichi explains, "we're very selective about who we offer ourselves to. It's a personal choice, but some of us only do it a few times within the span of our lifetime."

"In what circumstances is it appropriate?"

"Hm... it depends. Sometimes sources are established through a contract when we're children and before we even come of age at sixteen—which was the case with me and Ren. Sometimes we choose our sources based on personal preferences. Either way, the long-term intent is to bond. This is why I haven't secured a new source, Jae. Because they will one hundred percent request that I form a bond with them."

I nod. "So you've been sticking with the devil you know."

"Basically."

"But now the devil is demanding that you try bonding with him again?"

"Right." Jun surprises me when he lifts our hands from underneath his shirt. He gently tugs me forward, bringing my hand to his mouth and kissing my fingers. He pauses and looks up at me, serious. "I know I'm helping you through this process, but you should never feel beholden to me. Even after you've awakened, you are free to leave here and explore our culture—your new life and how you fit into the world. I think it'll be good for you to do, actually. So be careful about offering yourself, alright?"

He kisses my fingers again, closing his eyes. I hear what he's saying. I do. I see the logic in it, but... I scoot a little closer, looking down into his face. "I understand. And thank you for telling me those things, but... Jun, I want *you*. You give yourself to me constantly, so I want to give myself to you, too—to help you. I hate seeing you in this shitty situation with Ren, and I—"

I stop short because I feel the emotions bubbling up warm within me, breaking the surface and making my face flush. Three words. Rising up from nowhere, and I don't know if I should say them. If it's too soon, even though the fact that they're even in me now is validation enough.

But I swallow them down and take a breath. "I know that being free is extremely important to you. So if I'm satisfying for you, let *me* feed you, and then you can have your freedom... with me?"

My heart is beating like crazy in my chest and I'm embarrassed as I watch him. There's a moment of pause where Jun is staring back at me, not moving. Just as I'm wondering if I should run out the back door and impale myself on the nearest fence post, something truly remarkable happens. Something I've only seen once before with my own two eyes.

The black, liquid pools of his irises become brighter from the center—morphing and glowing like a dimmer switch is slowly being turned on. The moment I gasp at the drastic shift in color, he shuts his eyes tightly and brings his palms to his face, groaning. "Ay, Dios mííío..."

I sit up like a rocket, my eyes wide with shock. "Jun, what—what's happening?"

"No puedo creer que esto está pasando..."

I have no idea what he's saying, but he's so obviously riled up that it makes me smile as I reach and wrap my fingers around his wrists. "Jun, stop—I can't speak Spanish! Let me see?" I pull his hands from his face, but his eyes are shut tight. "*Jun.*"

I wait as he exhales a deep breath then opens one eye. I shake my head because it's breathtaking. He opens both eyes and looks at me. The weird melty feeling that had subsided shifts in me, like it's warm and bubbling deep at my spine. It's distracting, but I can't take my eyes off him. His irises are glowing in bright, vivid purple—like amethyst crystal.

He rubs his palm down his face. "Unbelievable..."

"Why? It's—You're *ravishing*. Christ, Jun. How is this scientifically possible?"

Jun laughs. "Wow." He opens his glowing eyes, but he shifts his head on the pillow, looking away from me and staring out through the glass wall.

"Why does this happen?" I ask, leaning over him. "I saw Haruka's eyes alight once—crimson. He was angry, I think. Are you upset?"

"No," Jun answers quickly. "I'm not."

"Then why?"

Jun takes another deep breath and closes his eyes. He breathes out through his nose, laughing again, but it feels self-deprecating. "Because my nature is developing a mind of its own, despite the fact that you're not even fully awakened yet."

"So this is a good thing?" I know that only purebreds' and first-gens' irises do this. Anyone ranked lower, human research assumes their blood potency isn't strong enough. So of course, we don't have any solid information on it since we rarely have the opportunity to work with higher-ranked vamps. The Harukas and Juns of the world don't divulge the secrets of their biology to human scientists and researchers. Why the hell should they?

He turns his head to look at me. I'm amazed yet again as his eyes slowly shift back into onyx marbles. "Yes, it's a good thing," he says. "And I accept your generous offer. Thank you."

I sit straighter, my heart still warm. "Good. You're welcome."

Junichi sits upright as well. I shift back to let him, but then he threads the fingers of one hand against the back of my head. He presses our foreheads together, and his breath caresses my mouth as he whispers, "If you change your mind once you've awakened, just tell me. I never want you to feel burdened, alright? You're not locked into this."

"I won't change my mind." I tilt my head and press into his full lips. His jaw drops and he holds me against the kiss even tighter, searching me with his tongue. God...

How could he ever be a burden to me? I want to tell him it's not possible and that I wish I *were* locked into it somehow. I wish that... he was officially mine and I were his—that I could wake up every day with that assurance. This bizarre path I'm on and its innumerable uncertainties. How wonderful would it be to know Jun would always be there? This vampire that I'm absolutely in love with would always be with me and I'd never be alone again.

Of course, I don't say any of that because I've probably said too much already. Instead, I just kiss him. Openly and like he means everything to me—because he does. Being with him, learning all these veiled insights within vampire culture, studying with Haruka and launching the surrogate program— it's all a dream, and Jun is at the center of it.

I'm kissing him, just hoping that somehow, he understands how I feel.

THIRTY-THREE

JAE

On Wednesday morning I'm sitting on the tatami in Haruka's office as per our usual routine. He's at his low desk table reviewing aristocracy requests while I'm reading a memoir written by a seventeenth-century purebred vampire. I'm exhausted, for some reason, but it's incredibly interesting.

This French vampire bloke intellectually fancied some human woman scientist, but drinking her blood was slowly killing him. He documents his decline and the impact of it on his body, questioning his choice of love over personal well-being. Haruka says the memoir is famous within vampire culture for two reasons. One, it was the first written account of what physically happens to ranked vampires when they feed from humans long term (in gruesome, step-by-step detail, might I add). Two, the key takeaway is that if this purebred's situation were truly love, there wouldn't be such a detrimental impact to his personal health and mortality.

I told Haruka that humans would view this account much differently—that his blatant self-sacrifice is romantic. True love and devotion "despite the odds." Haruka argued that it is self-destruction. More like a form of abuse colored with romanti-cized notions.

In the end, the purebred ditches the human woman and ends up mating with a first-gen female from Portugal. Haruka says they're very happy and healthy, and still live in Paris today.

A yawn springs up from deep within my chest. God. These things feel like earthquakes inside me, the way they take over. Lifting my glasses, I wipe the tears forming at the corners of my eyes with my fingertips.

"Are you feeling alright, Jae?" Haruka asks, watching me from across the room. "You seem exceptionally tired today."

"I'm alright." I pull my glasses off altogether. "I slept a lot last night, so I'm not sure why I feel so tired."

"Hm." Haruka looks like he wants to say something, but he doesn't. He just stares like he's assessing me. There's a knock on the open doorframe. When I look up, Nino is there.

"Hey, Jae." His eyes are amber and shining in the morning light. He looks fit in dark trousers and a rich canary jumper. All of these vampires are so bloody fashionable. I wonder if this is Jun's doing, or if this is just how they are.

"Good morning." I smile as he moves toward me, carrying a large manila envelope.

"This came from Giovanni this morning." Nino hands me the folder. "Feels pretty thick. Maybe it's a good sign?"

I accept the envelope with both hands, beaming. "*Yes*. Very good. Excellent. I'll review these, then compile them with the other candidates' paperwork I have. I think I'll have quite a few potential surrogates ready for your review next month." Between Haruka's local contacts and Nino's older brother's in Italy, I've started collecting surrogate data and applications. They don't know who they'll be a surrogate for, of course. But so far, the response has been outstanding. Haruka signed the intro letters, so I'm sure that has a lot to do with it.

Nino grins at me as he walks over to his mate. "Very exciting. Are you okay? You look pale today."

"I'm alright. Just a little tired. But thank you for asking."

"Sure." He pulls a sleek black smartphone from his pocket. I assume it's his, but he kneels down beside Haruka behind the table, places it on the surface and slides it toward him. "Why did I find this dead and underneath the bathroom sink? And last week, it was in the gap between the wall and the back of your nightstand."

Haruka blinks his burgundy eyes like he's just as confused as Nino. "I don't know?"

"Right. Will you please keep track of this today?" Nino asks. "I charged it. I'll text you if I'm running late tonight."

Haruka looks down at the phone, pouting, as if he's being asked to use some foreign, complex object. "Just... text Asao. He will tell me."

"No, tesoro. I want to text *you* today. *Tutto il giorno.*"

I don't know what Nino said since I don't speak Italian, but there is a distinct moment of pause. Like a stand-off. Haruka sighs. "Alright..."

Nino leans in and starts frantically kissing Haruka, like rapid-fire affection—on the bridge of his nose, then his forehead and cheek. Haruka turns his face away and Nino kisses his ear and against his temple. When he's done, Haruka is leaning away slightly, his face tightly scrunched in a smile.

Nino lifts his chin, grinning over him. "Ti amo."

Haruka turns to look up at him. "I love *you.*" He reaches and grabs a fistful of Nino's jumper at his chest, pulling him down into two quick kisses on his mouth. Nino grunts in a warm, satisfied sound, then stands and walks toward the door. He waves to me. "See you later, Jae."

I wave back, awestruck. When I look over at Haruka, he's shaking his head and rolling his eyes, but he's obviously amused. These two. It feels unfair. Everyone should be able to have this. Or no one.

"My apologies." Haruka sighs, picking up the phone and moving it to the other side of his desk.

"S'alright." I smile. I'm honestly accustomed to it at this point. Over the past month, I've observed that part of the charm in their relationship is Nino lightheartedly trolling Haruka. It's like Haruka needs it. A gentle reminder to not be so serious. When Nino does it, it's also a reminder to me that I can openly ask Haruka questions—that he isn't some impenetrable wall of purebred distinction and magnificence like he seems.

"Haruka... why do a vampire's eyes glow? What does it mean?"

"The cause of our eyes alighting is heavily contextual. Generally, some deep emotion has been stirred within our natures to trigger it. It can be positive or negative."

I nod. "Like if you're very angry or very happy?"

"Yes, put simply." Haruka sits up perfectly straight, folding his arms. "Our eyes alighting is a by-product of the manifestation of our vampiric auras, usually due to some significant emotion. For instance, true rage from the result of yourself or a loved one being physically threatened. On the opposite end, sincere love and passion—the inherent, deep desire for another creature. I am an exception to this general rule because I strictly maintain unique control over my nature. When I manipulate things with my energy, my eyes alight from that as well, regardless of my emotional state."

"Is Nino the same way?"

Haruka nods. "Increasingly. As he gains more control over our shared bloodline and nature. I should note that this only occurs within creatures who possess predominantly vampiric natures."

"Right, I know. Only purebreds and first-generations."

"Correct."

I slide my glasses back onto my face, thinking about the conversation Haruka and I had a few weeks ago about bonding. He's even let me read *Lore and Lust*. It's quite in-depth, and I'm still working my way through it, but it amazes me... the intimacy of vampire bonds. To be so deeply connected with another person that you can read their mind, or that *their* emotions register in your own body.

You drink each other's *blood*. I know that statement seems mundane in the context of vampires, and recently, Jun and I do it as well, but... sometimes I still like to isolate that thought, just to let the significance and weight of it sink in.

Jun and I drink each other's blood.

Insane.

"So, if your eyes alight for a person... maybe you'd want to bond with them?"

"Not exclusively," Haruka says. "But the prospect is unde-niably high. Your nature may tell you something—show you something fundamentally true. But there is always free will. We are driven by our natures as vampires, but we are not slaves to them."

"Right." Baggage. Mucks things up, doesn't it?

After Jun and I talked on Monday, I realized I've never said the words "I love you" to anyone but my mum. I can't even easily recall saying it to Dad. Maybe I did as a child. Probably. Of course, right? I had to have. But I clearly remember saying it to Mum when I was older. Especially as she got weaker and before she died. I said it all the time then.

I'm focusing on it because it feels like a phrase that's been kept in a vault inside me, and quite unexpectedly, it's tried to escape. These three words that I never put together in this particular, consecutive order. Not that I've ever said, "You love I" or "Love I you." That'd be weird.

"Bonding seems intense," I comment. "Like, two become one and everything is shared... You can't lie or cheat or hide anything, ever."

"Being bonded does not prevent a vampire from cheating, although there are heavy, painful consequences in doing so. And often, I do not disclose entire truths to my mate. However, he is the most intuitive creature that I have ever met, so my attempts at deception are more amusing to him than not."

That makes me chuckle. Haruka definitely put the phone under the bathroom sink.

"Why do you ask?" Haruka is looking at me pointedly. I'm not sure if I should reveal that Jun's eyes alighted in front of me (it was so gorgeous, sometimes I lie in bed and reimagine it). Jun seemed flustered in the moment. I'm sure he wouldn't want me blabbing on about it. Just as I'm about to evade Haruka's question, another deep yawn overtakes me, and I bring my palm to my mouth to cover it. Christ.

"Would you like to rest in the guest room before lunch?" Haruka suggests. "You seem depleted."

I nod. It feels weird, napping at Haruka's house, but if I'm going to do it, I'd rather lie in a proper bed than pass out in the middle of his office floor—have *some* dignity about it. What the hell is wrong with me?

"Thanks, Haruka, I appreciate it. I'm not sure why I'm so tired today. My apologies."

"No apology is necessary." Haruka smiles serenely, drawing his long body up from the floor. "Your body chemistry is drastically changing. Perhaps things are progressing?"

I stand up as well, just as another yawn comes over me. "Not sure. I feel fine... Aside from this notion of being slowly dragged underneath a sea of cotton, I'm brilliant."

Haruka guides me to a cozy guest room just off the back garden of their home. There's a giant, sprawling maroon-colored maple tree there, surrounded by a glassy koi pond and green grass despite the late season. It's lovely and peaceful—perfect for napping, so I leave the door cracked open a smidge to let the chilly air in.

I lie down in the soft bed, and that thick, cottony feeling suddenly overwhelms me. My body feels heavy and my mind is drifting off somewhere far away, like my consciousness is slipping too deeply and I'm losing sight of myself. It startles me, and I want to pull myself back, fight it off somehow.

In the end, though, I can't. I'm mentally kicking and screaming, but it's dragging me under. Forcing me to comply.

THIRTY-FOUR

JUNICHI

It's a little after one o'clock and I'm in between clients when my phone rings. Looking at the screen, it's Haruka. Twice now this year. Amazing.

"Hey."

"Hello, Jun."

"What's going on?" I almost add how weird it is that he's using his phone, but it's better to let him get to the point.

"I believe Jae is transitioning. It's time."

I stop dead in the middle of my studio, a sense of panic in my chest. I feel like my spouse is about to give birth. Are we ready? Where's the bag? Should we call the doctor? He *is* the doctor. "How do you know?"

"He has been immobile for the past two and a half hours. He seemed tired, so I thought perhaps he needed to sleep—which in and of itself is odd and unlike him, given the time of day. Now he is stirring wildly in the guest bedroom. Thrashing and sweating. You should come here if you can."

Shit. It's happening. God. I look at my watch. "Okay, I'll be there in fifteen minutes. I need to cancel my clients. Is he responding to you?"

"Yes. But he is obviously discontented—as if he is fighting with what is happening to him."

"Alright, I'll be there soon."

We end the call and I immediately dial out to my two o'clock client. I have four other calls I need to make afterward. Usually, I'm a stickler about cleaning up my shop and work-table before I leave, but I skip my routine today, turn off the lights and lock the door behind me.

When I arrive at the Kurashiki estate, only Haruka is there, with Sydney nervously shuffling around. Nino is in Kyoto and Asao is running errands.

"Tell him to stop resisting," Haruka says, preceding me through the outdoor breezeway and toward the guest room where Jae is. "He's fighting, and it is making the process more difficult."

"How do you know all this?" I ask. "You couldn't have read about this. You said it's never happened before."

"True. However, with what I *do* know, coupled with sheer observation, I am able to make educated guesses. He is resisting because he is afraid—which is understandable. But he needs to relax and submit to the process."

When I step inside Jae's room, I see exactly what Haruka means. He's lying on the bed, but his face is scrunched, chest heaving up and down with beads of sweat running down his temples. The room is showered in cool afternoon light as I walk forward. I look back to see Haruka leaning in the doorframe with his shoulder, his hands in his pants pockets, observing.

I sit down against the edge of the bed and take Jae's hand in mine. "Hey." His eyes flash open, panicked and wide. Frantic and delirious, like someone with a violent fever. He settles his gaze on me, and his voice is hoarse.

"*Jun*—something's *happening* to me and I—I can't think straight or move!"

I scoot in closer. "You need to try and relax. Don't fight it."

He shakes his head against the pillow, his gaze wild. "*No*— It... it feels like I'm *dying*. I don't want to die!"

Haruka's deep voice is quiet from the doorway behind me. "I believe he is dying, in a sense." I turn and frown at him. Not helpful.

I lean down over Jae's body and into his face so that our noses touch, because I know he likes this and it comforts him. "Sunshine, you need to let your body rest and do what it needs to do. If it wants to sleep, then let it sleep."

I can feel his breathing slowing, his body becoming slightly less tense. He deeply exhales, relaxing. When I lift, his gaze is soft, delirious, with heavy bags under his chestnut eyes. His hair is matted with sweat, but his overall demeanor is less frantic. He whispers, his voice brittle and dry, "I feel so heavy. Tired..."

"I know."

"Don't... Pl-please don't leave me."

"I won't," I say, smiling. "I'm right here." My heart is so warm in my chest that my eyes are threatening to alight and betray me again, but I inhale and blow out a breath to quell the rush of emotions. "When you wake up as a shiny new first-gen, let's talk about our life together." It's a bold thing to say, I know, but... I genuinely mean it. I want it. I want *him*. All of this—this bizarre, unprecedented circumstance is telling me that it's time to walk away from Ren and purebred blood for good.

Finally, Jae's expression eases and something like peace washes over his gaze. He smiles, his eyes drifting shut. "Life... together?"

"Yes." Leaning in, I kiss him softly on the tip of his nose, then on his cheek and up to his temple. When I'm done, he's deeply asleep. Calm and unmoving.

I sit up straight, watching him. My sleeping prince. Peaceful and lovely in the late autumn sunlight. Haruka walks forward now to stand beside me. He's looking down at Jae quietly when I ask, "Should he have submitted? Are you sure about this?"

Haruka shrugs. "Mostly."

"Wow."

"Is he not much more peaceful now than he was a moment ago?" Haruka reasons. "Regardless of the result, this is obviously better than his suffering."

"Should I have fed him one last time?"

"You could try now?"

Bringing my hand up to my mouth, I will my fangs out and bite down. When I gently pull Jae's chin with my free thumb and place the open bite marks down to his mouth, I feel his tongue lap against my skin, and he instinctively sucks. Amazing.

"Why have you decided that Jae will be first-generation when he fully awakens?" Haruka asks.

"It makes the most sense, doesn't it?" I say quietly, looking down at Jae's contented, sleeping expression. "Even if his mother was a fully repressed vampire, Jae's father was human. He can't help but be lower ranked. I think first-gen is best-case scenario... I'm aiming a little high because his blood tastes so good to me. Maybe we'll be equals? He could be second or third, though."

"Hm." Haruka turns and walks toward the door. I'm about to ask if he disagrees, but he cuts me off. "Sydney has lunch prepared. When you are finished, shall we eat and let Jae rest?"

I feel the holes in my palm heal, so I bring my hand up to

my own mouth and lick the rest clean. Jae is sound asleep. "Yeah. How long do you think he'll sleep?"

"I cannot be sure. Time will tell."

THIRTY-FIVE

JUNICHI

"Do I have to go back?" I've never thought of myself as a coward. But shit... maybe I am? "Can I just call? Write 'Fuck you' on some fancy letterhead and mail it?"

"No—you have to do it in person, Jun," Asao says, absently twisting his beer glass against the wooden table. "Don't say 'Fuck you.' Send the request directly to Ren's parents so that they're primarily involved in the meeting. Avoid talking with him alone since that doesn't seem to go very well. Haruka or Nino will need to go with you, too, since you're under their realm and your father is gone."

"Fuck *me*." I sigh, leaning my head back against the booth wall. I should have done this a long time ago. This is what I get.

"Is he still texting you?" Asao asks, bringing his beer to his lips.

"Every damn day."

It's Monday. One week since I last saw Ren. Five days since Jae fell asleep. He's still sleeping now at Haruka's house. I go to see Jae every day, and I'm close by now—in a bar in the historical quarter a couple blocks from the estate. Jae is lifeless and cold. His breathing is so shallow, I have to lean down and put my ear to his mouth to feel the subtle warmth of it. I do this every time I walk into the room. It's my new habit. It makes me anxious because he literally seems dead, but Haruka isn't worried about it, so I keep my cool.

Ren doesn't usually text me this much. If I'm home, his typical text pattern is once every seven days. He knows I'm probably running on fumes by then and thinks he needs to remind me that I need to feed—like I don't fucking know that. I still always push it two more days. Three if I can manage it. Just to spite him.

If I'm traveling in Europe, he doesn't bother me at all, because he knows I'm feeding from some first-gen or whoever. I'm not at my best when I do this, but it's fine—like what I imagine to be a bad case of seasonal allergies. I feel shitty and unfocused, but I can manage. Plus, Ren will be there to put me back in optimum health once I get home.

He's harassing me now because he's worried. Or he feels guilty? I'm not sure if Ren is capable of guilt. That would require his acknowledging fault in something. I went to him for our regularly scheduled feeding that day, and he decided to play fucking games and didn't feed me. Now it's been an extra week and I still haven't been back to feed. He's getting frantic.

What he doesn't know is that I fed from Jae the morning before he fell asleep. I admit, I was being greedy. I'd already fed from him Monday morning. Wednesday morning, though, he was naked and sprawled out on his back, taking up half my bed. Fast asleep. He'd been there with me all night, but it was like waking up to something sweet and delicious that had been delivered to me—warm, buttery pancakes with syrup and fresh peaches. Breakfast in bed.

I snuck down underneath the sheets, pushed his ankle up to bend his knee and bit down into the inside of his thigh. Right on the little brown mole that's always tempting me. He woke up on a sharp inhale, laughing in the golden sunlight and threading his fingers into my hair. Then I did some other things to him because he tasted divine and I couldn't get enough of him.

I find myself catering to Jae like this all the time. I don't know why... maybe because he doesn't demand anything of me, so it's easy to give freely? Or maybe because I find him so damn delightful? I *want* to comfort him and make him laugh. It's strange. I'm not usually a selfish lover, but I'm not usually this *unselfish*, either. I'm literally pleased pleasing him.

Even though that was five days ago, I still feel great. Stable and energized. My skin tone is the right color and I'm not drying out yet. Maybe this is what it's like when you're feeding from someone you don't secretly despise? Their blood nourishes you better. It soaks in because you're not internally rejecting it. You can last longer because you feed more frequently.

I asked Nino how long he can go without feeding from Haruka. At first, he said he didn't know because they feed from each other almost every day. The lovebirds. Must be nice. But then he remembered when he was abducted, it had been five or six days since he'd fed from Haruka and Nino's health tanked. His body was under severe stress during that time (and his tongue was eventually vanished from his mouth), so he's not sure if that's a good example. There was a lot going on.

I've been obsessively calculating and spreading out my feedings for decades now. It's strange to imagine not having to do that. Most vampires *don't* do it. I'm an anomaly because of the way I avoid Ren and try to maintain my freedom. This unattached lifestyle comes with a hefty price.

Feeding from Jae twice in the same week... I've never been able to do that. Never *let* myself do it, anyway. I'm sure Ren would be more than happy to feed me multiple times per week —to wrap himself around me like a snake and have me in his suffocating grasp more often. Fuck that. Fuck *him*.

"Contact his parents," Asao repeats. "You're ending a decades-long formal contract, so it's appropriate for you to do it this way—to sit down with all of them. *And* you can circumvent Ren's tantrum."

I sigh, picking up my beer. "Yeah. You're right. I have to do it that way."

Asao smiles. "This is good for you."

"Mm."

"You're officially choosing le petit doctor?"

"Stop calling him that."

"He's cute. He reminds me of a vampire in his twenties—excited and naive. He doesn't have that 'dead behind the eyes' thing we get as we grow older. Like he hasn't had his heart broken."

"Nino doesn't have that either."

"Nino's never had his heart broken," Asao reasons. "The first creature he truly loved, loved him back."

"I don't know, old man—we all have our cross to bear. Jae flares up at me occasionally. He has triggers."

"As do you. You're ready to bond now?"

My body naturally clenches up at this question. I've been thinking it. Letting the idea roll around softly in my mind for over a week now, but I haven't said it aloud.

"I don't know. Maybe." That's the best I can do for now.

"*Wow.*" Asao sits back, making a show of his amazement. "That's huge, Jun. Usually you can't say 'no' fast enough. Like you're flicking a damn gnat off your shoulder." He does this now, quickly flicks an imaginary gnat off his shoulder. "*No.*"

I laugh. "Yeah, yeah."

"Ren is a self-absorbed brat. But what about le petit doctor is changing your mind? After all these years?"

"Well..." I pause, considering. "He smells good. My nature is drawn to him—"

Asao waves me off. "No no no. This isn't the first time your nature has been provoked. You've ignored that before—coconut blondie, remember? What about Jae makes you *give in to it* this time?"

He's right. This thing with Jae... It's more than just instincts. It started out that way, when I first saw him and felt the immediate attraction and pull. But now, it feels different.

I rarely do work in America, because being a vampire, brown and male there is generally uncomfortable. There are many humans who take offense to that distinct combination, and they aren't shy about letting me know. But I got a request to design a gown for a pop star in Miami. For the Grammys. She was a purebred vampire of Puerto Rican descent. Pretty female with a small face, petite curvy frame and warm blonde hair down to the center of her back. She was nice and smelled like almonds and toasted coconuts. Delicious.

I didn't touch her. I felt the pull toward her inside me, my nature flipping all around in my stomach like a fish out of water. She watched me intently with large greenish-gray eyes. She felt it too. But I ignored it. Kept it professional, friendly, and finished the job without flirting with her at all. She was *purebred*. No fucking way. I never saw her again. She asked me to design another dress for her a few months later and I declined—told her I was too busy. I wasn't, though. I could have fit her in if I'd wanted to.

A similar thing happened with a first-gen male I met in Morocco. He was the same height as me with deep brown eyes and flawless black skin like midnight. Gorgeous. His scent reminded me of lemon bars with graham cracker crust. What the hell is it with me and desserts? God...

I *did* touch him. We spent a couple nights together. He offered his blood, so I fed from him because I was in dire need of a decent feeding at that point. His blood tasted like a zesty, creamy smoothie. It was so good it scared the shit out of me. I was only in Morocco for a week, but he got clingy fast. I ended it. I hurt him. He didn't understand it, and I could see why.

When you find that strong connection in our culture, conventional wisdom says you don't run away from it. You cling to it. You *bond* with it. Like I said, though, that's just never been what I wanted... until now? Maybe?

"Jae snuck up on me. He wasn't supposed to be a vampire."

Asao laughs at this and shakes his head. "He got you with your guard down. Le petit sneaky doctor."

I laugh because the ridiculous nickname is getting longer. Jae isn't even French. "He didn't trick me on purpose."

"Still. You haven't ditched him."

"Because he's *different*. He's a vampire with a human mind-set. He's not stuffy and uptight—over-concerned with blood-lines and ranking."

Asao nods. "That's true."

"And he doesn't make demands of me or constantly talk about bonding. He takes care of lower-ranked vampires and their health. I admire that quality in people. I've been living with him for over a month in my *home*. Asao, I never could have imagined this a few months ago—that I would let another person live with me. And I still don't feel oppressively chained to him, you know? I feel free, but I also have this intelligent and delicious creature flittering around my house. Like icing on a cake." Dammit. Desserts again.

"You're not bonded with him now though," Asao says. "You think it'll change if you do? Will the oppression set in?"

I frown. "I don't know. That's why I said I don't know. Maybe I'm not ready—maybe I am? *Shit...* I want him though. In my house. It's nice. Comfortable."

"Like a pet?"

"*No*—Why are you stirring the pot?"

"I'm not." Asao shrugs. "I'm helping you clarify your feelings. Getting down to the nitty gritty."

I smirk, picking up my beer again. "You're so old. 'Nitty gritty.' Who says that shit?"

"Shut up. You're in love with Jae."

I take a long sip of my beer. "Love is a big word. Heavy."

"You're not ready." Asao sits back, his arms folded. "I'll give you a tip. When you can admit that much, you're ready."

I lift my chin. "What about *you*? How long are you going to play old-man footsies with the yakitori lady down the street?"

Asao points, smiling. "*Oi*—that's grown folks' business."

"Dios mío. The hypocrisy." I'm rolling my eyes when my phone buzzes against the booth bench. I reach down and flip it over to quickly read the incoming texts, all from Ren.

[How long do you plan to do this!? Are you trying to prove a point??]

[You're acting like a damn child!]

[Get your ass over here NOW. Enough Violet. Don't starve yourself to spite me.]

[My conscious is too delicate to carry that weight.]

"Who's blowing up your phone?" Asao asks. "Is it Haruka? Is Jae awake?"

"No," I say, flipping the phone back over without answering. "It's Ren. Making demands and being oppressive."

———

WEDNESDAY MORNING, I'm getting ready to head to the studio when my phone buzzes against the kitchen counter. I'm still ignoring Ren's bitchy text messages and the entire circumstance of ending things with him. I pick up my phone anyway and read the screen. It's Haruka.

[Jae is stirring.]

I turn off the coffee pot, grab my keys and head out the door.

THIRTY-SIX

JUNICHI

A vampire's aura and the strength of it exist on a spectrum. Some people say that only purebreds have true auras. This is just some elitist aristocracy bullshit.

We all have auras to varying degrees. Obviously, purebreds have the strongest auras because they are the "heart" of our existence: the origin of where we as ranked vampires stem from. The power of a purebred's aura naturally draws the rest of us in toward them, acting as a kind of epicenter and creating a layered community of vampires around them. It's why Haruka and Nino's realm has grown from something like fifty to three hundred ranked vampires within the past year and a half since they've moved here.

As a first-gen vampire—one generation removed from pure-bred—I'm especially sensitive to the pull of their energy. There is a rule of thumb among snobby first-gen families called "keeping near the heart." It's an antiquated expression that's still being practiced, both intentionally and unintentionally.

In my case, I was raised very intentionally under this edict.

As an adult making my own choices, I am still operating under this system, albeit unintentionally.

The idea is that a family bearing first-gen children should make certain their children are connected, somehow, someway, with a purebred vampire. The purpose is to keep the family's bloodline as high as possible—God forbid your family line slips into second- or third-gen. So far removed from the heart of our natures that your generational bloodline is slowly crawling toward humanity, like a slug into a muck-filled and fruitless pit. It's why Ren was chosen as my source when I was young.

If you hook me up with a clean-blooded purebred in my developmental years, guess what I'll innately want and seek for the rest of my life? A fucking purebred. Even if things don't work out between Ren and I, what will I try to find? Another purebred. All the while maintaining my family's honorable and dignified bloodline.

This is why Hisaki is always questioning me about how to get closer to Haruka (even though Haruka is *clearly* not available as a potential mate—delusional twerp). How did I end up being close to Nino and Haruka? How is it that I can come and go to their estate as I please, when any other vampire in our aristocracy needs to make a formal appointment with them?

Part of it is likely my upbringing. The unintentional pull. The bigger part is that they're not like your average purebreds, and I'm not like your average first-gen. I think, somehow, our temperaments just match. We're friends.

They don't talk down to me or try to make me feel inferior, and I don't bow at them and speak in flowery, formal language. Both Haruka and Nino hate that. They don't judge me for sleeping with humans despite my rank, or for not bonding with Ren—although *a lot* of vampires in our aristocracy openly condemn me on that issue:

"Why on earth haven't you bonded with him and what are you waiting for?"

"How dare you keep Lord Ren waiting? Selfishly focusing on your own travels and career."

"Yes, your father was notoriously stern, but my God, isn't it about time you settled down?"

I have legitimately heard these things—and much more—at aristocrat functions. Usually from the older ones. Scolding me and ignoring the fact that Ren is a monster. Which, quietly, everyone thinks. He's *acting* realm leader for a reason. No one truly respects his authority. But he's *my* monster. I've been assigned to him, so I should do what's right and lock myself in the cage with him.

Damn that.

When I'm on the front steps of the Kurashiki estate, I stop dead, standing completely still in the frosty morning air with my breath fanning out in front of me. Usually when I visit, I sense the strong pulse of Haruka and Nino's combined aura, but... there's a second, unique energy now. It's weaker, but it's there. I swallow hard as I knock on the door. Almost immediately, it swings open.

"Hey," Asao says. His eyebrow is raised as he steps aside.

"Hey..." I respond, distracted.

"They're waiting for you."

"Is... is he alright?"

Asao smirks. "I think you know he's *more* than alright, Jun."

Frowning, I stalk past the old vamp and weave my way toward the back of the estate, down a long hallway, outside through the breezeway garden, and then I'm standing at the outer door of Jae's guest room. I slide it open and peek inside.

Jae is still in the bed but he's sitting upright. Nino is sitting on the edge of the bed, facing him. Haruka is standing behind his mate. They all turn to look at me. Nino's jaw drops in a panicked look. A silent scream that only I can see based on everyone else's juxtaposition around him.

Haruka smiles, calm as ever. "Hello, Jun."

I feel it. I know why Nino is silently screaming at me, and I want to scream myself as the reality of it registers in my mind. I want to scream and run out of the room, then maybe come back inside and try again. This *can't* be right.

Nino closes his mouth and quickly moves to stand beside his mate. I've stepped inside, but now I'm standing in the doorframe, frozen like an idiot with my stomach in knots. "Hey."

Jae is staring at me. Blinking. His hair is a mess from lying on it for seven days, but his skin is flawless. It might be my imagination, or maybe it's because the sunlight is pouring in through the window behind him and silhouetting his frame, but he looks celestial. A gorgeous, ethereal, creamy and messy-haired angel.

The angel speaks. "Jun?"

I blink and take a step forward. "Hi..." I move slowly, but eventually make my way to the bed, occupying the space Nino just vacated. When I'm sitting, I clasp my hands in my lap and hold them tight. "How do you feel?"

"Foggy," he says in his airy accent, lifting his hand to rub it in the wild nest atop his head. "Tired."

"You've been asleep for almost seven days." I don't know what else to say.

"Yeah." He breathes this answer, smiling. Warm, peachy air puffs out of him, and my body is so sensitive to it that it sends tingles all through me. My nature is going wild and my spine is hot. I want to stand up and move away from him because it's terrifying me. But I know I shouldn't do that. I can't. I feel so damn awkward I don't know what to do with myself.

Now we're just staring at each other in the white sunlight. I look away and inhale a breath, rolling my shoulders. How the hell is this possible?

"Can... Is it alright if I feed from you?" Jae asks, making me shift my gaze back to him. I used to think his chestnut eyes glowed. They didn't before, but they absolutely do now. They're radiant. He's batting them at me, and I can't tell if it's on purpose or not. I swallow hard and whip my head around toward Haruka. I need one of them to say something, to explain this situation to me.

Haruka gently grabs Nino's wrist. "We'll give you two some privacy." Nino follows his mate, but he's looking at me with wide eyes. My eyes are wide too because they're abandoning me. Leaving me alone with this confounding and alluring creature.

I literally watch them walk all the way out the room and slide the door closed, willing them to come back.

"Jun?"

I snap my head back around, blinking at him like I don't know who he is. Do I know who this is? This male emanating regal energy: antiquated and noble, like he's from another time and place. What happened to my feisty little doctor?

"What's wrong?" Jae asks, his brow furrowed. Now I feel bad, so I swallow hard and roll my shoulders. I have to get my shit together. I have to do this.

"Nothing." I smile. Try to act normal.

"Haruka said feeding might help with the fogginess I feel."

"Sure. Of course... Did he say anything else?"

Jae puffs out another breath and it hits me smack in the face. I close my eyes to stifle my nature's insane reaction to him. *Insane.* Like my body is on fire.

"He told me not to drain you."

My eyes are still closed, but I can hear the smile in his voice. I rub my fingers against the bridge of my nose, breathing and focusing. "Probably shouldn't kill anyone on your first day as a vampire." Jae laughs at this, the sensation breathy and sparkly. I swear to God, if he doesn't stop that...

"Christ, that sounds weird," he says. I open my eyes, and as I thought, he has a little self-deprecating smile on his lips. "Do you... do you think I'll be alright? Can I do this? How do I make my teeth come out? They're pulsing and hurt a little. It's weird." He raises his upper lip, sliding his tongue across his retracted incisors to get a feel for them.

"You'll be fine. And your teeth will know what to do even if you don't. Aside from the fogginess, what else do you feel? Anything?"

He pauses, flickering his vivid honey-brown eyes down, then back up at me. I swear he's doing this on purpose. "Honestly?"

"Yeah... what is it?"

"I *want* you," he says, pushing the covers away from his lower half and making me shift back slightly. "I always want you, but..." He crawls toward me and I sit back further on the bed, taken aback, my chest tight. He closes the distance, smoothly lifting himself into my lap to straddle me.

"Your scent is so strong now—pristine." Jae threads his fingers against the back of my head and into my hair, pressing his forehead into me. "I thought you smelled good before, but *God*... You're like lavender and winter and cypress trees all rolled into one. My whole body feels wired with electricity. I didn't feel like this until you walked in here, but it's *incredible*."

I'm frozen and not even touching him because I feel like I have an untamed animal in my lap. A beautiful and wild creature that doesn't know its own strength. His energy isn't radiating outward, but I can feel its power buzzing within him and pulling me in as he litters my face with kisses. The smell and heat of him are overwhelming my senses. "*Jae*."

He stops, blinking. "Hm?"

"Can you slow down, please?" I take a deep breath, placing my hands on his hips.

He grins, flashing a playful smile. "Sorry. Is my breath terrible? It's been seven days since I brushed my teeth—"

"No. You can feed. You have consent. Like Haruka said, don't suck too hard, alright? And... please be careful about your thoughts. Try to control them. Don't overwhelm me with the stuff in your head." Shit, I'm nervous.

He nods, his gaze soft. Sincere. "Alright."

I swallow and it goes down thick. "Go ahead."

He's still smiling as he leans down into my neck. He licks me. Then again and again, softly, like he's getting a taste for me and also trying to decide where he wants to bite me. When he puts his mouth on me, I feel his fangs pressing against my skin. They break through gently, and then his tongue is lapping against me as he controls the liquid flowing into his mouth.

Everything he's doing is so careful. Precise, like... well, a good doctor. After a moment, I feel his mind. The thoughts are radiant and soft. It reminds me of candlelight, the way it warmly swells and glows.

He loves me. Selflessly and truly. He's excited about life and he wants me. He's grateful to me. All of his thoughts, they're too pure and sincere. Too honest. My eyes alight and I shut them tightly against the burn. My nature is overwhelming me again, as if it has a mind of its own, fiercely responding to Jae and everything he's doing to me. I can't stifle it. Can't control it.

When he lifts his head, my body is trembling. Jae cups my face with his palms, so I open my still glowing eyes.

"Was it bad?" he asks quietly. "Why are you shaking? Your eyes are amethyst again... It's so lovely."

"I'm fine. You did great, Jae."

"Yeah?" He leans in, brushing a kiss on my lips. He lingers with his mouth touching mine, wanting me to respond.

"Yeah," I breathe, parting my lips for him. But he's pushing and lapping into me too soon—holding me tighter. I squeeze his hips and pull my head back.

"*Jae.*"

"Mm?"

"Just—You need to eat. Actual food. And probably shower. Does your head feel better now? Less foggy?"

"Yes." He grins. "Are you joining me in this 'probably shower'?"

Absolutely not. "No. Did you forget we're in Nino and Haruka's house?"

He laughs, bubbling with joy. "Quite possibly."

I peel him off of me and stand from the bed. "I brought a bag of clothes and underwear for you. Everything is already inside the guest bathroom next door. Shower and meet us in the kitchen, please?"

"Alright. Do you need to feed? You can if you want to—"

"*No.*" I say this, and it must come out harsh, because Jae's peaceful, happy expression drops and he draws back slightly. So I say, "Thank you, Jae, but I'm fine for now. See you in a bit?"

"Yes..." He nods. But I've blown whatever weak cover I had. He can tell something is wrong now. Unquestionably.

I leave Jae, make my way across the breezeway and back into the main house. When I turn the corner into the open kitchen, Haruka and Nino are sitting at the table. Haruka is expressionless with a cup of coffee. Nino's jaw drops in a silent scream when he sees me.

Staying calm, I make my way to the table and sit down. Haruka sips from his mug while Nino stares at me, mouth agape. I frown at him, annoyed. "You looking to catch flies like that?"

"Haru was *right*," Nino says, his eyes wide.

I turn my annoyed gaze to the coffee-sipping vampire at the head of the table. "You knew?"

He speaks in between sips. "I suspected."

"You could have *said* something. Warned me?"

"I was not certain."

"Jun!" Nino blinks. "Jae is *purebred*. Do you realize what this means?"

I'm fucked? I've somehow ended up in a situation I've desperately tried to avoid my entire life? I'm a source for *two* purebreds simultaneously—like a high-end trough? And I'm *centimeters* away from bonding with one?

"Jae is the *answer*." Nino says this with dramatic pause, like it's supposed to mean something to me. Jae is the answer? The truth and the light? What the hell is he talking about?

I lift my chin. "What the hell are you talking about?"

"Jae is British and a purebred." Nino blinks at me. "Everyone's been talking about this—trying to figure it out. Jae is the answer. They're probably *repressed*. They're generations removed, walking around and don't even know they're vampires."

"You've awakened a British purebred, Jun," Haruka says, his sangria eyes filled with delight. "The only one in the world that we know of. Congratulations."

THIRTY-SEVEN

JAE

How do I feel? How am I... I keep asking myself this, like a mental health check.

I feel *alive*. For starters. I'm not dead. Everything else is negligible, really.

At first, I felt ragged. When I opened my eyes, Nino was beside me. My mind was thick, like I was crawling up out of layers and layers of wet sand. Then I lay still in bed for a long moment, feeling as if I weighed a tonne. Out of nowhere, everything felt bright—too shiny—and it made my head pound.

All of that faded eventually, like the colors and sharpness adjusting on a camera lens. Now my skin is really tight... stretched? Pulled taut like cling film over a casserole pan. I don't know. Haruka told me I'd been asleep for six days, but on the seventh day, I rose. How biblical of me. He said Jun was on the way, which made me happy. The dry tickle at the back of my throat was agitating me. He'd help out with that.

Then Jun came into the room and *bloody hell*. It felt like someone flicked a switch. My whole body lit up inside like a Christmas tree. I have never felt so delighted and simultaneously horny in my entire life. It was all I could do to not crawl into his lap while Nino and Haruka were still standing there. He smelled *wonderful*, and it consumed me—every bit of me. I felt blinded by it.

But then, through the haze of my lust and euphoria, I noticed Jun was acting a bit strangely. Like... uncomfortable? I don't know why. I'm very anxious about it.

I get out of the shower and swipe the steamy mirror with my hand, examining myself. In addition to feeling stiff and heavy, my skin is also really clear now. I've never had bad skin, but it suddenly looks quite radiant. My eyes are more owl-like too. Brighter. Weird. My image is slightly fuzzy, so I still need my glasses. Annoying.

Inside, the melty feeling (formerly knotted feeling) by my spine is still there. Warm and tingly. It feels... happy? If that's possible. When Jun was in the room it went *wild*. Holy shit. Like lava in a volcano bubbling and spiking before it erupts. It made me giddy for him. Maybe that's what upset him? I'm not sure. I'll have to keep myself in check.

I remember... before I fell asleep, he said something to me. He told me that when I woke up, we could talk about our life together. *Together*. Me and him—both vampires. Honestly? It made me want to hurry up and go to sleep, just to get to the other side and have "together" with Jun.

Is that pathetic? To love someone so much and be truly excited? This is new for me, so I'm not sure, but... it's just how I feel. I really... I want to embrace it. And I want to finally tell him so that there's no question.

When I'm dressed, I walk out of the room and onto the breezeway. I'm moving, but I feel like I'm floating. Can I fly? *Am* I flying? I stop in the middle of the outdoor hall and spin. Now I'm laughing at how ridiculous I am. Have I awakened into the Tasmanian Devil? He can't even fly (not really, anyway... more like gliding?). Turning into a vampire has made me lose my mind. I blame the happy, melty thing inside me for this. Making me loony like a child.

I look up across the garden, and it's lightly snowing. Inhaling the clean, cool air, I can smell everything—the dampness of the grass juxtaposed against the icy koi pond, the earthy bark of the trees and bamboo stalks, the precipitation hanging in the cold, cloudy atmosphere. It's incredible. The first day of a new life.

When I've made my way to the kitchen, I peek my head inside. Five vampires are present—Haruka, Nino, Junichi, Asao and Sydney. They all come to a halt when they see me. I'm still giddy, but I calm myself and slowly walk toward the table. I feel like the outsider. I know I'm supposed to be a vampire now, and I do feel quite different, fundamentally. But I don't think I belong here. No way.

I pull out a chair and sit beside Junichi. I want to reach over and hold his hand, but everyone is just watching me. It's awkward. "Hello..."

"Are you feeling well?" Haruka asks. The young, queer, beautiful Japanese pope at the head of the table is looking at me with kind eyes. I have the urge to laugh at this description of him in my mind, but I clear my throat instead.

"I'm fine... Is everything alright? Have I done something wrong?"

"Of course not," Haruka says. "Why do you think so?"

"I'm not sure. The atmosphere is a little tense?" I look over at Jun as I say this. He's looking back at me. Onyx irises unreadable. He doesn't say anything.

"Do you know what you are, Jae?" Nino asks.

"I'm a doctor," I say automatically. "With anxiety—"

"No." Haruka smiles. "Your rank, Jae. As a vampire."

I blink. What is my rank? How the hell do I know? I'm so

busy trying *not* to lean over and lick this delicious-smelling man beside me. If I could just lick him once, maybe I could concentrate on other things? I know I licked him earlier—but that was earlier.

"I don't know," I admit. "Is this something you feel?"

Haruka sits back at that, then looks at Nino. Nino smiles like he's impressed.

"I guess you're right," Nino says. "When we're born it's just something we're told by the vampires around us... I've never thought about that."

"You're purebred, Jae," Haruka says simply. Then nothing else.

I heard the words—and the fact that he said my name afterward. But it doesn't feel like he's talking to me. I'm a doctor, with odd reactions to high-ranked vampires. Also, I like to drink Jun's blood. Also, I like to lick him... and sleep with him. That's all. Me in a nutshell. Oh, and I'm bisexual. But unless you're planning to date me, that's really none of your business.

"Jae? Did you hear me?" Haruka asks.

I nod. "Mmhm."

Nino suddenly laughs, breaking the odd silence. He shakes his head. "*Zero* reaction."

"Because I don't know what that means," I explain. "What am I to do differently? I know what it means within the context of your culture—"

"Jae," Haruka says, patient. "*You* are part of our culture. We are all ranked vampires in this house. You are *not* an outsider. You are one of us. You are purebred. Do you understand?"

It's silent. I'm listening and my heart is beating wildly inside my chest. My throat is dry, and when I speak, my voice comes out smaller than I mean for it to. "But my father... Even if my mother was possibly vampiric, for certain my father is a human. How can I be purebred with a human father?"

"Purebred vampire lineage is strong—particularly if it is clean," Haruka says. "This is conjecture, but imagine your vampiric nature has been crystallized and dormant, insulated deep within your DNA and continuously passed along from generation to generation. Powerful in its stasis but unable to truly flourish.

"When it received the resources it needed, the frozen entity cracked, seeped out and slowly overtook your humanity. I believe that genetic side of you was devoured by your vampiric nature, and that is why you slept for so long. That part of you died, and has slowly been dying for weeks now. There is no biological notion of humanity in you now, Jae. You sit before me, and *my* nature recognizes you as purebred. It has always been there—influencing your decisions and actions. Pulling you closer to us. Captivating Junichi."

That... is a lot to unpack. Definitely *not* what I was anticipating. At all. I look over at the elegant, tall and silent vampire beside me. Why isn't he saying anything?

"Jun's nature is conditioned to very clean, purebred blood," Haruka continues. "In juxtaposition with his affinity for humans and their culture, it is no wonder that he found you. That you found each other."

My chest is so tight, the anxiety I feel is almost suffocating me. I know what this sounds like: a set-up. Jun doesn't deal with purebreds romantically. He's made that very clear—over and over again. I keep staring at Jun's expressionless face. It's making me so nervous. "I did *not* do this to you on purpose. I didn't lie to you."

"I don't think you did," he says flatly. "But it sure as hell makes a lot of sense."

"What does *that* mean?"

"We'll talk about it later."

Christ. It feels as if my windpipe is caving in on itself, because I can't breathe.

What have I done? What is this? This shouldn't even be possible. *None* of it. The only reason I started to accept this insanity was because of Jun. Because I had this warm, fuzzy image in my mind of myself "awakening" and being a first-gen. Maybe even second? And I could be with Jun and we'd be the same—or he'd rank higher than me. I really don't give a shit about any of that, but he definitely does.

I could work at the hospital and expand the surrogacy program while helping all my patients. Sometimes Jun would stop by and snog me in my office until I couldn't breathe, then we'd see each other at home and I could cook and we'd dance. I'd get even better at bachata and we'd make love and have lazy mornings in bed and feed.

He'd never need to see Ren again because my blood is *good* for him, and I'd see him through breaking his addiction. It would have been hard, but I could have done it. I'm a doctor. And I'd have a long, happy life with this gorgeous, incredible person that I love and trust. Maybe one day he'd see how good we were together, and we'd quietly bond and it wouldn't be a big deal at all. We'd just be together forever, and I'd make spicy tofu soup for breakfast the next day as usual.

That vision is shattering in my mind, because if I'm purebred, that means Jun doesn't want me. It *absolutely* means he's done with me. Now I've submitted myself to this insane situation—and instead of whoring around and being alone for another thirty-five to forty years, I've locked myself into centuries of it. Plus, I have to drink weird blood and deal with an entirely new landscape where I have *no idea* how I fit in.

I jump when Sydney places an elaborate plate of food in front of me. "Are you okay, Doctor Davies?"

"You should eat to help regain your strength," Haruka says encouragingly.

Nodding, I pick up the fork beside me. I'm shuffling the food around on the plate, and I can't focus my mind at all.

I can't eat right now. I can barely breathe.

WHEN BREAKFAST IS FINISHED (I've eaten nothing), I get my bags and humbly apologize for falling asleep in their house for almost seven days. Insanely rude of me. Nino laughs at this, which is refreshing. For a moment, the sound cuts through the thick stress in my chest and throat. Haruka wants me to keep coming over to study and talk with him. He also wants me to keep a low profile, given I'm the only British pure-bred in the world. Fucking fantastic.

Jun and I are awkwardly quiet the entire taxi ride back to his house. I would give *anything* to hold his hand. I just want something, any sign to know we're alright. I'm scared to death of reaching over for him and him pulling his hand away. I honestly think I would die if he did that to me right now. I couldn't bear it, so I keep my hands to myself and take deep breaths.

How do you mentally, emotionally prepare for your heart to be broken? Usually in these matters, I think it just happens. It's unexpected. You don't necessarily see it coming and you have no time to prepare. Like someone reversing on you at a traffic light.

I *know* it's coming. I can feel it. But I don't know what to do. I've never... I haven't ever been in love like this before. I've never fancied a person this much—so strongly. Openly. I liked Cy a lot when I was younger, but it was an unrequited crush (although, turns out it wasn't). I never confessed it aloud or really gave in to it. Never let myself utterly drown in my feelings for him like I've done with Jun.

There's no experience for me to draw upon—like, "Oh, this is what I did the last time someone I loved dumped me. I'll do that thing again to cope." There is no last time. This is the *first* time I've ever just... lost myself in someone. *God.* I'm such an idiot. What the hell have I been thinking? I haven't been. That's the problem.

When we're in the house, Junichi is walking ahead of me. I still feel like I weigh a thousand tonnes with this new fucking tight-skinned body. And I've got the nerve to have that damn dry tickle in the back of my throat again.

"Can we sit in the living room and talk?" Jun asks, turning to glance back at me as he walks toward the kitchen.

"Yes." I'm dragging my feet behind him. No matter what, I will not cry. If I can at least make it through this conversation without blubbering all over myself in front of him, I'll consider it a success. This is the low bar I'm setting for myself on my first night as an allegedly purebred fucking vampire.

THIRTY-EIGHT

JUNICHI

"Do you want a beer?" I ask, holding the fridge door open in front of me.

"No thanks." Jae moves to the living room and sits on the couch, his back straight and stiff as he waits, like I'm about to read him a death sentence.

Shit. I haven't even said anything yet and he's already teetering on the edge of a cliff. My goal is to have a rational conversation without him flying off the ledge, but he's already there with his hands up, shouting, "Stay back or I'll jump." At this point, *anything* I say is going to push him over.

Once I have my bottle, I head toward the couch and sit beside him. The happy, playful creature from earlier is gone. Now he's like a prickly hedgehog sitting here. "Jae... would you *please* try to relax a little?"

"No." He shakes his head, staring straight forward, avoiding my gaze. "Just say it. You're done with me."

"Why do you say that? You said that to me before—"

"Because that's what it is. Plain and simple. I'm like *this* now... and you don't want this. You've told me over and over, so I don't need to have an elaborate conversation about it."

I set my beer down on the table, then twist my body with my leg folded against the couch so that I'm fully facing him. "I'm not 'done' with you. But can you understand that this is definitely unexpected for me."

"Right." He sighs, then runs his fingers up and through his dark golden hair. "Like this isn't unexpected for *me*. *All of it.*" I'm staring into his side profile, amazed. He was attractive to me before, but now there's a glow that radiates from him— aggressively pulling me into him. Making me want to touch and comfort him. Hold and reassure him.

I stand my ground. "I'm not thinking of you as a big bad purebred, Jae. I don't suddenly think you're like Ren. And I don't think you'll change and try to control me. It's not like that."

"Alright... then what *is* it like?"

"A few things. I think what's happened between us over the past two months has been a whirlwind. Really intense and *really* fast. I think... I was ready to wean my system off Ren with you. To transition myself into a normal feeding routine. But now it feels like I'm just hopping from one purebred to another—like a lucky tick."

He finally looks at me, his warm eyes sincere. "I don't mind, Jun."

"*I* do. I'm already codependent on him. It's toxic, and I've been like this my whole damn life. I don't want to have that same superficial dependency on you."

"It isn't superficial, though. It's what your body is accustomed to. You need to feed, your body prefers a certain kind of blood... I have it, and we're *not* toxic. So what's the problem?"

"It's just *preference*," I counter. "An addiction to iconic, super-luxury-level wine when premium should really nourish me just fine. It's been nagging me for decades... I just need to know I can break it. That I'm not some purebred-sniffing bloodhound cultivated and trained by my father. I'm my own fucking vampire and I make my own choices. I was ready to do that with you, but..."

"In the end, I'm purebred and you sniffed me out because I'm super-luxury-level wine, and you think that's why we're here. Why we've come this far."

"Maybe? I'm not completely sure." I think about all the ways I've been inclined to cater to him. The way I adamantly hunted him down when we first met. Was all of that just my instincts driving me? My nature easily recognizing and knowing what he truly was, even though I consciously had no idea?

Jae falls back, slouching against the couch cushions. He sighs, pulling off his glasses, tossing them aside and closing his eyes. He massages the bridge of his nose with his fingers.

"I'm also thinking... that you're like a brand-new vampire, and that's *incredible*, Jae."

"Mm," he breathes, the sound flat and his eyes still closed.

"You should explore this. Drink other vampires' blood and experience the aristocracy as a purebred—learn what that means to you and establish your new individuality. I don't think it's healthy for your identity as a vampire to be completely wrapped up in me and my blood."

Jae opens his vivid eyes, but he's staring straight forward. He folds his arms. He doesn't say anything, so I continue.

"I want to make sure we're together for the *right* reasons. Not because I'm a greedy, purebred-sniffing bloodhound, and not because I'm the only ranked vampire you've ever intimately been with and I awakened you. How do we know the exact same thing wouldn't have happened with another ranked vampire had they found you first?"

"Because they *didn't* find me." Jae finally looks at me. "*You* did."

"I don't think we should barrel into this. We've moved so fast... I think we should separate for a while and give everything that's happened some thought. Can you understand?"

"Do I have a choice?" Jae frowns, still watching me. "I think this is contrived."

"*What?*"

"You don't want me because of what I am, so this is your way of letting me down easy—gradually distancing yourself. You're telling me that how I feel about you is potentially artificial, but it's *not.* I'm not into you because you're the first ranked vampire to pay me some attention or because you're fit. There are *loads* of other reasons. This might be my first night as a vampire, but I wasn't born yesterday. I know who I am and what I feel. I'm not *confused* about it. It's all rubbish."

I'm shocked, staring at him and blinking. If nothing else, this male always surprises me. "I'm not ready for you, Jae. Not yet. Not right now."

"When *will* you be?"

"I don't know," I say honestly. "I can't give you a timeline... Are you demanding that I do? Is this an ultimatum?"

"*No,* Jun. *Christ.* I just—" He shakes his head and stands up from the couch. He's pacing now, running his hands into his thick hair. "I'm not 'making demands' of you. I would *never.* I don't know how to do this, alright? Be a purebred vampire. It's like I can't be myself because I know how you feel about me now—this *new version* I'm supposed to be or whatever. It's unfair. It's *bollocks.* If I'd known you'd be like this, I wouldn't have fucking gone through with it. I would have just tried to stay as I was!"

I fold my arms as I sit against the couch, watching him carefully. "So... you became a vampire for me, Jae? You blame *me* for this?"

Jae pauses. First, he's looking at me in disbelief. Then he shifts his gaze away and rubs his palm into his hair again. He looks like he's in pain. "*Shit.* No. I didn't mean that... I..."

He plops down against my live-edge coffee table. His head is in his hands and his back is hunched. "*Fuck.*"

"You still aren't registering the situation, and it makes me nervous, Jae. You had two choices—be awakened or die young. Embrace your nature or let it slowly eat away at you. You have *always* been a vampire. Regardless of whether or not I awakened you, you were one of us—you just didn't know it. You still don't *get* that. It's not sinking in and you're putting all your vampire stock in *me*."

He's silent with his back bent, elbows on his knees. I pick up my beer and take a sip before I say, "You know what I don't want? For us to bond, and then some weird shit happens in the aristocracy—because inevitably, it will—and you have a bad day. Then you come home and say, 'If I hadn't let that fucking Junichi awaken me, I wouldn't need to deal with this bullshit.'"

Jae sits up, frowning as he turns to look at me. "I wouldn't say that."

"You basically just did."

"I apologize."

Bringing my bottle to my lips, I tip my head back and down the rest of the liquid.

We sit in a long stretch of silence. Lulú eventually appears, slinks past me and hops up on the table, bumping her head into Jae's lower back. Traitor. She's taking his side. Or maybe she's giving him comfort when I'm refusing to.

He turns, petting the top of her head with his palm. She's nuzzling her nose into him. Showering him with affection. "What now?" Jae asks, focusing his gaze on Lulú and stroking her back. "I should sleep around the aristocracy and get a taste of everyone's blood on my path of self-discovery?"

"Generally, sleeping around in the aristocracy is frowned upon. But you're a purebred, so technically you can do whatever the hell you want... maybe not in this *particular* aristocracy? I don't think Haruka and Nino would appreciate that. But they are pretty chill about things."

"Is that really what you want me to do, Jun?"

"It's not about what I want. It's about you accepting who *you* are now. Whatever path you decide to take to get to that point. Again, your choice. I won't tell you not to."

I know what he wants from me—what he wants me to say. I *don't* want him to sleep around and feed from anything ranked that moves, but I won't say it. It's his journey. His decision, and I think it's necessary.

"I'd like for us to stay close, though," I say. "I'm not 'distancing' myself from you, like you said, and I *don't* want us to become strangers. It would be nice to know what you're doing —how you are. I don't want you to be angry with me. I just need time."

"I—I understand," he says. "I hear you..." Lulú is literally lying against him now with her legs outstretched. Dios mío. She sits up abruptly when Jae slowly stands from the table. He sighs. "I'll go pack up my room then."

I sit up straight, surprised. "What? I'm not kicking you out, Jae. You don't need to leave—you can take your time, and you probably need to feed again."

He shakes his head. "No... I'll figure something out. I'll leave tonight. It's best, I think." He tries to walk around the opposite side of the table, an effort to avoid passing me. I stand and quickly move to block his path. I put my hands on his shoulders and look down into his face.

"Are we clear that I'm not 'done' with you, or whatever the

hell you keep saying? That's *not* what this is. Do you really understand? It's just time apart to think and work on ourselves. Recalibrate."

"I understand," he says, avoiding my eyes.

In this moment, and in this singular day where I have decidedly not indulged Jae (after *weeks* of doing so), I take his chin in my fingertips so that he looks up at me. I lean down and brush my nose into him, slowly submitting to the intense pull I've been feeling toward him all damn day. Resisting it has been exhausting, and even giving in this little bit eases the tension in my spine.

I tilt my head and press our lips together. I'm kissing him, but Jae is totally guarded. He doesn't part his lips for me. He's awkward and not meeting my rhythm, trying hard to keep the kiss polite. Sterile. I decide to steal a page from his book. I move one hand up and into the thick waves of his hair, then move the other down between us to graze my fingers against the swell between his legs.

He opens his mouth in a gasp and I attack, licking into him and sliding our tongues together. He groans, exhales, and he's with me now, falling into our unique rhythm and moving his chin against mine. His hands are fisting my sweater at my waist like he's melting into me, or maybe we're melting into each other.

I'm getting swept away to where I can't tell where his mouth starts and mine ends, so I pull up. The back of his head is gripped in my palm and his eyes are clenched shut like he's in pain. I'm about to ask if he's okay, but his eyes open and my breath catches.

They're alighted in the most incredible shade of blue. Cobalt blue—lush and compelling. Like the sky over Santorini and the Aegean Sea, when you're genuinely not sure which is reflecting which.

He clenches his eyes shut again and tears stream from the inside corners. I don't know if it's because his eyes have alighted for the first time (and it truly does burn the first few times), because our emotions are running high or a likely combination of the two.

"Jae—"

He pulls away from my grasp, shaking his head. "Sorry—I need to pack up."

I reach out for him, to grab his wrist, step into his path again and wrap my arms around his shoulders. When he's secure in my arms, I say, "You don't need to pack right now. Just sit with me, alright? And don't leave tonight. At least stay until tomorrow and talk to me—about *everything*. If you're angry, if you're sad... if you think I'm being stupid and this is bullshit. Don't hold it in. *Tell* me."

It takes a minute, but slowly, he brings his arms up to my waist and wraps them around.

He's crying, silently, into my sweater as I hold him. It's good. I'd rather he do this here, with me, and then we talk openly as opposed to him being alone in his room—packing and pretending like everything is fine. That shit breeds bitterness and resentment. I want this separation to be healthy for us. Not a launch pad for toxicity.

THIRTY-NINE
EVA

October 2
Weather—cloudy

I finally told Jae-Hwa about the terrible dreams I've been having. I think it's been happening for a month now? Every time I have one, I wake up with terrible shakes and I'm sweating. I get shakes sometimes anyway, but this is rather unbearable—like I have no control over my body. I just wish that it would stop, but it seems as if it's getting worse.

Every night that I'm hit with it, my work morning is hell. Some of my students have even noticed and started asking me questions. That is the last thing I need right now.

My darling David made it as a finalist to the National Sciences and Innovation competition. He has a big showing tomorrow at Cardiff University. I told him I couldn't come... but the truth is, I've taken the day off for it especially. Both me and Jae-Hwa will be there. He's going to be so surprised. I cannot wait to see his face. I'm so proud of that boy.

October 7
Weather—cloudy, rain

I had another episode last night. Terrible. Jae-Hwa woke up with me and got a cold compress for my head because I was so hot, and then he held me. It's like a fever, but it's not. We went to the doctor again, but as usual, they've got nothing. Utterly useless lot, they are. If I told them what I really think is wrong with me, they'd have me institutionalized. Why aren't there any proper vampire doctors? Someone like that would actually listen to me. Maybe it's time I take matters into my own hands. I'll talk to Jae-Hwa about it.

David came in second place at the competition last week. He was disappointed, but I think he's incredible. Jae-Hwa was impressed, too. We took him for sushi at that posh Japanese restaurant in town, even though Jae hates sushi. I pushed for it because it was David's special night and he should get to have what he really likes, dammit. Jae-Hwa complained the entire way there, but thankfully, he shut it at the restaurant. It was a nice dinner.

October 20
Weather—partly cloudy

I'm in the kitchen and trying to enjoy my tea, but Cyrus is here with David and the TV is so loud the cottage is rattling like a movie theater. Christ. It's making my head pound and I'm two rooms over.

I need to be careful of the time. The last thing I need is Cy's mum breathing down my neck because I've let him stay too long into the evening. Haughty judgment, like, "I'm not sure how you raise yooour kid, but as for mine, he needs to be home before dark."

Piss off, lady. Ever think that your son is over here all the time because it's a much happier household? I wish I could say that to her. Matter of fact, I should. Stuffy little twit. Her husband is even worse, like a dyspeptic badger.

November 10
Weather—light snow

The school requested that I take leave today, and I'm gutted. The headmaster said I need to focus on my health, that I'm too pale and take too many breaks—that I shuffle to the loo too often. I can't believe this. All the work I've put in there since we moved here, and the kids love me. God, this is so frustrating. I feel like a prisoner in my own damn body.

Jae-Hwa let me try last week... to drink his blood. We kept the process clean and simple—a shallow cut to his finger and I licked the wound. It wasn't awful, but it's not really helping. We did it twice but nothing's changed. I'm still this weird gray color and the dreams haven't stopped. I don't know if I need to drink more, or if I should try with something else? Maybe a cat or a dog? God, I have no idea.

Jae-Hwa asked me if he tasted nice, and I said he tasted just alright. He said he was hoping I'd say he tasted like flavored soju or maesil, since I loved those things so much back when we were in Korea teaching together. I said no, sorry, you don't taste like delicious plum juice and alcohol. We had a good laugh about that.

It was nice. I can't remember the last time we laughed together. Everything feels so serious lately.

November 15
Weather—sunny

My son is beautiful. I watched him clean the snow from the lane up to the house with Jae-Hwa today. I stood in the kitchen, looking through the window. I swear the sun almost made him glow. Jae-Hwa doesn't like it when I tell David he's beautiful— even though he's always been. He discouraged me from telling him when he was a baby, saying he didn't want a son with a massive ego. I'd still whisper it to him when I was rocking him to sleep though. All the time. He's fifteen now, and he's still stunning and bright with this luscious head of ombre blonde hair. He's got lovely, clear skin that reminds me of French vanilla ice cream (my favorite) and eyes like swirls of caramel. And he's funny and sweet. I really lucked out with this kid.

Cy's mum came inside yesterday when she picked him up. She brought a big pot of osaman dal for us with fresh naan. I was shocked. What's more, she sat with me and asked how I was feeling, then told me she was sorry that I was too sick to attend school.

While David and Cy were still watching TV, she told me she and her husband are worried Cyrus might be gay. She asked if I'd noticed anything about David. Honestly, I have no clue. I'm much more concerned with whether or not he's going to survive and stay healthy, and if this sickness I have is hereditary. I'm not at all fussed about his sexual preferences—and that is most certainly his business. I told her as much. She nodded curtly, stood and called Cy to go home. That seemed to be the end of our sharing time.

I thanked her for the food. I still think she's a snobby twit.

November 30
Weather—snowy

I've tried pig's blood, chicken's blood and cow's blood. All of which have made me vomit. I tried having more of Jae-Hwa.

That doesn't make me vomit, but it doesn't ease the aches or stop the bad dreams and tremors. It does nothing, and I feel myself declining, fast. It's hard to get out of bed lately. David is tiptoeing around me now like I'm some fragile little bird. I've always been, but at least I could move about, travel and manage it. Take care of myself. I fell down the other day and I think I scared him. My poor baby.

I'm grateful he seems healthy. Whatever this thing is that I'm dealing with... it doesn't seem to have transferred to him. By the time I was his age, I was already having issues—visiting doctor after doctor with my foster parents and trying to figure out what the hell was wrong with me. The doctors didn't know then, and they still don't know.

What should I try? Who can help me? It feels like my body is rejecting and turning in on itself. Because of the nightmares, I keep thinking that maybe I'm something else. Or there's something inside me. I don't know how to give it what it wants, so it's slowly destroying me.

January 15
Weather—cold

December was awful. Today is the first day in weeks that I am out of bed, and I probably shouldn't be.

Now that Christmas is over, Jae-Hwa is at work again, so only David is here with me. He can't be overbearing and boss me about like his father, so I'm taking my tea in the kitchen. He's cooking for me, and it smells divine.

Secretly, he's a better cook than Jae-Hwa. Jae's pajeon is always a bit thick and too heavy, but David always gets it perfectly light and crispy around the edges. The room is warm. It smells like sesame seed oil and some delicious restaurant his father and I frequented in Seoul.

I wish I could have taken him there on a family holiday, and I'd show him the university where I met his father. I wish Jae-Hwa's family were more supportive of us, so David could meet them and know he has more family than just his father and me. I wish my body could have managed more children, so at least he'd have siblings to lean on and support him through this. I wish he didn't have to be so independent and adult-like while he's still just a teenager. I wish I'd told Jae-Hwa to stuff it and let David know how beautiful he is every day, because he seems to have no clue.

I'll tell him. As much as possible while I still can. I'll make sure he knows.

MARCH

FORTY
JAE

"Doctor Davies, you look different." Yukiko leans so that her forehead and eyebrows take up the entire computer screen. It's awkward. We're on a video call, but I lean back on instinct.

"Like... prettier," she goes on. "Are you wearing eyeliner?"

I am not wearing eyeliner. "Yukiko, this check-in is about you. Let's try to focus?"

"When are you coming back? It's been four months already!" She sits away from the screen. She's in her bedroom, which is also uncomfortable. I've asked that her parents set up these calls in the kitchen or some other common area within their home. But apparently her mother is having tea with friends. I can see a large glam rock poster of Hisaki-chan over her shoulder, taped to the wall. It triggers me slightly, giving me flashbacks of black licorice and angry, hissing, cat-like vampires.

Redirecting the conversation, I clasp my palms and lean on the desk with my elbows. "How was the outing with Vampire Teens United? You went to the movies, right?"

"Yeah. It wasn't bad. Some of the kids were nice. One guy was pretty cute. Whatever. I didn't hate it."

I smile. For Yukiko, that's a rave review. "Excellent. Will you join the next outing? What is it?"

She shrugs. "One of the girls wants to have a thing at her house. I might go. I don't know. It's whatever."

Now I'm nervous. I'm the doctor, but something parental springs to life in me. "That sounds wonderful, but remember, only feed from the bags we assign you at the hospital. Your nature is still stabilizing and we don't want you feeding from a person whose blood we know nothing about. Remember, your body isn't like a full vampire's, and you're still susceptible to blood disorders and diseases."

Yukiko sits back, her nose upturned, fully affronted. "*Ew, God*, Doctor Davies, *please*. I'm not going to feed from anyone —so embarrassing."

I absolutely think she would try feeding from someone. She fed from her dog. "Alright, I just want to give you the warning. Have fun at the party. I'll see you next week, same time."

She leans toward the screen again, not quite as close as before but enough to command my full attention. "*When* are you coming back to Japan?"

Taking a deep breath, I swallow. "Not any time soon, but thankfully, we have this technology to continue our appointments together. I'll see you next week, okay?"

Yukiko nods, seemingly satisfied with my ambiguous answer. "Okay... Thanks, Doctor Davies."

I end the call and start my notes on our session. I've got about fifteen minutes before my meeting with the hospital's CFO to talk about the reimbursement process for approved surrogates. We're only doing a test run now, one couple— Haruka and Nino—and using this process as a model for all others. It's been great, but I'm running into all kinds of snags and little details I hadn't foreseen during my initial proposal, which is natural.

"Oi, are you hungry? Should I order a pizza? Will you actually eat it?" Cyrus is leaning against the doorframe. "Are you in between meetings?"

"No, sure, maybe, yes." I stop writing and turn to look at him. He's grinning at me like a Cheshire cat as he walks into the room to stand beside me.

"I like maybe." He sits against the window ledge beside my desk. I've set my office up in the room off the back of the house, which was my old bedroom. It's nice because I have a view of our back garden and all the trees lining the edge of the woods. It's pretty and full of emergent green leaves. Not a full canopy yet.

"Eating is good, Jae. Your new purebred body is looking a bit thin—handsome devil, you. When are you getting your bloody hair cut, by the way? Is it in a little bun right now? *Jesus.* You look like a coffee shop barista in fucking Shoreditch."

I'm just staring up at him, because it's like he's having his own conversation and I don't need to participate. He smirks. "Now you're giving me resting vampire face."

"What do you *need*? I have a meeting soon." I told Cyrus what I was in early December, just before coming back home to Bristol. The lease I had with the renters in the cottage was up. Perfect timing, I suppose. I asked my supervisor at the hospital if he would let me see my patients virtually. He agreed, but only short term. I don't have a long-term plan at the moment.

Also, Cy wasn't very surprised when I told him I was a vampire. He said it actually made more sense than me being human, which I didn't know how to take.

"I wanted to ask you about dinner... and tell you that I'm having my fifth date later this week with Benjamin. Which is fantastic." Cyrus wiggles his thick eyebrows.

"I didn't know we were counting? Very nice, Cy."

Now he sits forward, resting his elbows on his thighs. "You know what I tried recently?"

"What?"

"Anal sex."

I choke. "Fucking hell—I thought you were going to say escargot or yoga."

Cyrus laughs. "I've tried both of those things, but I'd never had anal sex. It was just alright, honestly."

"I don't want to talk about this right now."

"Ah, c'mon, Jae! I don't have anyone else to ask—my parents and sister have been shockingly supportive, but I *obviously* cannot talk about this with them. I wasn't really into it, but it feels like I have to do it, right? Like it's mandatory."

"It is not. There are loads of ways to enjoy and have sex. You just need to establish as much with your partner."

Bobbing his head, Cyrus purses his lips as if he's deeply contemplating what I've just said, which is good. But then he looks at me and says, "So... do you have a preference—"

"Let's not, Cy, alright? Absolutely not."

He stands, laughing as he reaches and pats me on the shoulder. "You're even more tetchy now that you're a vampire. I'm going to order that pizza and warm up a blood bag for you, yeah? A new box just arrived. Stop obsessing over your work and come downstairs with me. Take a break, mate."

"After this meeting—" My phone buzzes against my desk and I lean to see who it is. Reading the screen, I take a breath, then pick my pen back up to finish my journal notes on Yukiko before the meeting with the CFO.

"Are you still ignoring Daddy Long Legs?" Cyrus asks. "He's persistent for someone who told you to shove off. How often does he ring you?"

"I don't know... maybe twice a week."

"Do you ever call him?"

"No."

"Hm. He genuinely cares about you, but old Cy is here to properly look after our man. You've only been a vampire for four months, Jae—*and* I'm older than you. You'll live on, but until the day I die I will always be older than you. Don't ever forget that. Respect your elder."

"God, that's depressing." I frown. "You're such a weird chap, you know that?"

Cyrus chuckles, walking toward the door. "Of course I am. My best mate is a fucking purebred vampire. There must be some side effects from being around you my entire life... like constantly standing in front of a microwave."

Shaking my head, I close my journal and place it aside, then grab my mouse and maneuver to the application for my virtual meeting.

Jun and I, well, we talk fairly often. He calls or messages me, and sometimes we video chat if our schedules match up.

My body... This new body is constantly talking to me. Not literally, but I have urges and sensations and very strong reactions to things. If I've gone too long without feeding, it makes this fact very clear. My throat aches and my incisors pulse and throb. I start to get that dried-out-sponge feeling, which scares the shit out of me. I still have PTSD from that first time.

I know now that all of this communication comes from my "nature." The twisty, melty thing that's always been in my gut is all through me, and it's *noisy*. Especially if I'm talking to or even thinking about Junichi. Just hearing his voice instantly sparks the visceral memories I have from being in his presence: what it felt like to be near his warmth and tangled between his thick legs on his cool sheets with the smell of him all around me. The taste of his sweet, lavender and earthy blood. Having his large hands sliding up and down my back or across my stomach—the intense pleasure of him pulsing inside me as his lips brush against mine.

All of it rushes back to me and consumes me, my nature writhing and having a fit from want of it. But I have to sit there and pretend like none of it is happening. Like I'm not about to burst at the seams from this intense desire for this creature that I cannot have. That helped to awaken me but doesn't want anything to do with me because of what I am.

It's shit, honestly.

I take a deep breath and roll my shoulders. I don't like thinking about Junichi because there's absolutely nothing I can do about that situation. I've shown him all my cards. I trusted him and was completely open with him. I kissed him with everything I had and I never held back—dancing bachata with him and cooking in his house. Buying new clothes and climbing into his lap after he'd bitten himself for me. Pathetic. I've had four months to obsess over my behavior, and every time I think back, I cringe. I feel like a complete idiot.

When you love someone like that and put your all into it but they don't reciprocate, that's all there is. I'd be a fool to keep chasing after him when he doesn't want me. I'm not doing it anymore.

———

I ORDER blood from a company called Premablood. This company has been around for a long time and was created to help discourage low-level vampires from randomly feeding off and attacking humans. It's worked well, actually. But they don't advertise in every country. In some markets they aren't needed because the vampire population is high and the community takes care of itself. For instance, in Japan, it isn't necessary, and I've never recommended it or used it for my patients.

In England, however, this company is absolutely necessary.

They never get requests from purebreds, so they needed to mix a unique blend of synthetic blood to meet my nutritional needs. And that's all it does—meets my basic, fundamental needs. It's nothing like when I would feed from Junichi. Imagine getting a plastic bag of cold, congealed, factory-made gravy with no spices. It's like that. If I warm it up, the consistency is a little better, but it still tastes like nothing.

I went to London two months ago to visit Cy. He always makes the trek out here to see me, but he finally talked me into coming into the city and going out with him. Haruka asked me to keep a low profile, and I do. But Cy kept pestering me.

Anyway, I ended up meeting a woman. Second-gen. Technically, her bloodline isn't high enough to satisfy me. Haruka explained as much before I left Japan (which he was not pleased about). The woman and I talked at the bar, one thing led to another, and she offered herself and I tried. She tasted better than the bags, but I felt wretched the next day. Horrible stomachache and chills. It's like my nature was irate, screaming, "Let's not do that ever again, please!"

When I'm done with my meeting and head downstairs, Cy has the pizza on the table in the breakfast nook and a mug of warm synthetic blood is beside my plate. He thinks he needs to come out here and check on me like this, but I'm alright. I'm just working on the surrogacy program and seeing patients virtually. That's all there is.

"How was the meeting?" Cy is standing over the sink, cleaning out the pot he used to heat my blood and looking over his shoulder. "Are all the surrogate things in order?"

I sit at the table and take hold of the cup. My teeth are starting to pulse, which is the worst. I take a quick sip of the warm, bland liquid. "Yes. I haven't told them yet, but we've found a match for our test couple. However, now that the surrogate knows who she'll be carrying for, she's refusing payment. We're having a small battle with her about it. We need to set a standard for how much vamps will be compensated—you know, get a sense of the typical expectation. She's not helping."

"Maybe this will be the typical situation?" When he's finished at the sink, he dries his hands and comes to the breakfast nook, sitting on the bench opposite me. He grabs a slice and lifts his chin. "*Eat.*"

"I'm not going to simultaneously drink blood and eat pizza." The thought turns my stomach. It's like I've forgotten how to eat. As time goes on, my body and senses become sharper and more vampiric. I don't have a strong urge to eat like before, but it's fine. Eating got in the way, taking up time and energy. Now, I can just heat up a cup of blood and keep working.

We sit in silence, with Cy eating his slice of pizza and me staring into space and cupping my mug in my palms, occasionally bringing it to my mouth. When Cy is down to the crust, he says, "Are you at least feeling a little more excited about Italy and the wedding next month?"

"Not particularly."

"Ah, Jae, it's your big introduction to the aristocracy! Maybe it won't be as awful as you're assuming? Maybe seeing Daddy Long Legs in person will be nice?"

I lift my mug and down the last sip of blood. It's lukewarm now. And tasteless. Sure. It will be nice to see Junichi. To pretend as if we're just best mates—like he hasn't ever been inside me. Looking forward to that.

Everyone who's anyone will be at Cellina and Giovanni's wedding next month. The two of them bonded last year, but the formal ceremony will be in Lombardy at a resort off Lake Como. I searched for images of it on the Internet and it's like something out of a fairy tale. Somewhere I don't belong.

Haruka and Nino will also be there, of course, but they can't babysit me, can they? So, no. I'm not looking forward to wandering around by myself, or talking to strange creatures three times my age.

My plan is to bring a nice present (what do you give as a gift to creatures who've been living for over a century? A new watch?), greet everyone properly, then store myself in a corner and out of the way.

"Hello?"

I blink, meeting Cy's doe eyes. "Sorry. What?"

He shakes his head. "You're so out of it, Jae. Has becoming a vampire changed you that much? What can I do? You rarely leave the house, you don't eat—and you're so serious all the time. What happened to my quirky and cheerful friend with all his cheesy jokes and weird observations? Is he in there somewhere? I miss him!"

I almost say "He died" to be funny, but it's not funny. Lifting my hands, I rub my palms against my face and underneath my glasses, feeling the familiar burn welling up in my eyes. I'm shaking my head and I don't know what's come over me, but I burst into silent tears. It just takes over sometimes, all the frustration, confusion and sadness I feel.

I don't know who I am anymore or what I'm doing. Cyrus is here and he visits me. He tries to help, I know. But it's like I'm on autopilot every day, and I've never felt more alone in my entire life. I could deal with this before, when I was human. I was accustomed to it. But now, the loneliness stretches into something like infinity. Like there's no end to it and I'm stuck.

"Ah shit—I'm sorry, mate. Dammit." Cy stands and comes to the other side of the bench where I'm sitting. He pats and holds my shoulder, then awkwardly pulls my glasses from my face. "Why do you keep wearing these? You don't even need them anymore. You said your vision was even better than twenty-twenty?"

Closing my eyes, I inhale deeply, then exhale to compose myself. I haven't spontaneously cried like this in two weeks. I thought I was getting better. "They're just... familiar. I've been wearing glasses since I was eight. I had clear lenses put in."

Cyrus is still gripping my shoulder. "Well, I kinda get that. Like a security blanket... But it's daft."

"Cheers."

"No, I mean, I think that's the problem. You keep rebelling against this new life in all these weird, micro-aggressive ways. If you embrace this—come out to London more, drink blood from *real* people, stop rereading your mum's depressing journal and get rid of these damn glasses—you'll feel better? Live the life your mum couldn't. You've been given something special, you prat. Stop pouting."

When I talked to my father and let him know that I was a purebred vampire, he didn't even question it. He told me to go upstairs in the attic and read my mum's journals. That was his first reaction to my big reveal. Turns out, she knew what she was. They both did. But they didn't know what to do about it. She didn't have a Junichi, Haruka or Nino around to sniff her out, because we lived in a country void of ranked vampires. I can't decide if I feel better or worse after reading about her last days. But it does give me some answers.

I take another deep breath, wiping my face again. I glance over at Cyrus. "I should try. You're right."

He squeezes my shoulder, his lips quirking up in a grin. "Of course I am, you beautiful vampire man... *God*, you're even hotter than you were before. I could kiss you."

"Please don't."

FORTY-ONE

JUNICHI

It's a cool, overcast spring day as Nino and I sit in the front tearoom of the Miyoshi Clan estate. It's doing that misty rain thing outside where it's enough to make you wet but not enough for an umbrella without making you feel dramatic.

There's a large window behind us, drenching the room in gray light as we sit seiza style on thick cushions, waiting for Ren and his father. They made me wait *four months* for this damn meeting because Ren's parents were traveling. I stopped feeding from him during that time, though. Actually, I haven't even seen him since November—since that day he restrained me and acted like a maniac. After Jae left, I started feeding from a first-gen I know locally: a friend of mine, so the arrangement is casual. I also started having the hospital draw my blood and send Ren bags so I don't have to see him.

It's been hell. I'm tired all the time and my skin is a weird color. I feed, but I never really feel satisfied in my nature. I needed to do this, though. To at least know that I'm capable, and that I'm not a slave to purebred blood. My life and decisions aren't just driven by the need or an addiction created by my controlling father.

"Why do you keep staring at your phone?" Nino asks, glancing over at me.

"Because I tried to video-call Jae two days ago and he hasn't responded or texted me back. He's ignoring me more and more. I don't like it."

Nino adjusts his shoulders, facing forward. "That's because you ruined his birthday."

I drop my hands and the phone in my lap. "Would you stop saying that? It doesn't help."

"But it's true. You broke his heart, then he ran away from us when he doesn't even know how to vampire. I can't imagine what he's going through right now."

"Listen, I wasn't ready," I express for the umpteenth time. I feel like all I do is defend myself around him lately. Haruka doesn't say anything about my choice, but Nino picks at me. It's like he identifies with Jae in some innate way. "If I need time, I need time. Plus, all this bullshit needed to be cleaned up with Ren. I didn't tell Jae to leave Japan. I *didn't* want him to go, but I can't simultaneously tell him I need space and ask him to stay close by, like an asshole."

Nino nods. "Exactly. Think about it, Jae died—physically and metaphorically, because everything he thought he knew about himself, and everything he knew to be true, flipped on its head in a singular day. He wakes up to a brand-new world, a new body, perspective and genealogy with nothing to hold on to, and on that same day, the one person he sincerely trusts says, 'Can you give me some space?'"

Groaning, I rub my palms against my face. He's been throwing comments like this at me for months. He's on a roll now, so I just let him get it out of his system.

"You know the night Haru and I bonded, he freaked out—"

"Yes, Asao told me that story. I know."

"But what Asao doesn't know is that Haru held my hand. He was so scared, Jun. Insanely distressed. I had never seen him like that before. I thought he might push me away or be cold toward me because he didn't want to bond at all. He'd told me as much over and over. But then *boom*, we ended up in that unexpected situation and he didn't push me away. He reached over and held my hand. That's the moment I knew we'd always be fine. That I could trust him and he would never hurt me."

I sit straighter, folding my arms. "Well, we can't all be perfect like Haruka."

"That's not what I'm saying. I get that Jae being purebred is unexpected. But... you can't push him away and also be crabby about him not picking up the phone when you call. Either you tell him you want space and leave him alone, or you push through your shit and keep him close. You can't have it both ways."

I exhale in a groan again because I know he's right. I *know*, but... "Your situation is less complicated because you and Haru are both purebreds. Haru had baggage, but you both came into the relationship on equal footing. It sets a tone."

"That doesn't matter," Nino says. "Haru and I are equals in formal ranking and within the privacy of our nest, but you know his bloodline is much older and cleaner than mine. When we're out in the aristocracy, it's subtle, but people treat us differently. When vamps greet us, they direct most of their attention to him. If we get requests for social events, they always request Haruka first. Everyone respects me, too, but that's just the way it is and how the aristocracy works. But I don't care about that. What matters is what goes on between the two of us, and Haru has never treated me like I wasn't his equal. And I seriously doubt Jae would ever look at you that way—"

The paper door to our left slides open, and we both stand up, watching as Ren and his father enter the room. Ren is angry, flat out. His forehead is crinkled and his butterscotch eyes are razor sharp as he looks at me. His robe is more formal today (another one that I made for him), and his hair is neatly pulled back in a sleek, long braid trailing down his spine. When he and his father are in front of us, we all bow at the waist, then sit down on our designated cushions. Ren sits on the cushion in front of me with his mouth twisted, never taking his eyes off me. His father sits beside him and across from Nino, who offers a cautious smile.

"Hello, Miyoshi-san." Nino politely dips his head. "Thank you for meeting with us today."

Ren's father is narrow like a plank, but tall. His silver hair is short, and although his face is cracked and weathered from age, you can still see the notes of beauty beyond the hard lines as he smiles. "It is a pleasure to see you, my young lord, despite the nature of the circumstance that brings us together. It is rare to terminate contracts such as these, but I suppose this has been a long time coming."

I'm watching Miyoshi-san, but I can feel the heat of Ren's gaze on my face. I won't lie, I'm terrified right now. At any given moment, he could flare his aura out and slam my head into the ground. It won't kill me, but I'd still like to avoid it, if possible. So I refuse to look at him. I just keep flicking my gaze between Nino and Miyoshi-san.

"These situations are rare," Nino agrees. "But amendable. Since Junichi is breaking the contract set between himself and your family, you can state the conditions upon which you'll allow this termination. Have you established your terms?"

Now I'm watching Nino as he sits straight, confident in his rust-colored sweater—his palms set calmly against his lap, revealing the beautiful watch on his wrist with a brown leather strap and rose-gold facing. We had a long discussion about who should accompany me as my realm leader and representative for this meeting. It's fucking ridiculous.

I'm a hundred and thirty years old, but I couldn't come to this meeting and speak up for myself because I'm first-gen. Even though this is about me and my life, I needed a purebred to speak on my behalf to the other purebreds. The even crazier thing is, I'm fortunate. If I had realm leaders who were assholes, they might make me stay in this arrangement—tell me to honor the contract because they don't want to waste their precious time dealing with my shit.

If my parents were alive, it would be their responsibility, since they originated this pact. In the end, we all thought Nino would be the best representative for me. Having Haruka here would have been like an extra slap in the face for Ren. It was a good choice, because he's agitated enough as is.

Miyoshi-san lifts his chin, his eyes unwavering. "Yes, my young lord. My partner and I have established two conditions. One, since Junichi is a subject under your realm and jurisdiction, we feel that you should take responsibility in arranging a new feeding source for our son. If we are breaking our arrangement starting today, this matter should be treated with the utmost urgency."

Nino takes a deep breath but nods. "Haruka and I accept those terms. And your second condition?"

Miyoshi-san looks at me, expressionless. "Compensation. We request that a fee of five million yen be paid as a small consolation. The two parties should have been bonded decades ago—our clan's resources and finances equally distributed. However, because of Ren's assurance, we have allowed this unorthodox arrangement to continue. Since, ultimately, our families' assets will not be combined, recompence for the considerable loss of time and opportunity is required."

I nod, exhaling a breath. I knew they would ask for something. I was thinking that they would ask for my family's estate on Miyajima island. We have a large property there on the mountain, deep in the woods. No one lives there, and I haven't been in forever to check on it. The structure is likely dilapidated, but old families usually go for property over straight cash.

"I recognize that my son is partially to blame for this failed arrangement." Miyoshi-san looks over at Ren, his face void of emotion as he speaks about his son like he isn't even there. "He has been blessed with outward beauty, but as our youngest, he is severely lacking in charm and grace. In that way, somehow, my partner and I have failed, and we are not ignorant to his distasteful character and poor reputation. And for that I will only require the direct cash payout."

I briefly flick my gaze over to Ren. He's staring down at his lap, the material of his robe clenched in his pale fists.

"Jun?"

When I whip my head to the side, Nino is looking back at me. "Do you accept these terms?" he asks.

Swallowing, I nod again. Five million yen as a direct payout for a failed relationship that's lasted a century is insulting. To Ren. "Yes, I accept."

"Good." Miyoshi-san stands, which causes a ripple effect, and both Nino and I quickly stand as well. Ren doesn't move. "Consider the arrangement terminated. Junichi, when your father proposed this marriage, I warned him of my youngest and his sour, spoiled temperament. I suppose I should thank you for tolerating him, and for preventing him from bringing us shame for as long as you did."

"May I speak with Junichi, please? *Alone.*"

The three of us are staring down at Ren as he sits, his chin lifted and his eyes locked on me. I don't want to be alone with him again. He's treated me like shit for years—strutting in here haughtily after making me wait for him, then pouring his inky-black feelings into me week after week—and I'm so close to leaving without having been slammed into the floor or vomiting.

"It's up to you, Jun," Nino says. "I can stand right outside."

Dammit. Why do I feel like I owe him this? Maybe it's because I never see Ren interact with his family, and seeing this surprises me: how careless his father is in talking about him and insulting him, right in his face. I've only ever thought about the monster that I have to deal with week after week. I guess I've never considered the environment that might have created him.

Running my fingers against the top of my head, I exhale. "Alright." I sit back down on the cushion, hating that I'll have to scream for Nino to rescue me if Ren decides to pin me to the floor. When Miyoshi-san and Nino are gone and the door is closed, I roll my shoulders. I'm about to tell Ren that this is for the best, for both of us, and it's way overdue. But he beats me to the punch. His words rush out on a breath.

"Violet, I love you." His butterscotch eyes are dead serious. I don't think I've ever seen him this solemn. "I *love* you. Why hasn't that ever been enough for you? What more should I have done?"

Now he's waiting. The air in the room is so still, as if time has stopped. Everything is silent, and it only serves to empha-size this moment. The smell of the rain and tatami in this plain room that I've come to week after week, year after year, to sit with him. All of those toxic feelings, arguments and insults—even those hazy early days when we were so young and we would actually make love. When I sincerely tried to please him and when he doted on me. There were times like that: sunny days sporadically peppered throughout the perpetual raging storm of our relationship. The rare calm where we sat in the eye together. I can barely remember those days, but I know they exist.

Ren is waiting for me to explain why. I know he gave every-thing he could—everything he was capable of. I realize this. I always have.

"The way you love suffocates me. It's painful."

Ren sets his jaw, his eyes glassy in the overcast, shadowy light of the room. "What does *that* mean?"

"You're possessive. You feed from me and every thought in your head pours into me, telling me that I belong to you. That I should love and want only you, and I can never do better. No one else can ever have me. It's manipulative and the same kind of shit that my father would say to my mother. Maybe that's how you love, but it's not the kind of love I want."

Because of Ren and my father, I didn't even want love for the longest time. If that's what love is, fuck it. I'm much better off without it.

But sometimes, something like a soft whisper would sneak its way through the thicket of thorns and bramble in my chest. I'd remember the sound of music and laughter, and the smell of cinnamon and fruit baking, chocolate and rainy days indoors when the estate was quiet because my father was gone. That was love, too. A different, softer brand that gave instead of took. That liberated instead of stifled.

Miraculously, I found that kind of love again. With Jae. Everything he is warms me and pulls me back to those good, quiet moments—pushing the joy, exhilaration and safety I felt to the forefront. His quirky, sparkling sense of humor and how he makes me laugh, his passion and sincerity for helping people and the way he slowly let all his walls down and trusted me completely.

But instead of holding on to that—to him—I got scared and pushed him away. *And* I ruined his birthday.

"So I'm giving you the wrong kind of love?" Ren scowls, the volume of his voice escalating. "I don't know what that means? I've given you *everything*. I've let you tramp across Europe for decades now, sticking your cock and fangs into God only knows who and what! Playing with your silly clothes and making your business—"

"Listen to yourself. You keep saying you 'let me' do things, Ren. But I don't belong to you. You don't own me."

"But I *do*, Violet." He sits straighter, and the light behind his eyes warms, slowly shifting into bright golden. "You are mine. You were given to me when I turned sixteen, and we've always been together. That is the contract—"

"The contract is terminated." I unfold my legs, because everything in me is screaming that I should get up and leave. I know my actions haven't been perfect toward him, either. I know. But he's not hearing me at all. There's no use explaining.

He leans into me, his voice low but laced with menace. "Fuck the contract. You can never walk away from me, Violet. I will *never* let you go."

He's too close to my face, so I move to stand up, but it's too late. He lifts his fingers and I inhale a breath just before my throat practically closes in on itself, as if there's a heavy brace or shackle wrapped around my neck but on the inside.

I can't breathe as I'm forced back down to the floor, onto my knees, and my eyes bulge and water. But a second later I hear the paper door slide open. I can't move or see anything, only Ren in front of me. He freezes, stiff as a board, and the pressure in my throat and body dissipates.

I drop down on all fours and heave, the air of the room burning as it passes through my aching, dry throat. When I'm able to glance up, Nino is there with his eyes alighted in that pretty apricot color and his hand outstretched toward Ren.

He's holding him completely still on his knees, and only Ren's eyes are darting around.

"Are you alright?" Nino blinks at me. "I'm so sorry, Jun— Haru was texting me and I got distracted. He rarely even touches his phone, you know? So I have to encourage that behavior."

I'm still on all fours, but now I'm laughing and shaking my head. "I'm fine," I breathe out. "I'm alright." Nino's ability gets more and more impressive every time I see it. He subjugated Ren easily, but I guess that's the power of two bonded pure-breds against one.

Nino brightens, still holding Ren in the sunset-colored grasp of his aura. "Haru had good news. Jae called him and they found a match for us—she's one of the refugees from Soco-tra! It's happening!"

I smile, genuinely happy for them, but also quietly noting that Jae has the time to call Haruka but not me. "That's great, Nino. Congratulations."

Before we leave the Miyoshi estate, Ren's father pulls me aside and offers to waive the contract termination fee entirely in exchange for me staying silent about the things Ren has done to me. I told him I'll pay the fee. I'm not going to walk around broadcasting any of this, but if someone asks me, I won't lie, either. There's no way in hell I'd let anyone walk into that situation blindly.

APRIL

FORTY-TWO

JAE

Taking a deep breath, I close my eyes, focusing on the warmth of the sun on my face combined with the soft chirping of birdsong just beyond the small window above my head. I can smell the woods, pollen and flowers in the air. Oak and juniper, wisteria and magnolia. The residual nighttime condensation settled on tree leaves and the dampness of the grass and soil. If I concentrate, I can smell and sense all of it. It's divine.

For a while, it bombarded me, like I was sensing too many things at once and they were attacking me. But as time goes on, I can pick each element apart—how different the atmosphere smells whether it's been dry or rainy, or whether the air is still or the wind is wild, and I can discern new scents floating in from the neighboring village or all the way from the bigger city.

I'm a dog in human form, essentially.

When I open my eyes, I'm staring up at the exposed ceiling. The room is flooded with morning sunlight—wide rays of it, with tiny flecks of dust floating and dancing in between the brightness and shadows.

My tablet buzzes on the floor beside me. I hesitate when I

see the name of the caller, but then I set it up on a box just in front of me and sit up straighter, folding my legs. I swipe my finger against the screen to answer the video call and smile. "Hey."

Junichi leans forward into the camera so that I can only see his cheek, which is partially covered in a dark, neatly trimmed beard. "What do you think?" he asks. "Better, right?"

"What am I looking at, exactly?"

"My skin. The shade is better, don't you think?"

I shake my head. Junichi is on this path. In my head, I call it "The Path of Mild Starvation." I know that what he's doing is very important to him, but he looks like hell. He has for the past five months. But he definitely looks better than he did in December. The first several weeks were especially rough on him.

"I'm not sure, Jun. It still seems a bit brownish-gray to me."

Junichi sits up from the camera, pouting. "Really? I swore I looked better today."

"Maybe I can't see well through the camera? It could be the lighting."

He folds his arms, grinning. He's sitting in his living room on that posh, velvety sunflower sofa. I miss that sofa. I have both very good and not great memories of that sofa.

"You're probably right," he says. "I *feel* good though. This week has been the best yet. It's been five months as of... yesterday?"

"Congratulations, Jun."

"Muchas gracias. And thank you for picking up and talking to me."

"I'm not busy at the moment."

"Good timing, then. I heard that you set up Nino's appointment to have his bio sample retrieved. He's freaking out about it a little."

This makes me chuckle. "Why?"

Junichi sits back against the couch, still smiling at me. "Because it feels more tangible to him now. They're *actually* going to have a kid in a few months. Before, it was all hypothetical. Plus, Nino said he feels pressure because Haruka has been adamant about him being the one to give the sample."

I grin because it's true. But I don't say anything. Patient privacy and all that.

"I have this feeling that he really wants the kid to look like Nino," Junichi goes on. "It's just funny to me. Haruka is so blasé about things—until the moment that he is *not*."

I'm laughing because I have also noticed this. "He was razor sharp whenever we played shōgi together. You'd think he wouldn't care about winning, but he definitely does."

We rest in the moment, grinning at each other, but only briefly before I look away to fumble with something. Distracting myself from the warm feeling sweeping through my body.

"You're in the attic today. Reading more of your mom's journals?"

"Yeah, and I was. But I'm just looking at some of her things now. Going through boxes."

"Have you spoken to your father about his heritage?" Junichi asks. "You said you were going to."

"I-I did. He... he told me that his great-grandfather was third-generation."

Junichi shakes his head. "Wow. You had it on both sides all along—"

"But I didn't know! My father doesn't feed and he never told me *any* of this."

"I know, Jae." Junichi's gaze softens. "You don't need to be defensive. I know. It's alright."

Jun never accuses me of lying, but I just... I get so defensive. My nature is getting all riled up, my skin feels hot and I'm honestly ready to hang up on him.

"I'm excited to see you next week," Junichi says. "Are you looking forward to the wedding?"

When I swallow, it goes down thick, like there's cotton in my throat. "Sure," I lie. I can't imagine what this is going to be like: how my body will react to him in person now that my senses are even sharper. It's already this intense on a silly video call.

"Everyone wants to see you," Junichi says. "Even Sydney told me he misses you and is looking forward to catching up. I miss you, too."

Now it feels like there's electricity running all across my skin—up my arms to my head and shoulders, down my torso and spine. It's so intense and distracting, but I ignore it and nod. "I'm looking forward to seeing everyone. Is Sydney coming to the wedding?"

Junichi smiles. "He is. What are you doing this weekend? Your flight is on Monday?"

"Yes, and... I think Audrey is coming for a visit. She says she's found a new recipe for cinnamon rolls and she wants to test them on me."

"The Vampire Audrey. Does she make you call her that?"

I laugh, which is a nice distraction from everything swarming inside me. "No. She only introduces herself that way. She's eccentric, for sure. She bought me a basket of the most delicious mangoes, but she refused to tell me where she got them from."

Junichi shrugs. "Maybe she stole them?"

"Do vampires steal mangoes?"

"If there's nothing better to do."

I laugh at this because it sounds utterly ridiculous.

"Your aristocracy of one," Junichi says. "They're flocking to you. With mangoes."

"I don't think one of anything can be defined as a flock."

He smirks. "Won't be long now though. Soon, the right person will get wind of you and you'll be featured in *The New York Times*, the BBC and the *Vampire International News*. I can already see the headlines—'British Purebreds, They Exist.'"

"God, I hope not. Christ."

"They'll be beating down your door with baskets of stolen fruit."

"Are you intentionally trying to make my anxiety flare up?" I smile. "Is this today's objective?"

"No. Definitely not. I'm happy that I can make you smile and laugh, though. That's a worthy objective for the day."

I'm still smiling, and that warm, bubbly sensation keeps rushing over my skin and through me. I don't know what to say when he's like this—throwing flirty remarks at me. The old Jae would say something quick and cheeky in response. Unabashed.

When I think about myself back then and how confident I was, I laugh. Cyrus confessed his feelings to me confidently—absolutely certain that I would reciprocate. I felt haughty toward him then, but didn't I turn around and do the exact same thing to Jun? Thank God I never actually told him how I feel. If I had, I wouldn't be able to look him or myself in the face.

Cyrus had all his queer hopes and dreams wrapped up in me, and I had all my vampire ones weighted on Jun. I didn't even realize how much I had let myself depend on him. It's humiliating.

My tablet buzzes, and it's my direct supervisor from the hospital. I hate to admit it, but I'm somewhat relieved. If I keep talking to him like this, I'll get too comfortable and it'll just be more painful for me later. "Hey, someone from the hospital is calling and I need to take it."

"Sure. Enjoy your day. I'm happy you picked up, and I really look forward to seeing you, Jae."

I nod, squelching and ignoring my nature inside me. "You too."

A FEW DAYS later it's Saturday afternoon. I'm sitting in the front room of my cottage with The Vampire Audrey. Spring rain is lightly tapping the windows and surfaces of the house, and my stomach is full of English breakfast tea and warm cinnamon rolls with raisins. She's telling me a story about how she once ran naked through Trafalgar Square for a cup of coffee in the 1970s. It is truly a fascinating tale, but I am distracted and officially concerned that I might be losing my mind.

"They didn't have cameras and all this fancy technology back then, so it was much easier to get away with little things—I reinvented myself over and over, just for the hell of it." Audrey takes a long sip of tea, then dabs a napkin at her ruby-red lips. "Those were the days."

"It would be much harder to do that now, absolutely." I squirm in my seat, trying to get my gut to calm down. It's not working.

"Oh, it'd be impossible to do it now. Everyone is a walking video camera! My streaking days are over." Audrey lifts her teacup to her mouth, but then frowns, focusing on me. "Darling, are you alright?"

I breathe in, and everything I'm sensing just feels more and more intense. "I don't know. I—I think I'm losing my mind."

"What's the matter? I'm not an expert in purebred matters, but I can probably help. I know a thing or two." Audrey is second-gen, and she definitely knows a lot. Much more than me. We met in the city one weekend three months ago when I decided to visit the larger chain supermarket instead of my small local one. She was shocked when she saw me—a British purebred. But she's kept me a secret like I've asked. She's very kind. Audrey visits me every Saturday unless I'm working. It's nice to talk to someone that's not Cy.

"I—Do you remember what I told you?" I ask. "About the vampire that helped to awaken me?"

"Junichi," she says, nodding. "Of course I remember. He's rather important."

"I don't know what's wrong with me, but it's like I can feel him. I'm not—I wasn't thinking of him, but it keeps getting stronger, and I can sense and smell him right now."

I run my hands up and through my hair, clenching my eyes shut and feeling my neck and face flush. It's overwhelming— like he's all around me. Why is my body torturing me?

"Is he here? If you sense him this way, he must be..." Audrey sets her teacup down, stands and moves to the front window, her long, silky skirt floating all around her as she glides to peek through the rain-dotted glass. "There's a black Jaguar pulling into your driveway. Are you expecting someone?"

Whipping my head around, I blink. "*No.*"

She's still staring through the window. "Well, someone is here. Oh—they're getting out of the car... rather tall fellow. Dashing. Sweetie, I think this is your vampire?"

FORTY-THREE
JUNICHI

I decided to surprise Jae in Bristol for two reasons.

First, there's no way he'd be comfortable going to the wedding alone. I didn't bother asking because I knew he'd tell me no and insist that he was fine. But walking into a major aristocracy like Milan on your own and as a brand-new purebred sounds like hell. Intimidating isn't even the word. Add to it, Jae has zero practice with being around other high-ranked vampires while being a vampire himself. He needs an escort. Without question.

Second, I wanted some time to talk and be alone with him before the wedding chaos. It's going to be an absolute circus when we get there, but I need to tell him how I feel. That I'm ready for him—for all of it. Everything... if he still wants *me*.

I was surprised when he left Japan right after he transitioned. Yes, his awakening and being purebred shocked the hell out of me. He was climbing all over me and his energy was so intense, it scared me—I admit that. But I didn't want him to leave altogether. I hoped he'd stay at the hospital while I worked through my shit with Ren, and that he'd keep learning from and visiting with Haruka. Our community is a good and safe place for him, so it was weird to me that he just fucked off and started doing all the surrogacy program work remotely.

Before he woke up and when I thought he might be first-gen, I had decided that I would be open to bonding with him. I just... needed some time to adjust. But it seems like in Jae's mind (and Nino's too, apparently) I outright rejected him. I didn't, though, and I tried to explain that to him the day he awakened, but his head was just somewhere else and I couldn't get through to him.

Maybe I was wrong to push him away at that exact moment. I get Nino's perspective. I understand. But I can't go back and change anything. All I can do now is reassure him—insulate him in the knowledge and confidence that he is loved, supported and not alone.

I rented a car at the airport to drive out to Jae's cottage. The area where he lives is quite a way off from the city—at least twenty miles. It's beautiful out here. The road in front of me is stretched like a thin line among rolling pastures, and everything is bright green and alive despite the steel clouds blanketing the sky. The wind is starting to pick up too, so the tree branches are bending and swaying in a hypnotic dance.

When I finally pull up the drive to the cottage, I laugh out loud. It literally looks like something out of a fairy tale. Jae is like a prince that lives isolated and in a storybook cottage with mint-green trimmings, ivy-covered brick and a mangle of red rose bushes flanking each side.

It's too much. Like he's intentionally set himself up here to be as dramatic as possible.

After I park the car, cut the engine and step outside, the minty-green door to the cottage slowly opens. Jae is standing still in the frame. His hair is a bit longer than I remember—

swept back and a little messy like he's run his fingers through it. He's wearing his glasses and he has on an off-white cotton sweater that fits his frame perfectly and dark khaki pants.

Across the distance, our eyes meet in an isolated moment. The wind is soft but chilly, still laced with the frosty edges of winter and damp against my skin—whipping my trench coat at the bottom edges. He moves down the walkway toward me, and I notice his ridiculously cute navy-blue leather boat shoes. This whole outfit suits him so well—it doesn't look like something he pulled off a mannequin.

Deciding to leave my suitcases in the car, the first thing I do is move to the back seat, pull out the large carrying case there and set it down so I can pop open the door. Enough is enough.

Immediately, she swipes at my hand. Ungrateful creature. She's been acting like this toward me since the day Jae left my house. Her chin is lifted as she slinks out of the carrier, then darts underneath the car and straight toward her target. I watch as Jae bends down, shocked as he pets the anxious cat.

"Lulú!" Jae's eyes are wide, and the cat lifts her head into his palm, her paws pressed against his knees. Dios mío. You'd think Lulú was *his* cat. I had to get her a passport, shots and microchip (she was *not* pleased about either of those), and certificates to get her cleared to enter the UK, plus she's been bitching at me the entire trip. Now she's happy as a clam.

Quicky grabbing my second surprise from the passenger seat, I move to meet him in the walkway. Jae stands slowly, looking at me like he's about to throw up. I have no idea what this expression means or if it's a good thing. "Hello, sunshine."

"Wh-what are you doing here?" He's staring at me with that same expression, but I'm now noticing his eyes. They're still the same vivid chestnut-brown color, but there's a thick ring of blue around them that I couldn't see during our video calls. When did that happen? Also, why is he still wearing glasses? I think he's very sexy when he's wearing them, but he told me three months ago that his vision had more than corrected itself.

"The cat gets a nicer greeting than me? If nothing else, I'm the one who brought her here." I open my arms, revealing the bouquet of flowers I was holding behind my back. It takes a minute, and Jae's expression stays unreadable, but he steps into me for a very stiff hug. God. We've been talking on the phone since he left. It didn't seem like he was angry with me? "I missed you," I tell him. "It's good to see you."

"You too," he says, hastily pulling out of my embrace. I hold the flowers in front of my chest. They're a mix of vivid blue and purple, long and elegant. I like them because they remind me of us.

"They're delphiniums. Do you like them?"

Jae finally smiles. It's weak, but it's there. He focuses on the bouquet. "They're brilliant."

"Since you told me bird-of-paradise were your mother's favorite flower, we'll have to decide what your favorite is."

He raises an eyebrow. "Do I need one?"

"Yes. Absolutely. Any cultured, sophisticated male who is confident in his personal style and tastes should have one."

Jae rolls his eyes, still smiling. "Right. What's yours, then?"

"Sunflowers. But you can't have mine."

"I don't want it. It suits you, though. The sofa."

"Exactly." I wiggle my eyebrows. I love that fucking couch. I based the design of everything else in the living room and kitchen off that couch. Why? Because my father would hate that couch. "Wild and garish." That's what he would call it— like the rocking of hips to the guitar and bongos.

Jae takes the flowers and lifts them up toward his nose. "Thank you for these... Why are you here? I thought I'd see you in Milan?"

"Jae. You're the only living British purebred vampire in existence and you've never been to an aristocracy event. I wouldn't let you walk into that situation by yourself."

There's an awkward pause where I sense he wants to say something, but instead he looks away from me, staring into the flowers. "That's very kind of you. Thank you... Do you need help carrying anything else?"

I raise my eyebrow. *Kind* of me? "I don't, no."

"Audrey is inside. You should come in and meet her." He turns, and I follow him up the charming cobblestone path and to the front door. Just before I step through the frame, I call out to Lulú. She comes bounding through the grass like a dolphin leaping in and out of the ocean, then trots past me and inside the house. It's obvious that she already loves it here. Too bad the owner of this stunning little home is less than thrilled about me.

"I HAVEN'T STOLEN anything in fifteen years," The Vampire Audrey exclaims. "It's too difficult nowadays. And prison has *never* been any fun. You won't catch this poppet behind bars. Not ever again!"

I'm laughing as the tea kettle whistles, the sound shrill and ringing through the warm sitting room. Jae hops up from his armchair and heads toward the kitchen with Lulú close at his heels. She hasn't left his side since we came into the house.

I sit back against the sofa, relaxing and breathing in. The whole house is drenched in his scent—warm and comforting, peachy and fresh—and it makes me want to bite him so badly. It's calling to me and my nature is responding, unequivocally.

"This sweet young creature..." Audrey's intense hazel eyes are on me, unblinking and framed with crinkly laugh lines. "He reminds me of a vampire that's barely come of age. He told me his story, and about you. He should *not* be out here all by himself." She's an older vampire, like Asao, but where my friend has led a fairly tame life—unexpectedly domestic, charged with raising and fathering his best friend's purebred son—Audrey has been out there, and then some.

"I agree."

"Purebreds are the *center*. They're the heart of our culture. They're not meant to be on the fringes and isolated—especially young pups like him who don't know anything."

Folding my arms, I smirk. "Audrey, based on your stories of streaking and stealing, I wouldn't have pegged you for a traditionalist—suddenly reciting classic aristocracy rhetoric to me."

She waves a hand, dismissive. "I have a laugh with dopey humans sometimes, but our community is sacred. We *need* each other, and purebreds much more so. I've never once met a happy and thriving purebred that was on their own. Not *ever*. Their need for camaraderie and companionship is ten times worse than yours or mine. The sliver of humanity we have allows us to tolerate isolation decently, but purebreds? Their natures demand otherwise." Audrey stands, grabbing her sling bag. "I hope you've come here to help him. This is no good for him—a *purebred* drinking false, factory-made blood. Horrible. I have never heard of such a thing."

"Well, I'll certainly try."

She stalks toward the door and opens it. In the frame, she turns to me again. The rain is sprinkling behind her, falling just a little heavier than when I first arrived.

"Don't just try, pussycat. *Do* it." She closes the door in a loud thud, and I frown. Why is this random-ass vampire that I just met telling me what to do? As if I didn't come here to try and convince him to come back to Japan with me anyway.

"Did Audrey leave?" Jae is standing in the entryway to the kitchen with a bewildered look on his angelic face.

"She did."

He pauses, looks at me, then looks away and runs his fingers through his golden-brown hair. He turns and goes back into the kitchen. Sitting in the front room alone now, I shake my head, then stand to follow him.

This kitchen is just as cozy as the sitting room. The white appliances are outdated, but somehow, this just adds to the charm of the clean space framed by rich robin egg–blue walls. There's a square window above the kitchen sink overlooking the front yard, and I can see a few of the red roses from the bushes outside peeking up and threatening to cover the bottom of the window.

Directly across from the appliances and sink, there's a white-wooded breakfast nook with bay windows and a curving bench. These windows showcase the back garden and forest—a portrait of rich, velvety green speckled with all manner of wild-flower. Everything is swaying and bending from the rain and an uptick in the wind. It looks like a storm is coming.

Jae is standing at the counter, overly focused on the teapot and tray of accoutrements. "I told Audrey that I was going to make another pot of tea. Why did she leave?"

I move to the bench and slide inside, glancing at all the raindrops dotting the windows in the gray late-afternoon light. "I don't know, but will you come sit with me?"

He doesn't respond, but continues fussing with things on the counter for another long moment. Lulú hovers around his ankles. When he finally turns, tray in hand, she precedes him and hops onto the opposite side of the bench. He scoots in beside her, removing our cups from the tray and avoiding my eyes. "I have milk, or mint. It's still growing wild out back from when Mum planted it forever ago, so that's lovely. There's sugar cubes as well..." He sets everything aside, and I keep waiting for him to look at me, but he won't do it.

"How was your flight?" he asks, pouring my tea.

"It was fine. I love you."

He overshoots in pouring the tea, and now it's puddled in the saucer underneath the cup and on the table, but at least he's looking at me with his celestial eyes. They remind me of the rings orbiting Saturn.

"I love you, Jae. I didn't come here because I'm *kind*. Or because it was my civic duty or whatever it is you're thinking. I came here because I missed you."

Jae is staring at me and holding the teapot like he's a wax figure, so I reach and pull it from his grip. "Can we put this down?" He jumps, but when the teapot is out of the way, I clasp both of his hands in mine on either side of the tray, making us both rest our elbows down against the surface.

"I apologize if I hurt you, or if you felt like I abandoned you when you needed me. That wasn't my intention, at all. Can you understand?"

Jae is frozen for another moment, then finally nods and breaks our eye contact. He says, "Yes," but I can feel that he's so emotionally guarded. He's sitting here, our hands are clasped and I'm staring at him, but he's never felt so far away from me. Like we're not even in the same room.

"Have I truly fucked this up? Have I lost you?" I bring one of his hands to my mouth and brush his knuckles against my lips, waiting. I'm watching him take short breaths, then he clenches his eyes shut and lowers his head like he's in pain. I have no idea what's going on. I'm about to ask if he's alright when he suddenly snatches his hands away from my mouth and out of my grasp.

"I-I'm sorry—can you please just give me a minute?" He stands, then swiftly disappears through the doorway of the kitchen. This time, Lulú doesn't chase behind him, but turns her head and stares at me.

I sit in silence, listening to the rain tap lightly against the windows of this beautiful cottage and realizing that maybe I truly have fucked this up.

Christ, this body. I feel like I'm about to spontaneously combust and I have no clue what to do about it—other than move away from the person who's setting me off.

I can't even process or be happy about what Junichi is saying to me because everything in me feels like a fizzy drink that's been shaken up—that is, if the drink were made with fire. I leave the kitchen as fast as I can manage and head to the bathroom down the hall from the sitting room. Inside, I close the door and grip the porcelain sink as I take slow, deep breaths. The surface of the sink is cool underneath my palms, which helps to distract me.

I don't know what's happening to me. I never know anymore.

This feeling... It was bad when Audrey was here with us, but tolerable, because I could focus all my attention on her. She was like a neutralizer compared to whatever Junichi is doing to me. But with her gone, it's harder to distract myself—and then he touches me and he's talking and I literally can't breathe because my heart is beating off the charts.

It feels slightly more manageable now that I'm in the bathroom, so I turn on the cold water and bend down. I pull my glasses off and place them aside before I splash the water against my face over and over, wishing I could wash this feeling away—this body. When I stop and stand up straight to look at myself in the mirror, droplets are running down my too tight, too perfect for comfort skin, and those weird rings around my irises that showed up a couple of months ago look like they're glowing.

"*Shit.*" I rub my hands against my face, willing it to stop. All of it. I feel like a fucking freak.

I stay in the bathroom for a long time, trying to calm myself. When Junichi is in front of me, it's like everything in my body is clawing and clamoring toward him. Even when I was human, I always wanted him. But this feels ridiculous.

By the time I leave the bathroom, I feel a little more in control. My weird eyes have stopped whatever they were doing, and my heartrate is calmer. I take a deep breath when I turn the corner to walk back into the kitchen. Junichi is still sitting in the exact same spot, and his eyes immediately meet mine. My body warms up, but I take another breath and stamp it down. I can't keep letting these feelings overrun me like this.

I force a smile. "Sorry about that..."

His gaze is intense but thoughtful. His tone sincere. "What just happened?"

"I'm still adjusting. I'm alright."

"If you talk to me and tell me what's going on, I can help you. I'm not Haruka, but I still know a lot and can explain things that might not make sense to you."

I believe him. I do. But... I don't want to dump all my shit into his lap again. I did that in the past, didn't I? He told me before that I could lean on him, and what happened?

I'll manage this and figure it out on my own. I will.

Slowly, I move forward and toward the bench, trying hard to keep my nature and body in check. I just need to focus. As I sit, Lulú is looking up at me with her golden eyes. She obviously can't talk, but it feels very much like she's worried and asking if I'm alright. Which is bloody weird.

"Thank you," I tell Jun, breathing steadily. "But I'm okay." I thread my fingers together in the gap of my legs under the table because it gives me something to focus on, and it keeps him from grabbing me and making my nature go berserk again. I take another deep breath. "About... what you said earlier."

"Can we take it slow?" Junichi asks. "You don't need to respond to me right now. You're adjusting, and I don't expect you to suddenly trust and open up to me again like a switch being flicked on. I know it doesn't work like that. But I'm here, Jae. Just know that I'm here for you—and this time, I'm not leaving unless you tell me to go. Deal?"

I don't think this will work anymore. I don't think it can now. But how could I ever tell him to go? This person that awakened me, and whose blood and presence make my entire body feel like I'm an explosive. I'm relieved, because he's saved me from having to admit that I'm a complete and utter mess. I can barely control my nature, and I don't know what's happening to this insane body from one minute to the next.

I love him, too. Of course I love him. I just... wish things were different. That I was still me—the me I know—or that I'd turned out to be first-gen or lower. Then I'd have some humanity left and Jun would be more comfortable with me. I'd be more comfortable with myself. Things would have been so much better.

It feels unfair.

I nod, taking another deep breath. I think I'm already getting better at controlling my nature. I can feel it. "Yes. Deal."

Junichi tilts his head as he stares at me, and a smile spreads across his mouth. "I can see your eyes better without the glasses in the way."

Instinctively, I reach up and touch the bridge of my nose. I must have left them on the sink in the bathroom.

"You told me your eyesight was perfect now, anyway," Junichi goes on. "When did the blue show up?"

Groaning, I rub my eyes with my fingertips. "I don't know. Every time I think I've plateaued, something else happens and I reach a new freakish level of abnormality." I'm rubbing the corners, but I stop and lift my gaze at Jun's silence. He's still watching me with that same soft expression.

"Not freakish. Your eyes are mesmerizing, Jae. Like an amber stone outlined by the ocean... I can't look away from you."

I swallow and take a breath before *I* look away. Then I stamp down on the warm feeling bubbling up my spine by focusing on the dark shadows of trees and brush swaying and moving beyond the window.

I don't think this will work, but... I'll try.

IF THE WEATHER had been nice, I would have taken Jun on a walk around the cottage. There's a path through the trees, winding toward a small lake, and it's stunning at sunset. But given the thick cloud cover, it got dark much earlier than normal. Now, the rain is pelting hard against the outside walls and windows. Thunder is rumbling in the distance, inching closer.

I decided to take him to the attic instead. He looked at Mum's journals and said he thinks Haruka would wet himself for that kind of research. Sorry, but I cannot imagine Haruka wetting himself under *any* circumstance. The very thought is offensive.

We had dinner (I made a simple stew with veg since he said he wasn't too hungry), then talked before retiring to our respective rooms. He didn't try touching me anymore, and we kept busy talking about things other than ourselves and this awkward situation between us, so I was able to maintain some semblance of normalcy. It was a relief—to know I'm capable of exhibiting some control.

I'm reading in bed now, which research says I shouldn't do. But I do. It's cozy for me, especially on violently stormy nights like this.

There's a bright flash of lightning in my window, briefly illuminating the darkness outside and the shadowed outline of trees. It's followed by a big boom of thunder, making the entire house rattle. Mother Nature is really cutting up tonight.

A soft knock on the door makes me lift my head from the book. "Yes?" It creaks open and Lulú pads inside. I'm about to freak out, thinking the vampire cat is capable of knocking and opening doors, but then Junichi pokes his head in.

"Hey."

I blink, staring as my gut starts twisting around in the familiar way. "Hey... what's wrong?" Lulú is already on my bed, nestling in beside me. There's another white flash of lightning. The boom of thunder that follows rattles the house again. Jun closes the door, presses his back into it with his eyes closed and takes a deep breath.

"What is it?" I ask once more.

"Don't laugh at me..." he says, his eyes still closed. "But I do *not* like thunderstorms. Do you mind company?"

"I..." Rubbing my hand against my scalp, I ruffle my hair to distract myself from the warmth that's suddenly pulsing in my groin and snaking up my spine. "I—Alright. But why would I laugh at you about that?"

There's another flash, and it jolts Jun into movement. He tries to play it off, but his walk is a little too brisk as he moves toward my bed. Just as the thunder hits, he climbs on and lies beside me, curling into himself a little. Once the house stops rattling, he says, "Because it makes me feel like a child. I'm too big to be acting like this—literally six foot one."

"Now you're just bragging." I smirk, looking down at him. He's cozy in a gray vintage-looking T-shirt and black joggers. He smells like something I want to rub my face in, but I ignore that. "I don't feel sorry for you. You've ruined it."

His head is on the pillow with his hands tucked underneath as he lies on his side. He blinks his onyx eyes up at me. "How tall are you? Five foot... five?"

"Um, five foot *six*, thanks. Please don't cheat me a whole inch."

Jun shrugs against the bed, grinning and closing his eyes. "Doesn't matter. You're perfect."

Right. Since when? A few months ago, he barely wanted to be in the same room with me. But now I'm perfect?

"You once told me," Jun begins, "that being here made you sad, which is why you stayed away for so long. Do you still feel that way?"

"Hm... a little." I close the book in my lap and set it on my bedside table. I pull my glasses off as well, massaging the inevitable mark at the bridge of my nose with my fingers. "It's not as bad as before, when I came back to check on it during uni. Now, it feels like I'm a kid looking after the house until my parents get home. Except they're not coming. It doesn't feel like *mine* yet."

"Mm. Maybe do some remodeling? Put your own stamp on it?"

"I'd like to." I lean to turn off the lamp, then settle down on my back beside him. "I have to make some life decisions before I do any big remodels."

"Life decisions? Such as?"

"If I'm going to stay here long term, or if I'm going to move into the city to work. Or an even bigger city where there are actual vampires I can help. How I go about the redesign and interior will be impacted by that—if it's done to my personal tastes or more generic for a buyer or renter."

"No matter where you go, Jae, eventually, vampires will naturally seek you. It just takes time to build your own community."

"Right. Audrey has said that to me as well. But do I want that? Who am I to run anything or lead anyone? I barely understand my own body and what's happening to me. As if I could ever 'lead a realm.' And maybe I don't even want to be bothered with all the aristocracy bullshit."

Jun laughs softly in the darkness. "I've been a bad influence."

"Maybe. Probably." I chuckle. The outside light from the storm flashes, then the house trembles again. It doesn't seem possible, but the rain sounds as if it's coming down even harder now. My breath catches when I feel Jun scoot a little closer, lying just at my side, a hair's breadth from touching me. But he's perfectly still there—the warmth and length of him weighted beside me. His cool lavender essence softly wafting through the air.

I clench my eyes tight and breathe in deeply. Christ. I love him so much and I *want* him. I keep trying to ignore the fact that his usually creamy, golden-brown skin is an odd shade—like cedar. Brown but with too much gray mixed in. Not enough warmth. Not quite right. I know if he fed from me, he'd be better. I could help him with that, and something inside me is telling me that it would feel so good to let him.

But it's all wrong now, because I don't even know how to behave anymore. That version of me from before, the one who flirted relentlessly and fed from his palm... I'm embarrassed about that person. I don't know if that Jae exists anymore, or if I even want him to.

"I have another question." Jun yawns, his face halfway swallowed by the pillow and his voice low against the static sound of heavy rainfall all around us.

"Yes?"

"Why does your mother call you David in her journals? And if your father is Korean, why is your surname English?"

I smirk. "That's *two* questions—"

I feel a quick pinch at the inside of my waist, and I swear I almost leap up from the bed and spontaneously combust. I'm sitting up on one elbow, looking down at Jun and breathing like a rabbit caught in a trap, but he's not moving. Just smiling and lying perfectly still with his eyes closed. "Humor me?" he asks.

Swallowing, I settle back down on the sheets, but my body is on edge. Trembling. "Sh-she wanted to name me David. But my father was worried about me having his surname and growing up here— that it would make things harder for me on CVs and applications."

"Racism."

"Yes." I take a breath. "So they compromised and she named me after him, but I have her surname."

"What's your father's name?" Jun asks, opening his eyes to gaze at me.

"Jeong Jae-Hwa. So in her mind, the entire time she was pregnant with me, I was 'David Jeong.' She kept calling me David even after I was born—so I came to understand it as a type of nickname? Anyway, I'm just grateful I'm not David

Davies, which would have added a devastating layer to my anxiety."

Junichi breathes a quiet laugh. Our entire conversation is so low, almost whispered and encapsulated by the rain and the night, the soft bedsheets and the warmth of our bodies and energies as we lie still. We're not even touching, but I can feel all of it against my skin—this cocoon we're somehow creating. The unintentional but undeniable pull and tangle of it.

It feels good and safe and intimate. It makes me want to curl into him and feel him even more, but I don't know what my body would do and that scares me. That fear is what keeps me from moving and potentially ruining this perfect moment. So I just stare at him beside me while he breathes with his eyes closed.

"Your mother chose well. David is a nice name," he says, then inhales before yawning again. He lazily opens his black eyes. "I think... any vampire or human I've met named David has always been of excellent character. It suits you."

I keep watching him, staring right back into the deep onyx pools of his irises. I let myself have this one moment since my nature actually feels calm—like it's sleeping, and unbeknownst to it, I've sneaked out for a little fun. "Cheers." I smile.

Jun's eyes close once more. "I really like the name Jae, too... Jae is sexy, but David feels endearing. Cuddly. You're both, like a... What animal is cute but kind of dangerous?"

"A racoon."

Junichi opens his eyes, frowning at me. But I laugh.

"*No*," he scolds. "You are not like an animal that knocks over and digs through trash cans."

"I might be. Give me some time." I'm still chuckling, but Jun doesn't crack a smile. "A skunk? Something rabid and unpredictable," I offer, lifting my eyebrow.

Jun stares at me, then huffs, adjusting his body and closing his eyes. "*Neither*—and I don't mean dangerous like violent. I mean sensual. Alluring. But I'm glad to know where you're at in your own head. I now have a clear understanding of where we're starting from and how far we need to go."

I scoff. "*We?*" My eyes widen. The snarky question slips out of my mouth before I even have a chance to process it, like I meant to say it in my head but it somehow passed through the wrong filter.

But Jun doesn't miss a beat. "*We.* You and me, sunshine. Unless you indicate otherwise."

There's a pause, and he opens his eyes again, looking at me and waiting for me to say something. When I don't, he snuggles down again. "Good night."

"Good night..."

The space between us falls silent, but the sound of the rain is still brash, the wind rushing against the outer walls of the cottage. The thunder and lightning have subsided as I lie there listening, fighting off sleep because I want this moment to last. For us to just live and exist in this peaceful, perfect space in the center of the storm.

***

JUNICHI LIKES MORNING SEX.

Before I was with him, I was accustomed to sex under the cover of nightfall—when all manner of unscrupulous behaviors tend to occur. As they should, I used to think. Like the things you do are hidden somehow and there's a mild sense of shame to them. Unspoken but universally recognized.

Not that I never had sex in the daytime. It just wasn't a regular affair. Nighttime felt more natural to me.

Not for Jun. First thing in the morning, when the sunlight would blaze through that ridiculous glass wall of his, he'd be touching and nipping at me. I'd wake up to soft kisses in the concave of my neck or down my naked spine, his long fingers stroking my sides. Once, I woke up gasping to a cheeky bite inside my thigh. Incredible. Jun doesn't have one bit of shame in his lovemaking. He'd revel in my body and the sunlight, as if it were a spotlight and he *wanted* the world to see what we did. How beautiful we were naked and entwined together and how excellent he was at driving me to the precipice of ecstasy.

Performance art.

It's morning. I'm lying on my back, awake and staring up at the ceiling. My nature may have been asleep last night, but it's wide awake now and practically roaring inside me—wild and hot, shooting up and down my body, across every pore and inch of my skin. I slept well through the night. Maybe the best I have in months. But now it feels like my nature is paying me back tenfold for that singular night of peace.

I'm about to get up when I feel Jun rustle beside me. His voice is groggy as he stretches. "Good morning."

"Hi." I sit upright. Him moving just a little is making his scent fan out and wash over me in waves. I take a breath to try and calm the insanity taking place within me. "D-did you sleep well? Do you want breakfast?" My voice comes out hoarse, and I swallow hard.

Junichi sits up slowly, then turns his head to look at me. "I did."

I nod. "Great..." When he doesn't go on, I repeat, "Breakfast?"

"You don't need to make anything for me."

"If I don't, who will?"

"I've been practicing."

Drawing back, I frown, but with a smile, skeptical. "Cooking?"

"Yes."

"Really?"

He lifts his chin. "Yes."

"What can you make?"

"Hm... rice, if there's a rice cooker. Boiled chicken and rice, beans and rice. Miso soup... and rice."

I laugh and shake my head, which is a nice distraction from the heat swirling within me. "So if I catch a cold or suddenly want to gain an absurd amount of weight, you've got my meals under control, yeah? Like an ill person's diet."

"I'm making progress. I can make quesillo—Dominican flan. It's easy, and my mom used to make it for me all the time."

I smile. "Very nice... But I don't mind it—making a quick breakfast."

Junichi surprises me when he leans into my space until we're nose to nose, and I'm blinking because he's so close. He's not touching me, but I stop breathing as he speaks low, the warm whisper of his breath rushing against my lips. "Is breakfast in bed an option?" He softly bumps his forehead into me, then tilts his head and caresses his nose against mine.

And that's all it takes. I can't breathe, and a fire ignites and flares inside me that I can't control—so intense like I've never felt before and everything goes to hell, quite swiftly.

FORTY-FIVE
JUNICHI

I don't think I did anything dramatic, but suddenly, the atmosphere of the room shifts, warms and intensifies.

The anxiety in Jae's body and demeanor is profound. I can feel his apprehension and his pulling away from me. The insecurities and doubts. His being guarded and very careful with me.

We're not bonded. I hear that these are things one can easily discern from their mate once you're bonded. Jae is not my mate, yet, but I can still read him like a damn billboard. He seemed relaxed last night while we talked. It was the most serene he's been since I arrived here. So this morning, I thought I'd try.

I *miss* him. He smells delicious and I just want to kiss him. I want him to kiss *me* in his profound, beautiful and trusting way. The way that only he can. I want to touch and feel him under my hands and against my skin and help him understand that he's not a freak, or a racoon or a skunk. That he's a unique, magnificent creation. He always has been. That he's kind, funny, endearing and frisky as hell, and I love all of that shit.

I figured I'd finally try, but he's leaning away from me now and his expression is one of pure dread.

It starts with his eyes. The ring of blue lights up along the outer rim before it melts into the center, drowning out any remnants of honey brown until his eyes are glowing in bright cobalt. Then I feel his nature fanning outward—pure and unfiltered in the same vivid blue, but as a thick haze encapsulating his body.

Soon, it's reaching out toward me, but also pulling at my nature within me and calling to me. My energy grows brighter, and I feel my eyes burn in response to what Jae's nature is doing. What it's communicating to me.

He wants me. Period. Deeply and sincerely, he loves and desires me. But it's not like Ren's aura—a thick, dank miasma laced with inky possessiveness. Entitlement, demand and discontent.

I sense Jae's desire for me, but there's no possessiveness at all. It feels more like an invitation. It makes my skin warm. It smells sweet and heavenly to my senses, as if he's the proprietor of a luscious shop offering fresh, delicious goods and I am welcome to enter. I'd be safe there and well looked after. I wouldn't ever want for anything.

I'm amazed at how *good* it feels as it radiates further outward, slowly engulfing my body and covering me. I want more of it—to greedily feel it and better understand the different layers and complexities of it—but Jae stands abruptly, staring at me with that horrified gaze still etched on his face. He backs away from me, and the warmth and sweetness disappear, like I've been shoved out of a door and left in the freezing rain. Was my existence always like this? Or is this some unique after-effect of being exposed to his aura?

Jae turns, walks across the room, goes into the en-suite bathroom and slams the door shut. I swallow and inhale a breath, still recovering from the loss of that feeling. My heart is pumping in my chest, but I push myself to stand and walk over to the bathroom door. I feel fucking bewildered, and my eyes are still alighted. "Jae?"

He doesn't answer me. After a moment, I knock, steadily taking deep breaths to settle my nature. "Jae? What are you doing?" I can feel his aura muffled through the door. Now, instead of being inside the shop, it's as if I'm looking in through a window. I can't feel it completely, but I know it's very good inside there. "*Jae—*"

"I-I'll meet you downstairs!"

His voice comes frantic and stifled through the door. When there's nothing else, I turn, walk toward the bed and drop down hard, lying back with my palms pressed against my face and waiting for my eyes to burn out.

Shit. I feel high. But not like a thick, cottony drug-induced high. More like I took some happy pills and the lingering effect is soft tingles across my skin and my heart being light. My body is amped up and now I *really* want to touch him. I knew his nature and essence would be good to me when I finally felt its true form. It was fantastic even when it was stifled and he was human. But this unfiltered, raw vampire energy of his... It's something else. Powerful and euphoric. Glorious.

Jae stays in the bathroom for a very long time. I don't know how long exactly, but by the time the door opens, I'm sitting upright with my arms folded, and my body is acclimated to living out in the freezing rain again. He starts when he sees me, even taking a small step back. He avoids my eyes and runs his fingers against the back of his hair

"I... I said I would meet you downstairs."

I watch him with my arms folded. When I don't say anything, he finally steps out of the bathroom, eyeing me cautiously. Totally guarded. "Sorry... about—"

"Why did you walk away from me?" I ask. Jae pauses. He looks at me, blinking. But slowly, he draws back, his face shifting and his brow creasing. I've seen this expression on him before. I haven't seen it in a very long time, but I do remember it. Distinctly.

"Why did I walk away from *you*?" he asks, the question laced with incredulity. "Have we forgotten that you walked away from *me*? That you told me to shove off five months ago because you wanted nothing to do with this?" Jae opens his arms, indicating his entire body with wide eyes. "You told me that you would *never* be bothered with ranked vampires—especially purebreds! And you told me plainly that you hated Ren's aura, and the fact that purebreds even have this ridiculous ability. But you show up here, unannounced and rubbing your face into me, and I'm supposed to what, exactly? Be overjoyed? Compliant? What the hell did you expect?"

He turns and paces a step, running his hands into his hair before he stops, looking away but still talking to me. "This won't work. I... I can't do this with you."

"Why?"

"Because I don't even know how to *behave* around you anymore." He turns his head to glance at me, and his eyes are glassy. But when he sees me staring back, he looks to the wall again, wiping his palm down his face and inhaling deep. "Anything I do, I'm worried it's coming across as bossing you or exerting my *rank* over you or whatever. And I know... I know how you really feel about me now. In this form. You don't like this, and I don't like it either. So why should two people try to exist together in a circumstance like that? It's toxic and it's painful."

He wipes his eyes, his shoulders rising and falling. Eventually, he looks over at me, frowning. "Are you listening?"

"I am. Is there anything else?"

He tilts his head. "Isn't that enough?"

I scoot over on the bed and pat the mattress with my palm. "Will you please sit with me?" At first, he doesn't budge. After a moment, though, he steps toward the bed.

If Jae had said all of this to me before I felt his physical aura, I might have believed him. He's been tense, guarded and uncomfortable ever since I arrived. Coupled with this declaration, I might have given in, thinking that this is what he truly wants.

But I've now had the immense pleasure of feeling the true inner core of his being. The soul of him and what he earnestly desires. Whether he realizes this or not, I don't know. But he's lying right now. Both to me and to himself. He wants this just as badly as I do.

When he's sitting beside me on the bed, I look over at him. "Everything you said is valid. But not all of it was true."

"What wasn't true?" he asks, staring forward and out the window—through the glass and at yet another gray, overcast sky.

"First, that I told you to 'shove off.'"

"You did."

"Did not. I said I needed space. If anything, *I* needed to shove off for a minute. I never wanted you to leave Japan. You could have stayed in my house and worked as long as you wanted. I just... I needed time to process and adjust, and I needed to fix the Ren bullshit. I would have been perfectly fine with you staying with me—"

"Sure. Right. I was supposed to just crack on. Walking around and pretending like I don't love—like I don't care." He takes another deep breath and runs his hands up and into his hair.

I smirk. "Like you don't *love* me, Jae?"

He drops his hands, gripping them against the edge of the

bed with his shoulders hunched. His skin is flushed and he doesn't say anything—guarded. I can't help but smile and shake my head. Does he not even realize what his aura is? Its function and what it reveals about his innate desires and needs? Nino was right. He doesn't know how to vampire. At all.

Which makes this all the more endearing, really.

"Second," I go on, since he's clearly done talking, "you said that I don't like you like this. That isn't true. It doesn't matter what you are. This outer shell is irrelevant. I love *you*, Jae Davies, and all the beautiful, intangible and marvelous things that swarm together to create the essence of who you are."

His skin is still rosy and splotched, but his grip against the bed eases. He's staring out the window, his face lit by the gray glow of the sky.

"Why?" he asks after a long moment of silence. "What's changed in the past five months?"

"Me." I smile, staring into his profile. "To quote someone that I deeply respect, 'I'm looking at you without all of my ridiculous personal baggage in the way.' Is that alright?"

Jae rubs his palm down his face. A weak attempt to hide his smile. "You can't use my own line on me."

"Why can't I? It impressed me when you said it. It told me that you were self-aware and working to change. Now, I am, too."

There's a moment of pause where the sunlight breaks through the clouds. I see the bright yellow ray like a spotlight, but it's only for a passing moment. Jae sits straighter, resting his hands within his lap. His voice is low. "I don't know who... or what I am anymore. And I don't know how to control this body."

I shake my head. "That's okay—"

"Is it?" He finally looks at me, his perplexing eyes distressed. "What if the thing you're afraid of is true? What if I *am* like Ren and every other purebred you hate, and it's only a matter of time before I change? Or something else happens to me besides my eyes shifting colors or this insane blue orb coming out of me? I don't know, Jun!"

"*I* know. I can feel you and you're the same, sunshine. You're just... getting in your own way?" I take a chance, because I *really* want to touch him. The way he smells and the pull of his nature are still there, tucked away but enticing me. Intoxicating me. I know a kiss is far off at the moment, but if I could just...

The second my fingers graze his against the bed, he snatches his hand away. I frown. "Jae—"

"Don't touch me! You'll just set me off and I'll be a blue fireball again. Jesus Christ, so humiliating. It took forever to calm it down. I need to talk to Haruka as soon as we get to Milan. There has to be a way to stop this."

"You could also *not* stop it and just let it breathe. It's your aura, and it's the physical manifestation of your vampiric energy. It's naturally responding to me. To us." I smile, but he's frowning and shaking his head.

"It's a freak show."

"It is not."

"You told me that you *hated* that feeling! And that it was forceful and controlling—"

"*Not* yours. It's not always like that, and I was wrong to only tell you that side of it. But there's another side, too. Your aura is also the essence of who you are, Jae—your true, unfiltered self all around me and communicating with me. Calling to me. It's pure and beautiful and I love it. It feels *good* to me." I finally have eye contact, so I take advantage and say, "Can we please try? I think we can absolutely do this, as long as we go slowly, and you truly forgive me for hurting you. Can you?"

Now that he's been honest with me and aired his grievances, I know we can do this. He's already less tense, and even though there are still hurdles to overcome, I can finally see the finish line in the distance. Somehow, I already know what the promised land looks like, and it is flowing with milk and honey. It is truly good.

When he nods, I exhale a breath that I didn't even realize I was holding.

"Yes," he says. "I forgive you... but don't touch me until I figure out how to control this thing inside me."

I bite my lip and look away from him because I do not want to make that promise. And *I* could help him learn and manage it, if he let me. Is he serious?

"Jun?"

I whip my head to look at his angelic face all frowned up. He's dead serious. Fuck. "Alright. I won't. Except..."

"What?"

"I have another surprise for you. To finish it, well, I might be required to touch you."

Jae raises his eyebrow. "What are you talking about?"

"I have a suit for you. It's almost finished, but I need you to try it on so I can make sure the fit is perfect. I estimated your height, but it seems I was an inch off."

He sits back slightly, laughing. "You're telling me that you've tailored an entire suit for me without my physically being present for measurements? How is that possible?"

I shrug. "This is what I do, and I've been doing it for decades. Besides, I'm quite familiar with the intimacies and dimensions of your body, aren't I?" I'm staring into his blue-rimmed hazelnut eyes, and in a pleasant turn, he doesn't immediately look away from me. He matches my hooded gaze, but then smiles in a knowing way as he stands from the bed.

"Fair," he says. "I need to respond to some emails for work, and I have meetings this evening. I'm trying to squeeze everything in before the flight tomorrow so I can be offline in Milan. I'll try the suit on a little later today."

"Sounds fine. I'll make some coffee?"

"Cheers. If the weather stays clear, let's walk out to the lake for lunch."

"I would *love* that."

He smiles as he walks past me, heading toward the door. Lulú, who has been curled up in the center of the bed this entire time, suddenly pops up, hops off the bed and pads through the door behind him. I shake my head. Traitor.

MILAN

FORTY-SIX

JAE

"You can let Lulú out into the garden if she wants to go, Audrey. She's... quite intelligent, and Jun is assuring me that she won't get lost."

Glancing out of the car window, Lake Como is a sparkling expanse of turquoise as we zip past. Across the water, the mountains are green and high, chock full of trees in multiple shades and set against a pristine blue sky.

It's unbelievable that I'm in Italy, riding in the back of this luxurious town car in a custom-made suit and driving toward a place called Villa del Balbianello. I did an Internet search of the property, and it looks like something out of a multi-million-dollar romance movie that is a hit with audiences everywhere. The house we're staying at (someone Giovanni knows) is also ridiculous. Correction, not a house. It's a medieval castle. Our bathroom is like if you dropped a large freestanding bathtub into the middle of a stylish greenhouse.

"Yes, all that is fine. Thank you for checking on her," I say into the phone. "Don't hesitate to call if you need something... Yes, we'll be back on Saturday... Okay, thanks, Audrey."

"Is everything alright?" Junichi asks. He's sitting beside me in the back seat. His suit jacket is a deep tan color, but his trousers and vest are black over a starched white shirt. The lapels have a black paisley design. As expected, it's all fashionable as hell, but subtle. The suit he's made for me is classic black, the only deviation being my tie and pocket square, which are the same rich tan color as Junichi's jacket. I laughed when I saw him, but honestly... it's nice, isn't it? Plus, if I get lost, it's a little bit like "please return to chaperone with matching jacket."

"Yes," I say. "Audrey is just nervous about the cat getting lost or attacked by wildlife."

Junichi sits back, adjusting his long legs, and I glance down at his beautiful, shiny black Oxfords. "Lulú might outlive all of us, and she can defend herself. Audrey has nothing to worry about."

"I suppose so, considering even your average cat has nine lives. How many more for a vampire cat?"

Junichi grins, nodding, then looks over and meets my eyes. "Are you nervous?"

"Yes. All of this is very surreal."

"How so?"

"I feel out of place. But... I don't know. I always have. Never quite fitting in anywhere. And now I'm here. It's preposterous."

"Well," Jun says, clasping his hands in the gap of his legs. "You've always had dormant purebred energy inside you. You were trying to live your life as a human, but that wasn't exclusively what you were."

"Maybe. But there are other layers, too. Like, when I was a kid in London and going to school, I couldn't ever find my footing. I was a bit too swirly for the white kids but not quite Asian enough for the others. When we moved to Bristol and I met Cy,

I felt a little more settled, but then Cy and I have our own host of issues, don't we?"

Junichi breathes in a laugh. "You have an interesting friendship, without question."

Glancing out of the window again, we're driving down a narrow road hooded with cypress and pine trees. The villa stands before us, large and square like a stucco palace. There's a long line of cars toward the front, and I can see fancifully dressed vampires stepping out of their vehicles and heading inside. The hum of all their energies radiates against my skin. If I focus, I can pinpoint my senses on any particular one. If I don't, all I sense and smell is Junichi. It's like always being covered by a soft, lavender-scented blanket, but if I want, I can lift up the edge and peek outside.

"I've had so much time to think," I go on. "About my life and what I've been doing. How much of it has been genuinely me, or my nature secretly driving me? Why things were a particular way. I realize... I only got into a groove when I went to Japan. I felt really good there—like I understood myself and the work I was doing. I was alone, but things finally made sense to me and I felt confident."

"You weren't alone, Jae. It's the opposite. You were finally interacting with and part of a large, thriving vampiric community, and though you didn't know it on the surface, your inner nature responded to that. It's what you needed all along."

Reaching up, I scratch the back of my hair. "I don't know." That sounds logical—and I know I've even told my patients to join local groups tailored to their specific circumstances. But why do I feel like a fish out of water? Like an imposter. Any minute now, this "purebred" skin will peel away, and surprise, I'm *actually* a lizard.

There's a buzzing sound, and Junichi pulls his phone from inside his jacket pocket. He reads the screen, types something out, then leans forward to address the driver. "If you pull past this line, there's a second road on the right that we need to take. The guard at the gate there will wave you through."

"Yes, sir!"

The driver does as instructed, smoothly moving past the line of cars, turning and pulling up to a large, rather intimidating but ornately designed iron gate.

I'm staring out of the window like this is my first car ride ever, but a question pops into my head. I turn to Jun. "Do you know Cellina and Giovanni very well?"

Junichi is still texting on his phone. "Giovanni not very, but Cellina a little more. I was her escort to a few society events when she was stepping in for Haruka last year while Nino was recovering. She's a lovely creature."

"I've met her once before at the hospital, but not Giovanni... Were you seeing her?"

He flicks his eyes up at me before looking back down at his phone. "No. I couldn't be bothered with ranked vampires, remember?"

I chuckle. "Ah. Right."

"Even though that was before they'd bonded, I'd seen the way Giovanni watched her whenever they were in a room together. I don't typically play by the rules, but there are some purebreds you just don't fuck with."

"Noted..."

Eventually, we're on the opposite side of the villa. There's a huge garden with all manner of flowers and rose bushes in every color, and I can see the greenish-blue glitter of the lake again if I peek through the trees.

When we step out of the car, the weather is perfect and there's a slight, cool breeze. A row of stone steps ascends before us, and at the top, thick pillars grace either side of an intricately carved wooden door. When I peek from underneath the metaphorical blanket of Junichi's essence, I know that Haruka, Nino, Cellina, Giovanni and even Asao and Sydney are somewhere up there, likely waiting for us.

"May I have your hand?"

Junichi is asking me and waiting, but his hands are in his trouser pockets as he stands there looking absolutely fucking delicious in his suit. He's clean-shaven, which doesn't really matter because I like him both ways. His curls are cut low against his head. I miss running my fingers into his hair.

My nature hasn't gone berserk since that first time in my bedroom on Sunday morning. He hasn't touched me since then, but... I want to try. I said I would. I reach out and he meets me, slowly clasping our hands.

"Is this okay?" he asks.

The warm tingles are there, shooting up my arm and reverberating in my chest and stomach, but I'm alright. "Yes." I nod. He adjusts and entwines our fingers, then pulls me toward the steps.

The door opens before we get there, and Asao is grinning on the other side. He's wearing a black suit as well, which fits his broad, square shape nicely. I'm suddenly wondering if Jun has dressed everyone in this room.

"Le petit doctor." Asao grins, his eyes full of old-man mischief. "It's good to see you again."

I blink, utterly caught off guard. "What?" I look up at Jun, and he's shaking his head at Asao, his lips pursed. Before I can recover from that, though, Cellina is floating toward me. Or at least it seems like she's floating because her stride is effortless with the sway of her hips underneath the steely-silver gown she's wearing.

"Doctor Jae!" She reaches down, taking hold of both my hands just as Junichi releases his hold. "Thank you so much for coming."

Cellina is quite gorgeous and smells like something that might bloom in the springtime. Her intense gray eyes staring at me from underneath heavy, dark lashes is making me blush. Which is humiliating. "I—You can just call me Jae, please! Thank you for inviting me." She smiles at me, and it's like her milk-chocolate skin is glowing. Radiant.

She pulls me over toward Haruka and Nino, who are both standing with a fairly muscular, tall and handsome purebred that resembles Nino—but a bigger, slightly scarier version. She's only holding one of my hands now, but I can still feel the heat radiating up my neck and cheeks. "This is Giovanni—my mate and Nino's brother. I don't think you met when Nino was in the hospital?"

I give a little bow. I have no idea why, but it feels like I should? This bloke's energy is like a thick wall, and he's standing here impeccably dressed and staring down at me with hazel-green owly eyes. "N-nice to meet you," I manage.

His gaze flickers down to Cellina's hand clasped in mine, then back up to my face. He lifts his chin. "Are you crushing on my mate right now?"

Bloody hell. "N-no—"

"G!" Nino turns to face him, his brow creased. "You're being *rude*."

Giovanni's stony face breaks into a smile, and he reaches up and clasps the back of Nino's neck in a rough but playful gesture. "I'm just joking, kiddo, calm down."

"It's not funny."

"Oh my God." Cellina's free hand is massaging the bridge of her nose as she shakes her head. "Could you just behave for five minutes?"

"Nope. I've been behaving my whole damn life." Giovanni wiggles his eyebrows, smiling at me and still gripping Nino's neck, pushing him in a downward, bowing motion. "Nice to meet you, Jae. I know you're new to vampire shit, but please remember that she's bonded."

"G!"

Giovanni only laughs, but Cellina lets go of my hand, and with lightning speed quickly flicks her mate in between his eyebrows. His palm releases Nino's neck and flies up to the center of his forehead. "*Fuck—*"

"You're doing too much right now. It's embarrassing." Cellina shakes her head and folds her arms as she looks him over.

"Hello, Jae."

When I hear the deep, calming voice of the vampire pope himself, I take a breath and relax my shoulders. "Hi, Haruka. It's nice to see you again."

He smiles. "You as well." I suddenly realize that he and Nino are wearing the exact same tuxedo. The color is similar to Cellina's dress, but their bowties and pocket squares are sage green. Giovanni's tuxedo is the same, except he isn't wearing a bowtie and his shirt collar is casually gaped open.

"How are you feeling?" Haruka asks. "You had expressed concern about coming here and how your nature would react to everyone."

Haruka and I have spoken at least once a month since I left Japan. But I try not to bother him too often because, well, I try hard not to bother anyone. I breathe in, assessing the environment as Nino comes and stands beside Haruka.

Giovanni's energy is like a hard, vertical wall in front of him. But it feels like... a façade? An immediate show of power, but he's exposed on the sides. There isn't anything to back it up. And as for Haruka and Nino, well... the energy coming from them pulses all around us. It's potent and drowns out everything in a strangely pleasant way. It radiates fully from Nino but feels stifled when I focus on Haruka.

I'm amazed at the varying levels of control and manipulation emanating from all of them. I suppose when you're born and raised vampiric, managing your aura isn't really an issue.

"Jae?"

"Ah—I'm alright. So far so good, although I would like to chat with you later, if you have the time?"

Haruka tilts his head. "Is that so? Nino has been adamant that I speak with *you* while we're here. Is your matter urgent?"

"Not really. I just... I'd like to know how to control my, er... aura. Better." It feels awkward even saying it. My "aura." Christ.

"No no, wait." Nino's amber eyes widen and he turns slightly, reaching out and gripping Haruka at his waist over his suit jacket. The movement surprises him, because he jumps at Nino's touch. "*I'll* teach you about that—controlling your aura," Nino assures me. He looks at his mate, and they exchange a pointed look before Haruka rolls his eyes. Nino scrunches his nose. "I'm good at controlling and manipulating it now, aren't I?"

"Of course," Haruka says.

"So I'll help Jae."

"What's the problem?" Junichi walks up and stands beside me. I was only vaguely aware of him fussing at Asao in the corner after we walked in. Seems like they're finished now.

"There's no problem," Nino says, leaning in toward Haruka's cheek. "But if Haruka teaches Jae how to control his aura, maybe you'll never see it again."

Haruka shakes his head in a laugh that registers from his throat. "That is not true."

"Mmhm," Nino snarks, then presses a quick peck against his mate's cheek.

"Well, I certainly don't want that," Junichi states. "But I don't think I have a say in it."

I look up at Jun, because it feels like there might be something hidden in the statement—some passive-aggressive undertone. But I'm immediately distracted by the luster and depth of his eyes staring down at me, and my nature (which had been very kind to me up until this point) does something like a somersault in my belly. I look away and take a breath. What were we talking about?

"They're ready for us," Asao says, standing by a door across the room.

"Okay, one more time." Cellina joins the huddle, and Giovanni and Sydney close the circle behind her. With all the commotion, I hadn't even noticed him. I smile in his direction, and he gives me a cheerful wave.

"Asao and Sydney are handling and orchestrating the waitstaff. First, Nino and Haru will welcome everyone with greetings as they enter the balcony, then Nino is standing with Haru while he reads the confirmation certificate, yes?"

Nino nods. "Yes."

Cellina faces me and Jun. "Will the two of you stand as witnesses to our bond with our friends—Matteo, Mia and Sergio, and my brother, Cosimo? Our parents will be there too. You'll all be sitting together in the first and second rows. You'll only have to stand up and say 'we do' when the officiator turns to you. He'll tell you when. Super easy."

I blink, taken aback that I have even the smallest role in this massive, fancy ordeal. Jun finds my hand and gives my palm a soft squeeze. "Are you comfortable with that?"

"Of course! Sure."

Cellina beams. "Perfect."

Giovanni takes hold of Cellina's waist from behind and leans over her shoulder as he addresses me. "You don't need to be worried today. Just observe and try to have fun. There are a lot of purebreds at this ceremony from all over the world, and nobody is expecting to find a British one. They'd only know if you spoke, and even then, by the time everyone is drinking, I'm sure nobody will notice. So relax."

Nino frowns. "Now you want him to relax? But you were rude as hell the second he walked in."

"That's because he walked in here looking like a skittish deer—that was a *joke*."

"How was that 'joke' supposed to help?"

"*Neither* of you are helping right now." Cellina is shaking her head again, and they both quiet down. Haruka clears his throat, and we all look at him.

"Shall we go?"

Still holding my hand, Jun pulls me toward the door as Asao holds it open for us.

FORTY-SEVEN
JAE

The ceremony took place on a large balcony overlooking the lake and mountains. Everyone was so poised and attentive, and their clothing reminded me of a scene from some classic film—back when everyone cared a great deal more about how they looked and dressed when they walked out of the house. *The Great Gatsby* or *The Age of Innocence*.

Giovanni and Cellina sparkled (not literally), and their love and commitment to one another as they read their vows genuinely made my heart flutter. Haruka's reading of the bond certificate was fascinating. The document outlined generations of Cellina's and Giovanni's respective families starting from the eighteenth century and leading up to today, creating a winding, storied path of how these two unique families came to be forever entwined. His rich voice was spellbinding, and it was as if everyone were frozen in time, not even breathing as we hung on to his every word.

By sunset, food has been served and devoured, drinks filled and refilled. I'm sitting out under the atrium with Haruka, but we're alone. Junichi is popular. I had a sense of this when I searched for him on the Internet, way back before our first real date. And again when I went to his shop and saw him beautifully posed on multiple magazine covers. But seeing it in person—having vampires call out to him from across the room or interrupt conversations to pull him away, gushing about the latest celebrity or icon he's dressed—it becomes quite tangible, doesn't it?

But he's stayed with me this whole time. He's never once left me alone, and when someone has taken hold of his arm and pulled him along, he's immediately grabbed my hand and pulled me right with him. Only when Haruka has found us and assures Jun that we won't go far does he separate from me.

Haruka and I are out on the balcony again, sitting in the front row of empty seats that overlook the now darkened water. It moves silently in the fading light, the sun setting behind the shadowed mountains. Little white and yellow lights from houses set in the hills are flickering on, their reflections dancing brightly within the water. The sky is a cool gradient of deep blue and soft yellow.

I inhale a breath, trying to feel the tranquility and beauty of this scene both inside my body and out. Maybe if I breathe in deep enough, I'll hold on to it and be able to use this feeling again later on when I need it.

"How is life in the English countryside?" Haruka asks, his voice somehow perfectly in tune with the calm atmosphere. Like a lullaby.

"It's alright. I don't have any complaints."

Haruka sits back to make himself comfortable, crossing his leg and clasping his hands in his lap. "I, too, lived in the English countryside for several years."

"Yes, I remember. Sidmouth, right? You told me that first time I had dinner at your house."

"Correct. I lived that life, but when I think back on my

experience, I was far from 'alright.' In fact, it was, frankly, a subpar existence. But perhaps your circumstance is much different than mine was."

I pause, letting that sink in for a moment. Contemplating how I spend my days—working, not eating, drinking factory-made synthetic blood, then working some more. Sometimes crying in the attic. Those are the worst days, of course. On better days, I walk out to the lake... But then sometimes, I sit there, staring at the glassy surface and wondering what it would be like to walk into it and maybe never come back out.

"I was miserable," Haruka continues in my silence. "I did not realize how miserable I was, though, until someone befriended me. It was like sitting alone in a dark room but then having the light turned on. Suddenly I could see, and it was impossible to sit there and alone again."

I smile. "Nino?"

Haruka returns the gesture, his ruby eyes sparkling in the ambient darkness. "Yes. It was unintentional on his part, but he showed me something important. Well, many things. But primarily, that I should not be alone—isolating myself, drinking blood unfit for my biological needs and living a generally malnourished life. I told myself for years that I was content existing this way, but when I reminisce and allow my mind to wander back to that time... I would not wish that life on anyone."

I understand what he's saying. I do, but... "So you bonded with Nino?"

"No." Haruka shakes his head. "Not immediately. First, I returned home. To my community."

"But... not everyone has that. A home and a community."

"*You* do."

I pause at that, because I'm pretty sure I don't. I have a

house… and Audrey when she's not traveling. But that's not necessarily what I meant.

"With us, Jae. Your community and home are with us."

"It's… it's not really my home, though. It's Junichi's. I'm just like… the friend who got to tag along to the party because he knows somebody with a real invitation." When I meet Haruka's eyes, he's looking at me like I'm nuts.

"No," he says. "That's not how it is. You awakened and were reborn under *my* realm. Nino and I have helped to guide both you and Junichi through this, so we feel a unique kinship and responsibility for your well-being and development. I had assumed that we also shared a unique camaraderie through our research interests and studies. Perhaps I was wrong and my amity was one-sided?"

"*No*—no, of course not! I appreciate you and Nino more than I can express, I just thought… I didn't belong there after what happened with Jun."

"You belong, regardless of your relationship with Junichi. You are always welcome within our home and society, but it is your choice."

"Thank you, Haruka." My hands are clasped tight in the gap of my legs now as I think of something I want to ask. Something I've been privately looking into but haven't had any luck with. I decide to take a chance. "Are there… vampire therapists? I mean, professionals that I can talk to who deal with vampire matters? I haven't been able to find anyone in Bristol or even London, and a human feels wildly inappropriate."

"There are. But they are rare—as rare as vampire doctors, perhaps? Our culture is progressive in many ways, but in some, we are severely lacking. Mental and emotional health resources being one of them. Both Nino and Sydney see someone in Osaka, occasionally. I'm sure they'd be happy to speak with you about it in more detail."

Brilliant. That possibility alone makes me feel more excited than I have in a long while, and I'm not sure what that says about my current state of mind, but here we are. As we sit in silence together and I take note of his soft energy beside me, I decide to risk another likely unorthodox question. "May I ask why you keep your energy stifled like this? I feel it flowing freely from Nino, but from you, it feels... muffled?"

He smiles his patient, pope-like smile at me. "Yes, it is simply a personal preference. When I am in the privacy of my home or with Nino, I allow my energy to flow freely. But in crowded spaces like this, I habitually stifle my aura. It is simply what I am most comfortable with."

"I understand." It makes sense. But I notice he's the only one who does it. Every other purebred here, their energy radiates outward to varying degrees. Some louder than others, as if they're trying to show off, maybe? Attract someone? I'm not entirely sure. I don't know enough about mine yet, but it's been largely dormant since the bedroom incident on Sunday. Maybe it wore itself out.

"If I may counter with an equally personal question?" Haruka asks.

"Sure."

"Of course, we are more than happy to help you achieve more finite control of your nature. However, does Junichi create a safe environment for you to experiment? To start, it would be best to learn and understand your energy while in an intimate space—letting it comfortably radiate outward and embracing the unique feel of it."

"I—Well..." Maybe? If I gave him the chance? The way he talked to me about it when we were in Bristol made it sound like he would. But I don't know.

"Haru—G wants you to meet someone." Nino is walking down the aisle, backlit by the bright lights pouring out of the inside hall. I can still hear the music of the live band playing, the sound floating atop laughter and animated conversation, glasses clinking and dishes clanging. It's like a layered cake of joyful sounds.

"Will you be alright for a little while, Jae?" Nino asks when he's beside me.

"Yup." I nod, suddenly noticing a staircase in the corner of the balcony that looks like it leads down to the first level and closer to the water and garden. "I'm just going to take a walk."

"Okay." Nino smiles. "Let's get together tomorrow sometime to talk about your aura?"

"Sounds good." I also thank Haruka as he stands, then watch the two of them link arms and slowly walk down the aisle, talking as they stroll back inside. Nino says something, because I hear Haruka's bubbly laugh echo just before they disappear into the crowd.

Everything feels warm and fuzzy here as I look up at the night sky. It's darker now, the glow of yellow all but vanished. The expanse is velvety blue with speckles of bright stars. I stand, stretch my arms and begin my descent on the winding stone steps. I guessed right, because I hear less of the music and chatter and more of the water splashing against the rocks as I reach the bottom. There's a winding path along the water with cypress and pine trees lining the opposite side. It's peaceful as I walk and simply breathe it all in.

I find a stone bench within an alcove of trees that overlooks the lake, and it isn't long before I distinctly sense my escort heading my way. I've probably wandered too far and he needs to make sure I'm alright. It makes me chuckle—how attentive Junichi suddenly is. I suppose he's always been that way, though. Even from the start. There was just a blip in the movie reel. Or maybe a scratch in the vinyl record or our song.

When he's close, I smile. "Hiya."

"Hey—are you tired of partying?" He sits beside me, unbuttoning his jacket and rolling his shoulders.

"No. It was nice down here, so I wanted to walk. You didn't need to leave. I'm fine, Jun."

He leans back against the bench with both palms behind him, then folds his leg. "I wanted to sit with *you*, Jae. If that's alright?"

"It's alright." I follow his gaze out to the lake. It's so lovely, and we both sit quietly, just listening to the water gently breaking against the rocks, over and over. It's soothing.

"How was your talk with Haruka?" Jun eventually asks, his voice low.

"Nice. He said some encouraging and insightful things to me. He's very kind. Nino said he'll help me with my aura tomorrow."

"That's great. I'm really glad."

I narrow my eyes. "That sounded weird."

He glances at me. "How so?"

"I don't know—like fake."

Junichi laughs, looking back toward the lake. "It wasn't."

I'm still watching him, unconvinced. "You're being awkward, which doesn't quite work because *I'm* the awkward one." He huffs in a laugh but still doesn't say anything. Just staring forward. "What is it?" I ask. It takes another moment, but he finally answers me.

"I would really like to kiss you. I want to touch you. You told me not to, and I respect that. But I miss you."

Him saying these things is enough to send off a flare of heat inside me, like flash photography. My skin is all tingly and the warmth of my energy is wide awake again. Truthfully? I miss him too. And of course I want to kiss him, but...

I swallow, trying to bite back the surge I feel inside me, but I already know it's useless. It's starting to register and burn in my eyes. Once it gets that far, I'm learning it's too late to turn back. "If we kiss, I will *absolutely* light up like a firework—"

"That's fine, Jae." He turns his upper body so that he's leaning into me but not touching me at all. His face looks pained. "If you're comfortable with it, I don't mind—I *want* it. Let me feel you..." He lifts his hands and cups my face, staring into my eyes and waiting. The heat is so intense inside me I can't even speak. There's no way I can stifle this now, and there's nowhere for me to run.

I nod in his hands, feeling the light behind my eyes intensify as my hands shake. "Okay." He caresses his nose against mine and I close my eyes tight. I love the tenderness of this when he does it to me. I always have. But I'm also scared because I can feel my nature swelling and radiating out of me now, hot and relentless. I open my eyes wide, and my chest tightens.

"*Breathe*, sunshine. Don't fight with it. Please just let it go."

My hands find the bottom of his lapels and I hold on to him, trying not to fight it, even though it's what I've always done. He kisses my face and I close my eyes again. Then he moves down to my jawline, gently pressing his lips to my skin and nestling his face into the curve of my neck.

As I breathe in and out, the raging heat eventually softens. It shifts into something cooler—less furious and intense. When I open my eyes, it's all around us. A distinct blue haze. Not thick or dense like fog. It's airy and light. Moving but hovering in place like magic.

Junichi lifts his face from my neck and looks at me, and his irises are glowing amethyst. Before I can truly admire the mystifying allure of it, he tilts his head and takes my mouth. My jaw drops as if there'd been a weight attached to it, and he's already lapping inside me. We fall into a passionate rhythm that hasn't been put to practice in a while but moves just as fluidly as it ever did.

We're kissing and moving so intensely that my mind flashes back to a room filled with sunshine. Suddenly, I'm in Japan, in Kurashiki, and the world feels new and fresh—like the morning after a night of heavy rainfall and the leaves and flowers are glistening. There's an overabundance of sensations. Everything is a little too bright, but I'm ridiculously excited. Absurdly so. Maybe this is the most excited I've ever been in my life, because I feel part of something now. I feel connected and loved and safe, and there's someone who's there for me and I'm there for them. He wants to be with me, and I with him, and there's truly no question or doubt in my mind. I feel full of life, and I never want this feeling to end. Somewhere inside me—somewhere deep that I don't quite yet understand—something tells me that it never will.

I open my eyes, and Jun is holding me with his fingers threaded in my hair and against the back of my head. His eyes are still glowing in vivid purple and I feel mine alighted as well. My energy is radiating outward and around us, holding us captive like a protective sphere. It doesn't hurt anymore, though. Now... it feels kind of nice. Tingly and soft.

He's not saying anything, just looking at me with heavy lids. When my head clears a little more, I say, "I don't know how to turn it off."

"You don't need to turn it off." He leans in and kisses me again, straight on. Then on my nose, then my cheek. "Just let it be free until it's satisfied."

I slide my hands from his lapels and inside his jacket, carefully resting my palms against his waist. "I'm assuming this isn't awful for you?" I smile, but I'm nervous.

He keeps kissing me all over, mindless with it like he's in a state of euphoria. "I love this. If I wasn't concerned about embarrassing you, I would undress you and make love to you right now on this bench."

My stomach clenches and the heat within me kicks up again. Well, that did something.

"Do you know what your aura is, Jae?"

Blinking, I think back to the textbook definition that he's given me a few times. "It's the physical manifestation of my vampiric nature."

Jun huffs in a little laugh. "Yes, but it's more complex than that. I told you before that it communicates with me. And that it reveals the most sincere and unfiltered parts of you and your desires. It calls to me."

I swallow, afraid of the answer but wanting to ask the question. "What... does it say?"

"That you've chosen me. That you love me and want me as your mate, and if I submit to you, I'll never want for anything."

Holy shit, that's embarrassing. Christ. I lean back, trying to break his hold on me. "*No.* I—I wouldn't ever ask you to—"

"Jae." His voice is soft, but he holds my head firm in his grasp, bringing our faces even closer. "Even if you don't say the words, or try to deny it, I know the *truth* and how you really feel. It's all around us... You said you forgave me, but why are you still pushing me away like this? It's confusing, sunshine."

"It's difficult—being this open and transparent."

"Because you're afraid?"

"*Yes.*"

He leans in again, pressing a swift kiss to my lips. "I understand. But I promise you don't need to be." Jun looks into my eyes, hesitating. "May I taste you? Technically, it's improper for me to ask you that question. I'm not supposed to, and I should wait for you to offer yourself to me. But I really just—"

I lift one hand from his waist and grip his chin so he stops talking, then I meet his gaze. "Yes."

He's right. I said I wanted to try and that I've forgiven him, but I'm still trying to protect myself. I'm guarded. That doesn't work, though, does it? You either love all the way or you don't bother. Half-assing it won't do either of us any good. It'd be pointless.

I'm surprised when Jun brings a trembling hand up to catch mine from holding his chin. This person who's always so cool, composed and unbothered is unraveled right now. I don't know how, but I can feel his hunger and desire for me—the depth and sincerity in his eyes when they meet mine.

He places my palm against his nose and inhales deeply before he licks the center. He tilts his head and bites down softly, then his fangs elongate and sink deep into my skin as he pulls and feeds. His eyes are closed at first, and he exhales a deep sigh, moaning with... relief? When he opens his eyes again and stares directly at me, I allow myself this moment. To completely trust him. I reach back to that feeling hovering at the edges of my psyche—that day when I first woke up to this new life and I had zero doubts about anything. Only promise and hope were stretched out before me.

Meeting his gaze, the stiffness in my chest softens. I might be insecure about this later, but right now, as he pulls from me and I nourish and give him the life he needs, I have faith in him. That he won't walk away from me again.

Just as my body is relaxing, something jolts from within my core, and it terrifies me because it's so unexpected. Jun stops feeding, looking at me as if he's waiting for something. I open my mouth to speak but I can't, because the heat inside me returns, but the dial is set to a hundred. A blazing inferno. My body goes rigid, but Jun pulls me in and holds me tight in his embrace, grounding me—or us—through whatever is happening. All I can do is watch as my energy shifts, deliberately pulling Jun's amethyst aura from his body. I can literally see the two colors converging and seeping into each other, like two shades of paint being mixed to create a new, brilliant hue.

When the colors are fused and one, the energy slowly shrinks down, pouring into us both like osmosis. It feels warm and liquidy as it seeps into me, and when it's finally finished, there's a heavy weight in my core. I still can't move because it's doing something. Adjusting? Like a bird settling into a new nest.

Eventually, the stiff weight lessens and my body goes lax, but Jun is still holding me in his embrace as I gasp—desperate to suck in air and swallow. His breathing is labored too, but he never lets me go. Not even for a second.

FORTY-EIGHT
JUNICHI

It's done. No more games.

I feel like an empty mug that's been poured into—filled with something rich, warm and more satisfying than anything I could fathom. To describe it would only shortchange Jae and his essence. The complexity and goodness of what he's given me.

But I also feel like a jackass, because I've been running away from this my entire life, and I even ran away from Jae for months. He's been offering me—a dying man—restoration and fulfillment, genuine love and refuge from an otherwise toxic and painful existence. A life where I've starved myself on a regular basis and willingly depended on someone who abused me because I thought there was no better option. I turned Jae down, blinded by my own stubbornness, prejudices and assumptions.

Fucking stupid.

The weight of the bond between us dissolves, warmly distributing itself all throughout my body. It's not heavy like an anchor. It was at first, but now it's dispersed, and I feel it running all through me like liquid feathers. It's incredible.

Jae lifts up from me and I loosen my hold on his body. I wanted this. I was ready for it. I know he was, too (somewhere inside, maybe deep down), because if he wasn't, it wouldn't have happened. But I'm preparing myself for a freak-out, because that's his MO.

He's staring down at my tie but not really looking at it. I slide my hands to his elbows and wait, watching him. He takes a deep breath. "Did I just..."

"Did *we?*" I correct. "Yes."

There's a long pause before he sits up a little straighter. Now I'm holding his wrists. He finally looks up at me. His eyes aren't alighted anymore, but they're still warm and celestial. Also, confused. "Are we bonded?"

"Yes."

"I... I thought you needed to have sex to bond?"

I've actually given this situation a lot of thought, so I'm not very surprised by it. "Well, yes. That's a requirement—along with other things between us that are more important. Plus, we had sex and fed from each other for *months*, Jae. You hadn't fully awakened, but... It's like we took advantage of the thirty-day free trial, and now it's time to pay up?"

"Did you just compare our relationship to a marketing strategy?"

I look away to poorly conceal my amusement. "I did." The moment he first woke up in Haruka and Nino's house, I felt it. The pull toward him was way too strong, and he was so open and trustful, his energy was practically reaching out for me. I think if I had fed from him that day—bam. It would have happened. But maybe not? I don't know. I wasn't ready.

Jae looks off and toward the lake. It's silent and moving

with an invisible current. Peacefully reflecting the moon and the night sky.

"Are you upset about this?" He turns, looking at me. "You didn't want this before."

I slide my hands down into his, clasping our palms. "Do I seem upset? We share a connection now. Can you sense me?"

His face is calm as he looks me over, examining. After a moment, he nods. "I can. A little."

"So?"

"You seem relieved and... horny?"

"Correct. I think your sense of me will grow stronger as you open yourself more. As you embrace and experiment with your energy?"

He nods in agreement, inhaling a deep breath but stifling a smile. Obviously, I can read him, too. And since I know what I'm doing, I can read him better. He's delighted. Thrilled. But he doesn't want to show it. He's worried about reacting too strongly and letting himself get excited. To protect himself and me, in case I get turned off by it—like I did when he first awakened.

Jae's energy radiates and speaks to me like an open book. He doesn't seem to realize this, because he's still trying to hide his real feelings from me. But that's okay. We'll get there. The hardest part is done.

"I came out here," I say, "because vamps are starting to leave. We're wrapping things up."

"That's odd. I would assume that vampires would party all night?"

"Vampires day-walk and have jobs. Shall we go inside and get ready to go back to the house?"

"Okay..." Jae pauses a moment, squeezing my hands. "Will they know? About this?"

"Yes."

"How?"

"Because our energies have changed. When we arrived, we had two distinct energies presenting from our individual bodies. But now we share the same one."

Jae reaches up, scratching the back of his head. "This is awkward."

"Slightly."

"Will they think we were having sex out here?"

I shrug. "Probably."

"Ah, bloody hell—"

"That doesn't matter!" I reach and wrap him in my arms again, grinning helplessly. "Who cares what anyone thinks? I love you and I have you, and you have me. We're *bonded*, Jae."

I want him to let himself be as excited as I know he is—as excited as I am. But he just holds me tight with his palms flat against my spine. I can feel the warmth and delight radiating from within him, but he doesn't say a word.

A LITTLE LATER, when we open the door to the back room of the villa, we're met with wide eyes across the board. Cellina is sitting on the couch with her bare feet in Giovanni's lap as he rubs them. Haruka is sitting in an armchair, and Nino is jacketless and pacing around behind him until he sees us and stops dead. Cellina sits up straighter on the couch as we walk inside.

"Oh wow! Congratulations!"

"Thank you," I say, holding on to Jae's hand. Giovanni cocks his head to the side.

"So you two were fucking in the garden? Who bonds at someone else's bonding ceremony?"

Cellina frowns, moving her feet from his grasp. "You are so out of control today."

"Actually, I only fed from his hand," I clarify.

"How they bonded is absolutely none of your business." Haruka is staring at Giovanni with that cold look he sometimes has—when the red of his eyes reads more foreboding than unaffected or playful. I rarely see this expression on him, but when I do, it shifts his entire demeanor, and I suddenly remember how old his blood is and what he could do with it if he chose to.

But Giovanni stares right back, then smirks. "You're calling me names inside your head right now, aren't you?"

"He is." Nino walks over to meet us, his amber eyes lit up even more by his sincere smile. "Congratulations. Does this mean you're coming back to Japan?" He's looking at Jae, but Jae starts and looks at me, then back to Nino.

"I don't know? We—we'd have to decide and talk."

Nino nods. "Alright, so you'll talk, decide, then come back to Japan?"

"My love, perhaps we should give them some space?" Haruka stands from the armchair and walks toward us. Nino runs his fingers into his hair and sighs.

"Sorry. I'm really happy for you, though. For both of you. This is great."

As Haruka walks up, he rests his palms against Nino's shoulders, leans and places a quick kiss at the back of his neck. Privately, I know that Nino is struggling personally—both with some kind of shift in the dynamic between him and his brother and with this kid situation. He's happy about the latter, but it's setting off some unexpected triggers inside of him and he's seeing someone to help manage it. His temperament has been wound a little tight lately.

"We were waiting for you," Haruka states. "We're ready to

return to Sergio's estate for the evening. Are you both ready as well?"

Jae and I both agree, and we keep a firm hold on each other's hands as we leave the villa, and even during the car ride back to the estate.

I've been to the Bianchi estate before. It's a sprawling property, like a small village unto itself, full of brownstone cottages and houses interspersed between beautiful gardens. This estate is much different. It belongs to Giovanni's friend Sergio, who is another kind of business tycoon, but not quite as famous as Nino's brother.

Sergio's house is a literal medieval castle—with a moat and drawbridge, tall rectangular towers, sweeping courtyards and crenellated walls—the whole deal. But inside, it's been gutted and everything is modern and cozy. There are glass atria, granite countertops and pine floors. The lighting is all recessed, so everything is cast in warm spotlights and shadows. It's a bold juxtaposition compared with the outside, but somehow it works, and I applaud his design choices.

When we all arrive, an after-party kind of gathering starts to form in the main sitting room. Giovanni plops down onto the couch in his suit and tosses his jacket aside. Sergio walks toward an impressive wall made of dark maple wood and glass that clearly functions as a large liquor cabinet. Cellina and Haruka are walking arm in arm toward another cozy-looking couch, while Nino trails behind them, walking beside Cosimo, Cellina's brother. Nino is clearly displeased as Cosimo passionately explains something to him that I can't quite catch.

Leaning, I whisper to Jae, "Should we join everyone? Or have you had enough for today?"

"A lot has happened today... I'd like some quiet time to process it."

I nod, then swiftly announce our retiring for the night and that we'll see everyone in the morning. Immediately, Giovanni calls out from across the room, "Is the deer feeling a little less skittish?"

I don't know why the fuck he keeps picking on Jae, but it's grating me.

"If he's a deer, then Junii is unquestionably a wolf." Matteo is smirking at me as he saunters past in his loud, sequined pants. He and I cross paths quite a bit if I'm working in Italy. He's highly sought after for the makeup he does in photo shoots for magazines. Apparently, he and Cellina are very close, which I wouldn't have guessed.

"I agree with that assessment." Jae is looking up at me all innocent and doe-eyed. Right.

I frown. "*What?*"

"That's not far off." Cellina is leaning on the arm of the couch, staring at me. "You're a little wolfish." Haruka is sitting beside her and tilting his head like he's about to say something, but I'm done with this.

Bowing slightly, I rest my free hand at my stomach. "I bid you all fucking goodnight." I turn, pulling Jae along behind me as everyone chuckles.

Our assigned bedroom is on the first floor, toward the back of the castle and through a small courtyard. It's very private, and the entryway is covered in hanging vines and ivy. At first glance, it looks like a room or closet that might have been forgotten centuries ago. But inside is a beautiful square-shaped bedroom with stone walls, lamplights and an oversized bed.

There are exposed wooden beams overhead supporting the low ceiling, and connected to the room and through a narrow archway is a glass atrium that serves as our bathroom. There's a private wooden area with a door for the actual toilet, but the large bathtub is freestanding, and there's a space with a shower head just off to the side. There are plants everywhere—hanging in pots from the ceiling, covering the floor at our feet and on a ledge that runs all the way through.

This part of the castle was likely a greenhouse and gardening shed that Sergio decided to convert into a bedroom. I can see how it worked in its original state, but it's been transformed exquisitely. Again, bold choices that I'm very impressed with.

"I feel like I'm in *The Hobbit*." Jae is standing in the middle of the bedroom and looking around. We arrived in the day, and it was bright and sunny here then. At night, it's taken on a different form. A fairy tale setting with soft lights, mysterious wonders and hidden treasures.

Meeting him in the center of the cozy space, I grin. "Are you tired?"

He shakes his head. "Not really." He steps away from me to examine one of the stained-glass lanterns on the shelf beside the bed. He's still nervous. Apprehensive. I can feel it pulsing off of him.

"I've never had a bath in a greenhouse," I announce.

"A greenhouse in a medieval castle off a lake in Italy?"

I chuckle. "Well, when you put it that way, it feels a little excessive."

"Quite."

"Nonetheless..." I slide my jacket off my shoulders and toss it onto a nearby chair, then move toward the archway leading into the greenhouse. "I'd like to take advantage. Will you be joining me? You can relax, and I'll let you know when it's ready? We should shower first, though. I can't help myself—it's an engrained behavior."

Jae laughs. "Okay, sure."

WE SHOWER, but I don't touch him in any significant way, because apparently, I'm wolfish and mated with a deer. Well, fuck me.

I don't touch him, but I playfully bump him a few times to take the obvious edge off. He laughs when I do this, and we talk about the day while we get clean. How beautiful the villa and entire ceremony were, how Giovanni is an asshole but he means well. How Nino's present anxiety is obvious, but he's going to be a great father and we're not worried about him.

The moon is high and so bright overhead that it lights up the night. I can see it as I settle down into the tub first. Jae's phone rang while we were in the shower, so he went to check it in case there's some emergency with the hospital or Nino and Haru's surrogate. I relax down, then notice a switch on the edge of the shelf holding about a million potted plants right by my head. Curious, I flick it. A line of tiny white faerie lights glows all along the shelves, their string hidden between the plant vines and leaves so that they appear to just float in midair. The water is perfectly warm, and the glass gives us a wide view of the courtyard, trees and flowers beyond this beautiful space.

When Jae comes back into the greenhouse, he's still naked and looking all around in wonder. "Well, this is something... Hopefully no one is taking a stroll back here."

"Indeed. Is everything alright?"

He stops at the opposite end of the large tub, then gingerly climbs inside, avoiding stepping on my feet as I draw them up a little. "Mmhm, everything is fine. It was my father. He left a message and was just checking on me."

"Did you tell him you were coming to Italy for the week?"

"Yes," he says, sitting and folding his knees up against his chest. "He wanted to know if I arrived safely."

"Did you tell him that you're bonded?"

He grins. "No, not yet. But I will later. That's a longer conversation."

"You told me that your father left and moved to Korea when you graduated high school, but he seems to keep contact with you fairly often?"

"Yeah, my father isn't a bad person by any means. He just didn't want to be alone in that cottage with me off in university. It made perfect sense for him."

"But it inadvertently left you alone."

Jae shrugs, running his wet hands up and through his hair to push it back. "I managed."

I don't say anything because I'm not sure that he did. Not well, anyway.

Silence falls between us, and crickets are chirping beyond the glass, the soft call of a nocturnal bird. I look at Jae, and he smiles politely before turning his head to glance away from me. I know what he wants: to come over here and be closer to me. But he's hesitating and doubting himself.

I don't know, maybe it's the wolf in me, but I'm starting to get a little frustrated. How many times do I need to prompt him like this?

Sitting forward, I reach underneath the water, grab one of his ankles and pull. He slides down, his arms flailing up in shock just before his head dips underneath the water. I know he's going through something right now and trying to get his bearings. I know. But I'm *really* over this shy shit.

He breaks the surface again, gasping and pushing his soaked hair back and away from his eyes. "*Shit*, Jun—"

"Why are you hesitating?"

He surprises me when he slaps the surface of the water, sending a wave directly into my face. "Because I bloody hesitate now! That's what I do!"

"You weren't like this before."

"That was *before*." He inhales a deep breath, smoothing his hair again.

I wipe my face with my palms. "You're the same, sunshine."

"Not biologically speaking. I'm quite different."

"You're overthinking."

He's looking at me like he's about to put up a fight—which is fine. I'd much rather he snap at me like this and be honest than politely conceal his feelings, like I'm some stranger he's sitting next to on an airplane.

Jae is watching me, but then his gaze softens and he slinks over to me through the water. He straddles my hips, and the moment he settles down, I wrap my arms around his ass and pull him even tighter into me. He leans down and kisses me, full on. No hesitation.

He brings his hands up to my head and slides his fingers into the back of my hair, gripping me as his mouth moves on mine—his tongue stroking inside me. The weight and feel of him on top of me is phenomenal. A relief, because I've been thinking about him and wanting to be close to him like this for months. I raise my knees up just a little so he's even tighter against me, and I can feel him warm and hard against my stomach.

My eyes are closed, but they start to burn the longer he kisses me. Breathing in his sweet scent, tasting him and having his slick, naked body in my arms—my nature and everything within me is on cloud nine. He raises his head from the kiss, and I open my eyes to see that his are burning too. The color has changed, but only slightly. The pristine blue from before is now more like indigo—blue but with a dark trace of purple. A little bit of me.

Jae brings one hand to my cheek, staring. "Your eyes changed."

I smile. "That happens. It's natural."

"Hm." He breathes out and kisses me again. Just a soft, sweet touch of our lips before he pulls up. "I like that you're a wolf."

"Good thing. It's a little late to turn back now."

He shakes his head. "I wouldn't ever... I want to talk to someone."

"About?"

"Everything," he says, his eyes slowly burning out and returning to normal. "This change and becoming a vampire... or awakening, rather. Feeling out of place. Not knowing where I belong."

I'm listening and lazily sliding my fingers up and down his lower spine underneath the water. I have something to say about this, but the timing isn't right, so I just wait and let him go on.

"Haruka said he knows of someone in Osaka," Jae continues. "A therapist. I'd like to talk with them, if possible."

"Does this mean you want to come back to Japan?"

He sits a little straighter, resting his hands against my chest. "Well, your work is there—"

"My work can be anywhere. If you wanted to stay in Europe, that wouldn't be a problem for me. I have lots of clients here, too, and materials can easily be shipped."

"Right." Jae inhales, thinking. "But the hospital and my work are in Japan, and it would be better if I was onsite to oversee the surrogacy program, and my patients. Remote is going alright, but my supervisor definitely doesn't prefer this arrangement."

I exhale a sigh of relief. Japan is the best choice. If Jae

wanted to stay in England, I already had some strategies planned out in my mind about how to make that work. We would have been fine, maybe. Truthfully? Jae needs more than me. After being with him for a few days and witnessing how this awakening has impacted him, I'm concerned. I think our bonding is definitely a step in the right direction, but it's not enough.

I hadn't anticipated how deeply traumatized he would be from all this, which was shortsighted of me. His entire life has been turned upside down. Separating from him did not help, but I can at least fix that part. That's a small piece of the bigger picture that I can manage.

"Is that alright?" he asks. "Me going back with you?"

Lifting, I kiss his chin and smile. "Of course. I like the house in Bristol though. Can we keep it? Maybe vacation there occasionally? Or if our schedules match up, you can join me when I come to Europe for work."

"I'd like that."

My hands are resting against his hips as I tilt my head. "You're not glowing anymore?"

He chuckles, tracing the contours of my stomach with his fingertips. "I don't know exactly, but... if I let it burn out like I did earlier, it's more manageable for a while afterward. It feels like it's sleeping now. Like a kid that's worn itself out after having a playdate."

I laugh at the imagery of that scenario—Jae's child-like indigo aura curled up inside him and napping because I wore it out.

"Can I release it for you?" I ask.

"What will it feel like?"

Bringing one hand up from the water, I rub the back of my neck, thinking. "I'm obviously not purebred, so I don't know for sure. I can't experience it, but I can do it for you. I hear it's one of the best things about being purebred—better than sex."

Jae is looking down at my stomach, still tracing. Silent.

"I don't have to if you aren't ready. We have lots of time."

"No," he says, looking up at me. "I'd like to try it. What should I do?"

"Let's look at this as an exercise in listening to your body and nature. Just relax and trust in it."

FORTY-NINE

JAE

Junichi sits up straighter underneath me, sliding his palms up my back to hold me against his chest and lifting his face toward the concave of my neck. I raise my hands from the water and embrace him, curling my fingers at the top of his spine. I'm nervous about him kicking the beehive when the bees have all finally fallen asleep. But if he says this will be a good thing, then I believe him.

He licks me just underneath my jawline—a long, flat stroke —then licks my neck and underneath my ear, tasting me before he bites. When Jun sinks his teeth in, he moans, and that sound and his hardness underneath me kickstart the fire inside. The heat of it is already pulsing up the length of my spine.

My eyes alight and I take a breath. For the first time, I can distinctly perceive Jun's mind and what he's doing to me. He's telling me I'm safe and that he loves me—I'm perfect just the way I am, and he'll never leave me. I never have to be alone again. The thoughts are so pristine in my mind that I can *feel* them. It makes me shudder in his arms, and my eyes water because my heart is overwhelmed.

Everything he's conveying and these warm, soft whispers swarming within me are what I need right now. I don't have the space to be embarrassed about this, because it feels too good to be denied. I don't want to shortchange it with doubts or insecurities.

He feeds and my breath catches. I hold on to him tighter, because he's pulling at something inside me and it feels as if I might be flipped inside out. It's scary because it's an unknown. I don't know what to expect. But there's too much goodness accompanying it to truly deny whatever is happening. He pulls again and I tense and groan, my eyes wide as I hold on to him. I think... I should let him take what he's pulling. My body is telling me to say yes. To submit to everything he's giving me.

When Junichi pulls the third time, he squeezes me even tighter against his hard frame in the water and I'm spent. I stop resisting. The fire inside me shoots up my spine, to my brain and groin and everywhere and anywhere it can go. I physically come against Jun's stomach, but it's so much more than that. It's like a weight has been lifted from me, or my very soul has been set free and I'm unburdened. It leaves me gasping and shaking, and the glow of my energy is purplish blue and all around us like a glittery haze.

My body is tense and caught up in a kind of glorious rapture for a long moment with everything in me pulsing outward. Slowly, the indigo haze dissipates and fizzles out. The tension releases, and I slump in Jun's arms, my arms going limp as he holds me tight. I breathe out, utterly euphoric. "*God...*"

"It's just Jun."

I'm in a daze. I feel as light as a feather, but I laugh, lifting my hands to cradle his head once more. When he lifts his chin to me, I kiss him with everything I have. With my whole heart. I haven't kissed Jun like this since I was human, but I remember how to do it and what it feels like. Shameless. Confident and uninhibited. Blissful.

When he finally pulls his head away from me, he's grinning. "That good, huh? I know I've done something well when you kiss me that way."

My lids are heavy as I look at him, and I don't know what's gotten into me, but I just can't stop myself. "I think you should stretch me..." I lean in to kiss him again, but he pulls away.

"How about you stretch me?"

That makes me sober a little. "Pardon?"

He slides his hands down my hips and along my thighs. "Make love to me."

In another unexpected turn, I laugh. "Why?"

"Why not?"

"Because... that's not what we do. It'll be awkward. I'm not a brilliant lead in bed like you are."

Jun chuckles, his black eyes shining in the warm, sparkling lights surrounding us. "Thank you for that. But I think you're an incredible lead, Jae."

Silence. I'm staring at him because I genuinely don't know what the hell he's talking about. "What?"

"When you let me have you, you set the pace, sunshine— not me. We *both* lead, but in different ways, and we listen to each other. I might make the house look aesthetically pleasing, but you're the foundation and you're amazing. Every single time."

Shaking my head, I stifle a laugh. We lead together and I set the pace? That's a paradigm shift that I'm not quite in the proper headspace for. I'll have to give it more thought later when I'm not sitting on top of this wolf, distracted and sincerely hoping we can stop talking so he can be inside me already.

In my silence, Jun whispers, "I want to do everything with

you. And this is something I haven't tried in over a hundred years of lovemaking."

"Not ever?"

"Nope. Could you give me that tonight? Our first night bonded together..." He kisses the corner of my mouth, then my cheek and down to my jawline.

Junichi is the designer. The one with the catalog of positions and seductive little moves. He's the wolf. I am not, but... I love him. And I want to make him feel good like he's just done for me. So, alright. I got this. Goggles on.

I lift my head from the barrage of kisses he's planting on my neck and face, then take hold of his chin. "Bedroom?"

He smiles. "Yes."

I'M SITTING on the bed, naked but dried from the bath and watching Jun (also deliciously naked) as he pulls a bottle of lube from his suitcase. When he turns and swaggers toward me, I scoff. "Seems a little presumptuous of you to have packed lube. And did this lube come all the way from Japan, or did you buy it in England? Is this bi-continental lube?"

He drops it beside me and plops down in a huff. He doesn't answer me, but shifts, bringing his legs up so that he's lying on his back behind me with his knees drawn up.

"Well?" I prompt.

His chest rises before he puffs out another deep breath. "You say presumptuous, I say optimistic. Like dressing for success." He adjusts his spine, resting his hands at his sides as he stares up at the exposed beams overhead.

I chuckle, shifting and eventually resting on my knees in between his gaped thighs. I place my hands on his shins, smirking. "Maybe *I'm* presumptuous for assuming the lube was meant for me."

"It's a safe assumption, considering I haven't been able to stop thinking about you for five months straight and explicitly came here with the intention of mating with you." He inhales again, then blows out another breath. "There isn't anyone else, sunshine. Only you."

My face warms and blushes as I listen, but the fact that he is very tense is slowly dawning on me. Physically, he's constantly adjusting and fidgeting. It's subtle, but more apparent in conjunction with all these deep breaths he keeps taking. I slide my palms up to rest against his knees. "Jun... are you nervous?"

Another deep inhale. "I'm not *not* nervous."

Sensing this is quite a bit more difficult for him than maybe he first anticipated, I scoot back a little so that I can sit and fold my legs. "Talk to me," I say. He lifts, using his palms to push himself upright until his back is resting against the dark, smooth and opulently carved headboard.

I know that Ren has treated Jun badly because he's told me about it in some detail—exerting his purebred power over him, manipulating him and dumping his emotions into Junichi when he feeds. Treating him like a place to rid himself of all of his toxic, possessive emotions.

Jun is here now and mated with me... but those kinds of scars run deep. I understand both professionally and personally that there's no simple fix for those wounds.

Jun runs his hand into the top of his thick curls. "I know... that I have trust issues. The majority of my existence has been spent under the direct supervision and manipulation of someone else. I've only been free for about fifty years... free from my father. Not from Ren, but he was easier to ignore since we never bonded, and I became the one responsible for the contract between us once my father died."

I'm listening, but a question I've been wondering about pops into my head. I have learned a lot about vampire culture and politics from Haruka and his extensive library, but there are some nuanced things I still don't understand. "May I ask a question?"

"Of course."

"You spent more than a hundred years with Ren and didn't bond with him. How was this okay with his parents and yours?" I was about to add "I'm no vampire, but that seems like a very long time." But that doesn't quite work, does it?

"Most arranged couples enter their contracts very young—with Ren, we were both sixteen, which was when our skin developmentally hardened and we could start feeding from each other. But the widely accepted maturation process for a vampire is a century. No one is taken seriously or considered a true adult until they reach one hundred. When Ren and I came of age at twenty-one, we were told to genuinely start attempting to bond. But no one expected us to be bonded that early. Some couples do bond right away, but most don't. We have lots of time, so there's no rush."

"Wait." I blink, processing. "Your father *told* you when to start having sex?"

"Yes."

"Yikes." I cringe. Christ. God.

"He told me with whom and when, and sometimes, early on, Ren and I were watched to make sure we were sincerely trying and doing it correctly." Junichi breathes. "That's how the arrangement worked. So when I was finally free, I only wanted to do things *my* way—and I've been refusing to compromise. But..." He rolls his shoulders, contemplating in the silence. I take his pause as a moment to interject.

"We never have to do anything you don't want, Jun. I honestly don't mind—"

"But *I* do," he says. "I don't want to be hindered by any of this anymore. I don't want it to affect me—or us and what we have—because I know that what we have is *good* and nothing like the shit I've dealt with. I'm sick of carrying it around. Can you understand?" He rubs his palms against his face, sighing.

Twice tonight I've seen these very vulnerable sides of Jun. He always seems so calm and assured. Confident and unshaken. But he's sitting here naked and baring his soul to me.

Leaning forward, I wrap my fingers around his ankles. His legs are still drawn up with his knees bent. "I understand. And we can take our time... Should we just go to bed?"

Jun chuckles. "I guess suddenly having deep introspection about my father isn't exactly a turn-on."

I dip my head and kiss his kneecap. "You talking to me like this is *always* a turn-on."

He raises his head, a glint in his inky eyes. "Can we take our time but not sleep?"

"Meaning?"

"I still want you to make love to me, but go slowly... please."

Unfolding my legs, I lift and lean toward him, pushing his knees farther apart so that I can crawl into the warmth of his face and look into his eyes. I tilt my head and softly press into his mouth, waiting for him to respond to me.

I *really* want this. I was caught off guard by it at first, but now that it's been placed in my mind, I want him badly.

Any time we've made love... I might set the pace, but Jun guides me—tightly holding the steering wheel like a Formula One driver. I love what we do and how seamless our movement and connection are when he's in the driver's seat, but this is my opportunity to discover and learn. Finally, his stunningly long legs, tight tummy and beautiful form will be stretched out before me like uncharted territory. I desperately want to explore him in a way that I haven't been able to.

The kiss is getting deep, with our tongues sliding and wrestling and tasting. When I feel Jun's hands on my waist and urging me into his lap, I gently break the kiss. He's already smiling.

"Sorry."

Grinning, I shake my head. "You can't help yourself."

"I can... but I love the way you feel in my lap."

"I know. Will you lie back down, please?" He does, biting his lip to stifle his amusement as he slides down. If I sit on him, it's over. I enjoy it, too, but I'll be trapped there and I don't want that right now.

When he's flat on his back and spread gloriously before me, I shift up to start from the top. Might as well? Put simply, my goal is to make him feel good, safe and comfortable with me like this. That much I can accomplish.

First, I kiss him—basking in the fundamental truth that I love the taste of his mouth. I feel hungry for it as I lick into him, tilting my head and breathing in his clean, cypress scent.

Jun is moaning against my mouth, his hands sliding across my lower back as I lift my head—leaving his mouth to trace down his cheek with my lips and over to his earlobe. I nibble him there for a moment while simultaneously running my fingers through the thick of tight, soft curls atop his head. I fucking love his hair. Sometimes it smells like coconut oil or some rich, buttery scent. Shea or cocoa.

He gaps his thighs wider, urging me down again and into his hardness and heat. I know what he wants, but it's breaking my stride, because I'm trying to move down to his neck. He does not want to give up the steering wheel, and I laugh. "*Stop it.*" He groans in response, squirming underneath me and playfully lifting into me and chasing my body. I didn't know Jun squirmed. It's a nice development.

Moving down from his neck, I kiss and taste his collarbone, then along the beautiful curve of his shoulder. I have no idea why, but I grab and lift his arm up over his head, then nuzzle my face into the soft hair of his armpit.

Jun giggles and I do too, but I inhale and bite him there before kissing down and over to his chest. It's crazy, but I literally want to taste every inch of him. My nature is burning hot in my belly and up my spine, encouraging me. I caress my palm down one side of his chest, indulging in the sensual, defined curve of his pecs and the soft, fuzzy hairs there. I'm busy on the other side with my mouth, licking and tasting his nipple—feeling it harden underneath my tongue.

Jun's hands are in my hair at this point, making it wild as I keep kissing down, dragging my hands against his body. He's saying something in Spanish as he breathes, but I don't speak Spanish (clearly, I should learn). It's fine, because I'm practically in a trance the way I'm so determined, and I love the way he's responding to everything I'm doing.

When I reach his tight little belly button, I really go to town on his flat stomach and the little curly hairs here, indulging and dipping my tongue in and out—pulling at him with my teeth.

"Jae."

I pause, looking up at him even though I'm very busy and particularly excited about the heat and fullness of his cock hovering right below my chin. I'm surprised to see that his eyes have alighted. "Yes?"

"Can you please come up here?"

"I'm not finished! You asked me to go slowly—"

"I know, but... *shit*." He throws his head back against the pillow, adjusting his spine, his chest heaving.

Dramatic. I kiss his belly again, grinning. "Someone is impatient."

He groans and mumbles something I can't understand, clenching the bedsheets in his fists at his hips. I really need to start studying immediately.

Looking down at him, it's obvious where I should go next. Quite obvious. And I want him, but I skip over his groin altogether and lick the inside of his thigh. Jun is still moaning and protesting, but I drag my fingertips down the undersides of his thighs and toward his arse, then flatten myself down against the bed.

His legs are drawn up, so his beautiful body is wide open in front of me. I've never seen him from this angle before and I am absorbed. Sliding my hands to cup his arse, I shift forward, close my eyes and very gently lick into the warmth of him—like I'm tentatively sampling a new flavor of ice cream on a cone. Jun shifts up the bed and clenches his body.

"*Shit. Fuck.*"

He jerks away from me, so I'm confused. "Should I stop this? You did this to *me*." When I look at him, his eyes are still burning and his skin is even a little reddened, which is usually not the case. I grin because I realize he's flustered. He's always the one who's giving, so it's like he doesn't know how to receive.

His voice is ragged as he stares at me with indigo eyes. "I know that, but... it's different. And if you keep going like this, I won't last much longer."

"Then don't last. And stop squirming away!" I smirk, dipping back down into him. I move up from his opening to tenderly bite and pull at the heavy skin beneath his shaft—which is very hard. He sucks in a sharp breath, but then says my name when he exhales and it is *glorious*. Fucking fantastic. I want to stay low and play a little longer, but now I'm distracted by the fullness of his cock. I lift up, licking the under-side of him in a long stroke.

Jun is swearing and breathing and saying my name, desper-ately, like the release he's been fighting is seconds from over-taking him—like the swell of an ocean wave about to crash onto the shore. I lower my head, gradually taking the length of him into my mouth and enjoying every inch, because Jun hasn't ever let me do this before, either.

He tastes... like how he smells. The same concentrated, delicious, sweet and woodsy essence that flows all through him —that wafts out from his skin and every inch of him. Christ. This has never been delicious to me before. Tolerable at best, but not distinctly enticing like this.

I relax my jaw, letting my tongue slide against him as he slowly lifts his hips up and into me. I grip him underneath his cock, willing him to finish so I can taste him fully. I realize I *want* it, and he feels satisfyingly thick and full in my mouth.

It doesn't take long before Jun grunts, his body tensing as I feel and taste him come. I breathe and swallow, relaxing my gag reflex until he's spent and finished. As he comes down from the high, I feel his fingers threading into my hair and gripping against my scalp. He urges me up his length and I blink, surprised. I was so focused, I hadn't realized that my eyes alighted while they were closed.

His chest is slowly rising and falling and his glowing eyes are soft. "I want you inside me." His hand moves down from my hair to caress and cup my too-warm face in his palm, and I smile. As I sit upright, Junichi lifts and slides the second pillow from beside his head so that it rests underneath his hips.

"I haven't even stretched you yet." I grab the lube, make quick work of wetting my fingers then toss it away.

"We can do that together."

"Together?" I ask, crawling my fingers toward his opening,

then very slowly push one inside him. He exhales and closes his eyes. I can feel him relaxing around my finger.

"Does this feel alright?" I ask. I'm carefully pulsing my finger in, then dragging it back.

"Mm," Jun breathes, his eyes still closed. "You're perfect. Are you alright?"

"I'm fine." I grin, steadily working. "I'm enjoying you—I always do—but... I don't usually get to do these things."

"Because I don't let anyone do these things."

Eventually, I draw back and ease two fingers inside. Jun groans, but then I feel him relax around me again.

After a couple of minutes of this, he surprises me when he moves his own hand between his legs, caresses his finger against my lubed hand, then slowly adds a third finger into himself to help me stretch him. Holy shit. He closes his indigo eyes tight and arches his neck to what we're doing. Gasping through parted lips, he's stunning, and I have to remind myself to breathe.

Our fingers pulse and stretch him, and with my free hand, I switch between caressing his tight tummy and gripping and squeezing his shaft. My aura has been pretty quiet since Jun pulled it in the bathtub, but watching him breathe and writhe underneath my hand is stirring it up again. Also, the urge to feed from him is starting to flood my consciousness. I've been focused on him, and my priority is that *he* feels comfortable with me and in this moment, but my hunger for him is slowly engulfing my senses like a dense fog rolling into a harbor.

"I'm ready." He groans, opening his glowing eyes. I swallow hard as we gently remove our fingers.

I crawl forward, and Jun glides his palms against my hips to bring me down and closer to him, but my voice is serious. "Tell me if I should stop."

He shakes his head against the pillow, biting his lip again. "You won't need to stop."

I grab myself as I rest lower in between his legs. My anxiety is present. I can feel it humming just at the edges of my consciousness, but I ignore it and stroke myself, trying not to get into my own head and focusing on this beautiful man underneath me.

When I place myself at his opening, Jun caresses down my skin and grips my arse with both hands, urging me inside. I slowly push through, watching him close his eyes and breathe with his mouth open slightly. He's so warm and tight, his large hands clenching me. It's honestly enough to push me over the edge right now when I haven't done anything. But I inhale and close my eyes, then blow it out, focusing.

Before I even have a chance to pump into him, he shifts his hips up and into me. My breath catches, and I rest down on my elbows so I'm just above his face. Our foreheads and noses are perfectly in line, gently touching. He grips and drives himself into me again—tight and hard. His breath is puffing against my lips as they brush together. There's no way I can keep this up for much longer. He feels too good, his scent is overwhelming me and my nature is hot and going wild. Everything is swelling like fire in my groin.

"Jun, I—" He grips me and rolls his hips up into my shaft this time, and I breathe a sound I only make when I'm with Jun.

He doesn't speak, but tilts his head and places the softest kiss on my mouth. I feel one of his hands crawl between my cheeks, and his finger is teasing my opening as he drives himself into me again. When he sweetly brushes his nose into me, that pushes me over. I groan and let everything burning in my groin flourish, let it simultaneously rush out of me and up my spine to my brain. It makes our connection even wetter inside Jun and it makes me tremble.

While I'm still in the throes of it, the urge to feed from him is crippling—the desire and need almost painful. I haven't fed from him at all since we've been back together, and I was afraid to ask, but now my body is shaking from want of it.

"Feed, sunshine. You don't ever need to hesitate."

I don't know how he knows, but all I can do is lean down and lap my tongue against his neck before I bite into him and feed gratuitously—completely indulging in his divine blood. This blood I was awakened with. This blood that is, has been and will always be an integral part of me. I love him and the taste of him more than anything, so I pour it into him, wanting him to understand how much he means to me. How grateful I am for him.

When I'm done, I open my eyes, and the blueish-violet light is surrounding us again. Warmly cocooning us and making the dimly lit room brighter. I lick his neck, but when I try to pull out of his body, he wraps his arms around me and holds me tight against him.

"Thank you," he says, exhaling. "For giving me this. All of this."

I'm about to tell him that I would give him anything he wanted. Everything. But his chest is rising and falling in a slow rhythm underneath me and his eyes are closed. His grip is still warm and tight around my back and waist, so I don't move. I let him hold me, even though he's gradually falling asleep.

FIFTY

JAE

In the morning, I open my eyes, and for a second, I'm very confused about being inside this posh cave. But I quickly remember where I am and what my life is now, so I inhale a deep breath to suck in the cool, damp air.

I can hear all manner of birds singing beyond the greenhouse just past the archway. The sun is shining brightly—practically pouring into the glass atrium. But from inside and where I'm lying in bed, it's more shadowed in a muted white glow. There are stained-glass lamps meticulously positioned on shelves throughout the room, and all kinds of other glassy bits and bobs that shine in the dim light.

I've been able to see and experience quite a few beautiful things since I've started hanging out with these vampires, but honestly, this bedroom with its en-suite glass-encased bathroom takes the cake.

Usually... well, before, when I was human, I never woke up first. Jun always did. But apparently, I wore him out last night, didn't I? Making our sex house look nice or whatever.

He's halfway on his stomach, half on his side next to me

and with his back to me. The white sheets are all bunched up low at his hips, so the full length of his spine is exposed. First, I run my fingers down the curve of it, because it's beautiful—the soft concave of it juxtaposed to his muscled shoulder blades. Feeling greedy, I place one arm over his body so he's trapped underneath me, then I kiss down the center of his back, enjoying the feel of his warm skin against my lips. When he groans and shifts, I pause. "Good morning."

His voice is groggy, muffled. "Morning."

I resume kissing the path down to his lower back, but I pause again to say, "You slept late."

"Mm."

"Did the skittish deer wear the wolf out?" I smirk. I'm not at all bothered by that characterization. It's better than a raccoon, and it makes me seem much more majestic and graceful than I actually am.

Jun flips and turns toward me so fast that my heart skips. He grabs my arm and pulls so that I slide underneath him, then rests the full weight of his body on top of me. He's heavy, and now I'm squished and flat against the bed, partially tangled in the sheets. I can only kind of move my arms at this point, so I press my hands to his chest and push. Honestly, I'm not putting much genuine effort into it though. "You're *heavy*."

In response, he locks his legs around mine, so now I'm really stuck. It's so warm like this, and the sun shines a little bit brighter through the archway. I just breathe, calm and pressed into the soft mattress and underneath his weight. His soothing lavender scent. After a moment, my eyes flutter closed.

"Jae."

"Mm?"

There's a pause, and I open my eyes. I can't see his face because his head is slightly above mine.

"I think it's a good idea for you to talk to someone. I know you have some things to work through, but know that you fit in here. You belong with *us*. You are one of us. Everything else aside, please stop questioning that. Do you understand?"

I swallow hard, because it's like he's just punched me in the gut without any provocation. Everything wells up inside me at once, and the next thing I know, there are tears leaking from the corners of my eyes. I only have one hand free, so I lift it to wipe my face as best I can. My voice comes out faint. "Yes."

He kisses the top of my head, then my forehead. He kisses the corner of my eye and I keep crying like a lemon, even though I'm happy. Really. He shifts down, still weighted on top of me but low enough to where his face is next to mine on the pillow. He doesn't say anything else, just watches me and reaches up to grip my free hand within his, entwining our fingers together. I close my eyes, inhaling and exhaling to stop myself from being so damn weepy.

When I'm finally calm, I ask, "Do you think there are others like me?"

"I have no idea."

"I can't be the only one."

He brings our hands toward his mouth, sweetly kissing my knuckles. "You're probably right. But how would we ever know? I think our situation is unique—maybe a once-in-a-lifetime chance that we found each other."

"That you sniffed me out?"

"Like any proper wolf would."

I laugh, but then inhale another deep breath, taking in this moment. "I'm glad."

"Are you?"

Turning my head on the pillow to meet his gaze, I smile. "*Yes.*" I pause, staring into his eyes. The light streaming into the archway is behind me, but Jun is facing toward it. For the first time, I realize that his eyes aren't achromatic. They've always registered as black pools to me, but... they're actually a lustrous, very deep purple—like black but with a prism or sheen of purple. I'm just staring at him because I'm amazed by it. Incredible.

He blinks at me. "What is it?"

"You're just... stunning."

His mouth quirks up in that rare smile that tells me I've caught him off guard. I'm on a roll now, so I put all my effort into pushing him off me so that he falls over and onto his back. He laughs openly and swears from the surprise of it, and I throw my leg over so I'm sitting on top of him. "May I feed?"

He's grinning like mad. "Oh, last night *and* this morning?"

"I'm hungry and you taste like heaven. Much better than those bags."

"That's a relief."

I lean down into his neck, feeling his hands stroke down my sides and eventually cupping my arse. As I lick him, he lifts his groin and grinds into me just a little. This wakes my nature up, and I feel the heat of it building and fanning out of me. But I don't stop it at all. Everything feels too perfect and sensual to interrupt it. I'm about to bite down when I hear Jun's voice.

"You're supposed to learn how to control this today with Nino, right?"

I pause, feeling it radiate warmly around us. My incisors are elongated and pulsing. My eyes are alighted, and Jun's hands are still lazily stroking me and he's hard underneath me.

"It might be nicer to just spend the day in bed and practice together... understanding your lovely, untamed aura. I think we could figure some things out? I can help you..."

My mind and body are set to full-on vampire mode at this precise moment, and I agree with him. The energy within me is already extended outward and resting. It's liberating, and I want to do this with him—to learn and explore myself with Jun. I know he accepts me like this now... well, not just accepts. It's much more than that.

I'll find Nino today and tell him never mind. At some point, anyway.

EPILOGUE

A year and a half later...

JUNICHI

"Ne, abeoji. Jega gugeul mandeulkkeyo. Jega modeun geoseul da hal su isseoyo."

Jae is standing on the small circular dressing stage in my studio as I finish up the bottom hem of his kimono. He's talking to his father on the phone.

"Aniyo. Jega tteogguggwa gimchileul mandeul su isseoyo. Gimchileul gajigo osil pilyo eobseoyo." Jae shakes his head, but he's smiling.

I've been studying Korean for the past year. After he talked with his father and told him that we bonded, he literally booked the first flight out to England to meet me. It was surprisingly very serious, and he brought his sister, too. Jae had never met his aunt before—or anyone from his father's side of the family. She was sweet. She cried and hugged him a lot, but she only spoke Korean. I felt bad about not being able to speak with her directly.

They're planning to visit us here, in Japan, after New Year's, so I'll be ready this time.

"Ne, goenchanayo. Abeoji kimchiga deo masijyo." He rolls his eyes before rubbing his palm down his face. Jae is telling him that he'll have the New Year's meal already prepared, but his father insists that his kimchi tastes better than Jae's. My mate is conceding.

"Algesseoyo. Abeojikkeseo banchaneul deo mandeuleo juseyo. Abeoji, gomawoyo. Najunge malsseum deulikkeyo... Annyeonghi gyeseyo." He hangs up, frowning. "I think my kimchi is better—honestly, he uses too much garlic."

"Are you going to tell him that?"

Jae laughs, tossing his phone away and onto the small couch just below the window. "No. If he wants to bring kimchi on the plane it's his prerogative. I'm not fussed about it." He's still glancing over at the window, his eyes wide with wonder. "It's snowing."

"It's supposed to snow for the rest of the night," I respond, talking around two pins sticking out of my mouth. Terrible habit, putting these damn things in my mouth. I shift toward the front of him as I sit on my small rolling stool, then sit up straight to adjust his belt. "Did Cyrus's plane land?"

Jae snorts. "Yes. He and *Sarah* arrived just fine."

I stop, pulling the pins out of my mouth as I look up at him. "Say what? What happened to Benjamin?"

"They broke up last week—again. This is someone from his office that he kind of fancies. He's just figuring himself out, which is fine, but I'd appreciate it if he didn't randomly swap out guests. I quite liked Benjamin."

"Did he tell her that we're all vamps?"

"Yes." Jae frowns. "She's 'chuffed' about that part in particular."

"Oh God..."

"I stopped by the Kurashiki estate earlier to drop off the

papers for the second round of surrogacy. Cellina and Giovanni were there."

"Oh yeah?" I say, before sticking the pins back in my mouth.

Jae nods. "Her belly is so round. She said they're having twins."

"Dios mío. Two of Giovanni's spawn at once."

He laughs. "Right? Poor woman." He takes a breath, and I can hear the smile and deep contentment in his voice. "This will be Nami's first temple visit—and mine too. It's quite nice..." As he glances out at the snow, he absently threads his fingers into my hair and caresses my scalp. Playing.

This is what Jae really needed. Community. A family. To feel like he's part of something stable and belongs somewhere. Purebreds are innately designed to be surrounded by other vampires. Their purpose is to serve as the epicenter of a varied and dense circle. It's kind of like their birthright.

But Jae was a repressed purebred that was forced to be alone—over and over again all his life. His mother dying, his father leaving, then being left with nothing but a series of callous, low-level vamp encounters and a toxic friendship with a person who has his own host of problems. It's no wonder he had anxiety and confidence issues. Of course he did.

He loves living here. He tells me fairly often, and even if he didn't, it's obvious. He still sees the therapist in Osaka, but only once a month. Between work and the surrogacy program, studying with Haruka, his dad's now frequent visits and playing footsies with me, he's busy. Still, he makes it a point to do some mental and emotional checks and balances.

This is why I love him. This vampire that still very much has a human mindset. He's weirdly, amazingly perfect—for me, anyway. I love his humility and kindness. His unique point of view, consideration of others and quirky self-awareness. I don't love it when he's crippled with shame or self-doubt, but that happens less and less as time goes on. He's always growing and changing, and I find that I am, too.

Tonight is New Year's Eve. We're all taking a trip to a small local temple together—me, Jae, Audrey, Cyrus and Sarah (apparently), Nino, Haruka and Nami, Cellina and Giovanni, Sora, Kosuke and the twins. Asao and Sydney are staying home to prep the food and drinks for our return (and knowing Asao, probably gratuitously sampling as well).

We all had a great time together during the week we spent in Milan after Cellina and Giovanni's wedding. We kept trying to plan another gathering, but it was hard to make it work with everyone's schedule. Finally, though, we're here, and we're thinking about making it a New Year's tradition—start this year in Japan, then maybe next year in England or Italy again. Cellina has already mentioned us potentially staying at her aunt's house just off the beach in Zanzibar, Tanzania.

I stand from the stool, satisfied with my work as I take in my muse. "That's it. What do you think?"

Jae slides his hands down from my head, then wraps his arms around my shoulders as he leans and falls into me. I catch him, embracing him at the waist. He presses his forehead into me and whispers, "I *love* it. It's the most beautiful piece of clothing I've ever worn."

I smile against the warmth of him. "Did you even look at yourself in the mirror?"

"I've been looking the entire time..." He lifts his chin into me, bringing our mouths together. I automatically part my lips for him, welcoming the sweet heat of his tongue inside my mouth. Jae kisses me like... he wants to melt into me. Like he would prefer it if we could truly become one. It's unapologetically honest, and his desire is so strong sometimes, it leaves me breathless.

Abruptly, Jae lifts his head from me, blinking his beautiful eyes. "Oh *God*..."

"What is it?" I'm a beat behind him, but a moment later I know what it is.

"Can—can I hide in the bathroom?"

"*No*, sunshine." I frown. "Absolutely not. It doesn't work like that."

The chime to my front door rings out. "Takayama Junichi? Your grace?"

Jae pulls away from me, but I grip his waist tighter, holding him as I smile. "No hiding."

When Hisaki appears in the doorframe, he bows deeply at his waist. Ninety degrees. Little fucker. "Your eminence. It is a pleasure to behold your beautiful countenance yet again."

Sighing, Jae rubs his fingers against the bridge of his nose. "Hi, Hisaki."

Hisaki lifts his eyebrow. "This kimono is exquisite. Your mate has done well to truly capture your radiance and elegant frame—"

"What the hell do you want?" I interrupt. All of this shit just makes Jae uncomfortable. Every time. "I told you last week that I was closed today."

"And yet you are here. Why is his grace dressed so formally? Is there a special society event today? Where are you going?"

"None of your damn business," I say.

He flicks his platinum ponytail, lifting his chin as if to speak past me. "Your grace? Is there a special event tonight?"

Jae inhales, then exhales an exasperated breath before he speaks in polite Japanese. "Hisaki, if Jun asked you not to come by today, why are you here?"

Hisaki blinks at the simple question "I... well. As you know, my lord, Junichi is often very *terse* in his manner toward me—"

"Maybe because you don't listen to him when he talks to you?" Jae reasons. "If he says don't do something, you should not do it. It's simple respect. I know you admire Jun, but you can't force a relationship with him. This behavior only makes things worse. Does that make sense?"

Hisaki pauses, then bows, his ponytail falling forward. "Yes. I understand, your grace... My apologies, Junichi."

"Mmhm," I grumble, pursing my lips. Hisaki stands and breathes a sigh. He wishes us a happy New Year and requests that we please take care of him again next year, then turns and leaves. I look at my mate, grinning. "Out of the mouth of a purebred—"

"Stop it." Jae frowns, switching back to English. "He's just young. Utterly clueless."

"You think he admires me?"

"Of *course* he does," Jae says. "You're stylish, creative and internationally recognized. It's what he wants to achieve but with his music. He obviously looks up to you—not unlike a big brother."

"No thank you."

"You could help mold him? Keep him from being an obnoxious prat of a vampire his entire existence?"

I wrap my arms around his waist again, bringing him into my hips and making him smile. "You have a soft spot for that little brat?"

He slides his hands around my shoulders to embrace me. "Maybe. I might've been just like him had I grown up a proper purebred and my family line had flourished. Some insufferable, entitled little twit walking around like the world owes me something because I come from an old English family rife with incest."

I'm staring at him with my teeth clenched. "You've given this some thought?"

"I wonder about it." He shrugs. "What life would have been like for me as a full-on purebred from the start. How much different I would have been—if I would even exist now as I am, currently. Maybe we never would have met... or if we did, you would have loathed me."

"Or maybe I would have seen through the bullshit exterior and somehow gotten through to the sweet golden core of your true nature—because no matter what, it would still be the same." I caress my nose into him, and he hums a happy little satisfied sound, closing his eyes.

"I love you."

"Oh yeah?" I smirk. "Show me."

He smiles, then kisses me in the all-consuming way that only he can.

THE PLAN IS to caravan over to the temple together, followed by food and drinks at the Kurashiki estate. The true tradition in Japan is to visit a temple in January, but we decided to do everything on New Year's Eve to beat the crowds (Haruka and crowds don't mix).

The snow is falling in big, powdery flakes by the time we reach the temple grounds, and the full moon is high. It's a chilly night—crisp, and the air smells clean. It feels like Mother Nature is showing off for us.

We're all walking the temple grounds together, through the massive stone gate, up the wide stone steps and along the pathway toward the main shrine. Aside from the few quiet whispers of conversation among us, it's silent as we move.

Peaceful. No humans or other vampires are here, so our unorthodox plan has worked. We have the entire place to ourselves with only the snow flurries, surrounding bamboo and stars overhead as company.

Jae looks magnificent in his layered kimono. I'm wearing one as well, except mine is black with very dark plum accents. He's in a state of awe as he holds my hand, looking all around. Nami is in Nino's arms beside me, doing the same thing—her warm, blush-colored eyes filled with wonder. But at sixteen months old, her short but thick coppery ponytails keep smacking Nino in the face every time she turns her head to watch the snow.

Nino leans his head back and frowns. "*Nami.*" Perceptive, the little girl focuses on her father, perfectly still. "Topolina, please stop," Nino says. She smiles and throws herself into him, wrapping her tiny arms around his neck. Haruka is there, stepping into Nino and placing a quick kiss on his mate's mouth before he lifts his hands. Nami senses him, flips and quickly transfers over into Haruka's arms. They signed papers today to begin a second process, this time using Haruka's bio sample and Nino's blood to nourish the surrogate and the baby. Maybe a year from now, they'll have number two.

"Vampires at a midnight shrine..." Jae whispers at my side. "This is brilliant. Are we religious? Do we think we're damned?"

I shake my head. Jae's fantasy book titles. The last one was *Mimosas and Vampires* when we had brunch over Sora's house two weeks ago. I told him *Vampires and Bloody Marys* would be better, but he argued that was too clichéd. Plus, Sora didn't serve Bloody Marys.

"No, we're not damned," I say. "We live excellent lives, and we don't carry sickness or disease. I'm not religious, but I'm not atheist. You'll have to ask each vampire how they feel about that."

Jae nods. "Okay, great—because I feel really good about all this. I'm not quite prepared to take on a 'cursed by God' mentality."

We all wash our hands in the large stone basin using the bamboo ladles. Haruka leans Nami down to carefully touch the black water. At the opposite end, Sora's kids slap their hands into it until Kosuke chastises them. Audrey laughs—she followed us here when we came back and lives in an apartment just outside the train station. She thinks the twins are a riot and often has them over to bake, giving Sora and Kosuke a much-needed break.

Cellina is watching it all unfold and shaking her head with her mouth gaped slightly open. Giovanni leans down and kisses the top of her head, reassuring her, then places his large hand flat against her belly outside her trench coat. She's been buddied up next to Sora all night, and I know Nino's father was a twin. He told me once, so I guess we should have seen this coming.

Cyrus and Sarah decided not to meet us out here. Cyrus said it's too cold, but Jae suspects Sarah's being "chuffed" about meeting all of us switched over to being afraid once she realized we were gathering at an isolated temple in the woods at midnight.

Slowly, we proceed inside to offer our prayers, coins and well wishes for the New Year. Haruka lets Nami grab and ring the shrine bell.

"Let's for sure do this next year in Milan," Cellina says to me and Jae quietly as we leave the temple grounds. Jae smiles and nods in agreement. I genuinely like the idea too. Maybe one year we'll host at the cottage in England. We'll have everything renovated and redesigned by then, and Jae can make a fabulous spread of Korean food. I'll make rice.

At midnight, the temple bells echo through the deep blue and starry sky, marking the peaceful transition into the New Year.

The End (For Now)

.

ALSO BY KARLA NIKOLE

Lore and Lust: A Queer Vampire Romance

Lore and Lust Series Book Two: The Vanishing

Love, Magic and Misfortune

Subscribe at LoreAndLust.com for book news, bonus content and store updates. Thank you for reading.

ACKNOWLEDGMENTS

Writing this book was such a joy to my heart (and also an important lesson in not worrying about word count, and simply writing the way that I want). I would like to thank everyone who has believed in me and encouraged me on this writing journey. From my parents, and amazing friends and family, to editors, artists, and all the wonderful people I have met on Instagram who send me beautiful messages every day. I share these books for you and only you, and I'm thrilled to know that this quirky, sweet and diverse family of vampires brings you as much delight as they bring me.

ABOUT THE AUTHOR

Karla Nikole has a long-standing love affair with Japan. They have always been very good to each other. Having lived in the country for two years and taken several extended vacations there, she is deeply inspired by the culture, language, landscape, food and people. A trip to Italy in 2018 for a wedding breathed new fire into her writing, eventually leading to the birth of Nino Bianchi and Haruka Hirano—two love letters to these beautiful countries. She has also lived in South Korea and Prague, and currently resides in the USA (although Milan is adamantly calling out to her).

 instagram.com/karlanikolepublishing

CPSIA information can be obtained
at www.ICGtesting.com
Printed in the USA
BVHW070920220921
617257BV00006B/97